The Historical Collection:

The Viking Enemy

SARAH RODI

MILLS & BOON

First Published in Great Britain 2023
by Mills & Boon, an imprint of HarperCollins*Publishers* Ltd,
1 London Bridge Street, London, SE1 9GF

www.harpercollins.co.uk

HarperCollins*Publishers*
Macken House, 39/40 Mayor Street Upper,
Dublin 1, D01 C9W8, Ireland

The Historical Collection: The Viking Enemy © 2023 Harlequin Enterprises ULC.

The Viking's Stolen Princess © 2021 Sarah Rodi
Escaping with Her Saxon Enemy © 2022 Sarah Rodi

ISBN: 978-0-263-31951-4

This book is produced from independently certified FSC™ paper
to ensure responsible forest management.

For more information visit: www.harpercollins.co.uk/green

Printed and Bound in the UK using 100% Renewable Electricity
at CPI Group (UK) Ltd, Croydon, CR0 4YY

About the Author

Sarah Rodi grew up watching old, romantic movies recommended by her grandad, or devouring love stories from the local library. Sarah lives in Cookham in Berkshire, where she enjoys walking along the Thames with her husband, two daughters and their dog. She has been a journalist for over twenty years, but it has been her lifelong dream to write for Mills & Boon. Sarah believes everyone deserves to find their happy ever after. Find Sarah: @sarahrodiedits, sarahrodiedits@gmail.com, sarahrodi.com

The Historical Collection

THE VIKING'S STOLEN PRINCESS

For Chris, Mya and Ayda

Chapter One

Termarth Castle, late spring, 821

Princess Anne ran along the ramparts of Termarth Castle like a hunted deer in desperate flight, her hair fluttering in the cool evening breeze. The battlements of the impressive fortress were meant to keep her safe from attack, yet in reality they had kept her prisoner her entire life. But it wasn't the place she despised, it was the man who held her hostage—her father, King Eallesborough.

He had shown her little kindness when she was growing up—it was male heirs he had wanted. But now it was as if Anne had blossomed into a shiny silver coin to be bargained with and he'd finally cashed in.

At the end of the north corner she came to a stop, gasping for breath and gripping onto the cold stone wall to steady herself. The sun was fading fast as she looked out over the sweeping countryside, where little fires from the tiny cottages were lighting up all over the land.

The people deserved better than her father to rule them, and so did she. Every day they heard more accounts about the Northmen and their devastating raids on defenceless villages, and even though she did everything she could to help—finding families shelter, sending out scraps from the kitchens and tending to the sick or wounded—it wasn't enough. Meanwhile, the King was only interested in safeguarding his lands and power.

Anne feared she was about to suffer the same lonely fate as her late mother, by being married off to a man she did not care for. She had been so dreadfully foolish to dare to dream of finding love. To want more. And her father had crushed those dreams just weeks before, when he'd informed Anne—and all his subjects in the Great Hall—that he'd brokered a deal for her to marry the Ealdorman Lord Crowe of Calhourn in exchange for an army of men.

Anne was distraught. Her happiness meant nothing to the King when weighed against him having soldiers to protect him from a possible invasion by the Danish warriors. She'd heard the attacks were drawing dangerously closer all the time. But it wasn't the Northmen's approach that had the walls of Anne's bedchamber closing in on her—it was learning that Lord Crowe had arrived at the castle to claim her as his wife the next day, so she had escaped to the battlement walkway to get some air.

She would never be ready to face him. She didn't want to lock eyes with the burly balding man who was twice her age.

The last warmth of the sun was beginning to ebb away, the vibrant amber streaks in the violet sky were gradually giving way to inky evening hues and the moon was starting to burn bright. Anne shuddered. Despite the unrest across the land, the kingdom was buzzing with excitement about her upcoming nuptials. There had been a constant stream of guests arriving, bringing ale, food, flowers and gifts into the city in celebration of a marriage she didn't want.

Her only solace was that the union would bring the people more security from the Northern clans. She had learned of some unfortunate Saxon women being offered in marriage to these Danish barbarians, to form alliances or in exchange for peace, so things could be worse. She would do her duty.

'*God kveld*, Highness.'

Startled, Anne whipped her head round to see who was there. She had been so wrapped up in her thoughts, she hadn't noticed anyone approach in the darkness. She struggled to see who the deep voice belonged to— she knew at once the man must be a stranger, for she did not recognise his silky tone. It was a voice from another world and certainly one that didn't belong here.

'Who's there?'

As he stepped into the moonlight, lowering the hood of his woollen cloak, Anne found herself staring across the passageway into the wild blue gaze of the most fearsome and fascinating man she had ever seen, and a jolt of awareness sent her blood soaring.

He was incredibly tall and very muscular, with long,

dark blond hair, braided and tied on top of his head, but shaven almost to his skin at the sides. He had a thick, well-groomed beard, secured with an iron band, and a deep scar ran from his forehead through his left eyebrow to his cheekbone.

This was the face of a man who had seen many battles. He epitomised the meaning of danger.

A shiver ran down her spine as it dawned on her; he had spoken in Danish tongue. A Northman had gained access to her private quarters.

'Highness,' he said again, with a slight inclination of his head and a knowing smile.

Anne reeled, the fierce need to protect her identity her immediate concern. 'I'm not Princess Anne. I'm afraid you are mistaken, sir.'

There had been many times in her life when she'd longed to be a normal village girl, with a loving family, true friends and freedom to do as she pleased, and now she could add this moment to the list.

'I think not. How could anyone fail to recognise the Royal Princess?'

Anne wasn't blind to the way his full lips curled slightly in disdain, nor unaware of the sudden erratic beating of her heart.

'You are as beautiful as people say, Highness, and you should not be out walking alone at night...'

She tilted up her chin in contempt. 'Well, it seems I am at a disadvantage. You appear to know all about me, yet I know nothing of you,' she said. 'Might I be enlightened as to who has interrupted my privacy before I call for the King's guards to arrest you?'

He grinned wolfishly, not even bothering to cast his eyes to the left and right, knowing there were no such soldiers. No one knew she was here, as she was supposed to be tucked up in bed, getting her beauty sleep for her wedding day.

'Your name, sir,' she pressed, lacing her voice with a confidence she did not feel.

'I am Brand Ivarsson of Kald, Highness,' he said, closing the distance between them.

One of her father's deadliest enemies. Here? No!

The shock of the realisation made her legs tremble. This couldn't be happening. She had heard stories of the warrior Brand Ivarsson. Everyone had. His reputation for being undefeated in battle had reached the kingdom of Termarth, as had rumours of his brutal raids on disarmed villages, his ransacking them for gold, and his ruthless sexual conquests.

'Brand the Barbarian'—that was what people called him.

Her pulse quickening, in a moment of determination Anne gathered up the layers of her silk nightgown and threw herself into one of the gaps in the castle wall. 'Don't come any closer,' she said, her entire body shaking.

The Northman stared at her for a moment, the dark warrior's kohl under his eyes making him look wild and formidable. His lips twisted in amusement. 'Don't be ridiculous! What are you doing, woman?'

'Step back,' Anne said bravely. 'I know who you are. I've heard all about you. You're a monster. You rape and pillage and have no care for anything or anyone. Now, step back, sir, or I'll jump.'

A muscle flickered in his jaw as he contemplated her threat. Thankfully, her words seemed to make an impact as he moved away slightly to peer over the next crenel in the wall.

Staring out at the dark, shimmering moat, almost sixty feet below, she realised it was a long way down. The faraway sound of laughter from the men in the mead halls, sitting around fires drinking, drifted up towards them. Would anyone hear her if she cried out?

'Don't do anything foolish, now,' the Barbarian said. 'It would be a terrible waste.'

She felt the slow ascent of his piercing gaze as he followed the points of her ankle boots up to her figure-hugging silk nightgown—and then, to her surprise, he frowned in disapproval.

'Come, get down from there. You have my word I mean you no harm.'

She shook her head vehemently. 'Then what are you doing here? What do you want?'

'To save you from making a grave mistake tomorrow, Highness,' he said, his face growing serious. 'I didn't come here to watch you jump to your death—it would certainly spoil my night.'

She sensed him edge closer again, like a black wolf silently stalking his prey. 'Well, I'm sorry to ruin your evening...'

'Give me your hand and I'll help you down.'

His eyes had turned surprisingly soft, penetrating, and his voice was gentle, but she knew it must be a trick. She had heard the Northmen were only ever cruel.

Anne gripped the wall even tighter. She dealt with ealdormen and knights all the time when they came to visit her father's castle. They weren't Danish warriors, and perhaps not as intimidating as the man who stood before her, and maybe she didn't have quite so much depending on those encounters as she did on this one, but she could handle this.

'Tell me what you want first,' she said.

'You, Highness,' he said simply, and her stomach flipped in response.

'Now it is you who is being ridiculous, sir. That will never happen.'

'You are to leave with me right now,' he said, crossing his arms over his broad chest, his eyes glinting in the moonlight.

The way her body was reacting to his ever-increasing nearness made her nervous, and she laughed, incredulous. 'And why would I do that?'

'For the good of your kingdom, Highness. You will leave with me quietly now, or my men—who have already infiltrated the castle walls—will begin to enjoy themselves however they see fit. They do so love a good wedding.'

She froze in horror. She'd heard of how these Northmen plundered villages, kidnapping people, making them slaves. But not before they'd had their fun. Fear chilled her to the marrow at the thought of what they might do to the women, the children...

'I'm not asking. I'm telling you,' he said, uncrossing his arms and taking a predatory step towards her.

She didn't have a choice, Anne thought bitterly. It was the bane of her existence.

And clinging on to the stone wall of the castle, in the now drizzling rain, with a sheer drop beneath her, seemed to be the most foolish choice of all. Just one wrong move and she would surely die. If she left with the Barbarian, she might just stand a chance—she hoped it wouldn't be long before her father and Lord Crowe would raise the alarm and come looking for her.

So she was still that frightened deer who had taken flight—it was just that now she was ensnared by a very different hunter. Was it her body or a ransom Brand Ivarsson was after? And just how much gold and silver would the Saxon lords have to pay?

Anne nodded. 'All right. Help me down.'

The Barbarian reached forward and took her hand in his, and the peculiar heat that rushed up her arm made her heart skitter. She faltered, losing her footing on the slippery surface—and screamed. Her stomach slammed against the cold, damp outer wall of the castle, her legs flailing, but two strong hands gripped her wrists.

She didn't dare look down, only up into his steady gaze, as he pulled her forwards—hard. With sheer strength the Barbarian dragged her over the top of the ledge and then her fall was broken by a broad, solid chest encased in smooth leather.

Anne was momentarily disorientated. She gripped

his upper arms to steady herself and his large muscles flexed under her fingers.

'What were you thinking?' he ground out, from where he lay beneath her on the floor.

She wasn't sure. She was shocked by what had just happened, and trembling with emotion. But those feelings were only heightened by the sensation of his warm, firm body pressing against hers, the invasion of her body space, and the stranger's spicy, musky scent wrapping around her.

She'd nearly fallen to her death but he'd saved her—which meant he couldn't want her dead. At least that was something. She must have some value, some use to him.

As she stared down into her enemy's brilliant blue eyes and felt his breath whisper across her face heat flooded her and she struggled off him, scrambling to stand. To occupy her shaking, tingling fingers, she ran the tips of them over her braids, which were becoming increasingly frizzy in the rain.

'*Helsike*, woman—you could have killed yourself!' he scolded, rising to his feet, his brow furrowed. He looked very angry. 'From this moment on you will do exactly as I say, unless you want yourself and others to get hurt. Here, put this on.'

He thrust a woollen cloak that matched his own into her hands and she didn't dare argue.

'We leave now. Keep the hood up and your head down. Follow me.'

'I have your word that if I leave with you now, no one will get hurt? Your men will stand down?' Everything she did was to protect her people. She wasn't about to change that now, even if she had to put herself at risk.

He levelled his gaze to hers. 'You have my word, Highness,' he said, before encouraging her to move with a firm grip to her elbow. 'Now, come.'

Anne knew she should be kicking and screaming. She should put up a fight and resist—pull away from his strong hold on her arm and run. But she couldn't bear it if innocent people were slaughtered because of her.

She nodded. She would go calmly. She would not fight him. Not yet.

His long, powerful strides were larger than hers, so she had to walk quickly down the narrow staircase to keep up with him. She felt as if she was being led down an unknown path, her sheltered, conventional life spiralling out of control. No one had heard her scream, and the realisation that no one was going to come to her aid—at least not tonight—slowly began to sink in.

Most of the royal household had stilled by the time Brand tugged the Princess down the endless stone steps, keeping within the shadows of the castle's keep so as not to draw any unwanted attention. They made it to the stables, where he had tied up his horse, and thankfully, disguised in their thick woollen travellers' cloaks, they were granted safe passage out of the gatehouse.

Once they'd crossed the drawbridge Brand gripped the reins of his faithful steed hard and applied his spurs to the horse's sides. His thighs tightened around the Princess's, and they began the long gallop towards Kald.

They continued over hills and ravines, putting as much distance between them and Termarth—and Princess Anne's impending nuptials—as possible.

Every now and again Brand allowed himself a furtive glance back at the castle, which was slowly shrinking on the horizon, to check that no one was following them. He knew they only had until morning, when the King would realise his daughter was gone and all hell would break loose. Crowe would soon come looking for her, wanting revenge—and that was exactly what Brand was counting on. Finally, blood vengeance would be his. For his father. And for his sister.

But for now they were free of the Saxon castle walls, and he finally allowed himself to relax his hold on Rebel's reins, and on his prisoner.

Heading for her chambers, but finding her on the ramparts, Brand had known it was Anne in a heartbeat. The epitome of elegance, he'd recognised her glossy dark brown hair, worn in two thick, long plaits, and her slender figure at a glance—she was unforgettably beautiful. He had been surprised to find her there, out on the castle walkway alone, and so late at night. And in her nightgown! Did she and her father have no regard for her safety? Where were the guards and her protection?

He had thought that when she saw him she might crumple and cry in fear—his scar and his imposing appearance, teamed with his reputation, had had that effect before. He'd expected dramatics—a possible fainting, perhaps. But in fact the opposite had been true. And the thrill that had flashed through him at her surprisingly stubborn highborn haughtiness had caught him off-guard. She was strong-willed, and he had enjoyed taunting her, provoking a reaction—until she'd almost got herself killed.

Skit! His blood had run cold. But even then she'd fought to keep control of her emotions, not giving anything away bar the trembling of her body.

He'd met her once before, a long time ago, when he'd been a teenage boy, and he'd shown no restraint tonight in stepping closer to take another look into those deep fern-green eyes that had once been tarnished with loneliness. She was still exquisite: a true English rose.

He remembered their first meeting as if it had been yesterday... He recalled the snarling of the bloodhounds and the shouts of the Saxon soldiers chasing him through the forest. And when they'd eventually caught him he had suffered the iron fists of the men over and over again, before they'd left him for dead.

He had been coughing and spluttering, gasping for air, with blood pouring from his nose and a limp arm hanging by his side, when a girl around the same age as himself, with two immaculate long braids, had tentatively approached him. She'd tasked herself with stopping the flow of blood, her hand to his face. Her kindness had calmed his fear, his rage—and his shame. And yet when the sound of fresh horses' hooves had drawn near, she had taken the ring his father had given him from his finger.

The wave of memories brought back the bitterness, the simmering anger that he'd been fighting to keep in check, and he gripped the reins hard once more.

It seemed the Princess didn't remember that boy, though she'd clearly heard rumours of the man he had become. He hadn't failed to notice her sharp intake of breath when he'd introduced himself—had expected it. So she knew the stories of his battles? *Good.* It was his intention to strike fear into the hearts of all Saxons, so they would stay away from his lands and his people. It was his duty to keep them safe.

Perhaps it was his reputation that was responsible for the Princess's demeanor now. She must be weary from travelling half the night, and the cold was beginning to seep through their clothes, but she still held her body stiffly away from him.

Instinctively, he pulled her against his chest. She felt warm and soft under his hands, and her long hair smelled of wildflowers and honey. As they hurried forward, through the dark, winding woods, jumping over gnarled roots and avoiding low, tangled branches, she struggled like a caged dove against his hold.

'Stop wriggling,' he barked. 'You don't want to fall again, do you? Next time it might not be such a soft landing!'

She stopped fighting him for a second, instead attempting to challenge him with words. 'Where are you taking me?' she demanded.

'The barbican on the bridge—your father's last line of defence. We'll rest there a while and regroup with my men.'

'Your men? The ones who were in Termarth?'

'Yes,' he said, and her relief that his warriors had left the castle was palpable. She almost sagged against him.

How strange, he thought, that she seemed to care more about the safety of her people than her own predicament.

'And then what?'

'Then we head to Kald. My fortress.'

'You mean a place you stole? A place you took from others by ending their lives?'

'You surprise me with your lack of knowledge, Highness. Kald was uninhabited when we arrived on these shores. We made it what it has become. Is it wrong to fight to defend our home?'

'This country will never be your home!' she bit out. 'You should go back to where you came from. Nobody wants you here.'

She was right. They'd hardly had a warm welcome from the Saxons. In fact, his people had suffered many attacks, and there had even been assaults on his clan's defenceless women and children when his men had been on a fishing expedition. Since then Brand had made everyone learn how to use a sword and shield— even the farmers and the very young.

'You wound me, Highness. But still, I think we'll stay. Perhaps you'll find you like our settlement too.'

She made every effort to free herself from his arms again.

'Stop it,' he said, with a voice full of cold fury. 'You'll just make it worse.'

For him, anyway. He was enjoying the feeling of her warm bottom nestled between his thighs a bit too much.

'I doubt I'll see much from the inside of a cage. I wonder…what is it that you plan to do with me when we get there? What is it that you want?'

Brand had the unsettling desire to reassure her, to tell her that he meant her no harm. He didn't want her to be afraid. But the less said the better. Now was not the time to be soft. She was his captive, and he must not forget himself. He must not lose sight of where her loyalties lay, who she was betrothed to. And yet, even knowing this, he felt his body disturbingly reacting to hers.

A loud clamouring of horses' hooves approaching snatched his attention, sending his adrenalin soaring. Tossing his cloak over his right shoulder, he reached for the hilt of his sword. His steed, Rebel, nervously cantered from side to side, and suddenly they were surrounded by half a dozen men on horseback, their weapons drawn.

'Brand?'

'Kar! Torsten! *Heill ok sæll.* I am pleased to see you,' Brand said, as their faces came into focus in the darkness.

'And us you. We have taken the tower on the bridge,' Kar said. 'We are glad you made it out alive.'

'Are there many dead at the outpost?'

'The Saxon fools saw us coming and left, running scared!' Torsten laughed.

Brand felt Anne shiver in his arms. But it wouldn't

hurt her to know they were not to be trifled with, should she have any notion of trying to run.

'They will raise the alarm. We must be on guard.'

He spurred Rebel back into action and led the way, covering the rest of the ground quickly.

Arriving at the barbican, he surveyed the old building for the second time that day. It was little more than a ruin, with a crumbling lookout tower surrounded by a small fort on the water's edge. There wasn't much to it but at least it offered the advantage of height and a good view up and down the fast-flowing river.

It would do for tonight. And he'd worked out that from here they'd be able to see if the warning beacon was lit at Termarth Castle.

'We'll make do here for the rest of the night and continue on to Kald in the morning.'

On his command, the camp became a hive of activity, with his men collecting wood, starting a fire, and unpacking straw and animal skins to rest on.

'Brand, do show us what treasure you have stolen from the Saxon King.'

His burly redheaded friend, Torsten, smirked, and the group all sniggered, but Brand felt an uncomfortable, prickling sensation down his spine. Had he made a mistake in bringing the Princess here? Perhaps he should have left her out of it. But when his eyes had fallen upon her familiar lovely face all reasoning had been lost.

He hadn't thought ahead to how his men might react to having a Saxon in their midst—especially one of such beauty. That had been foolish of him. He, of all people, knew what animals men could be—he'd witnessed it first-hand. And yet still he'd been so consumed with stealing Anne away and the insult it would cause to her Saxon lord… Plus, he had his people to think of. She would earn them quite a ransom—enough to keep many mouths fed for a long time. They were depending on him.

He motioned to his prisoner. 'This is Princess Anne of Termarth.' Brand climbed down from his horse, relieved to be out of her intoxicating proximity for a while, and began to lead Rebel and his passenger to a small lonely oak tree in the centre of the courtyard, where he tied up the animal.

'Let us see if she is as beautiful as they say,' Torsten said, stepping closer. 'Or if it would be better to take her on her belly.'

Unrestrained laughter broke out across the group again, and Brand wanted to wipe that smile off Torsten's face with a quick blow to his jaw. If Svea had been here, he felt sure she would have castrated him with a flick of her sword for saying such a thing.

Brand took a steadying breath. He knew his friend was only jesting and yet a fist had clenched inside his stomach. Torsten had been one of his father's closest friends and fiercest fighters, but he had a mind of his own, and a thirst for Saxon blood and women. This situation would only serve to bring out the brute in him, making everything harder than it needed to be, and Brand was getting bored with having to keep him in check.

'She is of value and my prisoner. She is not to be touched.'

'Are you saying she is spoken for, Brand?' Torsten continued to jibe. 'Are you not going to share?'

Brand made a swift decision. It would be easier if they thought he wanted to bed her. He trusted his warriors with his life, and yet he knew every man had a weakness…

All those years ago, it had only been when the Royal Guard had snatched Anne up and headed in the direction of Termarth, leaving him rubbing the black bruises that had begun to appear on his face, that he'd realised the girl who'd helped him was the Princess.

He couldn't fathom why she had robbed him of his silver. And he'd never forgotten her beauty or her kindness when he had been at his weakest. It had brought him back from the brink of despair and it had lived long in his memory. But she had also taken something that was precious to him and he intended to take it back.

All these years he'd kept his distance. She had been forbidden but not forgotten. But when he'd heard that Anne was being married off to the one man he despised, he'd seen it as an opportunity to take revenge.

He stared at the Princess, still sitting atop his horse, her back rigid and her haughty but pretty nose in the air, acting all prim and proper. And yet her cloak was hanging open to reveal the outline of her delicate frame in that virginal nightgown and silly little boots, and her face had turned ashen at Torsten's words.

Not so high and mighty now, was she? But her vulnerability struck him with an unusual pang in his chest.

She glared at him with contempt and he made his decision. If his men thought she was his property, they would leave her alone.

'She's mine to do with as I please, and no man is to lay a hand on her.' His voice carried the threat of violence—and they knew it.

He turned to Anne to get her down, but she refused his help. 'You make me sick,' she said, snatching her arm away. 'I would rather die than have you touch me.'

He gripped her wrist anyway and aided her descent. Her cool, soft skin under his roughened palm sent a shot of heat through his body and he set her down onto a stone step. 'Rest yourself...catch your breath,' he commanded.

'I am not tired. And even if I were, I do not think I could sleep,' she said. 'Not surrounded by a pack of wild animals. And certainly not in these freezing conditions.'

The men all looked at each other and laughed in amusement, and Brand felt his annoyance spike. This was not the time for her to be speaking so freely. He admired her wilfulness, and the fact that she was putting on a brave face in the circumstances. But the last thing he needed was for her to raise a reaction from one of his men, ignite a flame she didn't intend to. The effect she'd had on him from the moment he'd seen her again was disturbing.

'The cold won't hurt you, Highness, but your tongue might.' He used another length of rope to tie her wrists together and fastened the end to the same tree as his horse. 'Don't run away, now, will you?' He winked.

She tilted her chin up, revealing to him that there was more to come. 'You know, it's not too late to change your mind. You could have me back at the castle by first light. Any one of you,' she said, looking around at the group, who were now tossing logs of wood into a pile to add to the fire.

Brand raised one eyebrow, yet remained silent for a long moment, his cool gaze assessing her. Thankfully, he knew his men were loyal—they would never go behind his back. 'And why would anyone do that?' he asked.

'Maybe you can realise you have made an error in judgement. Yes,' she said, as if she'd come up with a great idea. 'We could put it down to a momentary lapse of concentration... I'm sure the King would forgive that. If I asked him to. Whatever you ask for—silver, gold—I'll make sure it's yours.'

It was a tempting offer. As an occupying force here on this Saxon island, it would certainly help to secure their power in Kald. They could live like royalty, and in safety. But all in good time...

'And just how much are you worth, Highness?'

'To my father and Lord Crowe? Priceless, I'm sure.'

Something that felt strangely like possession darted like poison through Brand's blood at hearing her talk about her fiancé—which was ridiculous, given how she was the one woman in the world who could never be his. He rose to his feet, tossing another log onto the fire. He instantly felt its heat. He lifted his gaze and their eyes met over the dancing flames.

'Which is why they'll be coming after me at first light,' she said.

'I'm counting on it,' he said, his voice dark.

The way he saw it, he'd done the Princess a favour. She would be thanking him if she knew the type of man she was betrothed to. Or perhaps she knew and was prepared to go ahead with the marriage anyway. Brand was determined to find out.

'So it is a fight that you want?' she said. 'You really are all the things I have heard about you and more? Well, you'll get your fight—you can be sure of that. And no doubt my fiancé will kill you, sir.'

The men fell about laughing again, knowing their leader and his skill with sword and axe. But Brand's lips formed a thin, hard line. He'd waited years to avenge his father, and there was nothing funny about that.

He wanted Crowe to suffer as he had suffered. He wanted him to be humiliated as his sister, Svea, had been. He wanted Crowe to lose all that he held dear— and if that meant stealing Anne away, then so be it. And yet even though he had thought of nothing but revenge for years, even now as he was drawing nearer to getting what he'd longed for, he was distracted. *She* was distracting him.

Strands of her long hair were flying free from her braids in the cool breeze, and he watched as she tried to blow them aside because she didn't have the use of her hands. How dare she mock him, with fire in her emerald eyes, even while she sat there in bonds before him, her arms wrapped around knees that were tucked up to her chin?

'You have made a bad choice in husband, Highness. I fear Crowe is not the man you believe him to be.'

Anne shook her head to cast her braids back over her shoulders. 'It is a good match. I'm certain my father wouldn't make it without cause.'

Frustration rippled through him. So she cared for her future husband? So what? The fact had no right to bother him one bit. But it did. The idea of her with any man, let alone that one, made rage boil over in his stomach. He had the urge to claim her for himself, to rid her of thoughts of any other man. What was wrong with him? He was acting no better than Torsten and he chastised himself for it.

'Mind you don't confuse his interest with ambition, Highness. After all, you can ensure his succession to the throne should something untoward happen to your father. You might even be worth more to him dead once your wedding has taken place.'

Anne inhaled sharply. 'What do you mean?'

'He is using you, Highness.' He shrugged.

Her nose rose in the air once more. 'Women always have a use, sir. I believe that is why I'm still alive. What would *you* use me for, I wonder?'

He ignored the smirks of the men and instead tried to crush the vivid imagery that had entered his mind on hearing her last words.

'You are indeed a most valuable prize, Highness,' he said, rounding on her, with the slow burn of resentment blazing in his blistering blue eyes. He crouched down before her and took her chin in his hands, angling her face up towards his. 'And as for the matter of finding a use for you… I don't think you want to put those kinds of ideas into my head, do you? Isn't it time you started valuing yourself and your safety more highly?'

Chapter Two

Anne had tried to sleep, but it was impossible while sitting upright on a cold stone floor. When she opened her eyes and finally saw brilliant sunshine in the clear sky above her, she realised it was perfect weather for a royal wedding. It was the dawn of what should have been the most momentous, if most unwanted, day of her life—yet here she was, tied to a tree and miles away from home.

'Morning, Highness.'

She started at the low, deep voice. She hadn't realised the Barbarian was so close. Disturbingly close. He was crouching down near to the burning embers of the fire, his body like a coil of power, trying to get the last dregs of heat out of them. Had he been watching her?

'You're right—the morning is lacking the "good" part,' she said.

He grinned. 'Did you sleep well?'

'No, not well at all,' she said, surreptitiously taking

in her surroundings, which were now bathed in day-light, and checking for any possible escape routes. If she managed to get away from the men, could she find her way home from here?

'Well, what bride ever sleeps the night before her wedding?' he mocked.

Anger heated her blood. How did he do that? How did he make her go from being calm to incensed within seconds? She squinted up at him. 'It wasn't the thought of the long walk down the aisle that was worrying me.'

'No?'

No…it definitely hadn't been thoughts of missing her wedding that had consumed her, or even bothered her. It had been her captors—especially Brand Ivars-son.

'She's mine to do with as I please.'

Did he mean it? She shivered, even as the warmth of the early-morning sun streamed down on her face. She tried to tame her unruly hair with her bound hands while looking at him, studying him properly. It was the first time she'd seen him in the light, and her mouth went dry as she drank him in.

He really did have no equal.

He had a taller, more formidable build than the rest of his men, and his hair, shaven at the sides, was more severe, with dark ink scrawled around his head. On one side there was a pattern that resembled a wheel of spikes, and on the other a curved ladder of symbols. But it was his eyes that made the biggest impact. There was something wild and reckless and yet vaguely familiar about them, but she couldn't quite put her finger on it.

She couldn't have met him before—she certainly would have remembered a man with such defined, carved features and a deep scar such as his. It was the scar of a warrior, and she found herself wondering what other scars lay hidden—scars that had made him the monster everyone believed him to be.

She searched the depths of her mind to find what she knew of him, what she'd overheard from her father and his witan talking. But, frustratingly, she came up with rumour and hearsay—no facts.

She had witnessed the injuries of the villagers who had suffered attacks by the Danes. Burned and bleeding, they had come into the grounds of Termarth Castle seeking sanctuary. Against her father's wishes, she had tried to help as many as she possibly could. She wanted to use her position to better the lives of her people—which was why she had reluctantly agreed to marry a man she didn't love or even like, having been convinced it would ensure their safety.

Was the man before her responsible for all that pain and anguish she had seen? He had the reputation of a barbarian, and yet he didn't frighten her as much as he should. Instead, she found herself fascinated… He reminded her of a magnificent dark bull standing in a field. His dominating presence made you want to give him a wide berth, and yet such was the power of his virility and strength you couldn't help but just stand there and watch. But if you took the risk and stayed, there was no telling at what point he might charge and destroy you.

'Here,' he said, tossing her an apple. 'Eat it slowly— we have a long ride ahead. But tonight we'll be feasting at my fortress. You should find it a lot more comfortable there than on those cold steps, anyhow.'

'Great,' she said sarcastically.

Did that mean a cell, or a cage, or worse? She shuddered. She had never done well in confined spaces, not since she was a little girl. But she would be careful not to mention that fact to the Barbarian, as he would no doubt use it against her.

She glanced around, trying to put those thoughts out of her mind. She admired the mature trees framing the sunlit ruins of the outpost and listened to the soothing sounds of the tumbling water. Her thoughts turned to how the Danes had fought off the guards last night, before she and the Barbarian had arrived.

'Your men...they were never in Termarth, were they? They were here waiting for you all the time.'

'Clever girl,' he said. 'We tend to stick out like a sore thumb among Saxons. I couldn't risk us all entering the castle walls.'

'You lied to me. Tricked me.' She winced, her eyes flaring.

He held up his hands in mock-defence. 'Guilty,' he said. 'But you wouldn't have come willingly otherwise.'

'I didn't come willingly anyway,' she bit out.

She shook her head. She had been a fool to believe him. She had given herself up so easily, believing it was best for her people. Perhaps he was right—she should take better care of herself, and not be so trusting when it came to Northmen and their word.

'So you still intend to go ahead with this insane plan of yours?'

'If you are so sure your betrothed will come to save you, you have nothing to fear,' he retorted menacingly. 'If you're lucky, he may even have you back at Termarth for your wedding night.'

He was trying to wound her with the mention of her ruined wedding, and yet she only felt relief flow through her as she digested his words and realised that the consummation of her marriage might not take place today. It was one small mercy.

She longed to make her own way in life—to marry a man of her own choosing. She hadn't even begun to live or to have any adventures of her own. She longed to see other places and meet new people, and when the time was right, to have a home to call her own and a husband and children to love.

But her status in life had ensured that was impossible. Her happiness was a small price to pay to consolidate the power of her father's kingdom. And this was the reason the King and Lord Crowe would come after her. And yet she couldn't be sure of it. The Barbarian might have picked the wrong Princess. Her father had always treated her coldly, keeping her out of sight and out of mind, and there was no love lost between her and her fiancé. It was a marriage of convenience on both sides, but she wasn't about to let the Barbarian know that.

'Fortunately, my father's price for my hand in marriage was an army. Ironically, the one that will now be used to rescue me and defeat you. What about you? Have you decided on your price for my freedom?' she snapped, suddenly angry.

She was sick of being a pawn in bitter men's lives. Her father was about to sell her off through marriage, as if she were an object, and now this stranger believed he had the right to put a price on her head too. Well, she was tired of being treated like a plaything, or as leverage, to help men get what they wanted, used as and when they needed her but cast aside the rest of the time.

So what he said next shocked her.

'No amount of treasure will do it, Highness. I want your Saxon lords to pay in blood, not gold. I'm afraid you will not be returning to Termarth until Crowe—or I—am dead.'

His brutal honesty took the strength from her readiness to fight him verbally. She had not been expecting that. In her mind, she had envisaged a rose-tinted scenario of her father emptying his chests of gold and silver and handing the treasure over to the Northmen in exchange for her freedom. She had thought the Barbarian a kind of pirate, wanting cold, hard money—not this… This sounded personal.

'I do not wish for any man to die on my account,' she whispered.

And it was true. She could not pretend to love or even like Lord Crowe, but she could never wish another man in the ground. And as for Brand Ivarsson… he was her captor, but did she want him dead?

'Sorry to disappoint you, Princess.'

Bristling at the injustice of it all, Anne tried to retaliate, but when she glanced back up at him she realised he was no longer looking at her.

He picked up his wooden shield and began beating his sword against it. 'Wake up,' he barked at his men. 'The warning beacon has been lit. We leave now and we ride hard.'

The men were swift and efficient, but they'd only just mounted their horses, ready to leave, when a maelstrom of arrows came whistling over the barbican walls. The horses began to snort, agitated.

'It's the Saxon fools we scared off last night,' shouted the ruddy-faced redhead they called Torsten. 'They've come back for more!' he grinned.

Was this some kind of game to them? Anne wondered, her heart pounding so hard she could feel its beat right through her body. The Barbarian had lifted her clear off the ground and onto his horse without giving her a moment's warning, and she was still smarting from the feel of his big hands cupping her back and the top of her thighs, her arm pressed into his chest. Her hands were still bound; she'd been unable to do a thing about it. And now he was pulling her against him again, in that firm but gentle and extremely disconcerting way he'd held her the evening before.

'They don't know the Princess and I are with you, so let's split up,' Brand yelled, readying his horse to gallop. 'Torsten, Kar, distract them and lead them along the main road. I will take the path through the forest. We will meet back at Kald by nightfall.'

* * *

They had been riding at quite a pace for a while, without a glimpse of the Saxon guards, when huge drops of rain began to lash down on them, obscuring their view. They hadn't seen a single person since the outpost and Anne was finding it increasingly unnerving being alone with the Barbarian again.

Last night, riding away from Termarth in the dark, she must have been in shock as they'd raced across the undulating landscape. But now she was aware of his every movement, of the taut muscles in his thighs gripping the steed, the warmth emanating from the solid chest that was rubbing against her back with every gallop, and her bottom shifting between his thighs. She had never been so close to a man before, let alone a Northman—and it was most definitely indecent! If her maids could see her right now they would have a fit.

She had been trying to concentrate on taking in the scenery of the meadows and the little brook, assigning it all to her memory so she could perhaps remember the way back. And she was trying to blot out the deafening silence between them and every curious and unsettling sensation, but her eyes kept returning to her captor's large, strong hands holding the reins. She was riveted.

It had been aeons and he hadn't said one word to her. Not one! And she was beginning to feel more and more agitated.

When she saw the straw rooftops of a farmstead on a hillock up ahead, she could have wept. At least she knew they weren't totally cut off from civilisation. But as they drew closer to the settlement Anne could tell that something was terribly wrong. The Barbarian slowed the horse as the acrid smell of smoke hit her, causing a bitter taste in her mouth. And then they came upon the heinous scene of homes destroyed and bodies of all ages strewn about.

'Look away, Highness,' the Barbarian ordered. 'Shut your eyes.'

She could not. Now that he was forbidding her from taking in the devastation, she had a morbid curiosity to see it. But as she glanced around she instantly regretted her decision, and realised he'd been trying to protect her from the horrors that lay before them.

She drew in a sharp breath as the desolation stormed her. 'Oh, my God. What has happened here?'

The Barbarian halted the horse and swung himself down. 'Stay here,' he commanded, as he quietly paced his way over to some of the bodies.

When was he going to learn that she didn't take orders from him? She slid down to the ground and watched as he went from corpse to corpse like a sleek, dark raven on the battlefield, moving stealthily. She was half expecting him to rob each one, but instead he surprised her by checking to see if anyone was breathing, running his hand over the women and children's faces, closing their eyes.

A sob began to rise in her throat. 'Did your men do this?' she choked.

He shot her a cold-eyed look. 'They didn't take this path, remember? And I thought I told you to stay put. It could be dangerous. Are you always this wilful?'

'Yes, actually.'

The inarticulate sound of someone groaning in pain distracted them, and Anne followed the Barbarian as he stalked over to where a man lay wounded on the ground.

'Stay back,' he warned her.

But she couldn't just do nothing. Instead, she quickly fetched a cup of water from one of the huts. Every task was made so much harder by the fact that her hands were still bound, the rough rope biting into her skin. But she knew the injured man must be a lot more uncomfortable than she was, so she hurried.

'What happened here?' the Barbarian was asking him, as Anne knelt down beside them and tipped the liquid into the man's parched mouth.

'Mercenaries…they passed through yesterday and ransacked the village.'

'What did they want? What cross did they bear?'

'Our food. Women. They wore black, with yellow markings on their shields…'

He coughed and spluttered, and then he lay back and shut his eyes. He was gone.

'Danes. Danes did this!' Anne exploded, violently jerking to her feet.

'You're wrong, Highness,' the Barbarian said coolly, standing to meet her anger. 'I'm not saying it's not something raiders from the North would do, but this is the work of Saxon soldiers. I've seen it before, and this man said so himself. Mercenaries. Men in uniform. These people were killed by their own kind— for loot, or for sport.'

She shook her head. 'I don't believe you. You've

come to our country and you are destroying it, ripping apart innocent villages. Just look at what you've done.'

His cool eyes considered her for a moment. 'Believe what you want, Highness. It makes no difference to me,' he said, walking back to his horse.

'Why would Saxons do such a thing? Why? They have no cause...' she vented, trying to keep up with his long strides.

'Because they can get away with it. Or maybe to blame us, to cause unrest and gain more power. Tell me, are more and more villagers who have lost their homes making their way to your father's kingdom?'

'Yes.'

'Then ask yourself what those once-farmers will do next? They'll make great soldiers, especially if they believe they have something to fight for, to take revenge upon. But perhaps they're being led down the wrong path.'

Anne gasped, and the Barbarian bent over to check something on the horse's side.

She couldn't believe it to be true. Yet why would he lie? After all, didn't the Northmen like to brag about their raids and conquests, wanting to strengthen their savage reputation? Why would he make up such a thing? Could it be possible? Surely her father wouldn't go to such lengths to create an army. No, she couldn't believe it.

'You should take off those wet clothes.'

'What?' she asked, her face swinging to his, horror-struck. Oh, my God, it was happening. All this talk of raids and unrest...and now he was going to attack her.

He looked her up and down, brushing his hand over his beard. 'There's another village up ahead and we don't want to raise any suspicions by having you parading around in wet nightclothes. You should change into something more appropriate. And dry.'

She looked at him, nonplussed. She'd always prided herself on her good sense, but he was messing with her composure, clouding her judgement. Her thoughts were a jumbled mess. Or perhaps she was just in shock from having seen what they'd discovered here. Yes, that must be it. She'd forgotten about the rain and her own drowned rat appearance. When they'd come upon the village, her own discomfort had paled into insignificance.

'You want me to steal someone's clothes?'

'I doubt they'll mind. I don't think they'll be needing them, do you?'

He strode off into a hut before coming back out and heading inside the next one. This time he came out carrying a long tunic and a pinafore.

'Here, go in there and put this on. And no arguing. You don't want to draw any unnecessary attention to yourself, do you?'

Anne hated to admit it, but he was right—she was cold and soaked through, and she had felt a bit foolish riding around in her nightgown. Plus, she really didn't want to turn up at the Danes' settlement wearing it— that was if they got that far. She'd be glad of something more substantial to wear.

The Barbarian took a knife from his belt and sliced the bonds that held her hands together. The abrasions from the rope were suddenly replaced with the gentle caress of his fingers circling her wrists, and for a moment time stood still.

'You didn't say they were hurting you.'

She snatched her hands back. 'Well, what did you expect?' she spat, yanking the clothes out of his arms and disappearing inside the hut, putting as much distance between herself and his soothing touch as possible.

She stepped out of her wet things and threw the clean and dry long-sleeved tunic dress over her head, but she couldn't fathom how to fasten the pinafore over the top. How did the straps work? She'd never worn such a thing and wasn't sure how to get the pinafore to stay up. She was becoming increasingly frustrated, her cheeks burning hot. What was she going to do?

'Everything all right in there, Princess?' the Barbarian called.

She had no choice; she'd have to ask for his help.

Cringing with embarrassment, she emerged a few moments later, still struggling with the straps. The Barbarian was busy tending to his horse, and when he saw her holding out the two long straps, looking perplexed and just a little bit flustered, he tutted. He stalked back into the hut and came out again, carrying two brooches. He came towards her and, stopping just a whisper away, put his big, beautiful hands to her chest. Then he set to deftly fastening the pins to hold the dress in place.

'I bet you've never dressed yourself before, have

you? Let me guess—you have servants to do that kind of thing for you,' he smirked.

How dare he mock her? Her silence spoke volumes before her chin tilted up in defiance again. 'If you must know, I've never seen such garments before. And I had no mother to take the time to show me how to fasten my clothes and wear my hair.'

He blanched, and when his face softened she realised his caring glances were much more dangerous to her than the mocking ones, so she babbled on.

'Anyway…how do you know how to fasten a dress? Had a lot of practice with women's clothes, have you?'

She had meant to be sarcastic, but when his full lips curved up into a wicked grin and she saw the amusement in his eyes, she felt the heat rise in her cheeks again. What was the matter with her?

She put her hands up. 'Wait, I don't want to know the answer to that.'

'There,' he said, stepping back to admire his handiwork. 'You look every bit the peasant girl. Now we just need to sort out your hair.'

'What's wrong with my hair?' She gasped, inching away from him, her hand coming up to curl over her braids. He reached for her again and her breath hitched. 'What are you doing?' she asked, panicked.

He tugged the bands from her two plaits, startling her, and raked his hands through her woven locks, releasing them. 'Peasants tend to wear their hair loose, like this,' he said, by way of explanation. 'That helps. Now you don't look quite so…lofty.'

Anne just nodded, mute. She was trying to come

to terms with the disturbing tiny tingles his fingers in her hair had sent erupting down her spine. She was glad when he turned his attention back to the animal.

'What's wrong with your horse? Rebel, is it?'

'I thought he was tiring quicker than usual. Seems he was hit by an arrow at the outpost earlier.'

'Oh, no, is he hurt?' she asked, coming up beside him.

She stroked the horse's muzzle while the Barbarian inspected the wound. 'It's just a graze.'

'Poor thing,' she said, and Rebel began nickering at his newfound friend.

'He'll be fine—he's had worse.' He inclined his head a little. 'I think he likes you.'

Anne was pleased. She loved animals.

'Come on, we're losing time and we don't want anyone to find us here.' He held out his hand to help her up into the saddle again, and before letting her go said, 'Whatever you might have heard about us Danes, Highness, my clan doesn't go about murdering innocent people.'

'No, you just go in for a little kidnapping here and there.'

He grinned again as he mounted the horse, and her stomach flipped.

'Let's get out of this place.'

It must have been mid-afternoon by the time the next settlement and the glowing amber light of a mead hall came into view. Anne was bone-achingly tired.

She had never ridden for this long before, plus she was starving—she hoped they were stopping.

As if he could read her thoughts, the Barbarian pulled the reins to guide Rebel into the stables at the back of the small building, and she instantly felt the loss of his protective body heat down her back.

Her eyes narrowed on him. 'Is this a good idea? Someone might notice me,' she said. And then she cursed herself. That would be a *good* thing, wouldn't it? She did *want* to be rescued, didn't she?

'Probably not. But we're a long way from Termarth, and you'll catch your death if we stay out in this rain all day. I imagine you're sore from being in that saddle so long, plus we both need something to eat. The journey is taking longer than I expected with Rebel being hurt—he could also do with a rest.'

Anne seized the chance to lower herself from the saddle while he tied up the horse—anything to avoid him helping her down and her having to touch him again… Every time he did so, a strange little ripple of heat shot up her arm.

Instead, the Barbarian's large hands came up to gently pull up her hood, startling her.

'Do you mind?' she said, snatching back the material.

'We don't want you being recognised. Keep your face covered and don't make a scene. Or there'll be trouble,' he warned.

'Do you know this place? Is it respectable?' she asked, taking in the exterior of the small drinking hall.

He smirked. 'You're miles away from home, having been taken hostage by me… Isn't that the least of your worries? It's mainly settlers, Danes… Most of them would probably love to get their hands on you, so don't draw attention to yourself.'

Anne nodded, suddenly nervous. She'd never been to an alehouse before. And as they made their way to the front entrance, she took a moment to compose herself before the Barbarian pushed open the door.

The noise of clinking tankards and the vile stench of men and ale reached out and hit her. If she stepped over this precipice and was recognised her reputation would be damaged for good. But she might also be able to signal to someone to send word to her father, although refusal to comply with the Barbarian's wishes would surely see her punished.

'Don't make eye contact with anyone,' he whispered, ushering her forward. 'We can't be too careful.'

He guided her to a table in a secluded corner by the fire, while she scoured the room for exits. She could try to make a run for it…

'Don't even think about it,' he said, as if he could read her thoughts. 'There's nowhere to go.'

Damn him, but he was so aggravating! She wanted to lash out at him, but she couldn't in such a public place.

'I'm going to see if I can find us some food. I won't be long,' he told her.

Scanning the bustling room, Anne cautiously took in a couple at a nearby table and men in chainmail and furs at the far end, seated around a long table, sipping from their full jars and joking with the serving girls.

But the goings-on in the buzzing room couldn't rid her of her tormented thoughts.

Would the Barbarian's plan last out the day? Or were Lord Crowe's men already out looking for her and hot on their tail? They couldn't be far behind.

Anne had lived such a reserved, sheltered life in the safety of the castle walls, and her loneliness had quickly turned to despair when her father had delivered his news about her upcoming marriage. Sickness swirled in her stomach. She hadn't even yet begun to live, and now she was to be handed over as a wife to a man she felt nothing for.

There had been moments when she'd thought life as an outcast, or taking the veil, would be better than even one night spent with Crowe as his bride. But her father had not heard her voice. And he'd played on her good nature and her desire to help their people in encouraging her to go ahead with the marriage.

If only there was another way… She didn't want or need any man. She was yet to meet one who would treat her as an equal, who would understand her thoughts and feelings—and who would offer her the freedom she sought. She bit her lip. Did such a man even exist?

She took a furtive glance across the room. She studied Brand Ivarsson, who was leaning against a post, in conversation with a lady. Even with his wet hair and sodden beard, his face streaked with mud, he was a striking, dangerous-looking man, all hard muscle. Did he have an even harder heart?

The buxom blonde obviously thought he was attractive, as two pink stains had appeared on her cheeks as the Barbarian spoke to her. He was talking in a deep, dulcet whisper that Anne found herself straining to hear, and she tried to curb her irritation as the woman giggled at whatever he'd said.

So what if he had impossibly broad shoulders and large, tanned hands, now braced on the wooden beam? Every now and again he would run them over his dishevelled hair, emphasising the muscles in his arms… She tutted blatantly, her frustration flaring. She was starving hungry—wasn't he? What was taking him so long?

He was the most masculine, intimidating man she had ever seen. He certainly lived up to his reputation. Yet so far he hadn't hurt her. And even though she couldn't believe her father's men were to blame, something made her believe that the Barbarian had had no part in those killings today.

She had been held tightly in his arms on horseback, and he had not once been rough with her as she'd thought he would. And he'd had every chance to drag her from the horse and attack her. Instead, he'd handled her with care—physically at least. But she knew he must have gained his nickname somehow. No one was called the Barbarian for nothing.

If she were to raise the alarm now, what would he do? She doubted anyone in the tavern would want to fight a man like him. And had he been telling the truth when he'd said most of the men in here would want to claim her for themselves? She tugged her cloak tighter around her and nudged up the hood.

When the blonde woman began talking animatedly again, and reached out to touch the Barbarian's arm, Anne's patience waned. She was annoyed with him—and with herself, for the peculiar feelings rushing through her.

One of the armoured men at the far end of the room put down his empty tankard, making her jump. He rose to his feet to signal for another, which confirmed she'd been waiting long enough, so she began tapping her foot in an impatient beat on the floor. Another shrill giggle escaped the blonde's lips and, feeling incensed, Anne added a cough for effect.

Finally, she saw the Barbarian's tall figure straighten before he turned and began to manoeuvre through the tables and benches, heading back towards her. As he came into the firelight, their eyes clashed, blue blazing into green.

'Is something wrong with your throat?' he asked.

'I do not appreciate being left alone in such a place,' she bit out.

He smirked and her heart skittered. 'If I didn't know better, I'd think you were starting to enjoy my company.'

She gave him a sour look. 'Definitely not. But one Dane is better than those five over there.'

Brand glanced over at the raucous men in the corner. Bringing Anne anywhere so public had not been part of his plan, and he was already kicking himself. They should have been almost home by now, but Rebel being hit had slowed them down, as had the driving rain.

He had been glad when they'd parted ways with

his men; he felt he could ensure her safety better on the journey on his own. But what he should have done was ignore his horse's injury, Anne's sodden clothes and his rumbling stomach. He should have thrown her over the back of his horse and ridden out at full gallop to Kald. Yet her whole body had been shivering, her soaking wet hair plastered to her face, and he'd become concerned—he still wasn't sure she'd make it without catching her death.

But her beauty was causing far too much interest in this hovel of a place. And he didn't like the way the men were trying to get a better look at her. In fact, a tall, balding man at the far end couldn't take his beady eyes off them. He didn't look like much of a threat, but Brand wanted to tear a piece off him anyway for ogling her.

But he couldn't cause a scene. The last thing he needed right now was for the Princess to be recognised.

He felt better when their steaming bowls of soup arrived. They ate in silence, and he avoided looking into Anne's accusatory emerald eyes, but that didn't mean he wasn't aware of her every movement. Every now and again her knee would brush against his under the table and she'd pull away sharply. Her wrists rested on the table, and it troubled him to see the faint red marks on her delicate skin where the rope ties had been.

That was his fault, he'd tied them too tight.

She kept wiping her palms on her dress. Was he making her nervous? He didn't know why, but the thought pleased him.

When he'd finished his food, he finally stole a look

at her face, and was glad to see the colour had come back into her cheeks and her new clothes were quickly drying out as they sat by the fire.

'How much further is it?' asked Anne quietly, as she mopped up the last of her food.

'It'll be a while longer, but we should still make it by nightfall if Rebel can keep up his pace.'

She nodded, and he was glad she hadn't fought him or cried out and sought rescue. Although he still wouldn't put it past her to try. She was spirited and courageous—he'd give her that. And she didn't seem to care about her own wellbeing, if her walking alone at night and squeezing herself between castle walls was anything to go by.

'What will your people make of me?'

He had been thinking the same thing. He wondered what Svea would make of her, and the rest of his clan. They would all be looking at him to set an example.

He shrugged. 'My people like Saxons about as much as you like us Danes.'

He thought he saw a slight tremble in Anne's fingers as she put down her spoon, and her wide green gaze swung to his in dismay. He relented. She had such a lovely, expressive face. He didn't want her to feel frightened.

'But you have my word you will not be misused or ill-treated.'

'The word of a Dane—can it be trusted? You've lied to me once already.'

The pulse beating fast in her throat intrigued him, and he had a strange desire to reach out and run his thumb gently over the base of her neck. But that would surely entice more scrutiny in the small mead hall, so he kept his hands to himself.

'About as much as a Saxon's, I'm sure. And I have no cause to lie about this.'

As they left the hall and Brand settled Anne back onto Rebel, he rolled his shoulders, letting out a long breath. They'd gone unnoticed, and now the rain had stopped they could finish their journey back to Kald—hopefully without incident. He'd be glad when he'd got his stolen Princess within the safety of Kald's fortress walls and she could warm up by the fire and get some sleep.

But just as they were joining the forest track, too late Brand noticed a tall figure jerking out into their path at a junction, taking them off-guard.

'Whoa!'

All at once, Rebel reared up, letting out a loud snorting sound from his nostrils, warning them of potential danger.

'Princess Anne?'

'Giraldus!' she gasped.

It was the balding man from the alehouse.

'Your Royal Highness! I thought it was you. Although I can hardly believe it. I thought my eyes were deceiving me. You can have no business being this far from home,' the man said to her. 'Where is your convoy? Is everything all right?'

Brand gripped her arms tight in warning, bringing the relief she must have felt at seeing someone she knew to a quick end. He reached for his sword and she tensed beneath him.

'Giraldus, my father has sent me on an important errand. I am afraid I require your absolute silence in this matter. I do hope I can trust you not to say anything?'

'Of course. Are you certain everything is all right?' Brand saw his eyes narrow as he tried to get a better look at the Princess's companion.

'Yes, I can assure you it is. We will pay you handsomely for your silence,' she added quickly.

Brand was furious with himself that he had not kept his hood up in the drinking hall, especially after demanding Anne did so. He had thought he was among other Danes. His shaven hair and ink markings would surely have given him away to a Saxon.

'There is no need for that. No need at all. Anything to keep you safe, Your Highness.'

'Thank you. I will see you very soon, I hope. Goodbye for now.'

As they cantered away, Brand released his grip on Anne and his sword. 'Who was that?' he asked.

'One of my father's loyal messengers. A good, kind man.'

'I admire your quick thinking.'

'Would you have killed him?'

'If I had to.'

'But he was just trying to help me!' she said, exasperated. 'He had done nothing wrong. You're despicable! Surely not everything needs to be settled with the sword?'

'Which is why I didn't. But I wouldn't be surprised

if he raises the alarm. He'll run straight to your father to say he saw you with a Northman. Now, let's get off this road.'

As they turned the corner, out of sight, Brand spurred Rebel into action. They made their way through the dense canopy of the forest, the afternoon sunlight dappling through the trees. Little primroses covered the ground in a vibrant yellow haze and Brand knew they would soon exit the woodland and hit the coast. Then he would breathe a little easier, as they could follow that familiar path all the way to Kald.

He hadn't slept in days, and longed to stretch out his muscles. He felt tense, and irritable, but not because he thought the enemy was on his tail—because he needed to get Anne out of his arms. She felt far too soft and perfect in his embrace, with her floral scent wrapping around his senses. With every gallop, her warm bottom was thrown backwards against his groin, and her small breasts kept rubbing against his arm that was wrapped tightly around her waist.

Talk about torture.

She must despise him, he thought. He'd snatched her from the safety and comfort of her home and deprived her of her wedding day. He promised himself he'd make amends for it later. And yet he couldn't fathom why he felt so protective of her when her acquaintances had deprived *him* of a family. Did she know what Crowe had done? What he was capable of?

They had travelled some distance from the mead hall when his heightened senses saw movement nearby. He had a clear line of sight through the sunlit forest corridor ahead, and right at the end he saw a swarm of Saxon soldiers, gathering in a clearing by a fallen tree. They were talking to Giraldus.

A sliver of anger sliced through him and he roughly gripped Anne's arms and pulled her back against his chest.

'What on—?' she gasped.

He wrapped his warm palm around her mouth, just in case she had the inclination to scream. '*Hold kjeft*. Quiet,' he bit out. 'Look! It seems the old man can't be trusted after all.'

Silently, he pulled the Princess down from Rebel and shoved the horse's hipbone, urging the animal to move forward without them. 'Go,' he said.

Although it pained him to let his faithful friend go, if they stayed with Rebel they would surely be seen. And he hadn't spent weeks planning all this to give Anne up now.

He tugged the Princess further into the undergrowth and gently released his hand from her mouth. 'Don't say a word.'

His hard hips pinned her against a tree, securing her to him, chest to chest, thigh to thigh, with his palms on the bark either side of her head. Her beautiful green eyes blazed up at him. *Skit*, up close she was even more stunning. Her skin was so pale and perfect, without even the smallest blemish, and her delicately arched eyebrows and long eyelashes looked as if they'd been spun with silk.

His eyes dipped to her full, lush mouth, which he realised he'd never seen curve into a smile. He *re-*

ally wanted to see that—to see her use those cherry-blossom-pink lips move in a display of warmth towards him. She had shown him kindness once, and he believed it was that which had stopped him from being entirely poisoned by his need for revenge.

As he continued to stare, his heart picked up pace.

'Your Royal Highness, it's Giraldus. Are you there?' the man called out into the forest.

Brand stilled.

He heard Rebel snort, and with a shift of annoyance realised his faithful steed was now in enemy hands. He vowed to himself he would get his animal back when the time was right. But that had been close—it could have been them. Now they would have to cover the rest of the ground to Kald on foot.

'Hand the Princess over, Dane, and you will not be harmed. There's nowhere to go.'

He needed to focus. To weigh up the situation. But he was finding it difficult to concentrate on anything but the nearness of Anne. Her breath was coming in bursts against his throat… He noticed her usually pale skin was flushed and her gorgeous big green eyes were dilated… The air surrounding them felt charged as he continued to stare down at her. His chest was almost pressing against hers… Was she as aware of him as he was of her?

'You should give me up,' she whispered. 'I will go to them and you can run. I won't tell them who you are or where you are going. I promise I won't let them hurt you…'

Brand's brow furrowed. Even now, at her most vulnerable as his prisoner, how could her thoughts be for him and not on escaping her situation? She was offering him freedom—despite the fact he'd kidnapped her. Well, she was a much better person than him—because there was no way he could let her go...not yet... He needed to see this through.

Brand felt her hand on his chest and stared down at her delicate fingers. It was the first time she'd touched him of her own accord, and his skin burned under her grip. He felt like a bull in silk chains. But his intuition, honed from years of fighting, told him she was about to push him away, as he'd done to his horse. She was about to make her location known to those men.

'Brand—'

No!

Instinctively, he lowered his head and covered her lips with his to stop her from making another sound. The moment his firm lips captured hers, his traitorous body gave up the battle it had been fighting since the moment he'd seen her again and all thoughts of the soldiers drifted away.

It was the little gasp that came from the back of her throat that did it—that allowed him to glide his tongue inside her mouth in a hot, silky, sensual tour. He waited for her to pull back, to struggle, but the hands that had been about to push him away instead splayed out against his chest, and the smouldering rage he'd felt when he'd realised she was about run to those men was transmuted into desire.

He drove his mouth down onto hers as his fingers twisted into the tangled mess of her hair. Her head tipped back into his hands and he angled her for better access, deepening the intensity of the kiss. He felt her whole body tremble as she surrendered with a backward sway, desperately clinging to his chainmail vest, and a spark of triumph shot through his body, right down to his groin.

The sound of galloping hooves leaving the forest and the feel of vibrations on the ground beneath their feet broke through the moment, helping him to recover his sanity. He stared down at her, his breathing ragged.

With fierce urgency she disentangled herself, finally pushing him away as she'd originally intended, dragging her hands over her face in flustered dismay.

'What was that? What on earth do you think you're doing?' she gasped. Her cheeks were a pretty shade of pink, her eyes wide with stunned alarm.

He shoved his tunic sleeves up his arms and ran a hand over his beard. 'I couldn't have you crying out to your father's servant, now, could I?' he said, backing away from her. 'It was the only way I could get you to be quiet.'

Her fingers flew up to her mouth as if he'd burned her. 'Never do that again!' she fumed, more than a little unsteady on her feet. She momentarily closed her eyes in what appeared to be an effort to keep calm and regain her composure.

Skit, he'd had no right to touch her. None! But he needed her to know he was a man who would do what was necessary, didn't he?

'No need to read anything into it, Highness,' he said, trying to shrug it off as if it was nothing. 'It was just a little kiss. Put it down as a mistake—one I won't be making again. And besides,' he added, 'we have bigger things to worry about. We're going to have to make the rest of the journey by foot. Can you walk, or do I need to throw you over my shoulder and carry you?'

'I'll walk!' she bit out, stumbling away from him. 'Just don't touch me! Don't ever touch me again!'

Brand was glad when he found the familiar wide track edged with mature hedgerows and the shoreline finally came into view. They walked in silence along the primrose-strewn path and he tried to focus his mind on the relentless roaring waves crashing onto the sand in the distance—not on the way Anne had felt in his arms.

He took in the wide stretch of beach surrounded by the dunes and heathland he knew so well, which had soothed his soul these past few years, when at times his only focus had been hate and revenge. But right now his thoughts were scattered—they kept returning to the taste of her lips against his...

He was such a brute! There was a vulnerability about the Princess that appealed to the hunter and the warrior in him, and yet since he'd seized her at the castle she hadn't made much of a fuss, nor begged to go home, nor even shed a tear. He'd seen a defiant strength beneath her delicate exterior, but also kindness when she'd tried to help the man at the settlement earlier today. She'd even tried to help *him*.

Brand was starting to wonder if she had a bad bone

in her delectable body. Her only vice seemed to be her choice of husband and the fact that she was a Saxon.

Her soldier comrades seemed to have taken the main track out of the forest, and he hoped if the two of them remained by the hedgerow they could stay hidden and one step ahead.

'Is that the ocean?' asked Anne, her voice a whisper on the wind.

It was the first time she'd spoken to him since the forest. Since he'd kissed her. What had he been thinking? He must not be sent off course by her pretty face, no matter how tempting she was. He'd told himself it was a temporary lapse of judgment—faced with the reminder of how she'd saved him once, and was offering to do the same again, he'd weakened. But it must not—could not—happen again.

When he'd threatened to throw her over his shoulder and carry her she'd looked appalled. She had charged on ahead, putting up a silent barrier between them by crossing her arms tightly across her body, as if protecting herself. Why had he acted like such a fool? The trouble was, she was making him act in all kinds of foolish ways.

'You have never seen the sea before?' He couldn't believe it. Didn't Saxon royalty tour their kingdoms and beyond?

'I have never been so far from home before.'

When he looked at her with disbelief in his eyes, she continued. 'My father forbade it. I've never left Termarth. So, no, I've never seen the sea. I have admired paintings of it, but it is so much bigger than I thought…so vast.'

Her gorgeous green eyes were wide with wonder and he understood it. Brand had always felt a connection to the ocean, since his mother and father had put him and his sister in a longboat and they'd all left Daneland, heading for new shores full of hope, in search of a better future.

There was no way his father would have left his woman or either child behind. And even when the sea had grown angry and fierce waves had crashed all about them, drenching them and tossing the boat around, taking his mother into its icy depths, he had felt in awe of it. It was loud and unapologetic. It was wild and untamed. And that was how Brand had gone on to live his life.

After losing his mother on their journey to this country, it had been even more important to his father that they found success here. So that she hadn't died in vain. They'd settled in Kald and tended to the land. They had built up a village and defended it over and over again from the Saxons with the loss of many lives.

They hadn't come here looking for a battle. Despite what the Princess thought, they were never the first to strike. They didn't have a thirst for blood like some clans. But, under witness of the gods, they would defend what was now theirs with whatever strength it took. And they'd been forced to do so many times.

After his father had been killed, the responsibility to protect their people had passed to Brand. He'd been young, and his father's closest friends, Kar and

Torsten, had helped him lead their people for a while. But since Brand had turned from a boy into a man he'd led *them* in building up the fortress palisades and the people had become self-sufficient—fishing and rearing their own animals and growing crops. But they'd recently suffered a particularly bad harvest, and an even harsher winter. And then the Saxons had slaughtered some of their livestock.

The people would need extra help this year, and they were looking to him for a solution. The responsibility lay heavy on his shoulders, but he'd vowed that his people would never go hungry. The gold he would fetch from a ransom for the Princess would certainly help...

'I'll take you down to the sea while you're in Kald. Just wait until you dip your toes into it,' he said in a conspiratorial tone, and was rewarded by her whipping her head round to face him, her long dark tresses cascading around her shoulders.

'I could not!' she said, her eyes wide. 'In our customs it is seen as scandalous for women to show their feet in public.'

He laughed freely at that. 'Then how do you wash, Highness?'

'In private, of course. We are not animals, like you.'

His smile grew wider. 'I think you need to be a bit more adventurous,' he said. 'What else have you never done?' He grinned, enjoying teasing her.

She strode on, her back rigid, her pretty little nose in the air, and a thought struck him.

He couldn't resist gripping her arm and tugging her

back gently. 'I know you're angry with me, for earlier…
But it's not as if you've never been kissed before…'

She yanked herself away, as if she'd been burned
by his touch, her chin in the air.

He walked faster to keep up with her.

'If you must know, I had never kissed anyone before
you ruined it for me,' she threw at him. Only her voice
didn't sound as if she completely meant it.

He stopped dead. 'That was your first kiss?' he
asked, his blue eyes wide. 'I'm sorry…'

He was going to say if he'd known he would have
been more gentle. He wouldn't have kissed her so hard.
But he didn't think anything could have kept him from
doing so, and he couldn't bring himself to regret it.

She charged on, but he kept pace with her. So she'd
never kissed Crowe…there was hope for her yet.

He took a step towards her, stopping her in her
tracks again, and cupped her face in his hand. 'It won't
happen again. I promise. But…' He grinned. 'Was it
really so bad?'

He knew she wouldn't answer, and a glimmer of
anticipation sparked inside him.

He glanced up at the dark clouds looming above.
'After I have fed and watered you, I will show you how
we bathe in Kald.' He winked. 'I think you'll like it.'

'I— You— You will not!' she said, as a brilliant
crimson blush spread across her cheeks.

In that moment he knew she was truly innocent,
and he felt a pang of guilt at his treatment of her. But
the painful tightening in his groin was his instant punishment.

Chapter Three

Anne was struck by how far removed the longhouse at Kald was from her father's Great Hall at Termarth. It was more like a barn, packed full of people braying with laughter, who seemed genuinely interested in each other. Where she had come from, no one seemed interested at all.

The celebrations to mark the warriors' return were in full swing, and she had to admit the Barbarian's home was not what she'd been expecting.

It seemed to have none of the stifling traditions Termarth was renowned for, and the people were so free and at ease with one another. A little too free, if the Barbarian's earlier actions in the woods were anything to go by! But she would not think about that.

Oh, what she would give to have the freedom to come and go as she pleased back at home. Perhaps to train in the art of healing, or to go riding whenever she wished, to mingle and make friends with the other women in the kingdom…to make a proper life for herself.

She shrugged off her thoughts.

The buildings here were basic compared to the castle she had grown up in, but much more homely, and as for the views... The circular fort of Kald was set in a commanding position on chalk cliffs and heathland, overlooking the sea and a vast stretch of sand below. And the ocean was even more incredible than she could have imagined. Just looking at it, she felt so far away from her ordinary life. She only hoped she hadn't let her wonder show...

When the imposing wooden gates had opened late that afternoon, the people had rushed forward to greet Brand and welcome him home. Anne had envisaged any number of scenarios—including being dragged to a cell and tortured, whored to the Barbarian and his men, or thrown into a cage and starved—but none of those seemed to be her fate. Yet.

Instead, the Barbarian had embraced a young woman with a warmth she hadn't expected him to possess, before asking her to find Anne some food and water, and to fetch clean clothes. And then he'd given her one last, lingering look before he'd turned his back on her and walked away.

The woman—Svea—had done just as he'd asked. She'd given her a plain underdress and a blue apron-style pinafore to change into, and thankfully this time Anne knew what to do with them.

Now, as they entered the large hall, Anne followed Svea through the throng of revellers, keeping her head down, trying to make herself as small as possible. Having heard of these pagan men and their ways with women, she did not want to solicit their attention. She would much rather have stayed in the small farmstead adjacent to the hall.

The noise of the raucous Danes made her pulse race, and though no one laid a hand on her, many pairs of eyes in the room turned to look in her direction. She was used to men admiring her in Termarth—most likely due to her royal position, not her looks—but this was a totally different experience. Yet it was only the man they called Torsten, with his red braided hair, who sneered at her as they passed and made her skin crawl. He looked at her as if she was a lamb about to be slaughtered...as if she was a juicy piece of meat.

Her senses were on high alert, with the hairs on the back of her neck like little needles, standing on end.

She took in the hunting trophies on the walls and the dancing flames of the huge firepit, her rumbling stomach reacting to the smell of spices and salted fish in the air. She noticed the large wooden doors were thrown open, overlooking the square, should she need to attempt to make a run for it—although she knew the high wooden stake walls surrounding the fortress would make escape almost impossible.

But mainly, she was aware of the Barbarian, who was sitting in a large wooden chair on a raised platform in the centre of the hall. She could feel his close proximity from across the room. Men, women and children filled the cloying space, chatting and laughing, and Anne felt so out of place, so overwhelmed.

When Svea motioned for her to sit on a bench in a corner, relief flooded her.

She sat there stock-still for what seemed like an endless amount of time, going through the motions, being polite, answering the questions the young woman threw her way and raising her voice to be heard over the rumble of conversations.

Svea placed a meal of fish and vegetables before her, and although Anne was starving, and knew she should eat, she could barely bring herself to scoop up the food with a wooden spoon. Instead, she pushed it around on her plate. She was finding it hard to concentrate on anything but the Barbarian, sitting just a short space away. His commanding presence was surely felt by everyone in this hot, oppressive room, with his piercing gaze surveying the scene. And when he rose to mingle with his men he was easy to locate in the crowd. He was so tall he towered above everyone else—which at least meant she could try to avoid him.

Serving girls handed the men overflowing tankards, smiling provocatively at them and sitting on their laps—all except the Barbarian, who just acknowledged them with that slight nod of his head Anne had already grown used to. He had all-knowing eyes that seemed to see right through people, and the way he stroked his beard as if he was deep in thought was equally unnerving.

She noticed how the other women looked at him, as if he was their god Odin himself. But none of them seemed to dare approach him, and neither did he solicit their attention.

'She's mine to do with as I please...'

The words kept echoing in her mind. Now that they

were here, what did he intend to do with her? It had shocked and disturbed her when he'd kissed her earlier today. She had never expected her first kiss to be with a Northman. And she had never expected it to be like *that*.

His warm lips pressed against hers, his beard grazing her skin, had lit a flame in her belly, with the heat coiling downwards, stealing along a new and disturbing path. And as his fingers had burrowed into her unkempt hair to draw her head closer, deepening the kiss, her skin had erupted in goosebumps—and yet it was strange…she had still felt hot inside, not cold. She'd thought herself like that hunted deer again—only this time it wasn't running, it was wildly leaping. And then she'd pushed him away…

It hadn't exactly been horrible.

And afterwards he'd astounded her by apologising.

She didn't understand. No one had ever said sorry to her before. Certainly not a man. And yet this man, who was more male than any other she'd ever met, with his wild customs and reckless reputation, who had stolen her away from her home and had the strength to do what he liked to her, whether she was willing or not, had tried to make amends for a kiss…even gently teasing her to try to win her round.

She shook her head, confused. Just who exactly was this man they called the Barbarian?

'They were pleasant to you on your journey, I hope?' Svea asked, disrupting her thoughts.

The woman poured her a cup of ale and Anne took a tentative sip. She had heard that the Northmen supped from the skulls of the dead and was very glad to see that wasn't the case! She rarely drank alcohol in Termarth, but right now she needed all the courage she could get.

'As well as to be expected.'

She nodded. 'That is good. Brand would have made sure of it.'

Svea glanced over at him as she spoke, a soft smile on her lips, and Anne thought it uncanny that she knew where he was; was there anyone in the room who wasn't affected by the man's presence?

She felt wrong-footed. This was not what she had been expecting. What was happening here? Where was the humiliation, the degradation that slaves or prisoners of the Danes had spoken of? Were they simply lulling her into a false sense of security?

'You are his woman?' Anne asked, and then heat flooded her face at being so bold. It was none of her business.

But Svea just laughed at the seemingly ridiculous suggestion. 'No, he's my brother.'

Anne allowed the information to sink in, a peculiar feeling of what couldn't possibly be relief washing over her. But of course they were related. Looking at the beautiful woman before her now, she could see the similarities. She was Brand's equal in height and looks. They both had the same striking blue gaze and dark blonde hair.

'He is fond of you, I think. Perhaps he is not as hateful as he makes out,' Anne said.

Svea smiled. 'He is a good man.'

'A good man who kidnaps women?' Anne argued,

and then instantly regretted it. Her mouth was running away with her again.

'You were saying?'

A low, silky voice came from behind her. The Barbarian. Anne's spoon paused halfway to her mouth. She went completely still.

'Don't hold back now, Highness...'

She felt the warmth of his breath on her cheek and goosebumps erupted all over her body. How had he crossed the distance between them so quickly? Slowly, she turned to face him. And, damn him, the familiar, earthy scent of him gave her a rush. She had been in his proximity for no more than a day and a night, but it had felt like an eternity of being pressed up against his solid chest on horseback, caught between his strong thighs, and she was disturbed by the strange feelings that his nearness had stirred in her.

She had never spent so long in one person's company before—not even her father's. He'd always treated her as a child, who might sometimes be seen but never heard. It had been as if she was invisible. Yet with the Barbarian, when he'd looked at her with his deep blue gaze in the forest earlier today, it had been as if he was truly seeing her, and her body had become heavy and achy. She'd tried to put it down to the long, rigorous ride, but as she felt the whisper of his voice on her skin now, heat raced up her spine again.

Cool, guarded eyes studied her. They were painted with that dark kohl around the edges, and yet they crinkled when he smiled in that wicked way that stoked her pulse, and she was acutely aware that she had stopped breathing. Was it getting hotter in here?

'The lady believes I'm hateful, yet I think she provokes me,' he grinned at his sister.

'Well, try being nice, then,' Svea berated him, nudging him jovially. 'I'm going to leave you two to it. I need to see how we're getting on with serving more food to greedy men.'

'Did you hear that? She said you have to be nice to me,' Anne mocked, but instantly regretted it when thoughts of just how 'nice' he could be to her made her mouth go dry.

What was wrong with her tonight? And why did she keep putting these ideas in his head?

The Barbarian grinned a slow, seductive smile, as if he could read her thoughts, and her breath caught in her throat. Anne had to tilt her chin up to glare at him. He towered above her, looking relaxed, exuding a confidence that was both maddening and intriguing at the same time. He was dressed rather differently from when they'd been travelling earlier. He'd lost the leather and chainmail vest and was now wearing a casual dark tunic that hugged his muscled chest, fastened with a belt. Her eyes were drawn to the open neck that accentuated the tanned skin at the base of his throat and hinted at the ink swirling beneath.

'We could both give it a go.' He raised his cup in a mock salute. '*Skol!* A toast to you making it to Kald.'

'Forgive me, but I don't really feel like celebrating. After all, I am a prisoner.'

'I don't see any shackles or chains—or even a cage,' he said, his large palms upturned.

She swallowed. 'So am I free to go?'

'Sure!'

He laughed, and her breath halted. She could tell he felt more relaxed now they were here in his domain.

'If you can find your way home in the dark. Or you can stay the night and see how you feel in the morning.'

She scoffed. An impossible choice. Again. Only a fool would try to walk back to Termarth in the dark. She was stuck here and they both knew it. She took a sip of her drink while struggling to think of something to say. She didn't know this man, or his customs, and she knew she was very much at his mercy. Still, she could try to be polite. Perhaps it would help her cause. She had been brought up properly, and could exchange pleasantries with him for a few moments, even if she suddenly felt the strange need to crush her thighs together.

Damn the man—his presence was stifling.

'So,' he said, sitting down beside her on the bench and lounging back against the table, his long legs outstretched. 'Are you going to speak to me, or are we just going to sit here having a staring competition?'

'Actually, I was planning on ignoring you.' As if that was even possible!

He gave a short laugh, which magnified his generous mouth. 'Very mature…'

Despite herself, she bit back a smile. So much for being polite…

She watched as he lifted his tankard to his mouth,

saw the pulse throb in his neck as the liquid slipped down his throat, but he didn't break eye contact. He leaned forward, sliding a little closer to her on the bench. He was analysing her with those intense, penetrating eyes.

She snapped her gaze away to study the beads of condensation on her cup and stroked her fingers through them, making patterns with the droplets.

'Why don't you tell me about your life in Termarth?' he said. 'What is it like there?'

She gave him a cool look. 'You can't be serious? You can't expect us to share stories about our land with each other now? Not when every week more devastated villagers seek shelter within our walls after one of your attacks.'

She frowned. She was struggling with this forced conversation. And it didn't help that her eyes were drawn to the curve of his mouth, her body to the warmth radiating from his closeness.

He sighed, but she couldn't stop herself now. She'd noticed she couldn't help babbling when she was in his company. 'Did you bring me here to learn of my father's weaknesses and how many men he has at his command?'

'Not at all,' he said, not rising to the bait. 'I'm interested in your life, not your father's. And besides, I already know my way into his home and how to reach his most prized possessions, do I not? It is my opinion he should take better care of them. And I certainly wouldn't have chosen you as my prisoner if it was battle insights I was after.' He smirked. 'Anyway, we have our own land…we are merely farmers, despite what you might think. The raids you speak of have nothing to do with us.'

Some farmer, she thought. Leader of a fortress of warriors, whose fierce reputation had travelled the length and breadth of the country, he was more powerful than a mere farmer and he knew it. How had he garnered such a reputation if he hadn't done these despicable things? He was certainly not a man you'd want to provoke. So why was she trying to do just that?

Anne took a large sip of her drink, grateful for the cool liquid lining her stomach, which was helping to ease the knots of nerves that had formed there. Snatching a glance at his face, she wondered at the duty and responsibility he must feel in taking care of all these people. He clearly wanted to protect them and his lands. Were he and she so very different?

'So you don't want to talk about your home. What shall we talk about?' he said. 'What about your lover, Lord Crowe?'

She didn't like the vitriolic way he said his name, or the way his stunning eyes narrowed on her.

'What about him?' She was just about to reveal that she and Lord Crowe were practically strangers, and that he was the last person she wanted to think or talk about, but she bit her eager tongue. 'You seem to know more about him than I. Tell me, why do you despise him so?'

The Barbarian shrugged, as if it was nothing. 'He's a Saxon, isn't he?'

'As am I. Do you profess to have a general hatred of our kind? Well, the feeling is mutual...' Anne smoothed down her dress with her clammy palms and took a deep breath. 'It's getting late. If you don't mind, I'd like to go to bed,' she said, rising and attempting to step past him. 'If you could just show me where I'll be sleeping—?'

He gripped her arm. 'Wait!'

She flinched. The touch of his skin sent a wave of heat through her body right down to between her legs, and her lips parted on a tiny gasp.

'Let go of me.'

She was shocked by his sudden touch, and even more distraught to hear the slight tremble in her voice at the feelings he triggered inside her. She suddenly had a compulsion to flee, but he was holding her fast. Scared to make a scene, she lowered herself back onto the bench. He loosened his grip, but instead of releasing her, he slipped his hand downwards, smoothing his thumb over the delicate skin on the inside of her wrist.

She fought against closing her eyes to the sensuous feeling. How could he make her feel such a mixed-up jumble of emotions?

'We seem to have got off to a bad start this evening— which is odd, as I thought you would be thanking me...'

Her eyes grew wider. 'Thanking you? What for?'

'For rescuing you from your wedding night.' He grinned.

Instant outrage shot through her veins, despite the fact she'd had the same thoughts earlier today. She was starting to wonder if one brute had been replaced with another. 'Rescuing me? Is that what you think you were doing?'

'Instead,' he said, ignoring her outburst, 'you shall be spending the night with me.'

Anne leapt out of her seat. 'I will not!'

The room was noisy, filled with the rise and fall of familiar voices, but all Brand could focus on was how absolutely perfect she was. And yet every pore of her gorgeous body screamed danger... Danger to himself and to his men. She was too much of a temptation and frustration rippled through him.

Right up until a moment before he hadn't been sure of his decision. But now that she was here, inside the walls of Kald, he felt responsible for the Princess's safety. If she made him this weak, how could he trust his own men to behave around her? He'd seen the way they'd looked at her as she had made her way through the crowd earlier and he didn't like it. He'd learned the hard way just how badly men could mistreat a woman.

A familiar wave of guilt washed over him from memories of not being able to protect his sister. No, he needed to keep Anne close, and there was nowhere closer than in his bed.

He'd made a promise to himself years ago: he might have failed when it came to Svea, but he'd be damned if he'd let anything bad happen to Anne.

Wasn't that the real reason he'd taken her from the castle? Yes, he'd called it a revenge plan to provoke Crowe, but he'd also wanted to get to know this girl who had once helped him—the girl who had consumed his thoughts since he was a boy. And he'd wanted to prevent her wedding to that monster from taking place.

But he'd acted selfishly. Bringing her here had put her in danger.

Brand was still holding her wrist, and as his fingers strayed over her skin he was sure she felt the same incredible spark he did. It was as if he could see every detail magnified: he noticed her breath hitch, her pulse quicken, her lush green eyes grow wider, darker.

He drained his cup and set it down next to hers on the table. 'Let's go.'

Gripping her hand, he led her in the direction of the door and out into the yard, despite her best attempts to tug herself free of his grasp and drag her heels every step of the way. But he wasn't holding her that tightly. He felt she could have swung free of him if she'd truly wanted to remain in the hall with everyone else.

The warm summer evening was dressed with the familiar salty scent of the sea and dark was closing in. There were only a few other people milling about outside, and Brand was pleased to see they were heading back indoors. He didn't want an audience for this.

As soon as they were out of view, Anne escaped from his hold and turned on him, her green eyes flaring. The neckline of the dress Svea had given her enhanced the pale swells of her breasts, which were rising and falling unsteadily, and the cotton dress, tied tightly around her waist, drew attention to her exquisite curves. Brand could see her pulse flickering erratically at the base of her throat, and as for the two tiny brooches fastening the front of the material…they were screaming to be ripped undone.

She pinched the bridge of her nose. 'I am tired and I wish to go to sleep now. If you could just direct me to where I will be sleeping, I can make my own way there.'

He stared at her. She was unbelievable! He couldn't have her walking about the place on her own! She was far too innocent and trusting. He didn't even trust his own men with her.

He took a step towards her, forcing her to take a step back so her shoulders grazed the wall of the barn behind her. 'Are you mad? Do you really value yourself so little?' If so, it made him wonder why. 'It would take a man less than a second to back you into a corner, just like this…'

'You told me I'd be safe here…'

'Yes, with me or Svea protecting you. Not wandering around the place all alone! You seem to forget, Highness, that right now I own you. You'll eat when I say, speak when I say, and sleep when I say…all for your own safety while you're under my roof.'

He could feel the anger vibrating off her. 'And I suppose I will have to bed you when you say, too?'

The rebellious heat and challenge in her eyes made all the blood in his body rush to his groin, making him hard, and for an insane moment he felt his body lean into hers. His face hovering over hers, he watched her tongue dart out of her mouth and tentatively trail over her parted lips.

So she was aware of such things, although he knew she had no experience.

He took a deep, steadying breath and took a step back. 'There you go, putting ideas into my head again,' he scolded. 'Now, come on.'

He pulled her across the square to Svea's farmstead, but he didn't make for her entrance. Instead, he began to lead her up a small staircase towards a door. It was an effort to get her to the top as she resisted him all the way, but she was no match for his strength.

He momentarily released her hands to grip her by her tiny waist and throw her over his shoulder, and she yelped. He took the stairs two by two and swung open the door at the top, before placing her down on her feet inside the room.

Brand had always been proud of the settlement he and his men had built here. It was the only place that had ever felt like home to him. He'd made his way out of the Saxon hellhole he'd been tossed into and he'd achieved his father's dream—well, most of it. But right now the cool caress of the sea breeze and the calming views of the bay through the smoke hole did nothing to ease the tension strumming through his body.

He drew a hand across his face. He was tired—the result of too many nights without sleep. And he'd gone too long without a woman. These days he could have his pick of Kald's most beautiful maidens, yet his interest never lasted beyond an evening or two. He had never allowed himself to care, nor even wanted to have a relationship with anyone. He'd learned that if he kept people at arm's length he wouldn't have to suffer any pain if anything should happen to them.

But Anne... Since last night, when he'd stolen her from her home, he hadn't been able to get her out of his mind and he hadn't even bedded her. He could never sleep with her—she was off-limits. He wasn't naive. He knew she would be worth more to her father if her virginity remained intact. Her father might not buy her back for a fortune if she was tarnished by the hands of a Dane.

When they'd finally arrived home this afternoon, and he'd handed the Princess over to Svea, he had missed the feel of her in his arms. He'd told himself he was being a fool, that it would soon pass, but this evening, when the door to the longhouse had swung open and she had walked into the room, his heart had literally stopped beating. It was insane!

Yet wasn't the sight of the Saxon Princess wearing a simple smock and a blue overdress that dipped subtly at the cleavage a vision to make any man question his sanity? Long, dark lashes framed her almond-shaped eyes, and her full, soft lips seemed pinker in the warm glow of his room. With a combination of small, pert breasts, a slim waist, and legs that seemed incredibly long in that dress, she was simply divine, and the desire he'd tried so hard to crush began to run riot inside him.

She had been so brave. And the stiffening in his groin made a mockery of any thoughts he'd had of being indifferent. Instead, that disconcerting, peculiar feeling of possession surged through his blood again.

Ulf, the youngest of his men, had lit the torches

on the wall and in the warm glow of the firelight he watched Anne's expressions as she took in her surroundings. The room was small, but comfortable, and a large bed dominated the space, which was lined with straw and covered with animal skins and fur. Still, the symmetrical dimples that had appeared as she'd smiled tentatively at his sister earlier this evening were nowhere to be seen.

His lips twisted. She had not yet extended that warmth to him. And as she looked up at him now, her green eyes clashing with his, his chest constricted. What had he been thinking? That her expression would slowly change from one of shock that he'd brought her to his room to one of pleasure? What a fool!

'These will be your new quarters,' he said, leaning in the doorway. 'Do they meet with your approval?'

'They do not.'

He grinned. He hadn't expected anything less. 'That's rather rude, given the room is mine. I do hope you will find it comfortable.'

'Do you live here with Svea?'

He nodded. 'She has the room below.'

'So you're not married?'

'No,' he answered, amused at the pink blush creeping up her cheeks.

'Why not?'

'Because I already have enough people to take care of.'

He had determined never to marry and have a family of his own. He couldn't be responsible for anyone else's life. And if you lived alone, you couldn't be broken by your enemy hurting someone you loved.

She nodded, seemingly satisfied with his response, and then her eyes came to rest upon the bed again. 'And where, might I ask, will you be sleeping?'

He offered her his best smile. 'I could sleep in here with you...' he teased, but instantly regretted it when Anne's exquisite emerald eyes widened in a flash of panic.

'You cannot. I will not. I'd rather you put me in a cage...'

He felt a muscle flicker in his jaw. 'That can be arranged,' he said darkly. 'And, believe me, that's where some of my men would like you.'

He came towards her, pushing his tunic sleeves up his arms. 'Look, you have nothing to fear. I am not in the habit of bedding Saxon women—especially ones who aren't willing... Where would be the fun in that?'

'But I thought—'

His blue eyes lanced her. 'You thought wrong, Highness. You shouldn't believe everything you hear. It seems to me you need an education in what Northmen are really like, based on fact, not rumour,' he said. 'Don't judge us on the actions of a few. And besides, you are not to my taste...'

'And neither are you to mine! You are the last man in the world I would ever want to be...intimate with.'

He felt as if she'd punched him in the gut as hard as a Saxon soldier might, and he sighed. 'If you stay in here you will not be harmed. You will not be touched. If you sleep out there in the hall I will not be able to vouch for your safety. Here, Svea will be just downstairs if you need anything, and I shall be watching the door.'

'Am I supposed to be grateful?' she spat.

'Mind who you're talking to, Highness,' he said, his voice like acid. 'Now, make yourself comfortable…get some rest. I'll have Ulf guard the door until I return.' He stalked over to the door and heaved it open.

'Where are you going?'

'To fetch my sister!'

Brand slammed the door and stormed down the stairs, heading back inside the longhouse and pushing his way through the throng of people. He wanted to head straight for the ale—he needed something to settle the rage and the lust coursing through his body. But he thought better of it. He needed to keep his wits about him.

All he wanted to do was go back to his room and coax her into allowing him to satisfy his need inside her beautiful body. But he was no barbarian, despite what she might think.

Anne's heart-shaped face had grown into that of a goddess over the years, and he wanted to take her long, billowing hair in his hand, twist it round his fist and pull her lips to his, silencing her far too talkative mouth.

But even as those feelings entered his mind, disgust also ripped through him. He should not be having these thoughts about her. She was a princess—spirited, brave and good—and he was exactly the type of person he should be protecting her from. Especially right now, when she was vulnerable. But their scorching kiss earlier today had caused a rush of heat to tear along his veins, making him wonder what one night would be like.

His primitive response to her was just as maddening now as it had been when he was a teenage boy, when they'd met for the first time. Back then, she'd stared at him—at his bruises and battered nose—as if he was something out of a nightmare. And perhaps she'd been right. Now he was covered in scars, both inside and out, so had he become the monster she'd once thought he was?

Yet everything he'd done had been for the good of his people, and in a way for Anne. Only she didn't realise it yet.

From a distance, he'd thought about her a lot. Too much, considering their first meeting had been fleeting. But now she was here, hadn't he made things a whole lot worse for himself? And for her?

He shouldn't have brought her here, and a wave of guilt crashed over him again. He knew only that he must keep her safe, and somehow he had manipulated the situation so she'd be sleeping in his room, in his bed. Yet he also knew all too well what would happen if he spent time with her alone—he wouldn't be able to resist her. And, disturbingly, it wasn't just her body he wanted to get to know. He found himself wanting to discover her hopes and dreams, what her life was really like. But she'd put up a barrier and avoided telling him. She was keeping her distance, and he had to do the same. He had to maintain control.

So much for getting some rest. He had the feeling he wouldn't be getting a lot of sleep tonight.

* * *

Anne lay awake in the darkness, listening to the sounds of the gathering going on in the longhouse. This bed was nothing like her grand one at home, but even so it had looked inviting and she'd curled up on it and shut her eyes, hoping slumber would come. But she was too warm, despite the balmy night breeze drifting through the smoke hole, and although she was exhausted, still sleep eluded her.

She had heard Svea enter the room downstairs and had listened to her moving around for a while before it all went quiet.

Anne hated to admit it, but she was waiting for the Barbarian to return. Enveloped in the furs on his bed, she breathed in the male scent of him, somehow needing to know and understand her captor better. He was certainly a mystery. Would he keep his word and guard the door? Or would ale reveal the rumours about his sexual appetites to be true? She had seen far too many of her father's advisors' real characters come out after they'd been at the mead halls in Termarth.

She imagined he'd retired to one of the back rooms in the hall with any one of those women who had been fawning over him...maybe he wouldn't even come back. And why did she even care?

But finally, as she lay there waiting, she heard deep voices in conversation, heavy footsteps on the stairs and a dull thud as if someone had slumped against the door. Her whole body tensed and she willed herself to lie as still as possible. She didn't dare breathe.

There was the sound of a sword being removed from

its hilt and being placed on the ground, a creak of the wood, and...nothing.

She waited again. She strained to hear his breathing. Was it the Barbarian? And was he asleep? What was he doing? Damn the darkness.

She couldn't bear this. She sat bolt upright and as quietly as she could tiptoed over to the door. She sat down, resting her back against it. 'Brand, is that you? What are you doing?'

'What?' His silken voice sounded in the pitch-black, through the wooden panel.

'I said, what are you doing?'

'Trying to get some rest—which is exactly what you should be doing after our long journey today.'

'Out there on the stairs? In the cold?' She felt hysteria rising.

'Someone has to make sure you're safe while you're here. What did you think I was going to do? I told you I won't touch you. I meant it.'

She couldn't believe it. He really did mean it. This wasn't the man she'd heard about, who didn't wait to be invited, who had a thirst for the conquest of Saxon villages and virgins.

She had been stoic throughout the journey here, trying to conserve whatever strength she had left to put up a fight should she need to. She would never have surrendered her body willingly to a man who would use her like an object. And yet he had surprised her by not even attempting to take her. He'd even confessed he didn't desire her.

'Why? Where would you like me to sleep, Highness?'

She tipped her head back against the door. Argh! He had to be the most infuriating man she had ever met. 'Out there, of course!' she ground out.

What was the matter with her? Of course she didn't want him to be in here, lying next to her—he was a ruthless killer who cared for nothing and no one.

And yet he did care about his sister. Images of him joking with Svea flashed through her mind, his wide smile and glinting eyes...and she'd seen the pained look in his face when he'd pushed his horse away earlier. He clearly cared for the animal. And he obviously wanted to keep his people safe. They certainly had that in common.

Was there more to Brand Ivarsson than she had originally thought?

'Fine, then we're both happy. Go to sleep.'

She reached out for a blanket from the bed and pulled it over her. He had somehow managed to awaken feelings in her she had never experienced before and couldn't even begin to understand. She didn't even think she wanted to—they were far too dangerous a response—and so she'd tried to push them down.

Perhaps it was just a heightened reaction to the terrifying situation. Maybe she'd feel better in the morning.

She played around with the animal furs, trying to get more comfortable.

'I do hope you're not going to be fidgeting around in there keeping me awake all night,' he said.

'You could always sleep elsewhere. Outside another room, perhaps?'

The wood creaked again and, straining to hear, she thought she heard him cross his arms over his chest.

'That's not going to happen.'

She sighed, and then decided she'd feel too guilty to sleep all night if she didn't at least offer him a blanket. So she stood and gently pulled open the door a little and peered around the edge.

'That staircase can't be very comfortable.'

'It's not. But I didn't think you cared.'

She could tell he was grinning in the darkness.

'I don't,' she said. 'But I don't want you to catch your death on my account. Here, take this,' she said, holding out the fleecy material.

His fingers brushed hers as he took it from her. 'Thank you,' he said. 'Now shut the door and go back to bed.'

She pulled the door closed and sank to the floor again.

'I said get some sleep!' he muttered through the door once more.

'I can't!' she fumed.

'Why not?'

'Why do you think? I'm miles from my home and I'm here—with you!'

'So you are homesick?'

'Not exactly,' she said.

'You do not like your home? Is that why you don't want to talk about it?'

'Of course I do! I would do anything for my kingdom, my people. It's just...'

'Go on,' he urged.

And something about the invisibility that came with being in the dark made her want to tell him. Perhaps he'd realised that she couldn't stop talking when she was nervous...

'It's just not as if my father will be sitting beside the fire, longing for my return. In truth, I fear you will not get the reaction you crave—he may not come at all. He might not think I am worth the fight.'

'He does not love you?' the Barbarian asked. 'I find that hard to believe. Among our people, family is everything.'

'He is not the man people say he once was. Not since he lost my mother when I was small. It is as if I am unimportant to him.'

She heard him release a long breath. 'I know what it is like to lose a parent. What happened to her?'

'She died in childbirth, having my brother. She never really warmed to my father, but he was obsessed with her. She was very beautiful. My brother was sickly and passed away when he was just a year old. I always felt my father wished it had been me who'd died instead.'

There was silence, and Anne bit her lip. She didn't know why she'd told him that. She was babbling again, but talking was helping to ease some of the tension of the past few days. In this absolutely absurd situation, it was helping her to relax. But she knew she mustn't reveal too much of herself—it would make her weak against her captor.

'That must have been hard on you. And your father,' he said. 'And yet I still think he'll send his men to fetch you. You *are* important, despite what you may feel.'

'As a bargaining tool, perhaps.'

And she wondered, not for the first time, how her life might have been different with a mother to love her and a little brother to play with. Would her father have behaved differently towards her and become a better king to his subjects?

She wondered if that was why she helped the people so much—to bridge the gap between them and her father. She had grown up understanding her position in the world, knowing she must heed her father's wishes and do her duty. Before the Barbarian had taken her from the ramparts all her dreams seemed to have been lost. And now... Now she wasn't sure about anything.

Did she really want to be rescued, to return to Termarth and marry Lord Crowe, now her world had been turned upside down?

'You are lucky to have a sister,' she said. 'To have the kind of welcome she gave you today. She would do anything for you.'

'And I her.'

'What happened to your parents?'

There was a long pause, and Anne wondered if she'd asked the wrong question, or if perhaps he'd fallen asleep. She stretched and curled her toes, waiting.

'My mother died on our voyage to England,' he said, his voice taking on a cooler edge. 'My father died not long after we arrived here.'

Her heart went out to him. 'I'm sorry for you too, then,' she said. And she meant it. 'No one should have to suffer burying a parent before their time.'

Her thoughts flew to how he must have had to grow

up quickly, to learn to take care of his sister and all these people.

He cleared his throat. 'All right—enough chit-chat,' he said. 'Now, please go to sleep. You must be exhausted.'

And at some point she must have drifted off, because the next time she woke the room was drenched in daylight. She opened the door, wondering if the Barbarian might still be there, but instead she'd found the young lad, Ulf, guarding her door. He told her he was under orders to keep her there, and she was still alone in the room by the time the sun was burning bright in the sky in the afternoon.

Anne paced the floorboards for what seemed like the hundredth time. She had watched through the smoke hole as the surprisingly beautiful kingdom of Kald had come alive. Children ran free, chasing chickens and a menagerie of other animals across the central square, and men and women emerged from their farmsteads and milled about chatting, milking goats and cattle, before heading off to the grain fields to farm.

Anne had been fascinated by the different clothing, their mannerisms and activities. It had been an education in Danelaw.

Svea had delivered her water for washing, breakfast, and lunch—but being cooped up was beginning to feel like torture. It wasn't the cage with bars she'd been expecting, but knowing she couldn't get out was making her start to panic.

She couldn't stay in this room all day, knowing she was trapped—she'd go mad. She needed to walk, to breathe in fresh air. But every time she tried the door handle it was locked, and the young Dane on guard on the other side of the door told her to stay inside, repeating that he was under the Barbarian's strict instructions not to let her out.

She was livid. He had lied to her again. He'd told her she wasn't a prisoner and yet here she was, locked up. She had seemingly swapped one prison at home, where she'd been caged by her father, for another. Well, she was sick of it!

She tried to focus on the view, on the sunlight dancing on the ocean in the distance, but that only made things worse. It was awful being this close to the sea and not being able to explore it. Her skin felt clammy and she was struggling to breathe. After pacing the room some more, she threw up her hands, exasperated, and made another try for the door.

Pulling and pushing at the handle, she felt it finally come free, and she fled past the young Dane and down the stairs.

'My lady, stop!' he said, struggling to keep up with her as she tried to calm her breathing, heading towards the longhouse full of purpose. 'You can't go in there!'

'Nonsense!' she said. 'I will not be locked up all day long.'

At home, she had begun to fight her father on the very same matter. But here she was surprised to find the hall empty, with just a few serving maids milling about. It had a different atmosphere in the daytime, with the fire slowly burning and animal skins strewn about, offering comfort and serenity.

She stepped back outside into the square, shielding her eyes from the sun with her hand. 'Where is he?' she asked, turning to the young lad.

'In the barn, my lady—but, please, you can't go in there. He told me you had to stay upstairs. You'll get me into trouble.'

He was really quite sweet, she thought. And she didn't want the Barbarian to punish him. But equally she would not stand being kept in a box. She would have to make the Barbarian see there was another way.

She headed in the direction of where she'd seen the men lead some horses and pushed open the door to the livery, which seemed to double up as a workshop. She found six men, some of whom she recognised from the barbican yesterday, huddled around what looked like a long, narrow boat, and her bravery wavered. She suddenly wondered how she'd had the gall to burst in here. But her irrational fear of being confined, of losing control, had propelled her forward without really thinking.

As she approached the group, they all turned to stare in her direction, some greedily looking her up and down, others bemused. Even the horses in pens on the other side of the barn started whickering at her flurried entrance. Undeterred, she concentrated on placing one foot after the other on the straw-covered floor as she drew nearer.

'My, my, what have we here?' Torsten sneered.

'I'm looking for Brand,' she said, finding her voice. She sensed these Northmen were in a rowdy mood—

perhaps they always were—and she tried to quell the uneasy feeling the redhead evoked in her.

'Is he here?' she asked, standing firm.

The group parted and stepped away from the vessel just as the very man she was looking for pushed himself out from beneath the craft, staring up at her from his position on the ground.

For a moment, looking into his steely blue eyes, she felt a bolt of unexpected heat strike low in her belly, and the sudden realisation that she actually found him attractive momentarily outweighed the anger he stirred in her.

She braced herself against it. 'I thought I'd find you here,' she said, taking a deep breath as she regained control of her racing heart.

He flicked his gaze over her, looking her up and down in that disapproving way she was growing used to, and she resisted rolling her eyes.

'Highness,' he said. 'This is a surprise. I thought I ordered you to stay upstairs and wait for my return.' An undercurrent of anger laced his voice, and he glared at Ulf. 'You have one moment to explain what you're doing here.'

She placed her hands on her hips. 'I came here to tell you that I will not stay locked up all day, waiting for you to grace me with your presence. I will not wait in a box until my father or Lord Crowe come to claim me. I will die of boredom!' she spat.

Annoyance lanced her as her outburst raised a laugh from the men.

'I'd be happy to keep you entertained, my lady, if Brand would only allow it!' Torsten grinned.

The Barbarian scowled and slowly stood in front of her, blocking the path between her and Torsten. He loomed over her, dominating the space between them. His sculpted frame, probably honed from fighting or from hard work on the land, seemed even more imposing than she remembered from the day before, and her heart began to pick up its pace again.

'So to what do I owe the pleasure of this little visit? Boredom?' he mocked, making her feel as if it was an inconvenience.

Not for the first time, she wondered why he disliked her so much. He didn't even try to make a secret of it. Was that why he'd been avoiding her—why he wanted her out of his sight? Well, the feeling was reciprocal. And it had grown ten-fold since he'd put her under lock and key. If Ulf hadn't let it slip that the Barbarian was working in the barn, she might never have been able to get near him. And she refused to be ignored! But she knew she needed to get him alone, to appeal to his better nature without these brutes being around.

'I was hoping we could talk. In private.' The words felt like blades in her throat, as she remembered what she'd spat at him last night—that he was the last man she would ever want to be close to.

He raised a dark eyebrow and Anne thought in that moment how he was rather like the stallions in the stables—no doubt a wild ride, but way too dangerous to take a chance on.

She anticipated that he wouldn't make this easy for

her. Why should he? He was wiping his hands on a rag while studying her face. Was he contemplating telling Ulf to take her away and lock her up again? She refused to give him the opportunity.

'It's important,' she pressed.

The crease between his brows deepened and he turned to his men, who were watching them with amusement. All except Torsten, who seemed to be looking at her in a hungry way that made her prickle with discomfort.

'Men, can you leave us?'

Anne released a long, steady breath. She was relieved, but also surprised. It was unusual for a man to honour a woman's wishes so publicly, wasn't it? Especially a prisoner. She didn't think her father had ever let her opinions be voiced. And yet didn't that make the Barbarian seem even more powerful—stronger somehow—because he wasn't afraid to let a woman be heard? She'd half expected him to throw her over his shoulder, take her back up to the room and chain her down. But everything about this place and her captor had caught her off-guard.

Then, as if for her benefit, he added the warning, 'This won't take long.'

The Barbarian busied himself with scrubbing a patch of dirt from the side of the wooden boat, and continued doing so even when they were alone, so Anne came round the craft to stand in front of him, crossing her hands over her body, feigning a confidence she did not feel.

He sighed. 'What is it that you want, Highness?'

It irritated her that he never used her name, Anne, yet at the same time, she liked the way Highness or Princess sounded like an endearment on his deep, velvety tongue. She wondered what else that tongue—that perfect mouth—could do, before stopping herself short.

Where had that thought come from? What was the matter with her? She'd had a taster of his kisses yesterday and she did not want more—did she?

She tossed her hair over her shoulders, and with it her appalling thoughts. She was a clever, strong, and capable woman, who just needed to keep herself sane until she was returned safely to Termarth.

'You can call me Anne,' she said. 'It might help me to fit in a little more while I'm here if you don't use my title.'

The Barbarian threw the rag onto the floor and finally turned to face her, bracing his hands behind him on the stable rail. 'I don't think you'll ever blend in here,' he said. 'But what is it that you want? I'm pretty busy here, *Anne.*'

She felt a tug in her chest—that same irresistible pull as when their eyes had met across the battlement at Termarth—and her mouth dried.

'Have you sent word to my father, to let him know I am here?'

He studied her carefully. 'That is no concern of yours.'

'I was just thinking… If it is a ransom you are after, you will need to let him know of my whereabouts.'

'I'm sure your father's dogs will sniff us out. We were careful to leave enough tracks. Is that all?'

She wrung her hands together. 'Last night you said that I didn't have shackles and chains because I wasn't a prisoner. That I was free to do as I pleased…' When he didn't speak, she rushed on. 'Well, you and I both know that I can't exactly walk out of here and find my way home, so I shall wait for my father's men to fetch me. Which will be soon, no doubt. But I cannot stay in that room, day and night, cooped up like one of your animals. I will go mad. Please…'

He must have noticed her pale skin, or perhaps even recognised the consternation in her eyes. 'What's the matter, Princess? Are you lonely up there? Needing someone to talk to?'

She tilted her chin up. 'If you must know, I'm scared of small spaces.' *Of having no way out.*

His eyes narrowed on her. 'Are you?'

He thought she was playing him.

'I mean it,' she said. 'I've hated it ever since I was young. I panic.'

He took a step towards her, concern clouding his blue gaze. 'Why? What happened?'

She sighed. She didn't want to tell him, but she knew he wouldn't believe her otherwise, and might send her back to that room in bonds.

She twisted her hands some more. 'After my mother died, my father would lock me away for long periods. He said he was worried that something would happen to me, and the only way to keep me safe was for me to stay in my room. I'd spend days and days up there, with no one to talk to and nothing to do. Then he'd soften and let me out for a while—until he had another one of his episodes and he'd do it again. Each time it happened I'd be up there for longer and longer, and I began to worry he'd forgotten about me. I started to pace and scream, begging to be let out, but it was as if no one could hear me.'

She thought she saw a flash of anger light up the Barbarian's eyes, but he didn't say anything.

'With you locking me in that room, I think it brings it all back,' she finished.

He took a step towards her. 'So what do you suggest? I can't have you roaming about the place—it's not safe,' he said, his eyebrows pulling together.

'Safe for whom? What do you think I'm going to do?'

'For *you*!' he said, exasperated.

Again, not what she was expecting.

'Some of my men have taken a shine to you, Highness. You may have no regard for your safety, but I do.'

'Anne,' she said.

'And some of them don't feel the need to be gentle with Saxon women, *Anne*,' he added.

Her skin chilled. 'I understand. Which is why I suggest you put me to work with your sister.'

For a moment he looked bemused. 'I do not put my sister to work—she does as she pleases.'

'Then I envy her,' she said. 'No man has ever let *me* do as I please.' He drew in a breath, but she carried on anyway. 'I can sew...or wash pans.'

He stared at her, incredulous. 'You can't be serious. You are a princess. I can't imagine you have ever done a day's work in your life!'

'Then you don't know me at all. Perhaps you need an education in Saxon women,' she said, twisting his words from the night before.

His amusement dried up. 'I am sorry if I've misjudged you, Highness, but I thought princesses drifted around in their palaces, being waited on hand and foot. They don't work.'

He picked up a tool, as if at the mention of work he needed to get back to whatever he was doing to the boat.

'This one does—even if my father forbids it. I can sew, or even cook. I need to do something. I know we don't exactly see eye to eye, you and I...' She waited for him to deny it. He didn't. 'But I'm serious. I need to keep busy.'

'Look,' he said, tossing the tool aside with a loud clatter. 'You're of no use to me dead, but if you promise to be careful, and not to leave Svea's side...'

She smiled at him then—perhaps for the first time. 'I don't especially want to end up dead myself...'

His lips twisted.

'Thank you,' she said. Then she turned her gaze to look at the boat. 'Did you build this?'

'I did.'

'It's beautiful. You're good at it.'

'Was that a compliment? From Princess Anne of Termarth?'

Her smile widened as she considered him. 'Brand the Boat Builder...' she said. 'It has a nice ring to it. What is it for? Are you planning to go somewhere?'

His brow furrowed. 'Ulf!' he called, and the lad came running in.

He obviously didn't want to tell her, and he was cutting their conversation short.

'Take the Princess to my sister and ask her to give her a job to do—or at least to keep her occupied until I am finished here.'

'Yes, Brand.'

'And don't let me down again.'

'No, Brand.'

'Thank you,' Anne said again, and began to walk away. Then she stopped and turned slightly. 'And for keeping your word last night.'

He inclined his head, narrowing his watchful eyes on her.

'I am starting to think you are not the barbarian people believe you to be.'

In fact, she was starting to wonder if any of it was true. Who *was* the man behind the fearsome name?

'Well, we can't have that...' He smiled. 'Perhaps I need to start living up to my reputation.'

Chapter Four

Brand knew he was letting Anne affect him more than she should. They were waiting for an enemy to arrive at his gates, getting ready for the battle he'd longed to fight for years, to take his revenge—and yet his mind was consumed with thoughts for this woman. His rival's woman.

But didn't they say you should keep your enemies close? Perhaps he should get to know everything about her, inch by silky inch. He found himself wanting to know more about the woman beneath the beautiful exterior too—the one who had handed him a blanket last night so he wouldn't get cold.

And yet he could not allow himself to care for her. He had a whole fortress of people to look after, and a sister he had vowed to spend his life making amends to. It was why he had determined never to have children of his own—he didn't need anyone else depending on him.

It had been hours since he had spoken with Anne in

the barn, and he'd kept himself and his men busy with reinforcing the castle walls, making more longbows and stockpiling food, preparing for Crowe and his men to arrive. But his thoughts were tormented. When she had smiled at him for the first time she had taken his breath away. She was more mesmerising than his beloved ocean. And more dangerous.

He needed to get some self-control.

He understood Anne's need to keep busy—he often sought solace in his workshop. His father had spent most of his time there too, tinkering away on whatever his latest project was. And it helped Brand to feel close to him.

His father had a lot to answer for... Ivar Bjarnesson was the reason their Danish shield brothers had joined them on their quest to England. They'd followed his vision, his search for fertile land and a good trading route. A better life. And it was why Brand was determined not to give up on what they'd built here.

Only he didn't know if his father would approve of his latest move of practically stealing a princess from her wedding bed...

The well-worn old longboat that had carried them to England was still here, and Brand smiled, running his hand over the bodywork. To anyone else, the bare shell of the vessel would have looked like scrap, but to him it was still beautiful, amazingly free from any major damage, just a slightly dented keel. A fierce dragon head was carved into the prow. One day he would strip it down to its core, discover its weaknesses—rather like Anne had begun to do with him last night...

Why did she keep interrupting his thoughts? Why was he letting her get to him? He needed to focus.

He knew he was purposely trying to keep his distance from her. Having just a piece of wood between them all night had been bad enough, but spending the day with her too? Hell, no. He'd been prepared to lock her up for the remainder of the time she was here, so he wouldn't have to be around her, until she'd stormed in here, refusing to behave the way he'd expected her to and breaking down his resolve. Again.

Everything she'd told him about her upbringing so far had shocked him, made him angry. How could her father have locked her away like that? Although wasn't he guilty of wanting to do exactly the same? Couldn't he understand why? When something was so precious, it was tempting to keep it tucked away, to keep it safe. And yet Anne had felt her father wasn't interested in her. The King had neglected her. And still, in spite of his harsh treatment of her, she had grown up to be kind-hearted. He'd seen it in the way she'd helped him as a boy and the way she'd cared for his horse when it was hurt.

He sighed, knowing he should seek her out, check that everything was all right and that his men weren't tormenting her. But when he headed into the square and inside the longhouse, there was no sign of her or Svea. They weren't in the cookhouse either. When he couldn't find them in Svea's room, his skin began to chill with alarm. His strides became longer and faster as he searched for her back in the barn, in the smokehouse and all the other houses. Nothing.

She wouldn't have made a run for it, would she? Yes, she was impulsive, strong-willed and tenacious— he wouldn't put it past her to try—but the gates were locked and his men were on guard. Someone would surely have raised the alarm. And Svea was nifty with a blade should an enemy have come close.

Then a thought occurred to him. The beach. He could tell she'd felt drawn to the sea—she hadn't been able to take her eyes off it on their journey to Kald. She'd been practically mesmerised. And although she had wanted to hide her fascination from him, she'd failed miserably. Would Svea have taken her there?

Fear thundered through him. Yes, the sea looked beautiful, and to a strong swimmer like himself or Svea it was glorious, but to someone unprepared for the currents—someone like his mother or Anne—it could be lethal.

He signalled for his men to open the fortress gates and then took off on the path that led downhill to the cove, picking up his pace.

Reaching the bay, sheltered on one side by the fortress, the rest a vast expanse of golden sand, he noted the tide was in and the waves were thrusting forward, rolling at full speed onto the shore. The sun was getting lower in the sky as he looked up and down the beach, but he couldn't see them.

Memories washed over him, of the boat rising over each crest then crashing back down, and watching his mother fall. He'd cried out to warn his father, but it had been too late—her head had slammed into the vessel, and he'd watched as her body had slipped beneath the surface. The last thing he remembered—would always remember—was the sound of his mother's last breath and the shattering of his own heart breaking.

In these past few years he'd been stronger than he'd known he could be—he'd had to be for Svea. He'd had to grow up quickly, and give over his time to making sure she was all right, that she had everything she needed. But he was certainly no replacement for their parents. And it had put him off ever being a father himself. The burden was too great. And should anything untoward ever happen to his own children, it would be more than he could bear. He often took comfort in the fact that his father had died without having to witness what had happened to him and Svea.

A movement near the rock pools caught his eye as a solitary figure began to walk towards him. He made his way in that direction, and through the fading sun he saw that it was Svea.

He cursed under his breath. 'Where have you been? I've been looking everywhere for you. Is Anne with you?'

'We've been here. I thought I'd allow our guest to wash while the men were otherwise occupied.'

'Good idea,' he said, relief flowing through him. 'Where is she?'

Svea pointed to the tidal pools, and as Brand registered the lone silhouette in the water he released his bunched-up fists, running his fingers over his hair and down his beard.

'Don't worry, she's safe,' Svea said, tapping her sword as if to reassure her brother.

These days his sister was one of Kald's fiercest warriors, and he was incredibly proud of the woman she'd become. Crowe had changed her, of course, as he'd changed them all. That man had torn apart the beautiful web his family had built, hardened their hearts, and he knew Svea longed for revenge, as did he.

If he could cause that man pain, it would assuage the guilt he felt for not being able to protect Svea and his father. And they'd had infinite patience, like a colony of spiders, constructing a new, beautiful but fragile home in which to take shelter, and it wouldn't be long now until Crowe fell into their trap.

'You know, if I didn't know better I'd think you had a soft spot for our prisoner,' said Svea.

His eyes narrowed on her. 'That's ridiculous.'

She grinned. 'Just remember she's a Saxon—you're a Dane. We stick to the plan.'

'How could I forget?' he said. 'You know I won't let you down.'

'Be sure you don't.' She squeezed his arm. 'Well, she's all yours. I need to go and see how tonight's food is coming along. See you up there.'

He paced over to the pools, needing to see with his own eyes that the Princess was all right.

'Anne?'

The water parted and she stood suddenly, in shock, water sluicing off her glorious body—and he froze. Never before had he experienced a shot of lust so strong, so powerful. He couldn't move.

They could use her as a weapon in battle, he thought, to paralyse men—she was that beautiful. He blinked his eyes, trying to block out the image of her loose dark hair cascading over her wet undergarments, the flare of panic in her green eyes.

He saw Anne glance down and gasp. The white material of her undergarments had turned see-through in the water and was clinging to her body in all the wrong places, highlighting the shadows under her small, pert breasts, the peaks of her rosy nipples. A little squeal slipped out of her mouth, and just as quickly as she'd stood her divine body disappeared beneath the water again.

'There's no need to stare!' she shouted.

He would have to disagree. But she was a little too perfect—especially for the likes of him. And knowing that helped him to keep his hands to himself.

He forced himself to be courteous and turn around.

'What are you doing here?' she screeched.

'I didn't know where you were. I came to find you to check everything was all right.' His back to her, he closed his eyes and tried to swallow down his lust, but it was futile. 'It's getting late. We should go back up before it gets dark. Svea's gone on ahead.' His throat felt incredibly dry. 'But you might want to get changed first,' he said.

Snatching up her cloak, he wondered how he had missed the neat pile of clothes on the rocks. He threw it to her and she stood again, holding the wool across her body, and with extremely unsteady fingers she reached for her dress too.

He was glad to have another moment with his back turned to pull himself together. He heard her hoist herself out of the water and begin to dress. There was the unmistakable sound of wet clothes dropping to the sand, and he heard her tussle with the wool as she dried her smooth skin. He could imagine every action and his blatant desire wasn't going away.

An agonising moment later, he heard her soft footsteps on the sand behind him.

'Are you decent?' he asked.

'I am now.'

Turning round, he knew he would never be able to erase the image of her perfect round breasts and the flare of her hips from his mind, as she rose out of the water like the Norse sea goddess Rán. And she'd definitely snared him in her net.

'I thought you weren't keen on bathing in public,' he said.

'I didn't have much of a choice, did I? And your sister assured me no one was here.'

'So how was it?'

'What?'

'The water?' He grinned, keeping up with her as she began to make her way across the beach.

He saw the faint flicker of a smile at the corner of her mouth. 'You were right. It was good—if a little cold.'

He knew how enticing the water could be. If it hadn't been for her teeth chattering and his stomach beginning to rumble he might even have tried to convince her to go back in with him. And not just into the rockpools, but the shallow surf.

An image of her body in his arms, slippery from the

water, made him hot and hard. He breathed in a lungful of sea air, hoping it would steady his racing heart, as they began their ascent up the steep, winding cliff path.

The dark fortress always took on a different character at night time. The light was rapidly beginning to fade and the tall wooden walls stood in a mighty silhouette against the setting sun. He wanted to know what she thought of the home he had built. He didn't understand why he cared, but he wanted to know if she liked it. It wasn't exactly like the castle she had grown up in, but it was still pretty impressive, and enough to put off even the fiercest of opponents from attacking.

Still, he knew Crowe would come. That man had a thirst for power and bloodshed. Brand had seen it first-hand. What was taking him so long? If Anne had been taken from *him*, he would have gone after her in a heartbeat. But he wasn't her rescuer, was he? He was her captor. And right now he wasn't sure he liked himself very much. He only hoped she knew by now that he wasn't going to hurt her. If anything, he wanted to protect her.

It was the gulls circling in the sky above them that first caught Brand's attention—and then he saw the field, well churned up by horses' hooves. Every muscle in his body tensed and his blood chilled. Out of the corner of his eye, not twenty feet ahead of them, he saw a wall of Saxon soldiers gathering on the heath.

He covered Anne's mouth with his hand, mirroring his movements in the forest the day before, enveloping her body in his arms as she tensed. If they'd carried on just a few steps more they would have been seen.

He nodded towards the field and she followed his line of sight. 'It seems your lover has come for you at last.'

He glanced over to the fortress gates. There was no sign of Svea. He reckoned she must have made it back just in time, thank goodness. If she had seen the Saxons, there was no telling how she might have reacted...

He backed Anne into the hollow of an old English oak where he'd played hide and seek with his sister as a boy. He manoeuvred her round to face him in the tight space, blocking her exit. She was enclosed, and he knew she wouldn't like it.

'Are you not going to scream, Princess?'

Her chin tilted up. 'I wouldn't dare. I know what my punishment would be if I tried.'

He grinned. He'd spent his childhood growing up in the marsh and heathland, so he knew this terrain inside out. The soldiers ahead of them looked like hired mercenaries, rather than free peasants fighting for their King. It would make them harder to fight, if it came to that, but Brand knew he had the upper hand having the fortress.

Only he saw instantly that those fifty or so men were blocking their way to the entrance of Kald.

Heading up the group was Crowe, and Brand felt a cold curl of wrath seep through his veins.

He reached for his sword.

'Don't!' Anne said, gripping his arm.

He glanced down at her hand, then back at her. 'What's the matter? Worried that your lover will get hurt?'

She shook her head. 'He is not my lover. If it was up to me, I would not be marrying him at all.'

He inclined his head. 'Worried about me, then?'

'I don't want anyone to get hurt. And you'd be a fool to fight all those men on your own. See reason!'

He would happily die trying... But, although he hated to admit it, he knew she was right. Now was not the time to fight. There were too many of them for him to take on by himself—even by his standards. No, he had to bide his time and first get back within the walls of Kald without being seen.

He released his grip on the hilt of his weapon.

'Do you have a death wish?' she added.

'I do not fear death, if that's what you mean. Every Dane wishes to fight with honour and to die bravely in battle.'

'But surely not yet? Not now?'

He nodded, taking her chin between his thumb and forefinger, gently tipping her face up to his. He was so close to her he felt her breath hitch. 'You're right. I should be patient.'

In all things, he thought, as he stared down into her eyes. He could get lost in their green stormy depths.

So what should he do? They could wait it out—see if the soldiers moved away, so he could signal to his men in Kald to open the gate for him and Anne to slip inside. Or they could return to the beach and make the hard climb over the rocks to the other entrance at the back of the fortress. But it was only accessible by water. Could Anne make it?

He peered around the oak and took another glance

at the men. They looked as if they were set to stay, so he made his decision.

Anne gasped. 'Brand, they're wearing black and yellow—the markings that man in the village spoke of.'

'I wondered if you'd noticed.'

She shook her head. She couldn't believe Crowe and his men would do such a thing. Why? Had Brand been right all along?

'I'm sorry I doubted you. What do we do now?'

He liked the sound of 'we', and he trailed his hand down her cheek, over her arm, and down to hold her hand in his. And when he thought she might resist, to pull back and protest, or cry out to Crowe, she didn't.

'They're blocking our route back. We'll have to go this way. Come on.'

Chapter Five

$\sim\!\!\infty\!\!\sim$

Anne supposed she should struggle against his touch, but she felt dazed and disorientated. She was sure that Brand had nearly kissed her for a second time. Would she have pushed him away? The way her body was reacting to him disturbed her. It seemed to have a mind of its own, burning for his touch, and she didn't understand it.

Was this what desire felt like? And why was she feeling it with this man?

Keeping low and quiet, so as not to draw any unwanted attention, Brand led her back down the narrow cliffside path and she let him, her tiny hand in his large, strong one. She wondered why she wasn't trying to escape. Why was she following this Northman down a dark, dangerous path when her fiancé's men had finally come to get her?

But if she'd made a run for it, or cried out, it would have led to certain bloodshed. Brand would have put up a fight and been killed, and she told herself she didn't want him or anyone else to get hurt. And wasn't there a tiny part of her that wasn't yet ready to go back to her old life? Back to Termarth to be married off to Crowe or the next highest bidder?

Her fiancé was practically within shouting distance, but she was no longer sure who was the enemy. Was Crowe a friend or a foe? Could it really be true that he and his men were responsible for the devastation of that settlement the other day? She felt sick. If he had killed all those people in that village, she needed to let her father know. Surely the King wouldn't want such an ally?

She wondered if Brand was right—were the Danes being blamed for Saxon atrocities?

'Where are we going?' she whispered.

'Back down to the beach. We can't stay here on the cliff all night, and at least there's shelter in the caves. We can get into Kald if we go the back way, but we might have to wait until first light. The rocks are lethal, even when you can see where you're going.'

Anne stopped dead, tugging her hand out of his grasp. 'You want us to spend the night on the beach? But there's no one else around.'

Maybe she was making a mistake. But she had her reputation to think of! She could not be alone with this man—especially when she was having such strong reactions to him. She thought she was even starting to like him. The yearning to have him kiss her again was becoming a concern, and as for the throbbing heat between her legs—it was terrifying her.

'What's wrong? Don't you trust yourself alone with me?'

He offered her a dangerous half-smile. Damn him,

how did he do that? How did he know what she was thinking?

'Come on, we don't have a choice,' he said over his shoulder. But he stopped again when he realised she wasn't following.

'We do,' she said, shaking her head. 'You could stop this madness and hand me back to my people.'

His face suddenly turned mutinous. 'What is it, Princess? You've caught a glimpse of your lover and are desperate to go back to him? Is that it?'

'I told you—he is not my lover. I barely know Lord Crowe and I do not care for him,' she bit back. 'All I know is that I can't be alone with you!'

Somehow her words and her anger seemed to appease him. He exhaled, slowly raking his hand over his hair. 'Look, I promised I wouldn't kiss you again, if that's what you're worried about, and I meant it. I'm not going to hurt you, Anne. I will hand you back to your father soon enough—I promise. But for now just keep walking. We don't want to be on this crumbling path in the dark.'

And, like a deer being led off into the unknown— either to freedom in the forest or to be made a sacrifice—she allowed him to take her hand again and she followed him.

When they made it onto the sand it had lost all the warmth of the sun and felt like a cool embrace around her feet, and yet Brand was right—it was much more sheltered from the elements down here. It was also out of sight of Crowe and his soldiers. Out of sight of anyone...

'Won't your men be wondering where we are? Won't they come looking for us?' she asked. 'Won't they attack Lord Crowe?'

'Svea knows we were at the beach. She'll realise we're stuck. And, no, they won't do anything without my command.'

Brand tugged her along the undulating sand to the opening of a little cave.

'Take a seat,' he said, motioning for her to sit on a smooth rock.

The sun was setting on the horizon and it was an incredible show of rich purple and glorious gold, casting a brilliant amber glow over the beach and illuminating the rippling water. When she was younger there had been so many times when she had longed for escape and had dreamed of seeing the ocean, of experiencing places and scenes like this one. But never had she thought she'd experience it with a Northman.

She had heard stories of men like Brand Ivarsson crossing the seas. 'Giant sea wolves', her father had called them. Unafraid of anything or anyone. Pagans to be feared and fought. And yet the man who stood before her now, trying to pull some green leaves from the rocks, was nothing like the men her father had described. Yes, he looked fierce and dangerous, but he was also extremely attractive—and she had not once seen him act like a barbarian. He had actually treated her rather well for a prisoner.

And, although she was deep in Daneland, Anne realised the barren beauty of the place was getting under her skin—just like her captor.

'What are you doing?'

'I'd normally spear some fish and cook it over a fire, but the smoke would give away our location, so we're going to have to make do with this sea spinach for our meal tonight. I hope you're not too hungry?'

Brand passed her a handful of green leaves with fleshy stems and she took a tentative bite. It wasn't too bad—she'd had worse. He ate a few stalks himself but he was quiet…brooding.

Was it because he had an army at his gates and knew battle was now imminent? But men such as Brand Ivarsson yearned for battles and glory, didn't they? They lived to fight—he'd told her so himself. Perhaps he was just desperate to get back up there and get on with it.

'We don't get sunsets quite like this in Termarth,' she said, trying to think of something to talk about. 'What an incredible view. I could get lost in it, couldn't you?'

'I could,' he said, but when she turned to look at him she saw he wasn't admiring the horizon. He was looking at her. And the more he looked, the more she babbled.

'I can see why you decided to settle here. What was it like where you originally came from?'

'Cold,' he said.

'Just cold?'

'Desolate. There were no crops, no harvest…' He shrugged. 'Nothing like this,' he said, waving a few of the green leaves around. 'I was just a boy; I don't remember too much. But I do recall we had no land. No land that wasn't waterlogged, anyway. And we were always hungry. There wasn't enough food. We came in search of a better way of life...better things.'

Anne thought how bad things must have been for his parents to make the decision to put two small children in a boat and travel across perilous seas—to risk their lives and start a new one. She tried to picture Brand as a boy, but struggled. She didn't like the thought of him being starving and cold, but then she wouldn't wish that on anyone.

'And is it?' she asked. 'Better here?'

'Some things.'

He was staring at her again, with heat in his eyes.

'I always longed to escape too...to get far away from home.'

'Is life as a princess really so bad?'

'I know I should not complain. I certainly cannot moan of ever being cold or hungry. But it's not all feasts and festivities either. There are so many rules and restrictions. It's lonely. I envy the way you and your people live so freely—the way Svea can do as she pleases. I spend most of my days lost in books, wanting to explore the places I read about, longing for an adventure of my own.'

'Are you not having one right now?' His lips curved up into a smile.

'Battles and bloodshed aren't really my type of thing...' she said, glancing away, trying to remind herself that she was *not* on an adventure, she had been abducted. Snatched from her home. And now her father had sent Crowe and his army to steal her back.

It was as if she was like some kind of toy the men wanted to play with, to throw around for a bit and see what bargain they could strike with her. If only they would leave her be to make her own life, to rule her own people. If only her father would see her as capable of doing that one day... But it seemed a husband had to be thrown into the deal.

Her thoughts flew back to her fiancé. 'What if we're not there and Lord Crowe attacks? I mean, Svea may not start it, but the Saxons might.'

'Worried you're missing the fight, Highness?' he mocked.

'No, I'd just hate him to storm the fortress for nothing. I can't bear the thought of innocent women and children getting hurt.'

'You are a good person, Anne.'

He placed a hand on her shoulder, trying to comfort her. And it did. She wanted him to keep it there, and yet she hated herself for feeling reassured by him when he was responsible for all this, so she shrugged him off.

'I told you—I doubt they'll attack tonight. Not after their long journey, nor in the dark—and definitely not if they think you're inside,' he said. 'They wouldn't risk it. They'll want to negotiate first. Anyway, no one needs to get hurt if your fiancé complies with my demands.'

She held his gaze. 'And what are they?'

'I told you. Crowe's life in my hands.'

As he began to rake the sand with his sword, she realised there was much more to this than kidnap and a possible ransom. She could tell that a burden lay heavy on his set shoulders and she wanted to know what it was. She had a right to know, didn't she? He was using her to get back at the man, after all.

'What is it driven by, your obsessive need for revenge? What did Crowe do to you? What scars did he cause you?'

He looked at her then, ice-cold. 'You're staring right at one.'

Her skin prickled. She studied the silver track carved into his face between his forehead and his high, defined cheekbone, interrupting his dark brow. It wasn't unattractive. If anything, it added a certain allure to his impressive face. But it must have been a deep wound originally.

'He gave you that? How?'

'I'm surprised you don't remember, Princess. After all, you were there.'

'What?'

He was practically glowering at her, his face taut, and she could feel the tension rolling off him. She felt as if they were each pulling one end of a tug of war rope, like those she'd seen the Danish children playing with in the square, and it was ready to snap.

'You don't remember me, do you?'

She stared back at him, felt a tremble starting in her knees. Whatever was coming, she knew it wasn't good...

'We met before, a long time ago...' he continued. 'You helped me when I was hurt.'

He stabbed at the sand with his blade again, as if

to give his hands something to do, his eyes something to focus on.

An image of a boy, battered and bruised, entered her mind. It was so vivid it took her aback. A boy with winter-blue eyes...

It had been a balmy summer's day and she a young teenager. She'd been walking outside the castle gates, where she hadn't been allowed to go. But she'd been desperate to explore, to see new things. It had been just after one of her father's episodes, and she'd been locked up inside for weeks. She'd thought even one afternoon of freedom would be worth getting caught for.

She'd heard barking dogs and male voices and had panicked, taking cover behind a little wooden shack in a meadow. She hadn't wanted her father's guards to find her, knowing she'd be punished, but then she'd seen they were soldiers from Calhourn, not Termarth, and that they were chasing a boy who was about the same age as herself.

She'd lingered to watch, to find out what all the commotion was about, and she'd seen them pummel his face and kick him, over and over again, until he'd stopped moving. She'd been horrified, clasping her hand over her mouth so she wouldn't cry out.

When the soldiers had finally retreated she'd crept closer, to check if the boy was still breathing. He'd been left for dead, his face covered in blood. Yet it hadn't been his terrible injuries that had shocked her; it had been his dark skin and long blond hair, and when he'd opened his pale blue eyes something about them had made an instant impression.

He was, without doubt, the most beautiful boy she'd ever seen—even with his appalling injuries. She'd sensed he was trouble. He didn't look like the usual boys who hung around the courtyard of the castle, and he was clearly a danger if the Saxon soldiers had been after him. And yet surely no child deserved that treatment?

Anne had felt a shift in her blood that day—a desire to piece him back together, to help him. But when she'd heard the sound of the Royal Guard approaching, sent to retrieve her, she'd realised how foolish that idea was.

Her hand flew to her mouth. 'That was you? And Lord Crowe?' She shook her head, allowing the information to sink in. 'I always wondered what had happened to you after they took me away.'

Before this moment she had never been able to imagine the warrior before her as a young boy. But now she knew with crystal-clear clarity that it had been him. And her heart went out to him for what he had suffered and the shadows that now haunted him.

'Well, now you know,' he said, frosting over, standing up as if to say their conversation was over.

But she hadn't finished. She shook her head, rising to join him. 'But why did he hurt you? For being a Dane?'

'You'll have to ask him that when you next see him, Highness. But, yes, I believe that was my only crime.'

She understood his rage now. Lord Crowe had nearly beaten him to death. And yet he'd lived to tell the tale. Yes, Crowe deserved to be punished, but she still couldn't see how taking the man's life would make things better. It would just make everything worse. Had the Barbarian told her everything?

'Thank you for explaining it to me,' she said.

He nodded. 'I have always wanted to thank you for helping me that day. I have never forgotten it. Never forgotten *you*. When I heard your father was marrying you off to such a man, I felt I needed to repay the favour… You have said you don't want to marry him. Hopefully you won't have to. Is it just him you're averse to, or the institution of marriage altogether?'

The question took her aback. No one had ever asked her opinion on the matter before. It was just a given that she would do her duty and marry whoever her father told her to, whether she wanted to or not.

'I had always hoped to marry for love, but as that cannot be I am prepared to marry for the good of my people, to help keep them safe. But now I see this marriage would not be good for anyone.'

'You know, we are not so different, you and I…' He smiled. 'You will marry whoever your father thinks will give your kingdom more protection. I will not marry for exactly the same reason—to protect my people.'

'Our people depend on us,' she acknowledged.

He nodded. 'Now you should try to get some sleep,' he said, drawing a line under their conversation. 'Whatever happens, it's going to be an interesting day tomorrow.'

She reclined against the wall of the cave, trying to get comfortable. Above them the magnificent sky glittered with faraway stars and the dramatic waves crashing onto the shore helped to calm the storm inside her. But every time she closed her eyes she was haunted by a pale blue gaze and a boy's bloodied face. He was hurt, and no matter how hard she tried, she couldn't reach him.

She shivered.

'Are you cold?'

'A little.'

'Here,' he said, passing her his cloak. 'Take it.'

Her brow furrowed. What was this—kindness now? He continued to surprise her.

As she took it, her fingers brushed against his. 'Don't you ever sleep?' she asked.

He muttered something under his breath, and she could have sworn he said, 'I did before you came along.'

Anne's head kept rolling forward in her sleep, and when she shivered for the hundredth time Brand made his decision. He sat down next to her on the sand and wrapped an arm around her, pulling her head into the curve of his shoulder. He drew her close, hoping his body heat would help to warm her up. He tucked the cloak around them and allowed himself to shut his eyes.

At least this way maybe he would get some rest too, without worrying that she might try to make a run for it or that she would freeze to death. She wouldn't thank him for touching her again, though, and the instant his body curved around hers, his hip resting against the side of her bottom, he didn't thank himself either. His erection was immediate.

What was it about this woman that made him want

her so much? Seeing her launch her half-naked body out of the water earlier had taken that desire up a notch.

And what was it about her that made him open up and tell her things? Things about his childhood that he'd buried deep, trying to forget them—like how his family had been starving and why they'd come here. All things that had made him the man he was today. Wasn't that why he'd vowed he would always keep the people under his protection fed and warm, whatever it took? And hadn't those memories of going hungry, and never wishing it upon another soul, led to him being here now, with Anne in his arms?

She could help him to help his people... She was valuable to her kingdom and her father would no doubt be willing to pay for her safe return. And yet he was starting to realise she was right. She really was priceless...

She muttered a few words in her sleep and turned into him. He could take her so easily. He knew that was what the Saxons expected of the Danes. Her tiny frame would be no match for his strength. But fundamentally he didn't agree with it—especially after what had happened to Svea. And he'd never had to use force to get what he wanted from women. Usually seduction came easily to him. But this was much more complicated.

If only Anne *wanted* to be with him... But that would never happen. She was far too good for the likes of him.

He must be insane... Here he was, stranded outside his fortress, with fifty or so Saxon soldiers at his gates, and he couldn't keep his feelings for this woman in check. Right under her fiancé's nose.

But wasn't there something deeply satisfying about that? Wasn't that part of her allure? He wondered if he would still want her if she wasn't engaged to Crowe, but as he stared down at her beautiful face, softened by slumber, he had his answer. *Helvelte*, yes. He wanted her. And now that she'd told him she didn't even know or particularly like Crowe, and didn't want to marry him, he desired her all the more.

In any other circumstance this would be an ideal setting to court a woman, with the backdrop of the ocean and the canvas of stars lighting up the night sky, the silk-smooth sand beneath their bodies... But he had to think of her and her reputation. He needed to stop being so foolish and he needed to rest, so that tomorrow he could focus on his vendetta.

He closed his eyes again and tried to put all thoughts of his captive out of his mind.

When Anne woke she felt warm, safe...and then she realised she was nestled into the side of a man's chest. A heavy arm was draped around her shoulder, a big hand curved around her waist, and she froze in alarm. Brand had promised not to touch her again and yet here he was, holding her in his arms. Arms that were solid and strong and seemed almost protective—or was their purpose purely restraint?

But as she listened to the steady beat of his heart, and felt the rise and fall of his breathing, she realised he was asleep. Heat was radiating off him, and he wasn't trying to harm her or imprison her. He was just holding her, perhaps to keep them both warm.

In the upstairs room he had told her he didn't find her attractive and she should have been relieved. Instead, it had hurt—more than it should. Was she unlovable? Her father had always been so cold, and he had made her feel that way. She had never had a close friendship with anyone except one or two of her maids, who were paid to look after her and be kind to her.

And yet this man, huddled next to her on the sand, had revealed that he had thought about her all these years—since they'd met as children... He had revealed he had stolen her away to protect her from Crowe. And now he was holding her, keeping her warm, and she had never felt so cherished.

She was lying here in the darkness, actually willing him to pull her closer into his chest and hold her even tighter, to run his fingers through her hair again, as he had done the other day. And her thoughts scared her, because she had only read about these feelings and been educated in how things were between a man and a woman through reading books—she had never experienced it first-hand.

Who was this woman she was becoming? She didn't even recognise her.

And as she lay there, trying to steady her erratic breathing, taking in the musky male scent of him, she couldn't help but nuzzle closer, enjoying the feeling of his solid chest muscles beneath her cheek, the heat of his thighs against hers.

But when she felt his breathing change and his arms tighten around her, her whole body tensed. She didn't dare move. *What had she done?* She knew she should act quickly and feign disgust at his closeness, but her body wasn't listening to her mind and she couldn't bring herself to pull away. And then, almost unbelievably, impossibly lightly, he began circling her shoulder with the tips of his fingers, sending goosebumps down her arms, making her shiver.

'Still cold?' he asked.

'No... You promised you wouldn't touch me again,' she whispered, turning her face to stare up at him. But her voice didn't sound as if she minded. Damn. Why couldn't she stir up some of that anger? 'You said it was a mistake...'

Sleepy hooded blue eyes gazed down at her. 'I didn't say I wasn't willing to make the same mistake again.' His husky voice was just a breath away from her lips. 'And if you don't stop looking at me like that I'm going to have to do something about it...unless you tell me to stop.'

But she didn't. She couldn't.

And this time Brand was gentle. His fingers brushed her cheeks as his firm mouth lightly grazed hers and her eyelids fluttered shut. Her thoughts were incoherent as her lips slowly yielded, giving in to the delicious sensations he was creating as he took possession of her mouth with persuasive, tender strokes of his tongue.

It was a kiss that seemed to start as a question, a soft enquiry, but soon deepened into a thorough examination of her mouth, demanding some kind of answer. And instead of pulling away Anne responded by pressing herself closer, bravely letting him know that she wanted this just as much as him. Her hands moved up to rest against his strong jaw, holding him in place as her tongue experimentally stole into his mouth too, over and over again, gliding against his in a deep, passionate caress.

Heat bloomed inside her—or was it hope?—and her hand slid down over his chest, brushing aside the material at the neck of his tunic so she could explore the feel of his skin, as hard as the rocks on the beach but as smooth as the sand. Brand moaned and dragged her down to the ground, so they were lying side by side, and then he tugged her body against him as he continued to educate her in the art of the perfect kiss.

As heat coiled down low in her belly she tried a little wriggle against him and he growled, his careful control seemingly about to snap. Drifting his hands down to her hips and cupping her bottom, he hauled her soft curves against the hardness of his length, binding her to him, and an insane need lanced her. She didn't want him to stop. She wanted him to put his hands on her. All over her.

Rolling her onto her back and hovering over her, he skated his fingers up her ribcage to curve over one pert breast. She knew she should pull away, stop this madness, and yet still her body arched into him, and a flutter of excitement blossomed between her legs as he kneaded her breast through the material of her dress, making her quiver.

She wanted more.

Her head rolled back against the sand as he left a trail of delicate little kisses along her throat, and then his thumb moved over her nipple, tweaking it into a hard peak. He pushed one knee between her thighs, his thick erection nudging against her stomach, leaving her in no doubt of his desire, or of where this was heading.

It must have been her little gasp of shock that made him pull back slightly. Anne's fingers were suddenly unmoving at the back of his neck as they stared at each other, their foreheads touching. And then, with an almost violent, urgent curse, he was up, leaving her lying on the sand, her arms outstretched, wondering what the hell had just happened.

'*Det var som faen!* We shouldn't be doing this. Not here. Not now,' he bit out, stalking away.

Anne's cheeks burned as she struggled to sit up, straightening her clothes. *What had she done?* She didn't know what had come over her, to act so brazenly. And yet still a part of her wanted to beg him to come back and finish what he'd started. But she had no experience when it came to things like this, and she'd certainly never expected to feel like that! Especially with Brand Ivarsson the Barbarian.

But she had welcomed his touch…willingly opened her mouth so his tongue could explore her. Her hands flew up to her hot cheeks. She had writhed against him, silently encouraging him to put his hands on her. What was the matter with her? After all, he was only doing all this to cause injury to Lord Crowe, wasn't he? Had their kiss been just a part of his revenge?

It hadn't seemed as if he'd been kissing her for anything other than his own pleasure. And surely if he wanted to wound Crowe he would have taken her already?

His touch had been potent, bringing her to budding

life, and as he'd held her against his chest her nipples had peaked as they'd grazed against him. She'd found herself holding on to him as if he was a lifeline, and then, just as quickly as he'd started, he'd pushed her away. He'd stopped. Whereas she would have continued.

She felt a little sob rise up in her throat. Oh, God. How would she ever find the strength to stand and face him?

He had his back to her, tying up his boots. And now she felt just as she had as a child, when her father had closed that door on her in the tower. Shut out and alone. She knew she should say something, but her lips were quivering and she felt tongue-tied. This whole situation was new and terrifying to her.

She stood on trembling legs and tried to focus on her footing, squaring her shoulders, trying to tear her thoughts away from him and the taste of his mouth on hers, the feel of his warm skin under her fingertips, his bearded jaw grazing against her chin.

Stop!

'Brand—?'

'We should go,' he said, cutting her off, his curt voice piercing her heart. 'The sun's rising and we've wasted far too much time here.'

Chapter Six

Brand hadn't been wrong about the hard climb over the rocks. It was a slippery scramble over ridges and little rock pools, and Anne reluctantly had to keep taking his outstretched arm to hold her balance.

He was used to the terrain and surefooted, easily making large strides from one boulder to another and then waiting for her, gripping her tight with his firm fingers as she jumped the distance to meet him. Her boots weren't appropriate, and as she landed on each uneven slab of stone she plunged into his solid chest and thigh muscles. Each time, she wasn't ready for the impact, and each time his big hands came up to circle her arms, grounding her.

'Steady.'

It certainly wasn't helping her to regain her usually cool poise. But if she was honest, she hadn't been in control of her own destiny since she'd met him. Yet she would like to salvage her self-esteem.

She scraped a hand over her face, as if to rub her

thoughts away. Was he regretting kissing her? she wondered. After all, he had described it as a waste of time. Was that why he was being so short with her?

The blistering hot sun beat down on her skin, making her overly warm, and still all she could think about was his lips on hers. She glanced out over the ocean and wished she could cool off in the water, like the little fish in the shallows, float away with the waves and be engulfed by something far bigger than her fear and shame.

When her body collided with his for the hundredth time her composure finally snapped. 'Don't you have any regard for keeping your distance?' she bit out.

'I didn't hear you complaining about that this morning.'

Her eyes narrowed on him. 'Oh, so you're acknowledging it now?'

'What?' His long legs straddled two seaweed-covered rocks.

'Nothing.' She sighed, suddenly thinking better of broaching the subject as he tugged her to join him. 'I just want to forget it.'

He moved on to the next boulder. She took a big stride and met him, meshing with his body again. 'You need to stop talking nonsense. I'd say it was pretty unforgettable, wouldn't you?'

Heat flooded her cheeks. He reached out to tuck a strand of hair behind her ear and she couldn't help but lean in a little closer.

He inclined his head. 'But that doesn't mean it was a good idea. It definitely was not.' He moved on again.

'I behaved badly. I'm sorry. I'm just not in the habit of abducting beautiful, clever, and spirited Saxon princesses and finding myself wanting to kiss them.'

Her breath caught in her throat. He thought she was clever! No one had ever considered her intelligent before. In fact, her father hated it when her nose was stuck in a book. He didn't believe she needed to be educated because she would have a husband who would make decisions for her. It had made her want to read all the more—even if it had to be done in secret, late at night by candlelight.

They continued on the rocky path in silence. Perhaps they both thought it safer, but from that point on he held her hand in his and didn't let it go.

The route seemed endless as they scaled huge boulders and clambered around smaller, sharper ones, being careful not to tread on the little creatures that lived among the rocks.

It must have been mid-morning when Anne began to tire, and Brand finally pointed to something up ahead of them.

'Look,' he said. 'We're almost there. Come on.'

She put up her hand to shade her eyes from the glare and see what he was looking at. She spotted a little jetty and a boat. But there was no path, no passageway into the fortress.

'Where do we go from here?'

'I forgot to mention…' Brand grinned sheepishly '…we have to sail around the headland the rest of the way, to take the mouth of the river into Kald.'

'Sail?' she said, her heart picking up pace. Her eyes

darted all around them, searching for an alternative route, a way to get out of this. 'I can't get into a boat! You know I don't like tight spaces. Brand—'

He continued to hold her hand in one of his, and tilted her chin up with the other, so she was looking up into his eyes. 'You're going to have to trust me, Anne.'

She swallowed. Easier said than done.

As they neared the crystal-clear water lapping at the jetty, she realised the long, narrow boat was just like the one she'd seen him working on in the barn. She felt redundant standing there, watching Brand jump knee-deep into the water to untie the vessel, while her mind made a mental tally of all the things that could go wrong if she got on board.

She reached up to feel that the back of her neck was damp with perspiration under her loose locks. She hadn't had a chance to braid her hair since she'd bathed at the beach last night. She must look a complete state.

Brand waded back towards her and held out his hand to help her onto the boat. 'Anne, it's perfectly safe,' he said, coaxing her towards him.

Chewing on her bottom lip, but accepting his help, she descended into the longship and as soon as she was in sat down on one of the benches to avoid making it rock. Brand pushed them away from the jetty before hoisting himself in.

'Welcome aboard the *Freyja*,' he said, and smiled.

'Named after one of your gods?' she asked, grimacing at the motion as Brand walked to the middle of the hull and sat down, taking up a pair of oars.

'Actually, my mother.'

Anne glanced at him in surprise. For such a supposedly unfeeling man, he had a tendency to say and do some rather sentimental things. 'She's beautiful. Did you build her?'

'I did.'

'Is she seaworthy?' she teased.

When he grinned in response, her stomach did a little somersault.

'Of course.'

'And you're sure you can row this thing on your own?' she asked, looking around at the oar holes which, if she'd counted correctly, were meant for thirteen rowers on each side—not one man. Even though the man in question was larger than life itself.

'I think I can manage.'

He began to rotate the oars to manoeuvre the vessel. She started at the sudden movement and gripped the side of the boat. There was no turning back now. Fortunately, there was no cabin, and although she was seemingly trapped in this prison on the water for a while, she was relieved that she didn't feel confined.

She pointed to the intricate carving of a sea serpent on the prow. 'You like these monsters. They're on all your ships. Are they meant to frighten people?'

'That's the *Midgard* Serpent—the world serpent.'

Her eyes widened. 'Surely such things don't exist?'

'Let's hope we don't find out!'

He laughed, and she began to relax as they glided through the shallow waves, the force of his powerful strokes meaning they were soon quite a distance from land.

'You asked me yesterday why I was building boats,' he said, and she wondered what it was about the sea that was making him more open. 'It was my father's dream, and is now mine, to build ships and use them to trade—to carry cargo in land or across the sea.'

She hadn't expected him to be a man of quiet ambition. 'I thought... I thought they might be for sailing to and raiding other places,' she said. 'I have overheard my father talking about Northmen landing on beaches and attacking monasteries and villages and then sailing away again.'

'You should know by now that's not what I do. Nor my people in Kald.'

She nodded. What other dreams did Brand Ivarsson have? she wondered. And why did he not want a wife...a family?

Images of gorgeous children with wild blue eyes and dark blond braided hair stormed her, catching her off guard. What was she doing? She was dreaming of the impossible, a Saxon and a Dane, when he had merely been telling her about boats. In fact, hadn't he implied he might even be leaving this island?

A vision of him sailing away from her caused a sharp pain in her chest.

'So, what do you think?' he asked, lightening the mood. 'Keep going and sail to distant shores, or go around the headland and face your fiancé?'

His joking, despite the subject, amazingly made her smile. It was actually a tempting offer... She realised this was what total and utter freedom felt like. They were out at sea and no one knew where they were. The scene around her was serene, the sound of the restless waves were gently rippling against the side of the boat, and it was hard to deny their newfound camaraderie.

She caught his gaze and heat snaked between her legs. Perhaps there *was* a sea serpent after all…

Brand seemed so at ease and carefree out on the water, as if this was where he belonged. His hard features had softened, and the only tension in his body was in the muscles pulling the oars, propelling the boat forward.

'Rowing suits you,' she said.

'I love being out here. Like you, I don't do very well stuck in a box.'

'Where's the furthest you've ever gone?'

'Apart from Daneland to England? Only so far as the little islands to the north and south of here.'

'What were they like? Will you tell me about them?'

She realised she might never get the chance to do this again, so she decided to drink in the moment. Leaning back, she tipped her head, turning her face up towards the sun and briefly closing her eyes, and felt her worries melting away under the heat as she listened to Brand talk.

He spoke of magical islands formed of forests and beaches, where no people lived, just animals. And he told her of grand monasteries and castles he'd seen while sailing along the coastline here. And as he rowed he pointed out shoals of fish swimming alongside the boat, or moonlike jellyfish with delicate dancing tentacles.

She delighted in his witty commentary and his observations, and she voiced her wonder at all the new sights and sounds. When he spotted a seal bobbing in and out of the waves she was overcome with a desire to get closer, and threw herself half over the side of the boat in awe, forgetting all about her earlier fear of its motion.

Brand stopped rowing, not wanting Anne to miss the seal swimming in the surf. Her rapture at seeing all the creatures of the ocean had him spellbound. He'd seen seals before, many times, but seeing one through her eyes made it much more appealing. Her face had lit up at everything he showed her and her pretty smile was genuine.

He wished they could stay out here forever. He didn't think he'd ever tire of her company, her sense of humour, and hearing her views on the world. When she'd stretched out catlike in the sun, his body had responded with force. He knew he should wipe the morning's kiss from his memory, but still his thoughts kept straying to the way her lips had sealed against his, to the taste of desire on her tongue and the feeling of her small, exquisite breasts pressed up against his chest, cupped in his hands.

He had instigated it, of course. He'd been the one to pull her into his arms and to press his mouth against hers. Then, staring down at her, seeing her cheeks flushed, he had come to his senses and pushed her away. And she'd looked confused—startled, even.

He had done some reckless things in his past, especially when he was just a lad, chasing fun and danger.

But he wasn't sure he'd ever done anything as hare-brained as this. He'd taken advantage of Anne's wedding to kidnap her and bring her to Kald. He was using her to get revenge on Crowe and now he was trying to seduce her.

Yet, clutching her so close, he hadn't had the strength to resist. One minute he'd been kissing her, going out of his mind with desire, and the next he'd been holding her at arm's length, unable to forgive himself. He'd never been so confused.

He was so irresponsible. He'd promised he wouldn't touch her again, but he'd broken his word and ruined her trust—what little he'd had of it. She must despise him for all he'd done to her so far, and she wouldn't thank him for what was to come, either.

And yet as she leaned over the side of the boat and skimmed her hand through the water she seemed content in his company, and he wanted to keep her to himself a while longer. Even though he knew everyone at Kald was waiting, he wasn't ready to take her back. He wanted this one moment, free of responsibility.

The instant they rounded the headland they'd be turning into the river and reality would come back to bite them. Anne would have to watch him fight her fiancé, and she would no longer look at him as she was looking at him now.

He didn't think Svea or Kar would engage in any kind of communication with Crowe and his men while he wasn't there. And he didn't think Crowe would attack or negotiate until he had some kind of confirmation that Anne was inside the fortress.

He hoped his gut instinct was right, because he was scorching in the burning sun, rowing a heavy ship, and the water looked too inviting. It was calling to him, and he made his decision. As they passed the secluded cove where he often came to be alone, he dropped the oars and put down the anchor.

Anne glanced questioningly up at him. And when he tore off his tunic, throwing it down by her feet, her eyes widened.

For a moment she just stared in astonishment at his body—in awe or in horror? He wasn't sure. His chest was adorned with dark blue ink, which also covered his entire torso and back, and he knew it was intimidating. It often struck fear into the heart of his enemies. He'd had it done when he'd become leader at Kald. He needed to know what she thought of the markings— whether she found them unattractive.

'What are you doing?' she choked.

'What does it look like? I'm going for a swim. Want to join me?'

He tugged off his boots. Next, his belt dropped to the floor. For a moment he reached for the tie on his trousers, and considered stripping them off and going in naked, but when he saw the consternation on her face he thought better of it. He'd probably shocked her enough for one day.

He dived over the side and the cool salt water instantly soothed his hot skin. He'd hoped the water might wash away his desire, but when he resurfaced Anne was dangling over the side of the boat again, watching in wonder, or concern—he wasn't sure which—and he knew that it hadn't.

'Well? Are you coming in?' he grinned.

'In this dress?' She shook her head vehemently.

'You're wearing undergarments, aren't you?' He smirked.

'I can't even swim!'

'I could teach you.'

For a moment she looked almost tempted. But then she shook her head again, biting her lip.

'Coward.'

He wanted to drag her in after him, to hold her in his arms, free and weightless in the water. But as his hands sliced through the water, while he swam to the shallows and back, he realised they'd reached something of an accord and was reluctant to do anything to damage it. He'd enjoyed her company this morning, probably more than he should. In fact, he was enjoying everything about her.

He wanted her, pure and simple, and that could only be resolved in one way. But taking her and satiating their desire was something he just couldn't do if he wanted a ransom for her safe return.

He made his body work hard, his muscled arms streaming through the water, cooling himself from the sun and his heated thoughts of his companion. By the time he finally heaved himself back into the boat he felt slightly more in control of his tormented mind and body.

Anne squealed as the ship lurched from side to side, then righted itself, and he noticed she did everything possible to avoid looking at his bare chest, suddenly finding the seam of her dress incredibly fascinating. Was she holding her breath? He grinned.

'Here,' he said. 'I got this for you.' He held out a large pink seashell with a smooth spiral core.

Now she had to look at him, and he enjoyed seeing a delicate flush appear in her cheeks. He crouched down in front of her and held the smooth open surface of the shell up to her ear.

'Listen,' he said.

At first, she looked confused, and then her eyes widened in amazement. 'I can hear the ocean!' She gasped, and he grinned again. 'It's the waves rolling onto the shore. How is that possible?'

He shrugged. 'I'm not sure, but it's yours. So you can hear the waves no matter how far from the sea you are.'

No matter how far away from me you are...

Anne nimbly took it from his hands. 'Thank you.'

She met his eyes and a moment passed between them. The tension in the air around them almost glittered, and it took every ounce of his strength to keep himself from leaning in and kissing her again. She was so close...

No! He stood and pulled his tunic back on, and she practically wilted with relief, making him grin even more widely.

'Ready to go?' he asked. He hoped she'd say no— that she wanted to stay out here with him for a while longer. But she just nodded and glanced away.

'Those clouds over there look a bit ominous,' he said. 'We'd better move on.'

She seemed to be analysing him as he rowed, running her fingers through her rumpled hair. He liked it. It reminded him of winding his own hands through it, drawing her lips towards his.

'What are you thinking about, Princess?'

She started fiddling with that seam on her dress again. 'Why do you cover your body in ink like that?' she asked.

So it was his markings that were playing on her mind. Did she find them off-putting?

As he pulled hard on the oars again, and they began to venture round the peninsula, the breeze began to pick up and the sea became choppier. But Brand was in full control. He knew it was rougher out here, where it was less sheltered. He hoisted the square sail to harness the power of the wind and help them pick up pace.

'We use ink to say something about our personalities and to honour the gods. Or, in my case, to cover up some pretty bad scars. I know it takes a bit of getting used to. Do you not like it?'

'I hadn't given it any thought,' she shrugged.

He smiled at the lie.

'What does your ink mean?' she asked.

'I will tell you about it some time, but right now the weather is turning faster than I'd predicted. I'm sorry. I shouldn't have stopped for that swim.' He stalked around the ship, holding on to the side, tying things down.

When a large splatter of rain landed on Anne's hair,

and then began pelting down into the boat, for the first time he felt real concern.

He didn't mind towering walls of water, the wind and the rain—in fact, there had been times in his life when he'd come out in search of a storm, wanting to test himself, war against the waves, even get lost in them. He'd buried a lot of his anger in this ocean. But he'd never have chosen to subject Anne to this. He was a fool, putting her in harm's way. They could have been home by now if he'd just stuck to his plan.

It wasn't long before the skies had turned grey and churning water was curving over the boat. He wondered if the gods were angry with him. It was the first time he regretted the open deck, where a woollen cover was their only protection from the elements.

He made a few more strokes with the oars, but it was becoming impossible to fight the waves. He couldn't believe it when he saw Anne bailing water with a bucket.

'What are you doing?' he asked.

'Trying to be useful!'

She never ceased to amaze him. She certainly wasn't the delicate flower he had originally thought. She always wanted to help.

'I'm going to have to take down the sail and lower the anchor again,' he shouted over the raging noise of the sea. 'We'll have to ride it out. Sit by the mast and hold on,' he instructed. 'I'll grab the cover.'

'Will the boat take it?' she asked, raising her voice so he could hear her. 'The waves are pretty big.'

'I built it to withstand storms like this. We should be fine.'

'Should?' she said, smiling.

It was her smile, even in these dangerous conditions, that made him feel a connection with her, and he stopped securing the oars and came to sit down next to her in the cramped hull. They huddled together and he brought his arms around her and the mast, holding them both tight as the boat rode the waves for what felt like an endless amount of time.

Swells of water rose and fell, taking them up to great heights, and then they'd crash back down with a bump. He saw Anne's face was turning greener by the second, and he felt like the world's worst person. He was worried she'd bump her head, or fall overboard, so he tightened his grip and she clung on to him. They were a tangle of limbs, but she didn't moan or blame him once.

He thought he would have preferred it if she had. He was finding her silence disturbing. And the way her body kept bumping into his was agonising. Although how he could even think of sex in these conditions was beyond him.

Suddenly she lurched forward and vomited over the side. He moved with her and held her waist as she did it again.

'Are you all right?'

A violent spray of water hit them, and she coughed and spluttered.

'I've been better,' she said, sagging down onto the floor, her eyes fluttering shut.

'But will you be all right?'

She looked up at him through the battering rain. 'The next time you feel like going for a swim, just don't—is that clear?'

He grinned. 'Clear,' he said, tugging her into his side and smoothing her hair. 'That's a promise.'

'You'd better swear it instead—you're not very good at keeping promises.' She smiled weakly.

He couldn't believe she was trying to make him laugh at a time like this. Who *was* this incredible woman he'd stolen and brought into his life? And how was he ever going to be able to give her up? She truly was a priceless gem. No amount of treasure would be enough for a woman like her.

After what seemed like the longest storm Brand had ever battled, the heavy rain began to slow and the dark clouds started to disperse. His heart lifted when a sliver of gold lit up their path towards Kald again. Anne might just forgive him yet. That was once she'd warmed up.

She was now sitting under the woollen cover completely wet and shivering again. He knew he had to get those clothes off her, but he didn't think she'd agree to that if he suggested it.

With a newfound burst of energy, he lifted the anchor and rowed the boat again, hard and fast, feeling the need to get back to the fortress as soon as possible now. And when the archway over the river into Kald came into view he breathed a huge sigh of relief.

He launched himself out of the ship and dragged it up the slipway to the boathouse before helping Anne out. She walked a few steps before sinking onto the grass, collapsing on her back, and he lay down beside her.

'I never thought I'd be so glad to see Kald again,' she said, her hand over her forehead.

Another flicker of admiration for the way she'd handled herself flashed through him. He rolled towards her and propped himself up on his elbow, staring down at her. He lifted a few wet strands of hair from her face, and was glad that she let him. She was either too cold to protest, or no longer so opposed to his touch... He hoped it was the latter.

But the moment was short-lived. The unmistakable sound of an arrow whistled overhead, and Brand was on his feet as fast as the storm had hit, his fight instinct kicking in.

'*Skit!*' he swore. 'Did you hear that? Something's happening. We need to get back. Do you think you can walk? It's just up the hill.'

She nodded, curling herself up to stand, and followed him as he took her hand again and began to ascend the grassy slope where remote farmsteads were dotted about, although the owners were nowhere to be seen.

'Is that Crowe attacking?' she asked. 'I thought you said he wouldn't.'

Brand couldn't believe it to be true. He wouldn't be so foolish to send arrows into Kald with the Princess inside, would he? Did Crowe not care for the safety of his bride?

Anger lashed through him. And yet even as these thoughts rushed at him he wondered if he was any better. Wasn't his imminent betrayal of her far worse? Would she understand if he said he was doing it for the good of his people? He doubted it.

A pain burned in his chest when he wondered what would happen when Anne discovered he was about to put a price on her head. That he was planning to sell her back to her family for gold.

They raced up the hillside, passing working horses and sheep grazing in the fields. It was tricky to run in her saturated clothes, and Anne felt her heart burn from the sudden exercise—or was it from the way Brand had taken care of her when she'd felt unwell, and how a moment ago he'd been staring down at her as if he wanted to ravage her mouth again?

But soon they reached a ridge and she realised they were back in the square, amid a flurry of chaos, the air tinged with a mixture of excitement and fear. Men were grabbing their shields and swords and taking up defence positions on the ramparts.

Anne knew their time alone was well and truly over.

They glimpsed Svea's retreating frame, and Brand dropped her hand as he raced to catch up with his sister. 'What's going on?'

'Where the hell have you been? I was starting to get worried,' Svea scolded him. 'They shot an arrow. It hit Ulf.'

'No...' Anne whispered, concern clouding her spirits.

'Come quick—he's in here.'

They raced towards the longhouse, where Ulf was

writhing in pain on a bench, an arrow sticking out of his upper arm and blood seeping into the animal skin he was lying on.

Anne's hands flew to her face in worry. 'This is your fault!' she said, turning accusingly on Brand, suddenly filled with anger. 'If you hadn't brought me here this would never have happened.'

'They shot just one arrow?' he asked his men, ignoring her and leaning over Ulf to inspect the wound and the weapon.

'This was attached to it,' Torsten said, handing him a piece of parchment.

Brand glanced at it before placing it in his tunic.

'They obviously want to get our attention, and they prefer to send notes rather than a messenger,' said Torsten. 'We need to cut off this arm. If we don't, the boy's not going to make it.'

Anne stepped forward. 'If you cut off the arm he will certainly die,' she said, speaking up bravely against the red-haired brute. 'He'll lose too much blood. I've seen it before.'

Brand looked between her and his friend. Unbelievably, his eyes settled on her. 'What do you suggest, Anne?'

Did he actually want her opinion? 'If we pull it out, the wood may come loose from the arrowhead and it could get stuck in his body. But I can try to cut it out...' Anne said.

'You?' Torsten mocked, his face darkening. He turned on Brand. 'You're not going to listen to the

Saxon witch? What's she even doing here? She probably wants the boy dead!'

Anger flared. 'That's not true!' Anne gasped.

Brand must know she wasn't lying. He'd seen her interact with Ulf. She liked the boy. Would he believe her?

He stroked his beard, taking a moment to think before giving her a steady look. 'Do what you have to do.'

'You've lost your mind! She's playing you—turning your head!' Torsten raged, and he kicked a barrel of mead as he stormed out of the longhouse.

'Anne, what do you need?' Svea asked, resting a hand on her shoulder to bring the focus back to the boy.

'A knife, a needle and thread, sage and garlic, if you have them—and some kind of liquor to numb the pain.'

Brand nodded to Svea. 'Go. And bring a blanket for Anne.'

'What are you going to do?' he asked, coming down to kneel beside her.

'Extract the arrow, then treat the wound. It's his best chance. But there's a lot of blood.'

'How on earth do you know how to do this, Anne?'

'I've helped my father's soldiers before…when they've been shot.'

'Unbeknown to him, I bet.'

She met his gaze. She liked it that he understood her. It was as if he knew her better than anyone. How was that possible?

'And did they make it?' he asked.

'Some… I'll do my best. Should we fetch his parents? Tell them he's hurt?'

Brand gave her an odd look. 'His parents are dead, Anne. He's a Saxon.'

Anne inhaled sharply. 'Ulf is a slave?'

Disappointment crashed over her like the giant waves had done earlier on. She'd thought Brand didn't buy people.

Svea came rushing back, holding the things Anne had requested. 'Here,' she said, and Anne took the items she needed first, while Brand reached for the blanket and placed it around her shoulders.

Ulf was murmuring now, squirming in agony, and Anne knew she'd have to wait for answers about the boy's family and his role here. She indicated to Svea to pour some alcohol down Ulf's throat, and then Anne doused his shoulder in the liquid.

'You'll have to secure him,' she said to Brand.

She wished she could tell him to leave, because he was a huge distraction. But she needed his strength to hold the boy down. If Ulf moved, she'd cut him and make his injury worse.

Had Brand really taken Ulf from his home and enslaved him? Ulf wasn't much older than Brand had been when Anne had helped him that day when he was in Termarth. She had somehow thought he was better than that—that he didn't trade people. It made her doubt him and his reasons for taking her.

But she couldn't think about that now—she needed to focus on helping Ulf.

It was hard, working in such subdued light, but she managed to cut the arrowhead out. The wound wasn't as deep as it had looked, but the loss of blood was proving tricky. She cleaned the wound and, using a needle and thread, carefully stitched it up, then sat back on her ankles to study her work. She hoped the herbal ointment would be enough to bind the flesh and stop any infection. Thankfully, Ulf was now asleep, and the wound looked clean at least.

'Thank you,' Brand said, resting a hand on her shoulder and giving her a squeeze. 'You have done well.'

His touch spread an unwanted warmth through her body. She turned to look at him and the rush of his all too familiar scent brought back the feeling of his lips moving against hers, his tongue filling her mouth, his hands on her breasts. Images of his half-naked body diving into the water flooded her mind.

When she'd seen that his muscular chest and back were completely covered in ink, at first she'd been shocked, and then she had been curious—transfixed. She'd wanted to let her eyes roam over every line, to explore the patterns with her fingers. And she'd wanted to know what they said about the man beneath. She'd been disturbed and enthralled all at once. Her pulse had been erratic as she'd watched his powerful torso channel through the water.

She had hoped this task—stitching Ulf back together—would help her to forget all about it. Incredibly, the storm hadn't, and she was sure he'd been about to kiss her again before they'd heard the humming sound of the arrow. She had wanted him to, and yet if he bought and sold slaves she would not be able to abide it...

She removed his hand and busied herself with clearing away the mess she'd made on the bench.

Brand reached for the note in his tunic and unrolled the bloodstained parchment. 'You can read?' he asked Anne. 'Will you read this to me?'

She nodded, astonished that once again he wasn't too proud to ask for her help.

'It seems you have no end of talents, Anne. You clearly like healing people, and are good at it.'

He was analysing her with those perceptive eyes. 'Is that so wrong?' she asked.

'It is not a criticism.'

She laid a hand on Ulf's forehead and was glad to feel that he didn't have a fever.

'After that day I helped you in Termarth, when we were much younger, I found myself wanting to study the art of healing. I read books on anatomy and herbs—anything I could find in my father's library,' she said, washing the blood off her hands. 'Not that he approves.'

'Surely he sees your knowledge as an asset?'

'Apparently not.'

'Then he's a fool.'

Anne's heart leapt. This man—this Barbarian—valued her education. How was it possible that he managed to bolster her confidence, her self-worth, more than any other person ever had?

'You didn't answer my question. How did Ulf come to be here? Did you snatch him from his home too?' Her chin tilted up in provocation, her eyes simmering with displeasure.

Brand held her gaze. 'No—I told you. I don't make

a habit of kidnapping Saxons. Is that what you think of me?'

'What should I think? You have a Saxon boy in your midst, helping you to do your dirty work.'

He came towards her, crowding her with his big body. 'His father attacked Kald—not the other way round. He brought him to the battlefield. A nine-year-old boy! He was left an orphan, so we took him in… treated him like one of our own. He doesn't know anything different now.'

Once again, he'd shocked her. 'Why would you do that?' she asked, her throat feeling tight.

He reached up to wipe a smear of blood from her cheek. She flinched. 'Because, like you said, perhaps I'm not the barbarian people believe me to be. I think children should be nurtured, not beaten or manipulated.' He inclined his head. 'Nor neglected and shut away and deprived of learning and adventures.'

Anne floundered at this hint to her own upbringing, suddenly feeling awkward that she'd doubted him. She nodded to the parchment to distract him—and herself—from the fresh curl of intimacy enveloping them.

'What does it say?' Brand asked.

'It seems my fiancé wants me back and he's prepared to fight.'

Chapter Seven

The longhouse was far from the jovial scene it had been the night Anne had arrived in Kald. She was washing her hands at the back of the room, and noticed that after dinner most of the women and children returned to their farmsteads, while the men were out on the ramparts, guarding the walls.

Brand's trusted few were gathered round the long wooden table in the centre of the room, deciding on their course of action.

'Crowe demands an answer and I say we spear the bastards!'

'They struck the first blow. Now we should darken the sky with arrows.'

'They should pay us in gold not to kill them while they sleep.'

So this was their great plan, Anne thought. And all this because Brand had taken a beating when he was a boy? Yes, the Saxons had left him for dead, but as he'd survived this all seemed too much, somehow.

Had he given her the full story? Was it really about Crowe attacking villages and blaming the Danes for it? He certainly deserved to be punished for that.

'They say we are to hand over the Princess or they'll send smoke and fire.'

'Then we take the fight to them!' Kar said.

'No.'

Brand's deep, authoritative voice cut through all the others. He had been sitting at the head of the table quietly observing until now, his long fingers steepled in front of him, and everyone turned to listen.

'I have said no one is to fight but me. I will make a square with Crowe. This is my battle.'

Anne felt a strange flutter of fear in her chest. She didn't want him to fight.

'It's as much mine as it is yours,' Svea said fiercely, stepping forward.

'It is a fight for all of us,' Kar said.

So they all loathed her fiancé. How could her father intend to marry her to a man who inspired such hatred?

Anne rubbed her temples. She was getting a headache…

'I know,' Brand said, placing a hand on his sister's shoulder. 'But this is how it's going to be. Kar, tell Crowe we will speak with him at dawn. If I go out there now there'll be no holding me back.'

'You should take the bed.'

'No, you take it.'

'I can sleep downstairs with Svea…'

'*Faen I helvete*, Anne!'

Brand and Anne were standing in the doorway of the upstairs room and he was losing the will to live. It had been a long day and he didn't want to argue with her any more—especially not in this small space and not about sleeping arrangements. His anger was causing a lick of arousal in his groin and that was the last thing he needed to feel all night, sitting outside her door. It would certainly hijack his ability to sleep.

He pulled off his boots on the staircase.

'If you're planning on fighting tomorrow, you'll need to sleep.'

Anne was talking a lot. He'd noticed she did that when she was nervous. And she was wringing her lovely hands.

'Are you always this stubborn?' he asked.

'Yes.'

'Well, stop it. With an army at the door I've got to keep an eye on the men through the night anyway, to check nothing is amiss, so you may as well take it. Now, stop talking and get out of those damp clothes. Put on the fresh ones Svea gave you.'

He closed the door and braced his hands on the wooden rail, releasing a long sigh. For the third time in as many days Anne was undressing just an arm's reach away from him and the constant ache in his groin was becoming excruciating, making him downright irritated.

A few moments later the door swung open again and he turned to find her standing there, in a fresh, plain white smock, minus the pinafore. She looked every bit the pure, innocent virgin. His mouth dried and he sighed. As much as he wanted her, he really did need to get some rest tonight. He had a date with destiny tomorrow. And tomorrow night he'd either be celebrating his revenge on Crowe, bathing in his enemy's blood, or dining in the Great Hall of Valhalla with the gods.

'I was thinking we could share the room,' Anne said, waving her hands about, looking flustered. 'I know you won't let me sleep elsewhere, but I can't let you sit outside all night either. And this...' she motioned to the animal skins and furs thrown over a chair in the corner of the room '...looks comfortable enough to sleep on.'

His eyes narrowed on her. 'What about your reputation?'

'Everyone is either on the ramparts or in bed! I doubt anyone will see or even care. They're not *my* people, after all. No one need ever know.'

'Stop babbling, Anne. But if you're sure, then I accept. With the Saxons surrounding us I don't really want to let you out of my sight, and that chair looks a lot more appealing than the floor out here.'

He took a last glance around the quiet village square, before striding into the room and shutting the door.

'I could do with getting out of these wet clothes, so if you don't want to watch me strip you might want to look the other way.'

He was half hoping she'd say she wanted to watch, but he knew she wouldn't. That was just a fantasy. Instead, she quickly turned around, facing the smoke hole, and he put on fresh trousers, leaving his torso bare. She'd just have to deal with it.

He poured them both some water from a jug and offered her a cup. She must have been thirsty as she drank it all in one go. He took the empty jar out of her hand and placed it down on the table. He caught her looking at his ink again, but he cut her visual tour short by putting out the torch flame.

He stumbled around in the darkness and cursed quietly as he crashed into the wooden chest before reaching the chair. He heard the bed shift under her weight as she got in, and he waited for what seemed like a moon's whole cycle, listening for the sound of her gentle breathing, waiting for her to go to sleep so he could finally relax.

He couldn't believe it, but he'd actually never shared this room with a woman before. The women he had were brief distractions, and they usually happened on mutual ground—either at the back of the hall or in one of the farmsteads. And, as leader of the clan, he always left before morning. No one needed to see him coming home after dawn.

But up here was his space—the only place where he could be alone, apart from out on the water, and having Anne here with him was both infuriating and...*nice*.

'Are you awake?'

He sighed. 'Yes. What is it, Princess? Do you need a bedtime story?'

'Will you tell me about the markings on your body? What do they mean?'

He knew she was fascinated by them. And he knew why. They were dark and intricate, and the sword on his chest and the ravens on his back were all combined together with trees and knotwork in a labyrinth of complex tangled lines.

He turned to face her in the darkness, his eyes adjusting to the blackness. With just the pale moonlight filtering through the hole in the wall he could see the outline of her beautiful face, just a stride away from him.

'The sword represents power, protection, and strength. And the ravens—they symbolise the death of my parents. But they're also a nod to our god Odin and his wisdom and intelligence, the good and the bad...'

'They're amazing. Who did them for you?'

'Svea. She's very talented.'

'What about the symbol on your neck?'

'That's *Ægishjálmr*—the Helm of Awe. To frighten off our enemies. Do they scare you, Princess?'

'No.' He heard her shake her head. 'Did they hurt?'

'We use wood ash—and, no, they didn't hurt. But then I have a high threshold for pain. Why? Are you thinking of having some ink too?'

She giggled at the absurd suggestion. 'No, somehow I don't think it would suit me.'

He smiled into the darkness. 'What design would you have?'

'What would you suggest?'

'None. Your body is too perfect to be covered with any kind of ink...'

He heard her swallow and saw her turn her face towards him.

'But if you had to choose one for me?' she pressed.

'Then I'd have to go for *vegvisir*, the symbol used

for protection…or a little primrose. It's our goddess Freyja's sacred flower. It also reminds me of our first kiss…'

The silence stretched between them. He wondered what she was thinking.

'You know, you really aren't anything like the person people describe you to be,' she said.

He ran his tongue over his lips. He was *everything* people thought him to be. He didn't know why he'd been trying to convince her otherwise. He was a brute and he was out for revenge; he would use her to gain wealth. Yes, he had taken her to protect her from Crowe, but in doing so he'd put her in harm's way. And right now he didn't like himself very much.

'Why do they call you that? The Barbarian?'

'Let's not talk about it now,' he said. 'You must be tired after our long day today. But you're safe to sleep now, Anne.'

'I won't wake up and find myself in your arms?' she questioned lightly.

He groaned. Now he had all kinds of images flicking through his mind—and he was hard. 'For pity's sake, don't put ideas in my head, Anne!' he said. 'Now, please, go to sleep.'

But if he wasn't mistaken, she'd sat up in the bed. 'I can't… I'm worried about tomorrow.'

He sighed, sitting forward, resting his elbows on his knees. 'How so?'

'I don't want you to fight.'

He reached out to catch her chin between his fingers in the darkness. 'Why?'

There was a long silence before she said, 'I don't want you getting hurt. It's all madness, Brand. If Crowe kills you, then it was all for nothing. And if you kill him, then what? Will you feel satisfied? Will it be over? No! You'll start another battle between Danes and Saxons.'

'It's a little late for that, Anne.'

She didn't need to tell him the stakes were high—he already knew. If he lost, Anne would belong to that man forever and Svea would never have peace… But if he triumphed, Anne would soon learn of his betrayal and he'd end up without her anyway.

'I don't see why it has to be like that. Why can't everyone just be friends?'

'Like us, you mean?' He grimaced.

He heard the bed shift again, and his whole body tensed when her hands came down to rest on his shoulders and she lowered herself into his lap.

His eyes narrowed on her in the darkness. Was she playing some kind of trick on him? He had the sudden notion that perhaps she was trying to deprive him of all reason now that rescue seemed imminent. Was this some idea she had to scramble his brain so he wouldn't be able to fight?

But he pulled her gently into his body and she rested her head against his bare chest. She placed a hand on his cheek. He should remove it. Hell, he should lift her body from his and put her back in the bed. But instead he turned his face into her palm and pressed a soft kiss to her skin.

'At least I can say it wasn't my fault when you wake in my arms in the morning. Now, please, stop babbling and go to sleep.'

Chapter Eight

The startling sound of a horn echoed around the fortress of Kald and travelled out across the land. Anne thought it was the most terrifying sound she had ever heard. It signalled a warning, a battle, death.

She was standing on the bridge, leaning over the parapet of the guard tower, above Kald's sturdy wooden gates. From there, she could see across the marsh and heathland to the vast expanse of golden sand and ocean. She longed to be back out there on the water again—not here, watching this harrowing scene unfold.

On any other day, she imagined the view would be breathtaking, but the sight before her now filled her with ice-cold dread. Her father had sent an army! Beneath them, it wasn't just the fifty men she and Brand had seen the other night—there were another seventy or so Saxon soldiers, all sent to fight for her release. But instead of feeling relief at her imminent rescue, she just felt numb.

'And you said your father didn't care about you,' Brand said, one eyebrow raised.

'Brand,' she said breathlessly. 'You must hand me back before anyone gets hurt. I'm not worth all this.'

'Actually, you are,' he said. 'Now, keep quiet. Stay out of sight.'

Brand was naked from the waist up, legs planted wide, a bearskin thrown around his shoulders. He held a wooden shield in one hand and a sword in the other. He looked like a ferocious warlord, all hard muscle and dark skin. His ink-covered body, although deeply fascinating, was enough to strike fear into his enemies, and his heavy brow didn't give away one ounce of feeling.

He looked like a different man from the one she'd shared a room with last night. Worlds apart from the man who had held her so tenderly, who had spoken of primroses and protection and stroked her hair as she drifted off to sleep.

Her throat felt thick. 'Why aren't you wearing any armour?' she asked, appalled.

'I have all the protection I need.'

'Don't you have any fear?'

'The only thing I fear is not being able to protect the people I love. I do not fear death.'

She wanted to throw herself down at his feet and beg him to stop this. She'd happily marry Crowe and be miserable for the rest of her life if it meant he'd spare Brand's life. But she knew he wouldn't retreat now—no matter what she said. This fight would go ahead. She was as certain of that as she was that the sun would still rise tomorrow, but by then her whole world would be changed.

Two figures emerged from the wall of Saxon men

and trotted forward on their horses. Anne recognised one of them to be Lord Crowe. He was the epitome of arrogance, playing with the gloves on his hands, cracking his knuckles. She had often thought he looked like a hefty dog, with a thickset body and a pushed-in nose. Taking in the black and yellow markings of his armour, she still couldn't believe that he and his mercenaries were responsible for the desolation of that village. It sickened her to the stomach.

She thought the other man, wearing a navy tunic over chainmail, was the Ealdorman Lord Stanton of Braewood. She had seen him before at the King's witans and knew her father thought highly of him.

Brand stared down at them from the bridge. 'My lords, welcome to Kald.'

'You must be the heathen they call Brand Ivarsson. I am Lord Crowe of Calhourn, and I believe you have something that belongs to me.'

Anne realised she had forgotten to breathe. Her heart was in her mouth.

'To you? No, I don't think so.' Brand shrugged. 'Though we have been enjoying the company of Princess Anne of Termarth.'

Crowe's lips thinned into a sneer. 'And how have you been getting on with my bride?'

'Very, very well,' Brand said, offering up a hard smile.

Crowe moved his neck from side to side. 'Well, fortunately she is not my wife...yet. If she has been touched, that will be most disappointing. I was so looking forward to breaking her in.'

Anne's stomach rolled. She saw Brand's fist tighten

around the hilt of his sword, so hard his knuckles began to turn white.

'But I doubt you have been so foolish as to touch her. You will know the King and I have no use for damaged goods. And you must be expecting some kind of reward for her safe return. No, if you'd harmed her, the fate of you and your people would have been sealed. I have no qualms about burning you all to the ground—the Princess as well, if she's been whored. But let it not come to that. Why don't you make it known what you want, Pagan? Why would you take such great pains to steal away my bride? Is it gold you are after? Or more of our land? Although I must admit she means little to me, so your price must be reasonable. I am prepared to make you a deal, but I wish to see my bride first.'

'There will be no deal,' Brand said. 'Tell your men to stand down and my men will do the same. Then get off your horse and fight me, man to man.'

Anne could tell Crowe hadn't been expecting that as his head snapped up. 'You wish to face me in combat, boy?' He smirked.

'You needn't have brought an army to fight your battle. It is only *your* blood on my hands that I desire.'

Crowe chuckled, spittle forming in the corners of his mouth. 'Very well—we fight. And to the death. But if, on the off-chance, I lose, you still won't win the Princess. My men have orders to attack if I am harmed. I must insist on seeing her first, though.'

Brand gently took Anne's arm, almost reluctantly bringing her into view on the bridge at the top of the gate. She stared down into Crowe's cold, flinty eyes and felt a flicker of disdain. She could smell Brand's musky skin and feel his heat, and she wanted to turn into him, bury her face in his shoulder and pretend none of this was happening.

'Highness,' Lord Stanton said, coming forward. 'I trust you have been well looked after?'

'I have, my lord. Thank you.'

'And is the honour and virtue of Termarth still intact?' Crowe barked.

She swallowed, feeling the heat of Brand's fingers burning into her arm. Thoughts of his lips against her mouth flooded her mind, his hand to her breast. For a moment she wished she could say no, then maybe Crowe wouldn't fight for her. But she thought of her father and knew she couldn't.

'It is, my lord.'

He nodded, and his gaze snapped back to Brand's. 'Very well, Heathen. We fight.'

Anne let out a little sob and her knees sagged.

'Take her,' Brand said to Kar, and she felt herself being pulled back, watching, helpless, as Brand made his way down the wooden steps.

She struggled against Kar's muscled restraint. 'They'll kill him,' she whispered, horror on her lips.

Kar shook his head, looking at Brand with admiration in his eyes. 'Brand is the best warrior I've ever known. Have faith, my lady...'

She watched, as if a pit were emptying in her stomach, as the huge wooden gates opened and Brand walked out into the fray. Something in the set of his shoulders suggested that he was bent on one purpose.

His hands clenched and unclenched on his sword and shield, and his nostrils were slightly flared.

Crowe had lowered himself from his horse and his eyes were narrowed on his opponent.

She strained to hear what was being said between the men. They looked like a bear and a wolf about to do battle, circling each other.

'Do I know you, boy?'

'I'm surprised you don't remember.'

And with a quick flick of his sword, which glinted in the sunlight, Brand sliced the Saxon's forehead open, through his eyebrow. It was an injury that matched his own. There was a rumble through the Saxon troops, the horses braying.

'I am the Danish boy you said you wanted to teach a lesson to a few years back...'

Crowe gave an animalistic growl as he touched a hand to his injury. Recognition lit up the deep-set eyes in his ruddy face. 'Ah, yes,' he sneered. 'A girl who screamed and a boy who watched. You, I presume? A good day. Just like today is going to be. Although I rather thought I had finished you off back then. I meant to.'

Anne's head swam. There was more to this than Brand had told her! What was it? Why hadn't he given her the whole story?

The men squared up to each other and began to cross swords, as all pairs of eyes looked on. Crowe's sword crunched against Brand's shield. Brand slammed Crowe against the wall, and metal clashed against metal. There was cheering from both sides, and Anne couldn't understand why the Saxons and Danes were enjoying it as if it was sport. Crowe rounded on Brand and he ducked, just missing his opponent's blade as it sliced through the air. Then Brand brought his weapon down on Crowe's shield so hard the yellow dragon splintered.

It was the most brutal, savage fight Anne had ever seen, and yet she couldn't bring herself to turn away. She needed to know what was happening. There was blood already, and she suffered every blow, wincing and gasping at every stab of their weapons. Brand was agile on his feet, dodging Crowe's sword, and his own iron kept striking his opponent's shield.

When Crowe was flung to the floor she could tell he was flagging—he was clearly no match for Brand's strength—and then Brand was on top of him. Crowe was pinned beneath his weight, his weapon discarded and his bare fists flying. Brand was wild and unrelenting, pounding and pummelling, almost overcome with rage, seemingly lost in revenge. And now she knew that this man, right here, was the Barbarian she had heard of.

Her hand flew to her mouth as they thrashed around on the ground and Crowe tried to crawl away. But he was pinned beneath Brand's weight again, writhing and convulsing in pain, and when Brand finally wrenched him up onto his knees the Saxon whimpered, begging for his life to be spared. Both sides looked on in hushed silence, waiting for the Barbarian to finish the job. He had earned his victory.

'Brand—no!' Anne said, launching herself towards him, her voice wobbling.

Lord Stanton cantered forward at the same time. 'Show mercy. Let us come to an arrangement.'

Brand glanced up at her, his eyes cold, devoid of emotion, his face splattered with blood. 'Get her out of here!' he yelled at Kar.

It was all too much. Anne heard wailing, and before she realised the sound was coming from herself she was being dragged across the courtyard and back to the upstairs room.

'Anne?'

Brand pushed open the door.

'Go away.'

She couldn't bear to look at him. The brutal scene kept replaying over and over in her head. Brand and Crowe's bloodied bodies and Brand seemingly going berserk.

She squeezed her eyes shut. She wanted to rid her mind of it. She wished she could return to this morning, when none of it had happened. How could she ever erase those images from her memory? No doubt he had finished the job and killed Crowe.

She was sitting on the floor in the corner of the room, hugging her knees to her chest, her face streaked with tears. She had never seen anyone fight like that before. Barbaric was the only word to describe it. So now she knew where his name had come from. If it was Brand's wish to stand out and be noticed by his gods, then he had achieved it with this bloodthirsty vendetta.

She had seen it too, and she wasn't sure she could forget it. But there was also a part of her that wanted to understand it better…to understand *him*. What had made him behave like that?

'Anne,' Brand said again, his hands on his hips. 'I've never pretended to be a good man, you know that.'

She bristled. He had seemed so devoid of feeling it had shocked her.

'It was a fair fight, Anne…'

'So now I know where you get your name from. You have fought like that, behaved like that before. How else would you have garnered your reputation?' She shook her head. 'Did you kill him? Oh, God, you don't know what you've done.'

He'd surely started a war. She was terrified of what this meant for Kald and for Termarth. What would happen next? The Saxons must be trying to break through the gates even now.

'No, I didn't kill him, but I should have.'

A cool trickle of relief flowed through her.

'You don't know what he did, Anne!'

'That's because you haven't told me!'

The silence stretched like the string of an archer's bow, until Brand came down on his haunches in front of her.

'You really want to know? I was trying to protect you from him. From the monster you were going to marry. The truth isn't pretty, Anne.'

'Tell me. I need to know.'

He stood and went over to the smoke hole, raking a hand through his hair. He was still caked in Crowe's blood and his wounds hadn't been seen to. How badly was he hurt? She wanted to reach out to him, but she couldn't. She needed to hear this first.

He took a deep, steadying breath before he began. 'When Svea and I were younger, our father took us to Termarth. He had a dream, as I told you, to build boats, to sell them, so we went there looking to trade. We managed to find a potential buyer and my father was in great spirits. His dream was coming true. Before we left for home we went to a mead house to celebrate, but just after we left the castle walls Saxon soldiers came out of nowhere, surrounding us. One of them had taken a shine to Svea and he made it clear what he wanted.'

Brand had started pacing as he spoke, the tension rippling off him like a raven shedding its dark feathers.

'My father didn't stand for it, of course,' he continued. 'He would have done anything to protect us. He drew his sword, but that gave them the excuse they were looking for to strike. They beat him, ten to one. They waited till he was broken and on his knees, and then they...'

He drew his hands over his face, and it was as if he had the weight of the world on his shoulders. She wanted to tell him to sit down, to rest.

'Sorry,' he said, his voice cracking. 'I don't ever talk about the events of that day. It makes me feel a mixture of hatred and shame... Because they killed my father, Anne. They severed his head from his body. And then they grabbed Svea and made me watch as they took turns with her. She had just turned twelve.'

Anne felt as if an archer had released his arrow and

it had hit her in the heart. She couldn't believe what she was hearing. It was tragic. Horrific. Her heart lurched for poor Svea, for having to go through such an ordeal. And it ached for Brand.

'That was Crowe? Crowe did that?' She wanted to reach for Brand, to comfort him, but he was so deep in thought, dark and brooding, she wasn't sure he'd want her to.

'Yes. Afterwards, they beat me, but somehow I managed to get away and run.' He stared down at a spot on the floor, his neck bent forward. 'They came after me—as you saw. But I thought I deserved it because I hadn't saved my father, or Svea. I deserved to die for not protecting her.'

Anne shook her head furiously. 'Brand, it's not your fault. There was no way you could have fought all those men on your own. Unarmed. They would have killed you. They tried to kill you!'

'After they left—after *you* left—I spent the next few days looking for Svea. I was so ashamed that I'd run out on her. When I eventually found her she'd been cast out onto the streets and she was in a really bad way. I stole a horse—the only crime I'd ever committed up until that point—' he laughed bitterly '—and got her home. It took a long time for her to recover. They'd hurt her. Badly. And I vowed that when I was strong enough I'd make that man pay for what he did.'

Anne didn't trust her voice to speak. Her throat was aching. How could Lord Crowe have done that?

'Brand, I had no idea,' she said, fresh tears pooling in her eyes.

Deep down, she wondered if a part of Brand held her responsible—after all, they were talking about her father's ally, her fiancé! *Ex*-fiancé. How could her father have wanted to marry her off to such a man? Did the King know what Crowe was capable of?

She shuddered.

'After that day, I vowed never to let another Saxon hurt my family or my people. I learned how to fight like a warrior, so the next time the Saxons attacked I could protect the people I loved. And I did. Those first few years after my father passed away I lived for the fight. I was filled with hate and desperate to punish any Saxon for what Crowe had done. I took my anger out on them. When the Saxons repeatedly tried to get us to leave Kald by laying siege, part of me was glad. I wanted to fight them with fury, to kill them. And so my reputation grew. And if that's what's needed to keep my people safe, then so be it. If my name instils fear into Saxons and keeps them away from our lands—good. But I never provoked the battles, Anne. I was just defending my people from your people. And as the grief eventually passed, and the years wore on, I realised there was only one man I truly wanted to destroy...'

So this was why Brand had taken her...why he had provoked this fight. And she was glad he'd won.

'Why didn't you kill him?' she asked.

He ran a hand over his beard. 'Because to kill a monster sometimes you have to become one,' he said quietly. 'And I didn't want you to see me like that. You have always soothed my rage, Anne. And I held Crowe's life in my hands and I made my decision. But

there are always consequences, aren't there? I had just
thrown down my weapon when I heard a guttural roar
come from behind me. It was a sound like no other
I've ever heard before. One that held grief and pain
and torment. I turned and saw Svea running towards
me... She must have sensed me pull back, decide to
spare his life. It all happened so quickly, but I kicked
Crowe to the floor and grasped hold of Svea and she
broke down in my arms.'

'Is she all right?' Anne asked, concerned.

'I've just been with her, holding her as she wept,
trying to calm her down. At first she was furious with
me, but now I think she's just relieved that he's finally
been seized and is no longer a threat. That he can no
longer hurt anyone else. Deep down, she's tough.'

'Where is Lord Crowe now?'

'He's in chains in a room at the back of the hall. I've
been waiting years for this moment, and today I've settled my promise to my sister and avenged my father's
death. I shall send Crowe back with you to your father,
and I ask that you tell him of all the atrocities he has
committed—against my people and yours. I hope your
father will punish him accordingly.'

Anne's head shot up and she stared at him. Brand
was standing on the other side of the room from her,
his hands braced across his chest. She'd been wondering what he would do with her, now he had got what
he wanted. Now she knew.

'You're sending me home?'

Wasn't that what she'd wanted? Or had she hoped
he would ask her to stay? But that was surely impos-

sible. He was a Dane and she was a Saxon. And yet, did she not mean anything to him?

As she stared at him, there seemed to be a giant void between them, a great chasm opening up.

'That is what you want, isn't it?' he asked.

'Of course,' she said, tears welling in her eyes. 'It's time.'

He gave a curt nod and stalked to the door and pulled it open. 'It's been a long day. I'll leave you in peace now, Anne, while I work out the arrangements.'

Chapter Nine

Brand knew the exact moment Anne entered the
longhouse—and the exact moment she discovered
that he had always meant to sell her for a price.

She had come into the hall with Svea, but while his
sister had joined the men at the large table, Anne had
made a beeline for Ulf, at the side of the room, who
was now sitting up and looking a lot brighter.

Her wispy floral scent alerted Brand to the fact she
was close, and the hairs on his arms bristled in anticipation. But jealousy smarted when she smiled at the
boy and tended to his wounds. Had *he* not suffered far
greater injuries today?

Brand had washed the blood from his skin and inspected his multiple cuts and bruises. The worst was a
deep gash to his arm, which Svea had tried to patch up
as best she could. And he thought he might have broken a bone in his foot. He was having difficulty bearing any weight on it, which was making it increasingly
hard to walk, but he would tolerate the pain.

It was Anne caring for someone else and saying that she wanted to leave that he couldn't handle. His blood had been up ever since.

He knew everything had changed. The intimacy that had blossomed between them had been crushed by his brutal behaviour. She had thought the worst of him, thinking he had killed Crowe, and she'd even shed tears over it. She'd said she wanted to leave and, frankly, he was as angry as hell with her.

But even so, when she'd stepped into the hall and he'd seen that she no longer had a red, puffy face, that she was composed and in control of herself, she had detonated his desire all over again. How did she do that?

Mainly, he was furious with himself. He knew she was safe from Crowe, but that meant he now had to give her up—and he wasn't sure how to go about it in a way that would keep both her and his people happy. He had promised them a reward. He couldn't let them down. But he didn't want to let Anne down either.

'I say we stick to the original plan and demand five hundred pieces of gold for the witch!' Torsten was saying, trying to work the other men into a fury. 'That was always the plan—what's changed? We tell the Saxons we won't murder them all while they sleep, and that in exchange for our leniency they can have her back once they give us the gold.'

Brand saw Anne's back stiffen, saw the realisation of what Torsten was saying dawn in her eyes—that Brand had intended to fetch a ransom for her all along.

Her chin thrust upwards sharply, in that proud, dignified way it always did.

A wave of fists began banging on the table by all those who were in agreement with Torsten, and now Brand felt the swell of rage against his men as well. He understood that they wanted gold, to provide for their families, but it was his decision to make—not theirs. And he'd grown weary of fighting. He longed for peace and stability—didn't they?

'Enough!'

The air in the room was so thick that it seemed almost tangible, but Brand placed his hands flat on the table and the pounding stilled. It was strange... He'd got his vengeance—they should have been celebrating—but he felt dissatisfied. He still hadn't got what he wanted. But what exactly was that?

He glared at Torsten and felt the tension between them simmering. 'What's the matter with you? Your thirst for blood is even worse than usual! Do you have something you want to say?'

'Aye, I damn well do.' The older red-haired man stood up. 'You've been getting your cock wet with that Saxon whore this whole time,' he said, his hands on his hips. 'And you've become fixated on her. Cast your mind back a few years. We followed your father to richer lands and we were promised an equal share of any spoils. Land, treasure, slaves... Is she not a treasure? I demand that you share her before we give her up and then share the ransom you get for her. You owe us that.'

Brand saw Svea blanch, and he put a hand on her

shoulder to reassure her he would deal with this. He studied his old ally, his cool eyes full of disdain, and felt the anger vibrating off his body.

It had been one hell of a day. He'd beaten his enemy in the most brutal of fights, he'd had words with Anne and watched his sister cry, and if he didn't negotiate with the Saxon soldiers soon, they would no doubt attempt to breach the fortress walls. But he wouldn't stand for Torsten giving him orders, or speaking to him as if he wasn't the leader of Kald. It was *his* leadership that had kept them all safe these past years, and he expected loyalty now.

Quiet rage had him rising to his feet, squaring up to his father's old friend. He realised theirs was an acquaintance that had run its course. 'Like I said right from the start—she's mine to do with as I please. If I want to bed her, I will, and if I want to sell her, I will. *I* will decide what happens to her, not you. You're far too hot-headed, Torsten. You always think with your cock, and therefore you make bad choices.'

His adversary glowered at him, his face turning puce.

But Brand continued. 'You'd like to sleep with her? You'd like a bit of fun? Well, you're a fool. You'd be selling us short. The minute any one of us touches her, she loses her worth. She's nothing.' His eyes lanced her across the room. 'We'll make much more gold for her if we return her to her father, the King, her virginity intact. And that's the prize here, yes? Gold—not her body. So go and take a mistress tonight, but keep your hands to yourself when it comes to the Princess. Now, are you with me or against me? What's it going to be?'

As he glanced around, his men's fists began pounding and pummelling the table in agreement...

Anne rose to her feet and met Brand's steely gaze. His final insult had taken her breath away. She had felt his anger from across the room as soon as she'd entered the longhouse, but she hadn't been able to understand why it was directed at her. There had been a hard edge to his voice and words, and she'd felt the blow of each and every one. When Torsten had mentioned the ransom treasure they were all expecting, her heart had frozen over.

She felt rooted to the spot. Now she knew Brand's desired outcome in this dark game he was playing. This was the truth.

She took in his set jaw and unreadable eyes and felt her temper spike. He had deceived her. He had told her he'd taken her to provoke Lord Crowe, in revenge for the wrongs that man had done, and to protect her from marrying a monster. But all along he had been planning to sell her back to her father for gold, which he'd said he wouldn't do.

She felt winded by the betrayal and by his cutting words. He'd called her nothing. *Nothing!*

She had stupidly convinced herself he felt something for her, and had begun to believe she cared about him too. But it was all lies. It had always been about the treasure. He was no different from her father—or any other man. He was treating her as an object for his own gain and she felt like such a fool. She'd let him kiss her, touch her... She'd even thought about going further... Yet he had held back, and now she knew he would never have taken her anyway, because then he wouldn't have earned his gold.

Oh, God! She felt tears sting her eyes and furiously blinked them away.

He'd promised he wouldn't hurt her, but right now she felt more wounded than she ever had before in her life—as if he'd pierced her heart with his iron sword.

But Anne had never been one to keep her mouth shut when she felt she'd been wronged.

'You bastard!' she said, as she placed her cup down on the table and rushed from the room.

The men all around him cheered, back in good spirits, but for an awful moment Brand was at a loss, as if he had made an enormous mistake. He rolled his shoulders. He was so wound up. The thought of Torsten laying a hand on Anne had spiked his rage. He'd said what he'd needed to say to ward off his once-friend from following through on his dark desires. But had he gone too far?

He rubbed his chest. He'd lashed out at his friend and then at Anne, wanting to hurt her as he was hurting because she'd agreed to leave. But then she had looked at him, her emerald-green eyes two wide pools of vulnerability...

He really was a bastard.

He pushed himself away from the table. 'I'll go and make our demands known to the Saxons,' he said, and stalked out of the hall after her, leaving the men to their revelry.

He followed Anne, a mixture of rage and lust propelling him forward as she fled across the square, and finally caught up with her in the stables, just as she threw herself against one of the horse's sides, her fingers curling over its mane.

'Anne—wait.'

'For what, Brand? For you to enlighten me as to why you're such a brute?' Her stare was full of judgement, her cheeks wet as she wiped away a tear. 'This was all about gold the whole time… But not everything has a price. You're no better than my father.'

His brows knitted together. 'Anne, we need to talk… What I said to the men, I didn't mean it. It was just to keep Torsten's wandering mind and hands in check.'

'So you're not going to ask for a ransom?'

He paused before answering, and she laughed bitterly.

'Oh, but of course you are.'

She dug her heels into the horse's sides and mounted the animal. It reared up. He was forced to step back as he realised she meant to ride it—without reins or a saddle—and she sped off in a cloud of dust across the square.

For a minute, he felt off-balance, stunned. There was a connection between them that made her so familiar to him this whole situation felt absurd. Part of him wanted to rant and rage, tell her off for daring to run away from him, and another part of him wanted to pull her to him and thank the gods she was still here. Safe.

And yet without a saddle she could fall off that horse and—*Skit!* When was she going to start taking care of herself?

The spike of irritation in his groin spurred him into action. He mounted one of the stallions and tore off after her, across the yard and over the grain fields, down to the track they'd come up earlier that afternoon from the boat.

He was livid, his boots digging into the sides of his horse, and he was gaining on her, travelling at speed over the long grass, down the hill, the horse jolting and jerking over the uneven terrain. His arm burned, his foot was agony—but he didn't care. Where the hell did she think she was going?

The stallion's nose was finally aligned with Anne's mare and he swerved to the right, recklessly making contact with her. Steering into her, he forced her to turn abruptly, backing her against the boathouse.

When her surprised horse came to a halt, she flung herself off the animal and he jumped down too, meeting her anger with his.

'Are you out of your mind?' she yelled.

'Quite possibly.'

And as he stared down into her blazing eyes he knew she wanted him as much as he wanted her, and he hauled her to him, crushing her mouth with his.

He thought for a second that this was what insanity felt like—wanting someone so badly that you didn't have a choice. Her stifled gasp sent a warning signal to his brain that he shouldn't be doing this, but he'd already made his decision. And, by the way she was pressing her body against his, she had too.

He'd half expected her to shove him away, had even hoped she would, to put a stop to this madness. But she was responding with fire. He grabbed her round bottom and almost welded their bodies together, his length pressing into her flat stomach, and she groaned—a delicious, needy sound that made him want to cause more of a reaction.

He carried her a few strides to the boathouse and, placing her on her feet, pinned her up against the wall. Her hands were around his neck, and as he ravaged her mouth with his tongue he put his hands possessively over her breasts. She whimpered, and his need for her was like an excessive thirst that he had to quench.

He tore his lips from hers, and as he ripped open the brooches that fastened the straps of her pinafore together, letting the material cascade to her waist, he said, 'I didn't mean any of what I said to my men, Anne. I was just telling them what they wanted to hear. Believe it or not, I'm still trying to protect you.'

Her under-gown was still in the way of his destination, and he urgently tugged the collar down over her shoulders, peeling away the material. Small, pert swells of creamy skin spilled into his hands. At last. She was so beautiful...so pale and perfect under his tanned palms. He kneaded and stroked her sensitive flesh, and loved it when she groaned, her head rolling back.

Staring down at her thrusting pink nipples, he realised they were too much of a temptation, and he lowered his head to take one hard bud into his mouth and suckle. She let out a gasp at the indecent torment he was creating, and his hot tongue and teeth tugged at her sweet and salty skin, his beard brushing against her.

She held his head to her chest, her hands roaming through his hair. 'And what about the gold, Brand?'

'To hell with the ransom, Anne. It's you I want.'

Her hands slid over the taut muscles in his shoulders and down his broad back, securing his body tighter to hers, and then they began to roam up and under the material of his tunic, exploring and caressing the ridges of his solid but smooth skin. Her tantalising soft caresses were torture. They weren't enough. He wanted and needed more.

Pushing up her dress, seeking out her other intimate places now, he wrapped one of her legs around his thigh so that he was right there, his hard shaft pressing against the already damp heat of her undergarments. And the last shreds of his self-control were gone.

'I've been fighting this with all the strength I've got, but it's not working. This is the only way...'

And as she wildly, desperately grasped for him, her hands under his arms, pulling his chest closer to hers, the ache in his groin grew hot and heavy. He had to have her. Now.

'Then take me, Brand, and put us both out of our misery so we can move past this.'

He longed to spread her legs wide, his weight holding her down, to thrust deep inside her, to rid himself of this rage and longing. But her words had sliced through his fierce need. He didn't want to just take her and move on, and the thought brought him up short. That was a first.

What he really wanted was to savour every moment of her sweet submission. And, realising this would be her first time, he wanted it to be special—not a frantic moment up the side of the boathouse.

Anne's hands slid over the taut muscles of Brand's stomach and around his broad back, securing his body tighter to hers as the soft material of his trousers brushed against the bare skin of her inner thighs, making her hotter by the second. And when she felt his thick erection nudge against her most intimate places, waves of heat spread like a raging inferno through her body.

Brand lifted his head to meet her lips again, his tongue filling her mouth, entwining with hers—but something had changed. His caresses against her skin became less urgent and his touch was suddenly excruciatingly tender, gentle, as he stroked her neck, her breasts, teasing her nipples between his fingers.

It was driving her mad. She wanted more. It wasn't enough. She never wanted him to stop. He was stealing her away to places she had never even known existed. And maybe this was what she needed—to forget everything, just to feel total, utter pleasure.

She believed that he had said those things to warn off his men. And now she knew that if he continued to lay his hands on her, if they carried on down this dizzying path, she wouldn't be worth a ransom...

She flattened one of his hands against her breast

before pushing it down over her stomach, and lower, guiding him over the bunched-up material of her skirts to reach between her legs. Her eyes opened and met his blue heated gaze. His lips curved up into a dangerous predatory half-smile as she encouraged his fingers to carry on their descent, leaving him in no doubt as to where she wanted him to touch her.

She grazed her mound against his hand, impatient. She had no idea what she was doing—she just knew she needed him to touch her right there. Now. The ache that had been throbbing between her legs the past few days was becoming impossible to ignore.

'I wanted to touch you here that night on the beach.'

Her hand still covered his as he skilfully drew the material of her underwear to one side, and her breath caught in anticipation of his intimate touch. 'Then why didn't you?' A breathless whisper.

Momentarily, she felt fresh air drift over her exposed sensitive skin, before it was replaced with his warm, strong fingers. Parting her with one slick slide of his thumb, making her legs buckle, his thighs held her up and in place as he gently pushed one long finger inside her.

Languid heat bloomed. Need lanced her. 'Oh, God…' Her head fell forward, her forehead against his. So this was what it felt like. She had never imagined it to feel so good.

As he drew his finger out, bringing with it a rush of wetness, he masterfully, mercilessly, circled her sensitive nub, slowly, incredibly gently, making her head spin.

'Because I was waiting for you to want me as much as I want you...' he said.

She would have responded, only he'd ruthlessly pushed two fingers back inside her again, causing her to cry out in shocked pleasure.

'Quiet,' he said, before he caught her mouth with his to stifle her moans. 'We don't want to wake the villagers.'

His fingers weren't acting as if he wanted her to be quiet. They were unrelenting, seeking, pulsing in and out of her, demanding more of a reaction, and her leg curled higher and tighter around his, holding him to her, never wanting this to end and yet at the same time urgently wishing for the release only he could give her.

Her head fell forward on a sob of swelling emotion and pure white-hot blinding bliss, her teeth sinking into his shoulder to stop herself from crying out. His fresh, musky male scent enveloped her and the boathouse wall bit into her bottom, grazing her as she rode his masterful fingers, which were bringing her to the mind-blowing brink, and she cried out into the curve of his neck.

She didn't know how long they stood entwined like that, neither of them moving. He must have been giving her time to get her breath back, but it was a while before he spoke. He smoothed her damp hair either side of her face.

'I'm sorry for all that I said in there, Anne,' he said quietly, cutting through the haze of lust and the torrent of pleasure strumming through her body. 'I was angry with Torsten for the way he was speaking about you. I wanted him to back off.'

He sighed and took a step away from her, the last of his anger seeming to ebb away. He helped her to straighten her clothes while she still clung to him. She didn't think she could stand without his support. Her legs were still trembling. She gripped his upper arms to steady herself, and he blanched beneath her grasp, grimacing.

'You're hurt!' she gasped.

'It's just a little cut.' He grimaced again.

'I don't believe you. How bad is it?'

'Don't worry about me, Anne.'

'But that's the problem. I do…' She brought her hands up to his jaw and drew his mouth down to hers, and their tongues found each other again in a long, lingering kiss.

His hands stroked down her arms to find her hands, and he tugged her around the side of the boathouse, leading her to the jetty so they could take in the view of the moonlight shimmering on the water. He pulled her back into his chest and kissed the top of her head.

'What are you going to do about my father's army, Brand—and the ransom you've promised Kald? Your men are talking about the price you want for me, but where does it end? What about the cost of all this conflict between our people?'

He sighed. 'The men expect me to earn a ransom for your safe return—but I promised them the gold before I got to know you, Anne. I wish I could take it all back… Now, if I send you home and they come out of it empty-handed...' He shook his head. 'Try to remember they don't come from a life of privilege, like you.'

She inhaled sharply. 'That's no excuse.'

'You're right,' he soothed, his arms tightening around her. 'And I don't intend to go through with it. I shall have to provide for Kald in some other way. I will come up with something. I promise that I'll make all this right, Anne.'

He tipped her head back so he could access her neck, placing soft little kisses along her jawline, and she moaned softly. She could feel his hard length pressing into her back and knew she had to be brave and touch him too. And she wanted to—she just didn't know what to do. What if she didn't please him?

So she turned in his arms and forced her trembling hands to stray downwards, tracing the thin line of dark hair that descended from his stomach, and then she plucked up the courage to flatten her palm over the ridge in his trousers.

He groaned, resting his forehead against hers as he began to run his hands down her body.

'Anne, you are so exquisite... I want to cover your body in kisses,' he whispered into her ear, and he pushed open the door to the boathouse and pulled her inside.

She had no idea what she was doing. She just knew she wanted to accelerate the intimacy between them. She wanted to drive him as wild as he was making her. So she tugged open the tie fastening his trousers and moved her other hand beneath the material to take hold of him, wrapping her hand around the intimidating, huge, hard length of him.

He growled. 'Anne, you're driving me insane. Can you feel how much I want you?'

She pushed him back against the wall she gave him a few quick strokes before he moaned into her mouth, but he stilled her roaming fingers.

'Anne,' he whispered. 'Not here. Not yet.'

How did he have such control when she was losing her mind?

Brand lowered her to the wooden floor on her back as he kissed her, stroking her arms as their tongues continued to tangle. He pulled away slightly to look at her in the mellow moonlight, sprawled beneath him, her hair cascading across her shoulders, and when she smiled up at him, trying to pull him back towards her, he'd never seen anyone or anything as beautiful in his whole life.

He gazed down at her as his fingers traced the edge of her dress, over her cleavage. He lowered his head to follow the path with his tongue. If he wanted to kiss her everywhere he needed her naked, so he found the hem of both her garments and rolled them up her legs, tugging her up so he could gently peel them away from her chest and over her head.

And when he lay her back down on the straw he allowed his eyes a moment to linger over her body, soaking it in in the moonlight, before he dipped his head to her naked breasts. She was perfect, so pink and pert and soft, and he showered her sensitive skin with endless kisses, making her nipples wet, swirling his tongue around them, causing her to writhe beneath him and arch her back, wanting more.

She moaned softly and his cock soared. He stretched out beside her, his hands trailing over her flat stomach, his fingers moulding to the gentle curve of her hips and moving round to squeeze her smooth bottom. But his exploration didn't stop there. His fingers dipped further below, to her soft, silky entrance, once more.

'Brand…' she spluttered.

This was exactly where he wanted her. Compliant, wet and willing. His for the taking. He knew that if he wanted peace between Termarth and Kald, as she did, he must take her back pure and chaste. But he could still make love to her with his mouth, couldn't he?

Leaning over her, he let his eyes glance down to take in the intimate dark curls at the apex of her thighs, and his mouth watered to kiss her right there.

His mouth had left her lips and begun to kiss an indecent burning trail down her body, not leaving any part of her skin uncovered. His beard tickled the soft, sensitised skin of her stomach, while his fingers skated up and down her parted thighs. And then, before she knew what was happening, he'd hooked her legs over his shoulders.

Too late, Anne realised his intention, where he was planning to kiss her next, and despite her gasps of shock and her half-hearted protests he held her fast. She threw her arms over her eyes and gave in to the burning intimacy and the incredible sensations his tongue was causing as it swirled over her silky thighs, keeping their course upwards.

Finally, he bent his head and placed his lips where she wanted him the most. He ran his tongue over her most sensitive nub. She bucked, but he ruthlessly pushed her thighs further apart to give him better access. And when he flicked his tongue down her crease, opening her up to him, she cried out, letting him know he was driving her wild.

She reached down to clasp his head, never wanting this to end, and as his tongue inched inside her fingers bunched in his hair in disbelief and her bottom arched off the floor, rising up to meet him, demanding more. She had never known such things were done, or even possible.

Her muscles began to clench and her thighs quivered. He must know she was on the brink. But still he didn't stop. His clever tongue continued to lick, tease and torment her, tipping her over the edge, and he brutally gripped her hips to hold her in place as she cried out in her intense swirling climax.

He dragged his head up her body until he was hovering over her, his hands braced either side of her shoulders, and he was so hard. But he just pulled her into his arms and kissed her gently, until the tremors stopped coursing through her body.

A while later, she allowed him to deftly pull her under-gown and pinafore back into place, sorting out the straps. She watched as he fumbled with the pins. Were his hands shaking?

She bit her lip, suddenly shy. 'What of your needs?'

He smiled. 'I want you, Anne, but not now—not here,' he said, tucking her hair behind her ears. 'Not when your father's men are still banging on my door. And not until I've made amends. But before this is over, Anne, I will make you mine.'

Not long after that Brand left Anne talking with Svea in his sister's room. Svea seemed in much better spirits, and he was glad. His heart warmed as he watched her and Anne busy themselves with making hot drinks and a fire. It took all his strength to leave the cosy scene, but he knew he must come to an agreement with the Saxons before it was too late and things took an ugly turn.

He exited the fortress gates and began to pace over to the soldiers. They were readying themselves to fight, and as he approached the men bristled like the hairs on a huge hog. He couldn't blame them—they'd all seen what had happened between him and Crowe, and as far as they were concerned he had two Saxon hostages.

He asked to speak to the man in charge, and as he waited, with an army of men staring him down, all he could think about was what had happened between him and Anne. The realisation that she wanted him as much as he wanted her made him restless, and even had his fingers shaking.

Just remembering the way she'd felt in his arms, the way his fingers had moved deep inside her, made his blood heat. She'd practically demanded that he touch her, then shown his hands the way to the secret parts of her body. And he'd needed no further encouragement. He'd had his tongue down her throat, her bottom backed up against the wall, her dress gathered up around her waist and his long fingers buried inside her within seconds.

Did he have no shame? To seduce a virgin Saxon princess against the boathouse wall? And yet he couldn't bring himself to regret it. His fingers had fitted her tight body so perfectly, and she had been so responsive to his touch.

He had wanted to claim her from the moment he'd first laid eyes on her. She had been his dream girl as a boy, and she was still his fantasy as a man. He'd thought that when he brought her to Kald those feelings would soon pass, as they had always done with other women. He took them to bed, he grew bored, he moved on. But his need for Anne was becoming greater, not less, and he hadn't even made love to her. All he wanted to do was shove down his trousers and lose himself inside her. He wanted to make her his forever. But a little voice inside his head made him hold back.

She stirred feelings inside him that he'd never felt before, and he knew that was dangerous. Especially when she would be leaving him soon. Now Crowe was in chains Anne was free to marry someone else…and he knew he had to return her to her father to have any hope of making things right. He just wasn't sure how he was going to let her go.

She had made him remember the love his parents had shared. She'd stirred up his memories of the happy times they'd spent together as a family when he was a boy. Did he really not want what they had had—did he not want a wife and children? Was he going to deny himself all that love and joy just because he was fearful of losing all that he would cherish and hold dear?

He raked a hand over his head. He wasn't getting any younger. What was he doing with his life? When this was all over, he needed to get his priorities straight.

Chapter Ten

'Fire! Fire!'

Anne had been sitting at Svea's table, sipping a hot drink and listening to her talk about her and Brand's childhood, enjoying the stories of Brand as a boy, when they'd heard shouting coming from outside. They'd dropped their cups and rushed out of the hut to find hordes of villagers gathered in the square, some scurrying about, looking up in horror at the wild blaze atop a section of the fortress ramparts.

Spitting and smoking, the flames were now blindingly bright and fierce, illuminating the dark night sky. Leaping from the battlements to the turf and timber rooftops of some of the farmsteads, the fire seemed furiously out of control, its thick smoke making people choke.

'Are we under attack?' someone cried. 'What's happening?'

The villagers were running around in chaos, gathering up children, animals, and their belongings, trying to get them to safety.

Anne was momentarily stunned. Where was Brand? Was he safe?

But when she saw Svea filling buckets with water she rushed to do the same, wanting to do something to help. But she didn't make it to the well. A large figure grabbed her from behind and clamped huge clammy hands over her mouth. As she was picked up off the ground and carried through the air, everything moved too quickly for her to process.

This was not Brand's firm but gentle touch, and fear lurched through her. Was this her father's attempt at a rescue? Had the Saxons set the fire as a distraction? And if they had breached the walls, what had they done to Brand?

Despite her kicking and screaming, her captor didn't throw her down to the ground until they were inside a building. He closed the door behind him—and locked it.

Dread pounded through her veins. 'What are you doing?' she asked, trembling. 'Who are you? Let me go!'

Eyes darting around, she tried to work out where they were, but she couldn't see anything in the blackness. Then the pungent metallic odour of hanging meat and fish hit her and she retched. They were in the smokehouse and she was trapped.

'What am I doing?'

The rough voice sneered, making her shrink back from it. It was Torsten. She knew it without a doubt, even before her eyes adjusted to the dark and his outline came into view.

'I'm going to show Brand that he doesn't always rule

the roost around here. Not any more. And I'm going to show *you* that you're nothing but a piece of meat.'

She felt sick, her skin crawling with fear. She had to stall him. Stop him doing whatever it was he was about to do.

'Did you set the fire to distract everyone?' she asked, playing to his ego, trying to keep him talking.

Her breath was coming in short, sharp bursts, and she was sweating. She was having difficulty focusing—the panic of being confined as well as being attacked by this man was overwhelming her.

He laughed. 'It should keep them occupied while I have my fun. And they'll think your Saxon fools did it,' he jeered, reaching out for her.

She dodged him, grappling around on the floor, searching for something—anything—to defend herself with. 'But when they realise Brand will come looking for me. He'll come storming in here at any moment,' she said, her survival instinct kicking in.

'Then I'd better be quick,' he spat.

He launched himself at her, grabbing her arms, and she struggled against him, lashing out and screaming. But he smacked her across the face, sending her into a crumpled heap on her back on the floor.

'I don't believe he has any intention of fighting your army. Or of sending you back and claiming our gold... You've turned his head, witch. Well, I've had enough of waiting.'

Shuffling backwards, and still fumbling for something to use as a weapon, Anne grabbed anything she could lay her hands on—pots, pans, cooking instruments, even a fistful of salt… But she was no match for his weight. He grabbed her hands and pinned her down, his vile breath hissing over her face. He smelled of stale sweat and ale, making her stomach churn, and she turned her head, struggling to gasp some air. He was rough as he tried to manoeuvre his big body in between her kicking legs, but she made it as difficult as possible for him.

'Get off me! Stop it!' she cried.

She could hear the tremors in her voice. She couldn't remember a time when she'd been more afraid. Brand had never made her feel like this.

But her resistance was making Torsten even more angry, and he hit her again, this time blackening her eye, knocking the wind out of her. He took the opportunity to grab her by her wrists and bind her with rope, then dragged her across the room and bent her over a table.

And then she realised she'd rather be dead than have this man take her.

'I've never known a Saxon woman to have such influence over a man. Let's find out what all the fuss is about, shall we?'

When she heard Torsten unfasten his trousers she gagged. *This is it*, she thought, bracing herself.

And then he was gone, pulled back by a force she couldn't see.

'What the hell do you think you're doing?'

Brand.

Her body almost sagged in relief.

'Taking a piece of what's rightfully mine! What I'm owed.'

She heard the crack of bone hitting bone. '*Dra til helvete!* She'll never be yours.'

'You've broken my jaw. Over a Saxon whore?'

She heard another blow and saw Torsten stagger backwards.

'Pick up your things and clear out your house. You'll leave Kald tonight. And if I ever see your face again it will be too soon.'

Anne could hear the anger vibrating in Brand's voice. She whimpered, the rope beginning to slice into her wrists. She could tell a crowd had gathered just beyond the door. She needed to get out, to get away.

'You're choosing her over me? I gave my life to your father. I've given years to you.'

'No, you have followed your own path of rape and pillaging. That was never mine or my father's. We are not the same, you and I. Now, get out!'

Anne realised with relief that the fire must have been extinguished if everyone had gathered round the smokehouse to see what was going on. She hoped no one had been hurt. She could just make out Svea, Ulf and Kar. She couldn't believe Torsten had set the buildings of his own village alight as a distraction, so he could attack her. He could have burned them all down to the ground.

'Get out!' Brand roared again.

She watched Torsten begin to stalk away, but as he did so she saw him slide Ulf's sword out of its hilt.

'Brand, watch out!' she cried.

And in a flash Brand, Kar and Svea all turned their weapons on him. The red-haired brute slumped down to his knees, dropping Ulf's blade in defeat.

'Take him away,' said Brand.

Anne felt a hand on her waist and she jerked.

'It's just me.'

Brand.

And that was when she felt an uncontrollable trembling start in her legs and the tears began to roll. And as Brand untied her and pulled her to her feet she collapsed against him, throwing her arms around his neck and clinging to him, never wanting to let go.

Chapter Eleven

'You're bleeding.'

'It's nothing. I'm fine.'

Brand had carried Anne up to his room and they were sitting cross-legged on the bed, face to face. Her skin had turned almost colourless, and she was bruised and dishevelled, her hair all over the place. But she was still so proud and dignified, still so beautiful, and it hurt to look at her.

When he'd seen her bent over that table in the smoke-house, looking so tiny and fragile, he'd felt an uncontrollable blinding rage shift through him. The thought of Torsten or any other man taking her against her will, hurting her, had filled him with nauseating horror. The warrior in him had thought only of helping her and he'd wanted Torsten's blood.

As he'd enveloped her in his arms her whole body had trembled, and she had clung to him, burying her face in his shoulder. He'd wrapped his arms around her and stroked her hair, soothing her for a long while.

Svea and Kar had dealt with Torsten, and the crowd had begun to disperse and make their way to their homes.

Brand had told them he'd come to an agreement with the Saxons and they wouldn't be attacking tonight. They were all safe. And then he'd scooped up Anne and brought her back here.

He pressed a damp cloth to Anne's split lip and she winced. He felt as sick as a dog. He'd broken his promise. He said he'd keep her safe. But it was his own selfish actions that had brought her here and put her in harm's way. By taking her from her home and bringing her to Kald he'd let a brute prey on her. This was all his fault. He'd failed to protect his sister, and now Anne too.

'Did he really set the fire to distract everyone, just so he could lure me away?' she asked, shaking her head.

'Looks like it.'

'Is there much damage? Was anyone hurt?'

'Anne, you've just suffered probably the worst attack of your life and yet you're worried about other people?' he asked, offering her a half-smile before it collapsed again. 'Danes?'

'I don't see your people as any different to ours. In fact, I've grown fond of a few of them,' she said quietly.

His heart lurched. Did she include him in that count? he wondered—and then stopped himself short. *No! Enough.* He must not wish for something that could never be. He had to let her go. He had to return her to her people, where she would be safe. His worst nightmare had come true—he had had a taste of what it would be like if something happened to her and it was more than he could bear.

'When I saw the fire and felt someone grab me I thought it was my father's men, making a rescue attempt.'

He nodded, moving the cloth to the cut near her eye. She flinched again. He wished that had been the case. He wished they had rescued her instead of her having to go through that ordeal. He should have been there with her, guarding her at all times. But now he'd lost her trust.

'Then I realised it was Torsten and I knew it was going to be bad...'

'I'm so sorry, Anne.' He hushed her, his mouth dry. 'You know we're not all like that,' he said, staring steadily into her eyes, his brows drawn together.

But even though he knew he wasn't like that—that he would never act the way Torsten had—he also knew with absolute clarity that he wasn't good enough for her.

Her fingers came up to take the cloth, brushing against his.

'Torsten gives us Northmen a bad name.'

'I know.'

And as if to prove it she leaned in and kissed him. It was the sweetest kiss to the lips, and one he definitely didn't deserve.

He cupped her face in his hands as he pressed his mouth against the tiny cut next to her eye, kissing it better, and then his lips moved back to her mouth, gently touching the cut there too. It was meant to be a goodbye kiss, and it took every ounce of willpower to pull away from her.

'I should leave you to get some rest,' he said, rising off the bed.

'Leave? Don't be absurd—this is your room,' she said, gripping his arm. He winced again. 'You are badly hurt, Brand! Let me see.'

'I have told you I'm fine. It's you I'm worried about.'

She pouted just a little. 'I've let you tend my wounds—you could at least let me do the same for you.'

The fact that his arm actually hurt like hell, and knowing she probably wouldn't let it go, made him relent, and he sat back down on the bed. Plus, he wasn't ready to leave her just yet. Would he ever be?

'Take off your top,' she said. 'Let me look.'

He rolled his eyes, but did as he was told and turned his bandaged arm towards her. Slowly, ever so gently, she peeled away the wool and he heard her breath catch.

'That is not just a little cut,' she scolded him. 'It's deep. Who stitched it for you?'

'Svea. But I fear she doesn't have your skills.' He smiled.

'I would have done it for you. Why didn't you let me?'

'I was being stubborn.' He shrugged.

'You? Stubborn?' She smiled too.

She cleaned the wound with water, and then reached for the ointment on the wooden chest—the one she'd made for Ulf. She applied it with the delicate tips of her fingers before wrapping the bandage around his muscular arms again.

'Svea has done quite a good job, actually. I'm impressed. There—how's that?' she asked.

'Better. Thank you,' he said, and as their eyes met the tension in the room was so thick he thought he could slash it with his sword. Or smash it to smithereens with a kiss.

But he didn't dare kiss her again. He must never kiss her again.

'You should get some rest now, Anne. Actually, we could both do with some rest.' He tried to stand again.

'Will you stay with me, Brand?'

He knew he shouldn't. He should walk out through the door and never look back.

'Please?'

It was the 'please' that was his undoing. He couldn't resist. Because what she was asking for was all that he wanted. He wanted to hold her and stroke her and make everything all right. He wanted to show her that Northmen could be gentle. And he knew that if this was going to be the last night they spent together, he wanted to hold her in his arms.

He gave a short nod and she moved over to one side of the bed and slipped beneath the furs. He did the same and pulled her to his side.

He could stay like this forever, he thought. This was what he wanted for his future, he realised. Anne at his side, always.

And this was what could never be now that he'd let both her and himself down. He could never forgive himself for that.

* * *

Anne woke with a start to see Brand fully dressed and leaning over her, his forefinger to her bruised lips.

'Don't talk, just come. Get dressed,' he whispered. 'Quietly.'

'What's going on?'

'No questions,' he said. 'Just do as I ask. Don't make a sound.'

It was barely light and she glanced at him, wary. She'd had just about enough drama to last a lifetime. Why was he dressed and wearing his leather and chain-mail vest over his tunic—the one he'd worn the night they'd met on the ramparts? And the shadows under his eyes told her he hadn't slept well. That was strange—she'd had the best night's sleep, wrapped in his arms...

She clearly wasn't awake yet—she couldn't think straight. Her limbs felt heavy and she wanted to stay in the warm cosy bed with him. Why was he pulling her to her feet and helping her pull on her pinafore over her smock? Why was he slipping her feet into her ankle boots?

And then she reached up to pat her hair, to see how much of a state it was in, and realised it was braided.

'Did you plait my hair?' she asked, incredulous.

'Not very well.'

'While I was asleep?'

'I used to do my sister's hair...after my parents died.'

A giggle escaped her lips. The Barbarian had plaited her hair. He would never cease to amaze her, she thought.

And then he was leading her down the steps and

across the square to the gates. The pink and golden early-morning light was hazy, just like her mind, as she watched Brand signal to Svea and the fortress guards, who were up on the bridge. They raised the wooden bolt, and then slowly the huge wooden gates began to open.

'Take care, Princess,' Svea said. 'We'll miss you. Come and see us some time, won't you?'

And Anne suddenly realised what was happening. This was it. Brand was sending her home.

Her heart exploded in pain. She didn't know what she'd been expecting—but not this. She had thought he cared for her, so why was he sending her away? She was now wide awake, and she spun round to Brand, ready to say—what?

'Not now, Anne,' he said, purposely avoiding her eyes, and with his hands on her shoulders he propelled her forward, towards the awaiting convoy of Saxon soldiers.

She was completely taken aback, struggling to come to terms with what was happening. She felt like a caged bird, flapping its wings, desperately trying to escape— and yet it looked as if she was no longer a prisoner. She was being released, set free from his hold.

What was Brand thinking? Why was he sending her back after all the incredible things that had happened between them the day before?

Tears threatened, so she bit the inside of her cheek. She could not make a scene—not with the Saxon soldiers approaching—and he knew it. What she wanted to do was to grab him and shake him and yell at him, but mainly she just wanted to throw her arms around him and beg him not to do this.

Didn't she deserve an explanation? Shouldn't they have talked about this?

And then the ice-cold clench of betrayal gripped her. Had he made a deal after all? Had her father paid him a ransom? And, despite the explicit things he'd done to her yesterday, how he'd made her feel so special, she realised he still hadn't made love to her. Was that because, as he'd said before, she was worth more if her innocence was still intact? She felt sick.

Lord Stanton, who now seemed to be in charge of the Saxon army, cantered towards them on his horse. He nodded at Brand in recognition, then turned his attention to Anne.

'Your Royal Highness, I'm not sure if you remember me. I am Lord Stanton. I'm very pleased to see you.' A look of consternation crossed his face when he saw her swollen lip and blackened eye, but he refrained from commenting on them. 'Your father has missed you. It's time to take you home.'

Her eyes narrowed on them both, and a rage burning like the fire on the rooftops last night swept through her. How dare they make decisions for her? And yet it was as if she had an invisible gag on her mouth. She couldn't protest. What could she say? That she didn't want to go home? That she wanted to stay?

She couldn't. It wasn't appropriate, was it? And she didn't even know what Brand's thoughts were on the matter. For all she knew, he couldn't wait to be rid of her. Had their shared intimacy over the past few days not meant anything to him? It had meant everything to her. She had thought she was falling in love with him.

Instead of saying what was in her mind and in her heart, she took a deep breath, schooling her features. 'Thank you, my lord,' she said. 'I appreciate you and your men coming to fetch me. But might I ask what deal you have struck for my release?'

'Your father was willing to do anything to ensure your safe return, Your Highness.'

Anger seeped through her blood. She was livid now. If she had been sold like one of Brand's animals at a farmers' market, didn't she at least deserve to know what price her father had paid for her and how rich he'd made the Barbarian?

She swung a look at Brand and, damn him, he was acting so cool, so remote. This whole situation felt unreal. Especially as just yesterday she'd let him do unspeakable things to her naked body. He'd made love to her with his mouth—and now he was selling her like an object. Whatever the amount, Brand had made her feel dirty and cheap—like a slave.

And then she almost laughed. He didn't even have slaves. Most Northmen bought and sold slaves, yet this man didn't—it was beneath him. No, he only sold princesses.

Anne wrestled with her emotions, trying to keep them in check. She was on the edge of hysteria. Of course she wanted to go home—didn't she? She couldn't expect to stay in Kald forever, living as Brand's mistress. She was a fool to have entertained the idea, even for a second. It would destroy her reputation. And yet the things he'd done to her yesterday...

She had stupidly thought that he cared for her. That he wouldn't want to let her go. She'd thought he might even marry her. But all this time he must have been scheming behind her back. She didn't want to believe it, and yet the truth was there, right before her eyes, as the Saxon soldiers began to move off the heathland.

Her throat felt thick with the tears she refused to shed—she could not let him see her cry. She wrapped her arms around her midriff and determined not to look at him again.

Her father's messenger, Girladus, who they'd encountered on the way to Kald, came towards Brand, leading Rebel.

'I believe this steed belongs to you?'

'Thank you,' Brand said, taking the reins.

The horse was pleased to see her, and Anne could have wept. She nuzzled the animal's neck, needing the comfort, while Brand busied himself readying Rebel for her to ride. He moved to help her mount the animal, but she put her hands up in a warding-off gesture.

'I can do it,' she said curtly, backing away from him, increasing the distance between them.

'We'd like you to ride in the middle of us, Your Highness. It's the safest place,' Lord Stanton said.

He had treated her with respect so far, and she wondered if, after Crowe, he was next in line on her father's list for her hand in marriage. She imagined most women would find him ruggedly handsome—he had an attractive face—but for some reason he left her feeling cold. There was only one man who had ever stirred her heart and her desire.

Unwanted tears welled in her eyes and she suddenly lost the strength and the will to argue. She didn't even have the energy to talk. She spurred the horse into a trot and took her place behind the new leader of the army. She was pleased to note he was still wearing the navy uniform of her father's men, not the black and yellow that Crowe's close comrades wore.

When she saw Brand turn back towards the gates of Kald, for an awful moment she thought he was heading inside, walking out of her life without even so much as a goodbye, and the pain took her breath away. But then she saw Svea leading out two black stallions, one with a forlorn-looking Lord Crowe positioned on top, his hands bound.

She noticed Brand was hobbling. Did he have another injury she didn't know about? Why did she even care? Brand and his sister seemed to be having a heated conversation, and then Svea threw her arms around him, holding him tight. Why did Svea look so distraught? And then Brand mounted the second horse and fell in behind Anne in the convoy.

She couldn't understand it. None of this was making any sense. She rubbed her temple, where a dull pain was starting to throb.

'What are you doing?' she demanded, turning round in the saddle to speak to him, already breaking her own rule of not looking at him.

'I wanted to see you safely home. And Crowe locked up.'

She sat up straight. 'I was safe at home until you came along! My father's men can look after me from here.' And then a thought struck her. 'By escorting me home, you'll be putting yourself in danger. You might be arrested by my father's men the moment you set foot in Termarth.'

He shrugged. 'I've decided to come anyway.'

And as the snake-like trail of soldiers in navy uniforms began to leave the kingdom of Kald she knew she must withdraw from him. She could never forgive him for this. Any of it. And yet she still couldn't help but worry about what would become of him once they arrived at the castle.

They rode all morning in silence, along the coast she'd grown to love, and she wished he'd never come into her life and taken her away, opening her eyes to everything the world around her had to offer. Even the storm hadn't dampened her fascination with the sea, and she didn't think she'd ever tire of its wild beauty. Not seeing it every day would cause her great pain. Not seeing Brand every day would be…

No! She must not do that. She must not think of him.

Her mind kept running over the past few days for any signs she'd missed of his betrayal. He'd completely fooled her, and she resolved not to let it happen again. She knew she had to get away from him to process what had happened, but he was riding right behind her, keeping her in his sights, so escape was impossible.

It was unnerving—like having a constant dark shadow looming over her. She could feel his blue gaze burning a hole into her back and it was making her ridiculously agitated, her fingers trembling on the reins. She felt exposed, vulnerable, and sat rigid, trying to block him out. Everything about his nearness reminded her of how she'd felt in his arms last night, and in the afternoon, how she'd flourished beneath his touch. How he'd brought her to aching, throbbing life like a flower blooming in the sun, opening her up to a world of beauty and possibility.

And now he was tearing her down and she was literally shrivelling and closing up, making herself impenetrable.

But what surprised her and disturbed her the most was that she still wanted him. How could she still feel that way after all he'd done? She loathed herself and shuddered at her own weakness.

Suddenly Brand was right there, riding beside her. 'Are you warm enough, Highness?' he asked. 'You're shivering.'

She bristled at the formality of him using her title. 'Why are you still here?' she bit out, rounding on him.

She saw the Saxon soldiers raise their eyebrows at her furious tone, but right now she didn't care. She'd had enough of men and all their schemes, their thirst for power with no regard for anyone else's thoughts or feelings.

'Now that you have what you want, why don't you just leave?'

She thought she saw him recoil slightly from her words, but his eyes remained cool and steady. 'I told you—I promised to see you safely home.'

It was like looking into the unwavering gaze of one

of the carved heads of those monsters mounted on his ships. How could he be so cold, so unfeeling? She had the sudden desire to lash out at him, to try to hurt him as he was hurting her, to provoke a reaction.

Her chin tilted up. 'Lord Stanton, after the fall from grace of Lord Crowe, and therefore the cancellation of my wedding, are you aware of my father's plans? Does he have any other potential suitors lined up for me?'

Brand's eyes narrowed on her and she saw him tighten his grip on his horse's reins.

'I'm afraid I don't know. You'll have to ask your father that, Your Highness, when we arrive back at Termarth.'

'I'll be sure to do that, Lord Stanton,' she said, smiling sweetly, cutting Brand a look. 'As soon as I get home.'

She knew she was being childish, but she couldn't help herself.

The time seemed to drag, and when they finally stopped for a rest, and Lord Stanton tied up Rebel and helped Anne down from the horse, she made sure she stayed away from Brand. He tried to approach her and offer her some bread, telling her she should eat something as she had missed breakfast, but she shunned him.

'You're so wilful—do you know that?' he said, raking his hand over his hair.

'I pride myself on it.'

He grimaced, stuffing his hands into his leather vest and stalking away. It was then that she realised, in dismay, that they were surrounded by a swathe of pretty yellow primroses. They'd stopped in the forest where they'd shared their first kiss. And, no matter how much she wanted to hate him, her heart still ached for her Barbarian.

Every sight or sound on this journey stirred a memory, and Brand was finding it increasingly difficult to keep up a front.

He shifted in his seat. Anne had been travelling further and further ahead of him for the past few hours, ever since they'd stopped for a rest in the forest where he'd first kissed her. He'd been a brute since that first night, proving she could definitely do better than the likes of him. But when she'd mentioned her father finding another suitor for her it had felt as if she'd taken his axe and swung it into his chest, ripping it open.

He knew this journey would be different. For a start, Anne was no longer his prisoner, and she was surrounded by the King's men and their protection, not nestled in his arms, between his thighs. And she was heading back to Termarth. He was not whisking her off to Kald, bringing her home.

This time, the journey would be slow and steady, and she'd have people to look after her every need. He knew this was how it should be, and yet he longed for it to be as it had been before—just the two of them. He wanted her as much now as he had when he'd pulled her into his chest that first night. Actually, he wanted her more.

By the time they stopped to pitch their tents that evening, in a sheltered redwood grove, his mood was black. Listening to her talk to Lord Stanton and some of the other men, rather than speaking to him, was infuriating. He was glad she didn't have to sleep out in the elements, surrounded by monsters like Torsten, and yet watching the Saxon men fall over themselves in their attempts to help her off Rebel, or to show her to her tent, was maddening.

He nestled down to rest against a tangled tree trunk, far enough away from the soldiers cooking meat over a fire and close enough to Anne's tent to keep an eye on it, to check she was safe.

Yesterday at the boathouse it had been incredible, and he wanted to relive it over and over again. That was where he'd choose to spend his life—in her arms, with her looking at him as if he was her whole world. But last night, as he'd held her and soothed her to sleep, he'd told himself it was for the last time. He'd proved he couldn't protect her...that he wasn't good enough for her.

He'd hardly slept, watching her sleep, playing with her hair and wondering if he was doing the right thing.

He had made no deal with the Saxon soldiers. He realised he had never really wanted a ransom for Anne—he'd just used that as an excuse to get to know her. But if she wanted to believe he had accepted a reward for her return, then so be it. It was his way of gently pushing her away, of letting her go.

He had been honest and told Lord Stanton that Crowe had killed his father, and when he'd insisted on escorting Anne home the man had been decent, agreeing to him joining them on the journey. Brand knew he was risking capture and punishment when he reached Termarth, but he was prepared to take that risk—he would do anything to ensure Anne's safety.

And if he did make it out of this alive, he would just have to find another way to appease his people and provide for them.

He should have told Anne about his talk with Stanton and about her leaving Kald before he'd slept beside her all night, but he'd put it off. There had been a large part of him that had wanted to break the agreement and sail off with her into the sunset this morning, but he'd known that was impossible.

She didn't belong to him. She could never be his. He had to hand her back.

But he wouldn't be without her until he'd deposited her into the hands of the King. Yet being this close to her and not being able to talk to her, or touch her, was torture.

He knew she was furious with him for making a deal behind her back. He could tell she was trying to distance herself from him by the way her body stiffened every time he came near her, by the way her chin tipped up, the way she stumbled away to avoid touching him. And that was the way it had to be—what needed to happen. But knowing that didn't help. It still hurt. It wasn't what he wanted.

They'd barely spoken since they'd left Kald, and now Brand wanted to storm into her tent, take her in his arms and kiss her. To cut through the tension. To forget everything else and just seek pleasure in each other's bodies. But he knew the guards wouldn't let him anywhere near her. Hell, she might not either. And saying goodbye to her tomorrow would be easier if she was still furious with him.

He was just settling down for another uncomfortable night, watching the entrance to her tent, when the canvas was cast aside and she stepped out. Their eyes collided with the force of two shields clashing, bringing him to attention, before she turned and headed in the direction of Lord Stanton and the smell of roasting meat. He saw the ealdorman offer her a plate of food and she accepted it with a smile. Jealousy burned.

He took his knife out of his belt and began to sharpen it against a stone...just for something to do. He knew the Saxon men were wary of him, and he didn't blame them. They'd all seen his fight with Crowe. It seemed Crowe's men had returned to Calhourn, though, and Stanton was responsible for his own *fyrd*, who would do the King's bidding.

Would Stanton be King Eallesborough's second choice of suitor for Anne? he wondered. He would probably be considered much more attractive to a woman than Crowe, with his easy smile and his full head of dark hair. Had Anne had these thoughts earlier—was that why she'd mentioned it?

The thought of her with any man except him made Brand incensed and he ran the blade harder across the stone, foolishly slicing his finger open. *'Skit!'*

'Are you all right?'

He glanced up to see Anne coming towards him.

'It's just a scratch,' he said, popping his finger in his mouth to draw off the blood.

'You should be more careful. Here, I've brought you some food.'

He looked up at her, suspicious of her kindness.

'I'm fine, thanks. I can fend for myself.'

'And you have the nerve to call me stubborn?' she said, shaking her head. 'Well, just for once, why don't you swallow your pride and eat what my father's men have cooked and be grateful?'

She bent over and set the plate down on the grass next to him.

'Is this where you're planning to sleep?' she asked.

'Why not? It'll be the third or fourth time I've slept out under the stars this week. I'm getting used to it.'

'Lord Stanton says he can find room for you in one of the tents if you like.'

He narrowed his eyes on her. 'How kind of him. Will you be finding room for him in yours?'

'What?'

'He seems to like you, and you him. What's stopping you?'

He knew he'd gone too far. He saw it in the wounded flare of her eyes, the stricken set of her mouth. But he was hurt. And he was angry—but with himself mainly.

'How dare you?' she spat, her quiet anger unfurling. 'After all you've done. How can you sit there and criticise me? I hate you. I—I think I shall go to my bed early. And I shall ask if I can ride at the front tomorrow, so we don't have to see or speak to each other again.'

She turned on her heel, started to walk away.

'Then they'll really know how I affect you, Princess.

Bringing me food, then complaining about being in my company... They'll think you're afflicted.'

She stopped and glanced back, her lips pursed together. 'I don't care what they think. All I know is that I was wrong about you. And if I ever have to speak with you again it will be too soon.'

She stalked back to her tent and threw the canvas flap shut.

Well, at least she hadn't gone to Stanton, Brand thought wryly. He ran a hand over his face. What the hell was he doing? He didn't even know why he'd said those things. He didn't mean any of it. But if he was trying to keep her feeling furious with him, he was certainly going about it the right way.

When the walls of Termarth finally came into view the next day, Anne was surprised at how much the sight of the castle comforted her. The dramatic silver stone walls around the tower had always made her feel trapped before, but when the drawbridge was lowered and the gargantuan wooden doors opened up, she felt as if the walls were giant arms, reaching out to capture her in a welcoming embrace. Despite her lonely upbringing, it was still her home, and after everything that had happened, she felt so weary and out of sorts.

She had stuck to her word and ridden at the front with Lord Stanton today, rather than in the middle of the convoy, so she didn't have to talk to the Barbarian. And she'd forced herself not to look at him at all—even though she'd found it excruciatingly hard. Just as water was vital to her survival, she'd found herself needing to drink him in, to check he was still there. But the cruel words he'd spoken to her last night had struck deep, and she knew she couldn't forgive him for all this.

She took in the familiar landmarks of the pulsing kingdom, trying to lift her spirits. People lined the streets to celebrate the safe return of their Princess, cheering and waving, and she plastered on a smile, moved her hand to and fro in the air. But her mind was in complete and utter chaos.

She had been gone for less than a week, but she had changed so much in that time. Everything was different. She would have to face her father and pretend everything was fine when it was far from it, and she didn't know how she would be able to move on with her life. She couldn't picture her future without Brand in it.

Most of the army dispersed when they were inside the city walls, and just a small group of Lord Stanton's trusted soldiers, as well as Brand, escorted her to the steps of the castle keep. She was shocked when she saw her father was waiting for her, his eyes shining with tears.

As Lord Stanton helped her down from Rebel the King extended his hand and his thanks to the man, before enveloping Anne in a warm hug. She couldn't remember the last time her father had embraced her like that, and she was momentarily stunned.

'I'm so sorry, Anne,' he said, holding her close. 'I thought I'd lost you and I was so scared. Are you all right, daughter? Have you been hurt?'

'I'm fine, Father,' she whispered.

But a sob threatened to escape, and then she couldn't

hold it in any longer. It was as if his embrace had melted the ice on the winter hilltops, and suddenly her tears and pain were like unstoppable water, rushing down. He put his arm around her and began to lead her up the steps to go inside.

But just before she reached the door something made her turn back and look. She had to see him one last time.

And as she glanced over at the group of men who had seen her home, she saw Lord Stanton talking with Brand. He met her gaze over the other man's shoulder. Was he leaving and about to walk out of her life forever? Or were her father's men going to restrain him? Panic stirred in her chest. Either way, she knew she might never see him again, and that was the worst pain of all.

Chapter Twelve

Brand paced up and down in his room. He'd never slept in a castle before, and the room was impressive. Stanton had apologised, saying it was the best he could do at short notice, but Brand had been expecting nothing more than the servants' quarters.

He hated to admit it, but he liked the man. If the King had him in mind as a suitor for Anne, he knew he couldn't have chosen better himself, although the thought caused him pain.

Turning his attention back to the room—anything to try to rid his thoughts of her—he tried out the large bed for comfort, and then inspected some kind of barrel contraption up the corner. But the view was what made the room superb—of the rain-washed green and verdant pastures past the city walls. But although it was beautiful, the scene just served to remind him of the colour of Anne's beautiful eyes, so he was glad when finally it became cloaked in darkness.

He wasn't very good at being on Saxon territory, but

the King had requested a meeting with him the next morning. He hadn't been able to say no—after all, he was grateful he hadn't been thrown into the castle dungeon. He didn't expect that he could return the Princess to her home, after kidnapping her and fighting her betrothed, and be excused.

He wondered what would be said. If he'd been the King, after he'd taken one look at his battered and bruised daughter he would have rammed a sword through the man who was responsible. He should be dead by now, he thought. And if he was going to die he had just one regret. He should have made Anne his lover while he had the chance.

After his harsh treatment of her the night before she'd been true to her word and turned her back on him all day—right up until that last moment, when she'd given him a final glance over her shoulder as she'd entered the castle.

As he lay on the bed, staring up at the ceiling, he could hear Svea's voice ringing in his ears. 'If you take her back, they will be sure to kill you,' she'd said to him by the gates as he'd hugged her and said goodbye.

'It's something I have to do,' he'd told her. 'I have to make amends.'

And he had, in a way. He had seen Anne safely home, as he'd promised. And for Svea he had made sure Stanton had taken Crowe to the dungeon.

If he were to be set free from Termarth he would make things right with his people. He wondered how they would feel when they found out that he'd handed Anne back without earning a ransom for her.

He started when he heard a light knock at the door, and he swung off the bed and pulled it open.

A small, hooded figure stood in the doorway, and after looking from side to side along the corridor tilted her head up to face him.

Anne.

Anne had come to see him.

'Can I come in?'

He stepped back to allow her room to enter, and once she'd crossed the threshold he closed the door behind her. When she lowered her hood, his heart exploded in his chest. The bruise around her eye was beginning to turn a bluish yellow, but even so she was still the most exquisite woman he'd ever seen.

She had obviously just bathed—her glossy dark brown hair was still damp, although it had been braided into two immaculate plaits on either side of her head. She was dressed in a ruby silk gown that drew in her waist and had long flared sleeves and a full skirt. She looked every bit the pure and perfect Royal Princess and his mouth turned to dust.

'You shouldn't be here, Anne.'

'Neither should you,' she said. 'The Saxons won't like a Northman staying in the castle. They could hurt you. You may not be safe.'

He smiled wryly. 'Still worrying about me, Anne?' He shook his head. 'You know I don't wound easily. Whereas you... Your father—?'

'Is asleep. No one saw me come here.'

He released a breath and saw her swallow, watched

the pulse flicker at the base of her throat. What was she doing here?

'The King—was he pleased to see you?' he asked.

Brand was surprised to see her eyes swim with tears. 'Yes.' She nodded, smiling. 'He confessed that he had missed me. Can you believe it?'

He smiled. 'I can. I knew when I saw the size of that army that you might have misjudged the extent of his feelings for you.'

She wrung her hands. 'He apologised for his treatment of me since my mother died. Apparently, I remind him of her. He said that sometimes it's too painful for him to look at me. And after she passed away he became obsessed with wanting to protect me and keep me safe.'

'I can understand that,' he said, his lips twisting.

He thought perhaps he and the King might just have something in common. They would both go to great lengths to keep Anne safe.

'He has admitted he went the wrong way about it, though. He said he saw how the people cared for me when I was gone, and he has even asked me to be a part of his witan. He said I have such a loyal following he believes my opinions and ideas should be heard.'

Brand nodded. 'I am glad he has seen sense, Anne. But now you must too. You need to turn around and leave. You mustn't be seen here with me.' He motioned to their surroundings, hoping she'd understand what he meant.

'You can't give me orders any more, Brand. Not here.'

His brow furrowed. 'I'm thinking of you. Reputation is everything, surely?'

'To you. So much so that you let me believe you're some kind of barbarian,' she accused. 'And you did it again when we left Kald. Why did you let me think the worst of you, Brand? Why didn't you defend yourself? Lord Stanton told me... Why didn't *you* tell me you hadn't taken the gold my father offered?'

He ran a hand over his hair. So she knew the truth. She knew he had kept his word on that, at least.

'Everyone believes all kinds of things about me. It's not my job to set them straight.'

'Even me? After everything we've been through? I think you owe me a better explanation than that.'

He stood with his hands on his hips, his head bowed. 'I did promise my men a ransom for you, Anne. So I am all the things you believed. And I thought it would be easier saying goodbye to you if you still thought badly of me. But, no, the gold was never important to me.'

'If it wasn't the gold, what was it?' she asked, closing the gap between them. 'You could have killed Lord Crowe the night you came to Termarth if you had wanted to. Instead, you took me... If it wasn't for the ransom, why didn't you just leave me out of it?'

'And where would have been the fun in that?' He grinned, but his smile didn't quite reach his eyes. 'When I heard you were going to marry him, I guess all rational thought was lost. I wanted to hurt Crowe, and I knew I could get to him through you. But I'd be lying if I said I didn't take you for selfish reasons. I wanted to get to know you, Anne. You, the girl who helped me when I was at my lowest. I'd thought of you so often. And I'm ashamed to say I wanted to stop your wedding… But the more I got to know you, the more I realised *you* were the real treasure—not the gold or silver your father could offer.' He reached out to stroke her face. 'You really are priceless, Anne.'

Her eyes were swimming with tears again, and one slipped down her cheek. She turned her face into his palm and it felt so good to touch her again.

'My father says he and his witan will be speaking with you in the morning. I will talk to him, Brand. I will ask him to treat you well.'

Brand wondered what they would do to him. Would he be put to death, or would that be too good for him? Looking at Anne now, he didn't really care. Now he'd lost her, he had lost almost everything.

'Please. Don't worry about me, Anne,' he reassured her. 'I've made my peace with whatever happens now. I just want you to know I'm sorry. I hope what I have put you through hasn't caused you too much distress. I wanted to make it up to you and see you back home safely.'

Anne toyed with something in her hand, and he saw her swallow before taking a deep breath.

'Here,' she said, holding something out to him. 'This belongs to you.'

She placed a silver ring with a Y-like symbol on it into his open palm.

His head shot up. 'You kept it?' He shook his head. 'All these years you have kept it safe? Why did you even take it?'

'I heard the soldiers coming and I saw the rune on it. I realised you must be a Dane so I took it, hoping they wouldn't see it and…and finish you off.'

His eyebrows pulled together. 'My father gave it to me. It's the symbol of the elk. It offers protection. I thought you'd stolen it.'

Anne blanched. 'I would never—'

She had kept the ring safe in a little trinket box for years. She had often thought about that beautiful blue-eyed boy she'd met in the meadow. She'd just never put two and two together when she'd met Brand on the castle ramparts.

She knew that returning the ring to him wouldn't be enough to heal his hurt or fill the void of losing his parents, but now, standing here, she wondered, even hoped, if she could. Faced with his closeness, she realised she still wanted him. She loved him. And she wanted to heal his heart.

It was mad to think it had only been a week since they'd met. So much had happened…so much had changed. But the only thing that mattered was whether or not he still wanted her.

'Brand, I have to tell you something,' she began bravely, although she couldn't help but play with the tassels on her dress. 'In the hut with Torsten, I shut my eyes and wished to be somewhere else. I longed to be back on that boat with you, free from all this. All I could think about was you and whether I'd see you again.'

'Anne—' He shook his head, couldn't look her in

the eye. He knew what she was about to say, and he knew he should stop her now—before he did something reckless. Something insane.

'Brand, I know you blame yourself for what happened to me, just as you do with Svea, but you mustn't. I'm fine. You got to me in time.'

He closed his eyes briefly and Anne seized the moment to bravely step forward and wrap her hand around his beard, tugging him closer.

He inclined his head in that smouldering way she'd grown used to. 'Brand, I want you to kiss me.'

His eyes dipped to her lips. 'Here?'

'Yes.'

'Are you trying to get me killed?' he whispered, as he bent his head and his lips lightly touched hers. 'It would be worth it.'

His arms came around her waist and he kissed her slowly, trailing his tongue along her lips and stealing it into her mouth, stroking against hers in an intense, deep, sensual exploration. She sank against him, a melting sensation making her knees weak, forcing her to wrap her arms around his shoulders to stop herself from falling.

When he finally raised his head she was breathless. Their faces were so close she could see tiny flecks of gold in his dilated blue eyes. And his skin smelt of musk and the sea.

'Do you still want me, Brand?'

'More than I've ever wanted anything else in my life. But it would be wrong, Anne.'

'If it's wrong, why does it feel so right?' she asked,

as she raised herself onto her tiptoes and pressed her curves fully against him, as if she'd been starved of his touch.

He groaned. 'Anne...'

'Make love to me, Brand.'

He briefly closed his eyes, as if that was all he needed to hear, and then he drew her even closer to him, so their entire bodies were touching. And when he kissed her again she knew he'd made his decision. Because this kiss was different from any other. It was raw and unapologetic. And his tongue didn't hesitate to invade her lips in the most impassioned, frantic open-mouthed kiss...as if he was determined now to give them both what they wanted at last...as if he'd finally been given permission to take what was his.

The kiss detonated a fire in her stomach, sending a flame of butterflies soaring, but while her tentative, trembling hands stole over his cheekbones and into his hair, his confident, reassuring fingers travelled over her hips to grasp her bottom, moulding her to his intimate ridges. And she revelled in the feeling of being in his arms again, coming to life under his touch.

His large palms curved round her front, grazing up to cover her breasts, but the thick, expensive material of her dress was annoyingly in the way.

He nuzzled and nipped at her neck. 'You're wearing far too many clothes, Anne.' When he kissed her again, he tugged at the cords at the back of her gown to loosen it. 'Turn around,' he said.

On unsteady feet, she slowly spun, so that her back was to him and he could unlace the material, and it felt incredibly intimate. Her heart was in her mouth. The sleeves fell from her shoulders first, allowing him to place little kisses there, and then the gown dropped down her arms, loosening around her waist and sinking to her hips.

Brand used both hands to push it down over her bottom so it pooled at her feet. She heard his sharp intake of breath and swallowed in anticipation of his touch, tiny tingles rushing down her spine. She felt his breath on her neck first, and then one arm came around her waist, tugging her back towards him. She tipped her head to rest it in the curve of his shoulder, further exposing her bare upper body to him, and his handsome hands came up to play with her breasts.

He was gentle, but demanding, clearly desperate to feel every inch of her skin, hungry to roll her achingly hard nipples between his fingers as his lips moved over her collarbone.

She could feel his erection nudging between her buttocks and she wanted to explore him, as he was exploring her, so she roamed her hands down to feel the hard muscles of his thighs.

He growled and twisted her round to face him, pulling her into his large, muscular body. His fingers hooked beneath her undergarments, pushing them down to the floor to meet the rest of her clothes. Now she stood before him completely naked, and she felt so exposed under his heated gaze.

She shivered, and yet she felt incredibly hot at the same time. 'Brand…' she whispered, trying to cover herself up with her tiny hands.

He reached for her wrists and gently pressed them to her sides. 'I've never seen anyone or anything so beautiful in my whole life. Don't hide from me, Anne, let me look at you.'

He stepped back to rake his eyes all over her body and then dealt with his own clothes quickly, as if he couldn't wait now. He pulled his leather vest and his tunic over his head, tossing them to the floor, unfastened his belt, and she was transfixed by his body.

'Help me, Anne. Undress me.'

She reached out, fumbling with his trousers, fiercely tugging the cord and pushing them down so they bunched around his calves—and he laughed at her eagerness. And finally there was no material barrier between them and it was her turn to explore him. She ran her gaze and fingers over all the old and new scars on his torso. She wasn't shocked—she'd seen them before. Maybe she didn't have all the facts, but she had a vague idea. She determined to find out about the story behind every single one.

Her palms roamed down his back and over the firm globes of his bottom. And she allowed herself to luxuriate in exploring his warm, solid skin, which felt amazing pressed against the smoothness of her own. His fingers trailed over her thighs and up, reaching between her legs to find her secret heated places. She parted her thighs to allow him better access, but she wasn't sure she could stand up while he touched her. Her legs felt unsteady and her knees nearly gave way when his fingers stroked and delved inside her.

Throwing one arm around his neck for support, she

could feel his hard length pressing into her hip, and she mustered up the courage to move her other hand down between their bodies to take hold of him in her palm.

He groaned, resting his forehead against hers. She pushed him back against the wall and dropped to her knees to take him in her mouth. A string of expletives tore from his lips. With one hand braced on the wall, the other in her hair, he drew her head closer, over his length, and she knew he was going slowly out of his mind. *Good.* She wanted to torture him with pleasure, just as he had done to her the other night.

'Anne, stop!' he said, desperately tugging at her shoulders, trying to drag her back up towards him.

'Don't you like it?' she whispered. 'Am I doing something wrong?'

'It feels incredible,' he said, his wide blue eyes staring down at her. 'But I want you…and any more of that and you'll take me over the edge.'

He cupped her bottom and she wrapped her legs around his hips as he carried her over to the bed.

He laid her on the furs and came down beside her, kissing her slowly, his hands trailing up and down her back, as if he were giving her time to change her mind. He kissed her so tenderly she wondered how such a strong, fierce man could be so gentle. How could she and everyone else have got him so wrong? She wanted them to know what she knew. She wanted to shout it from the castle ramparts.

He caught her wrists between his hands again and pressed them to the bed above her head. And then he kissed and stroked his way over her lips, her heaving breasts and her taut stomach, and she knew he was preparing her for what was to come. Every stroke was making her hot with need. She wriggled closer, wanting to feel more of his silky hardness against her thigh. She wanted him inside her. She knew she was ready.

His palms drifted up her silky-smooth calves and he pulled her leg over his hip. Rolling on top of her, he pushed her thighs wide apart with his knee, holding them open as he reached between her legs to touch her again. He parted her intimate folds and slid his fingers inside her, and she gave a feminine growl of disbelief. Drawing them back out, he found her nub and teased it with his thumb, making her writhe with pleasure.

'This is your chance to change your mind, Anne. You can still leave… I'm not going to try to convince you that this is the right thing to do. We both know it isn't. But I'm no saint, Anne. I want you anyway.'

He was making her feel hot, feverish, needy. She was spiralling out of control, and she knew she must be making way too much noise as he gently put his hand over her mouth.

'Shh.' When he removed his hand he kissed her slowly, deeply, as he guided himself to her entrance. 'Are you sure, Anne?'

'Yes. Please, Brand, now.'

He thrust inside her and she tightened around him, her arms coming up to grasp his shoulders. He stilled, his forehead resting against hers for a second, giving her time to adapt to the feel of him. With the next thrust he breached her wall, edging deeper inside her, possessing her. And it felt so good, so right. He continued to kiss her and stroke her until her body began to relax around him.

He set the rhythm, every thrust allowing him a little deeper inside her tight body. Pure toe-curling pleasure shafted through her. And when she wrapped her legs around his hips, finally taking him all the way in, he groaned. She was totally impaled, pinned to the bed by his hips, which were thrusting faster and faster, his own urgency increasing.

'Oh, God, don't stop, Brand. Don't ever stop.'

Her hands were in a feral frenzy now, her nails tearing into his shoulders, down his back, gripping his bottom, pulling him into her. Their bodies were slick with sweat. She wanted him deeper, harder, faster.

And then her whole body tensed and shivered, and she screamed as her orgasm took her over. Brand felt every muscle in his body tighten. He thrust into her one last time and her name roared from his lips as the explosive rush of his climax pulsed powerfully inside her.

When Brand finally stirred, he realised he was still inside her. What the hell had just happened? Had he lost consciousness? He felt shaky, and didn't even have the strength to withdraw from her body. He wanted to stay like this, buried deep inside Anne, forever.

He felt her chest rise and fall—was she sleeping?— and violent emotions ricocheted through him. It had never, ever felt like that before. He'd never had such a fierce need to take someone so thoroughly, to possess her, make her his.

He had spent his life consumed with vengeance, and

in the space of a week Anne had torn down the fortress he'd built over the years... Now he was consumed with something else entirely. Was this love?

He was worried he was crushing Anne with his weight, so he gently rolled off her, pulling the curve of her back into his chest, his fingers lightly tracing over her stomach.

'You're awake,' she said, covering his hand with her own.

'I think I blacked out for a while.'

'Is it always like that?' she asked. 'So intense? So incredible?'

'It's never been like that for me before.' He planted little kisses along her shoulder.

'I guess you've never had sex in a castle before.' And then she giggled.

'You should know by now that I have expensive taste,' he said.

She laughed again. 'What else don't I know about you?'

He stroked his hands up to cup the weight of her breast, and she wriggled her bottom back against him. 'You're playing a dangerous game,' he warned. He stroked the soft skin of her chest and torso some more. And then, 'What's that over there in the corner?' he asked, nodding at the barrel, trying to distract her from torturing him further.

'Ah, now, that is how we like to bathe. We fill the barrel with hot water and get in it.'

He raised his eyebrows into her hair. 'Much more civilised than the sea, then.'

'Yes, I can't see you using one of those.' She laughed again, and it was infectious. 'You're much too wild.'

'I could be wild in that.'

She made that little movement against him again, as if to torment him, and he growled, rolling her onto her stomach and plunging all the way into her from behind. She gasped at the sudden intimacy. But he loved it when she raised her bottom to meet his next thrust, as if she wanted to feel him deep inside her again.

He lifted her smooth thighs up off the bed, so he could access her secret places with his hands as he rocked into her, and she cried out. Brand hushed her, whispering all the things he wanted to do to her into her ear. And she surprised him when she came up on her knees, pressing back against his chest, deepening their connection. She curled her arms back around his neck and he revelled in having full access to her body.

He squeezed her breasts with one hand, tugging at her hardened nipples, working his other hand between her legs.

'I told you I'd make you mine, Anne,' he whispered as he thrust deeper inside her, taking her with him into an excruciating spiral of pleasure he never wanted to end.

Chapter Thirteen

The next time Brand woke he saw that a shaft of daylight was streaming into the room. His limbs were heavy, yet relaxed, and his body felt sated at last. But when he turned his head towards Anne she wasn't there. He was alone in the bed.

He sat bolt upright. She wasn't even in the room. When had she left him?

He wondered if he might have dreamed everything that had happened, but then he realised he was naked, and he could smell her floral scent on the furs. Plus, he didn't think he could have dreamed something as amazing as the night they'd just had together.

He dressed, and waited to be taken before the King, like Stanton had said. He hoped the King was a man of his word and he wouldn't just be fetched and walked to the gallows, hung as the whole kingdom of Termarth looked on. Including Anne.

Now Anne had let him take her he felt more alive than ever, and he didn't think he was ready to die just yet.

It was the longest morning of his life, but the guards finally came to fetch him. His pulse picked up pace as they led him through long stone corridors and a large wooden door into a grand hall. The King sat in a wooden throne at the head of the ornate room, monopolising the attention of what looked to be his council. And at his side sat Anne, dressed in an elegant burgundy gown.

Brand felt a punch to his gut. Would his reaction to her always be like this? he wondered.

As he strode forward, with all eyes upon him, his senses were on high alert. He was aware of every movement. It was as if the witan had never set eyes on a Dane before. They all seemed to balk or cringe at the sight of him, turning their gaze away. And he couldn't blame them. They were looking at the man who had abducted their Princess and imprisoned the leader of their army.

When he reached the steps in front of the King on his raised platform Brand stopped. Nothing could have prevented him from taking another furtive glance at Anne as the all-too-familiar scent of her wrapped around him in a kind of warm embrace. She looked radiant this morning, her skin glowing, her eyes bright. Her robes were as beautiful as her personality. And yet she still had that blue bruise around her eye—a reminder to everyone in the room of her attack. Of him not being able to protect her.

He wiped his hands on his trousers.

'I sent for you, Brand Ivarsson of Kald, as I hoped to satisfy my curiosity in meeting you at last,' the King said.

'It is an honour to meet you, King Eallesborough.'

The King was a tallish man with a slight build, grey hair and a neatly trimmed moustache and beard. He had a calm demeanour and considered Brand with thoughtful green eyes.

'I have heard much about you and I am yet to decipher which parts are true. But tell me first—why did you take my daughter from me?'

Brand wasn't used to defending himself, or his actions, but right now he knew that he must. He owed it to Anne and her father.

'At first it was for revenge. It was my ambition to wound your ally, Lord Crowe.'

The King took a sideways glance at Anne. 'My daughter tells me Ealdorman Crowe hurt your family.'

'Yes. He killed my father and hurt my sister. He also desolated other Saxon villages, blaming the Northmen. I believe in order to send people your way and make more men willing to fight for you—against us. Where I come from, things cannot be put right until blood has been repaid. It is my right to take revenge.'

'Where you come from? And yet here you are in Termarth. Here, we do not take things into our own hands—things are not resolved this way. And you took my daughter as part of this feud?'

'Yes, King Eallesborough.'

He couldn't bring himself to look at Anne again. Did her father know he had taken her in every sense of the word? Brand had once hoped that after he'd had her he would grow bored and move past his desire, but now he knew that would never be possible. The infuriating, unrelenting longing for her was still there. Worse, even, because it wasn't just her body that he longed for. He wanted her by his side always. If he were ever to take a wife, she would be the only woman he could marry.

'But I realised it was wrong to have involved the Princess, so I have returned her safely to you.'

'That you have...but I see she is much changed.' The King glanced over at his daughter and his eyes softened. 'Why, I wonder, did you involve her at all?'

Brand felt a flicker of irritation in his jaw. What did the King want him to say? 'At first it was in the hope that you might pay a ransom for her. We had a bad harvest and a cold winter in Kald this year. And Saxons slaughtered our animals. Perhaps I wanted to earn back what had been taken from us.'

'But now?'

'I don't want your gold.'

The King's eyes narrowed on him. 'I wonder what it is that you do want?'

'I am willing to accept any punishment you see fit to bestow upon me for taking your daughter. But as for what I want... I wish to protect our land in Kald—and I want peace. We came here for a better life, hoping to farm, to trade...'

'Is that all?' asked the King wryly, and Brand had an inkling that he knew much more than he was letting on. 'And my daughter has helped you come to this conclusion?'

For the first time in his life Brand felt as if his emotions were being exposed—as if a blade had been brought down on his head to reveal all the deepest, darkest thoughts and feelings hidden beneath the surface.

Anne was toying with a tassel on a cushion and he tried to tear his eyes away from her beautiful fingers as they reminded him of how they had played with his body last night. But when his eyes moved up to her face, her lips, he remembered how she'd taken him in her mouth, those soft, full lips curling around him...

This was not helping. He needed to focus. Just being in the same room as her was torture—could anyone tell what he was thinking? Could anyone tell that he loved her?

'What else has my daughter changed your opinion on?' the King asked, but it must have been a rhetorical question as he then turned to his council. 'She seems to have a way of changing opinion. When you took her from us, there was uproar among the people here. I had never realised how much she meant to them. She seems to be a symbol of hope.'

Brand nodded—hadn't she been the same for him all these years?

'You took that hope away, and yet I am grateful that you have brought it back.' The King turned to his witan. 'My lords, Anne, you may now leave us. I would like to talk to Brand Ivarsson alone.'

'Father—' Anne began, rising to her feet.

She was wringing her hands in that way she did when she was nervous, or concerned. Was she worrying about him? Brand wondered.

'It's all right, Anne,' the King reassured her. 'We are just going to talk.'

Brand was almost relieved when Anne performed a little curtsy and reluctantly walked away, her skirts swishing behind her. He could breathe again...think clearly. When the last of the ealdormen had left the room, the King strolled over to a table and poured two goblets of red wine. He pulled out a chair and sat down, before motioning to Brand to take the seat next to him.

'Some of my witan believe I should have you killed for stealing the Princess.'

'It would be no more than I deserve.'

'Ah, but my daughter would be most displeased,' said King Eallesborough, his hands steepled in front of him. 'She tells me you treated her well—were kind to her. Even protected her.'

Brand swallowed. *Not very well*.

'It seems you have saved her from an unhappy marriage. And brought to my attention a thorn in my side in Crowe, for which I thank you. You are a boat builder, Brand Ivarsson?'

'I am.' Brand's brow furrowed. This was not going the way he had expected the conversation to progress. He had thought he'd be dragged in here and beaten, or beheaded. But instead Anne's father, the King, was talking of his beloved ships.

'Your boats can sail on the ocean as well as up rivers?'

'Yes.'

'I would like to see these ships. I have long believed boats are a necessity in protecting this island that we live on, and that they will also help with trade. I believe our river here in Termarth leads to the ocean, where your settlement is? These two sites, adjoined by water, are of strategic importance.' He picked up one of the goblets and handed it to Brand. 'I would like to talk about you building me some ships and setting up a trading route.'

Of all the things Brand had thought would happen, this was not one of them. This was his father's dream. *His* dream. Had Anne had some part to play in this?

'I would be honoured.'

'I am trying to work out, Brand Ivarsson, if you are a lion or a wolf. Which is it? My daughter has clearly made her decision... So, in atonement for all my past sins against my child, I will concede to her wishes and set you free. But we will come to an agreement. You will not invade our lands and we will not attack yours. And we shall seal this deal by me giving you a title. You shall be Ealdorman Brand Ivarsson of Kald.'

'I have no need of a title.'

'That is where you're wrong. You cannot marry my daughter unless you have land, wealth—and a title.'

Brand's head snapped up. 'You wish me to marry your daughter? But I am a Dane.' His brow furrowed. Was he still dreaming?

'At a price—and in return for your protection. I believe there is much to be gained from forming an alliance... calling a truce between Termarth and Kald. It would help to safeguard our lands and our power. My daughter has told me how your men would follow you into battle, and how you are not like the majority of your kind. We have seen the destruction and devastation that clans from the North and even our own Saxon neighbours have caused to villages across the land, and the threat grows greater every day. I seek order, peace and prosperity—just as you have told me you do. I can help with your food shortages, land and wealth. And in return you will provide me with warriors who will fight for me when I need it. And we will bind this deal with the hand of my daughter.'

Brand allowed himself a moment to let the King's words sink in. He agreed with all the points this seemingly wise and open-minded man had made, bar one. 'You have my loyalty, King Eallesborough, and you have my word that I will protect Termarth. I believe we have both come to realise that the greatest riches are here, inside these walls, and need to be kept safe. But, even so, I cannot marry your daughter.'

He couldn't believe what he was saying. Wasn't this everything that he wanted? But, no… All along he had wanted Anne to want to be with him. He wanted it to be her choice. He didn't want her to be sold in marriage, as she would have been to Crowe.

From the moment he'd met her he'd made bad decisions, over and over again. And even though he couldn't regret making love to her last night, he knew he must now do the right thing by her—even if he inflicted pain on himself.

'And why is that?'

'Because your daughter is a priceless treasure—not an object to be gifted to any man, to do his bidding. I believe she should be free to make her own choices to ensure her happiness.' He inclined his head towards the King. 'So I will accept your terms of peace, and I shall build your boats, but I implore you to allow the Princess to decide her own destiny.'

The King studied him for a long moment. 'You are, as my daughter has said, a surprising man, Brand Ivarsson. I would like to get to know you better. But for now, let us shake on this deal.'

King Eallesborough stood in his elegant red and gold velvet robes, his hand outstretched. And Brand rose to meet him, towering over him, and took his hand, sealing their alliance. Mutual admiration glimmered between them.

'I am very pleased. I only hope my daughter is as content with this accord.'

Anne was in the stables, grooming Rebel and feeding him carrots, when a shadow fell over the wooden shelter.

'You're spoiling him.'

She turned to see Brand leaning in the doorway, watching her, and her body almost sagged with relief and happiness. Her father had been true to his word. He had not hurt him.

The brush in her hand stopped mid-stroke. 'He deserves it.' She smiled, her heart thundering in her chest.

It had taken every shred of willpower to extract herself from his arms this morning, to leave his warm bed and get dressed. She had known she had to get back to her chamber before the household awoke, and yet leaving him had been torture. She'd had the best night of her life, and she didn't even mind the raw, aching feeling between her legs—it was a reminder of where he'd been and what they'd done together.

She had spoken with her father and begged him to show mercy to the Barbarian. And when Brand had stalked into the Great Hall her chest had almost imploded. She knew with every breath that she was helplessly, foolishly, in love with him. But she had no idea if he felt the same.

'How did you get along with my father?' she asked.

'He was far too lenient with me, if that's what you mean. I have not been punished enough for what I did, how I behaved. The King is different from how you described—as if he's learned the error of his ways. I hope he will be good to you now, Anne.'

He took a step towards her, tucking a wispy strand of hair behind her ears, and her breath hitched at his touch.

'He has asked me to build him a fleet of ships and to open up trade between our fortresses—I believe I have you to thank for that, and I'm grateful to you.'

She was delighted Brand and her father had come to an agreement. This was exactly what she had been hoping for—that Brand would build her father's boats and her father would in turn see the kind of man Brand really was...what she saw in him. But she didn't want Brand to be grateful. She wanted so much more from him...

Rebel nickered, as if to say *Keep brushing*, and Anne realised the brush was still suspended in mid-air.

Brand inclined his head, nodding to his faithful steed. 'Will you look after him for me when I'm gone? I think he should stay here. He likes you much more than me anyway.'

Pain lanced her, swift and hard, in the heart. 'You're leaving?'

She didn't know what she'd been hoping he would say, but it wasn't this. Never this. She shook her head a little, as if to say it couldn't be true, but when she looked up into Brand's eyes her stomach seemed to sink like one of his boats, landing with a thud at the bottom of the ocean. And she knew, instantly, that he meant to say goodbye.

He'd taken her to bed, made love to her, and now he was about to ride out of her life. How could he?

She felt the agony of a million arrows hitting her. She wanted to lash out at him, yell and beg him to stay, but her pride would never allow herself to do that.

'I must. I need to go home and make amends with my people...put things right.'

What about him making amends to *her*? She wanted him to start by taking her back to bed and making love to her all over again.

'But you only arrived here yesterday! I was hoping to show you the castle.'

She'd been hoping he'd stay a while. Forever. She had hoped he might get to know her father, win him round until the King accepted him as one of their own.

Until the King accepted him as suitable husband material...

But it had all been nothing more than an unrealistic hope. Of course Brand wouldn't stay. He wasn't the type of man to bow down to the rules of another, and he had his own lands and people to protect. She wouldn't want him to abandon them—and yet she couldn't bear it if he abandoned her either. She had been foolish to hope of having any kind of future with him. He had told her once he would never marry, so why had she begun to hope otherwise?

She didn't trust her voice to speak any more. A huge lump was growing in her throat. She had been mad to think that it could ever work between them. He was a Dane and she was a Saxon. They could never be together—her father would never allow it. Their people wouldn't like it. And yet she knew now it was what she wanted with every beat of her heart.

Brand gave her a cool smile. 'We have a harvest to focus on in Kald, and now new boats to build.'

He kissed her lightly on the lips, and it was almost her undoing. She nearly threw herself down onto her knees and begged him to stay. But she had too much dignity. So she just stood there, watching him saddle his stallion, watching him mount the horse.

'I wish I could go back and change what has happened. I really am sorry for everything. You'll always be my regret, Anne. I hope that you can one day forgive me.'

Her whole world was unravelling and yet she was rooted to the spot, nodding under his gaze.

'I do. I have.'

And then he inclined his head one last time, his blue gaze raking over every inch of her body, drinking her in as if to fix her in his memory, and then he was gone.

Chapter Fourteen

'Don't slouch, Anne.'

'Sorry,' she muttered.

Anne and her father were having dinner together in the Great Hall, but she wasn't very hungry. She had lost her appetite weeks ago and she wasn't sure it would ever return.

'Oh, for pity's sake, girl, is everything all right?'

'Yes.'

She offered her father a little smile, because that was what he expected. But it felt false, as if it had been carved across her face with her meat knife.

'You've been pushing that meat around your plate for the past God knows how long. If you don't want it, feed it to the dogs!'

'Don't curse, Father. I'm fine,' she reassured him, not wanting to talk about it. She saw no point in bringing up old wounds.

He sighed. 'You're lying to yourself and to me, Anne. You keep saying you're fine when you're clearly not.' He put down his own knife and sat back in his seat. 'When you returned from Kald with my men I was relieved. I had been so worried the Northmen had hurt you, or worse. I wanted to make amends. The people wanted their Princess back and I was desperate to have my daughter home, to make right all my wrongs over the years. But you are not my daughter! All I've got is a shell—a hollowed-out version of the girl she used to be!'

She stared across the table at him, her tears threatening to spill over. The summer had dragged on and on, and finally the leaves on the big oak trees outside the windows were beginning to fall. She felt bad upon hearing her father's words.

She'd been so pleased that he had wanted to make things up to her and get to know her properly. He'd been making such an effort. And she'd tried, she really had—throwing herself into tasks like reorganising his papers, or taking afternoon walks with him, going out riding together. She'd also thrown herself into studying the art of healing those in need. Finally, she felt needed, wanted…useful. She was no longer invisible to her father or his subjects.

She'd even made the King parade around his kingdom, meeting the farmers and traders to find out more about them, and they'd hosted a banquet in the Great Hall to reward the soldiers for her safe return. But it had all been with a false kind of enthusiasm. She'd hoped it would take her mind off what had happened, distract her from thinking about Brand, but it hadn't worked. Nothing worked. Her Danish warrior consumed her thoughts.

'If I'm not mistaken, you have not been yourself since Brand Ivarsson left to go home to Kald,' her father said.

Just the mention of Brand's name was enough to spur an onslaught of memories. She didn't want to talk about him. She couldn't. It hurt too much.

Watching him ride off into the distance had been awful. It was as if he'd ripped out her heart and taken it with him. She'd felt a terrible sense of loss and had sagged against the wall in the stables, sobbing. And it hadn't left her since. She hadn't been able to eat properly, and when she slept she dreamed of his voice rolling over her, like the gentle roar of the waves.

He had left her the shell he'd found for her in the ocean that day they'd been out on the boat, and she spent hours lying on her bed, its cool surface pressed up against her ear.

'I don't know what you mean,' she said.

'Don't you?' Her father leaned towards her. 'You've been shuffling through these halls with a vacant, lost look on your face for weeks. You don't eat, you don't sleep, but most of all, you don't smile, Anne. You don't know what to do with yourself!'

'That's not true... I've attended your witans, helped with the kingdom, and the banquet, and—'

'And you are always distracted!' He finished her sentence for her, throwing his hands up in despair. 'You're in love with the man, Anne. Admit it.'

'Father! How can you say such a thing?'

He sat back again, steepling his hands in front of him, as he always did when he was deep in thought or about to say something profound. 'I wasn't going to tell you this, but I think that now I must. I offered Brand Ivarsson your hand in marriage as part of our truce.'

'What?' Her knife slipped out of her hand and clattered down to the table.

'Not just because he can help to protect us, form an alliance, but because I could see what he meant to you. It was my way of making amends to you. You have to marry someone, Anne. And, yes, it should be someone with lands and a title, an ally to Termarth. But most of all it should be someone you love—and who loves you.'

'Wh-what did he say?' she gasped, not caring about letting her real feelings show now. She was too miserable to care. 'He must have declined.'

Her father took a gulp of his wine and swallowed it down. 'He said you shouldn't be any part of a deal between men. Instead, he made me promise that you'd be free to make your own choices, to marry who you wanted. And I agreed.'

Anne stared at her father in shock. She couldn't believe it. Brand had done that? Fought for her freedom? It was everything she had ever wanted… She was overwhelmed by what Brand had done. A man had put her needs before his own. She should be grateful to him. And yet none of this helped to make her feel any better.

'Why are you telling me this now?'

'I was selfish. I wanted to keep you to myself for a while before you left me again. Perhaps I had hoped you might take a shine to Lord Stanton. He is a good man, and he's a Saxon. But that was a fool's hope. I can see it now, as clear as day. You love the Barbarian and you won't be happy without him. And as our lands are now relatively safe—or as safe as they can ever be—you should be free to marry for love, Anne, not to bolster our kingdom's power.'

A tear slipped down Anne's cheek. It was everything she had ever wanted to hear. But there was one problem.

'He didn't want me,' she said, wiping the moisture away with the back of her hand.

Brand had given her a great gift, and yet she felt as if he'd taken something far greater from her at the same time.

Her father sat back in his chair. 'Surely you don't believe that? I certainly don't. I could have killed him for taking you from me, Anne. But when I saw how you felt about him I was willing to give him the benefit of the doubt. And then, when I met him, I saw a man standing before me who, in pursuit of revenge, had crossed his own moral boundary—and couldn't forgive himself. And in his determination to set things right he had to give up the thing he wanted most. You.'

She stared up into her father's wise eyes and stopped trying to wipe away the tears. She just let them roll freely.

'He had to set you free to make your own choices. I thought you might have told him what he meant to you, what you wanted, before he left...no?'

She shook her head, horrified. She hadn't even tried to stop him from getting on his horse and riding out of her life. She'd just let him leave without telling him how she truly felt.

'I loved your mother greatly, Anne. I know now that she might not have felt the same about me, and I would do anything to have another day with her, to try to win her heart. After she died, I was in so much pain. I couldn't bear to lose you as well. But I went about everything the wrong way.'

Hearing her father's words, she knew now that this was how Brand felt. She knew he blamed himself for his father's death and Svea's attack, and that he must feel he'd let Anne down too. Had he pushed her away to punish himself?

'Don't waste your life, Anne. I have caused you many unhappy years. Well, no more. Go after what you want, daughter, with no regrets.'

'What are you saying, Father?'

He put down his glass. 'I'm saying you have his horse, don't you? I'm sure it knows the way back to Kald. And I'm sure Lord Stanton would be happy to escort you there. I could even ask him to take you under the pretence of checking how my boats are doing. So, go, Anne. You have my blessing.'

The King had been right. Rebel hadn't forgotten the route to Kald and seemed happy to be heading back that way, his tail swishing freely as she and Lord Stanton and a number of the King's men galloped over the meadows and undulating hills.

If only Anne could borrow some of her loyal steed's confidence, all would be well.

She took in the vibrant, earthy tones of the countryside, signalling that autumn was almost here. The first fallen leaves crackled beneath the horses' hooves and the golden branches of the amber-coloured trees creaked in the cool afternoon breeze. The hedgerows were laden with delicious wild berries, but it seemed Anne was destined never to fully enjoy or appreciate this journey—her thoughts were always consumed by one thing…or rather one man.

The closer they got to the fortress, the more Anne's courage began to waver, and she started to doubt her decision about making this journey. It had been many weeks since Brand had walked out of her life, after convincing her father to set her free so she could choose her own path. And this was the path she had chosen to follow: this sunlit avenue through the forest and along the coast to Kald, back to her Barbarian.

She wondered what his reaction would be when he saw her. Would he curse softly in his deep, Danish tongue and pull her into his arms, telling her he'd missed her? Or would she blurt out how she felt about him, and then he'd tell her to stop babbling, before scooping her up and carrying her up to his room to make passionate love to her all night long?

She closed her eyes as if in silent prayer…

She wondered if the biggest battle she would face would be with his conscience—after all, that was what had kept them apart these past few weeks, wasn't it? What if his self-loathing for all he'd done wouldn't allow them to be together? Then she would have to soothe his worries and show him that they deserved to be happy.

But she was scared, shaking like the leaves rustling

around her in the trees. What if her father was wrong, and Brand didn't care for her at all? What if he'd simply wanted to bed her and then get away from her as fast as he could? If that was the truth, it would hurt like hell, but at least she would know and could return to Termarth and try to move on.

Her mind began to torture her, running through all the worst scenarios. What if she arrived and found him in the arms of another woman? Her heart screamed at the thought. What if he wasn't pleased to see her? Then she would have to be brave and put on a front, show an interest in seeing her father's boats and then make her excuses to leave.

But what if he was? Oh, what if he was?

When the small convoy left the forest and the ocean came into view, Anne began to feel better than she had in weeks. This was where she wanted to be—where she belonged. She took strength from the steady ebb and flow of the thrilling waves, and the trilling sound of the sea birds gliding overhead. The fiery autumn sun was beaming down on her, so full of promise, and just like the pretty little toadstools that were flourishing all around her in the undergrowth, hope mushroomed inside her.

It was a while longer before the high, imposing wooden walls of Kald came into view. She slipped down from the saddle and the men led the horses along a weed-strewn path and over the heath where Crowe's army of Saxon soldiers had gathered. Anne heard the horn signalling their arrival and felt as nervous as she had when she'd stood before Brand naked. Once again, she was about to lay herself bare.

Damn, she must have brushed against some stinging nettles. Her legs had begun to burn...

'Are you all right, Your Highness?' Lord Stanton asked.

'Yes, I think I've just landed in a mass of nettles. It's nothing—just a little prickle.'

There was no time to focus on that now. Approaching the tall wooden gates, she looked up to the parapet on the bridge and saw Kar staring down at her. He grinned, and she raised her hand in greeting. Her heart was in her mouth as the gates slowly opened, her entire body trembling.

As the convoy made their way into the settlement, many of the villagers rushed forward to greet them. Anne was pleased to see them all—especially Svea, Kar, and Ulf. Svea hugged her tight, and Anne instantly noticed a difference in her—she seemed free, happy...perhaps because she knew her attacker was locked away. Anne was glad. Ulf proudly showed her his battle scar.

'It's wonderful to see you. You're very welcome,' Svea said.

Anne scanned the central square, her eyes full of enquiry. *Where was he?* And then, out of the corner of her eye, she saw a tall, dark figure emerge from the doorway of the barn and her heart bloomed inside her chest.

Brand.

His towering presence was enough to make them all turn and stare, and Anne's reaction was the same as it had always been. Her heart took flight and she knew there was no point trying to contain it. He looked more dangerous, more formidable, more magnificent than she'd ever seen him as his steely gaze assessed the scene before him.

She struggled to work out what he was thinking. Those penetrating eyes she'd dreamed of every night since she'd last seen him regarded her coolly, and she realised this was not the welcome she had imagined or hoped for. And when he began to stalk towards them, all power and lithe legs, her carefully rehearsed words abandoned her.

'*Heil ok sæl.* Hello, Anne... Lord Stanton.' He inclined his head. 'This is a surprise.'

So much for scooping her up and spinning her round in his arms. She just nodded, revelling in seeing his face again and hearing his velvety voice. Since when had she ever been rendered mute?

'What are you doing here?' he asked.

'Lord Stanton and I have come to see how you are getting on with my father's boats,' she said, with a strained, overbright smile.

He didn't look pleased to see her. If anything, he looked angry. And he must know the King wouldn't have sent her—someone who didn't know the first thing about boats—all this way to check on his ships. It was a ridiculous excuse. She cringed and a blush burned her cheeks.

His icy gaze continued to rake over her, then lanced Lord Stanton.

'Perhaps you and the King's men would like a cup of ale and something to eat by the fire?' Svea asked.

Anne could have hugged the woman for cutting through the tension as Svea took her elbow and steered her in the direction of the longhouse, away from Brand's dark judgement.

But neither the fire nor the meal Svea served them helped to warm her up. Brand's glacial gaze had sent shivers through her, and a cold hand had reached into her chest, squeezing her heart. They were all seated around the large wooden table, but Brand was talking about ships with Lord Stanton, and even though Svea was asking her questions about Termarth, and her summer, Anne felt as if she had been cast adrift, totally and utterly miserable.

She knew that she'd made a mistake; she shouldn't have come. Brand didn't want her here.

'I am surprised you have made this long journey… King Eallesborough told me he didn't want the boats until the spring.' He was talking to Lord Stanton, but his gaze rested on Anne.

So he wanted to know why they were really here? They were here because she hadn't thought ahead, that was why! She'd thought only of her wants and desires, her hopes and dreams—not his. Hadn't he told her once he never wanted to marry? Why had she thought she could convince him otherwise?

When a pretty young serving girl topped up Brand's tankard, smiling at him, flushing scarlet when he thanked her, Anne's heart felt as if it was being trampled on. Had there been women since her? Why had she thought she was different and meant anything to him? He must take women to bed all the time—perhaps a different one every night. There was nothing stopping him.

Oh, God, why had she come? She'd just made the agony worse by seeing his fascinating face again.

She stole a look at him. His hair had grown even longer since the early summer, and it was tightly fastened with bonds at the back of his neck. His skin was a golden colour and she noticed he wore his father's silver ring. He looked fit and well—had he not missed her at all?

Her father had offered Brand her hand and he'd declined. The King had convinced her it was because Brand loved her, but that was just his opinion. How could she have come all this way on a whim, hoping he might feel the same? He was being so distant and aloof...surely she had her answer? He didn't.

And now she was trapped. She couldn't just leave; they'd travelled day and night to get here. Her Saxon men would at least want a good night's sleep before they returned home.

And then a thought struck her. Where would they sleep tonight? Where would the Danes put them? Would Brand send her to sleep in Svea's house while he took that serving girl up to his room? It was all too much to bear...

She shot to her feet, clumsily knocking over her drink.

'Is everything all right, Your Highness?' Lord Stanton asked. 'Is it the sting?'

'Sting?' Brand asked.

Anne waved her hand in the air. 'It's nothing—just a few nettles.' She'd almost forgotten about that; it was her heart that was hurting.

Brand's brow furrowed. 'Still putting yourself in danger at every turn, Princess?'

She sighed. 'Everything is quite well. I think I just need some air,' she said, seeing all eyes upon her. 'Please excuse me for a moment.'

She headed out of the hall and across the square, making her way down the grassy slope towards the boathouse. Whichever way she turned she was taunted by memories, and she realised she had fallen in love with this place—the purple heather covering the heath, the undulating farmland, the endless expanse of sand and the rollicking waves.

But she had fallen for Brand first.

When she reached the little jetty and saw the longship they'd sailed in weeks before still tied up and bobbing about on the water, she smiled wistfully. She carefully lowered herself into the hull and sat down on a bench, no longer concerned by the gentle rocking movement. She wished she could conjure herself away to that day when they'd sailed around the headland, right back to the moment when he'd asked her if she wanted to sail away with him...

'Planning on going somewhere?'

Brand. She whisked round to face him, and the boat toppled a little.

She shrugged, suddenly feeling more than a little

silly at being caught sitting in a moored boat. 'I was debating my next adventure. Are you following me?'

'It wouldn't be the first time,' he said darkly. 'I would have thought you'd done enough travelling for one day. And why are you roaming about the place on your own? You should know better than to do that.'

'Well, I'm not on my own, am I? You're here. But you can't always be there to protect me, Brand. I don't expect you to be.'

His eyes narrowed on her. 'Come on—get out of there. Show me your nettle sting, I have something for it.'

She stood up slowly and made her way towards him on the jetty. But she refused his offer of help. She didn't trust herself to touch him.

She lifted the hem of her dress to show him the red rash that had appeared on her shin.

He let out a gentle curse and busied himself on the bank, looking for something. A moment later he came back towards her, brandishing a leaf, and knelt down to cup the back of her leg in his palm.

She swallowed. 'I can do it.'

'It's fine,' he said, as he used his other hand to rub the leaf over her skin. 'I've done it now.'

He took a step back and crossed his arms over his broad chest. 'The rash should start to fade now.'

'It feels better already.' She tried to smile, but she couldn't quite manage it. She wanted him to always take care of her like this—and her him. 'Thank you.'

Although the leaf had cooled her skin, her leg was still tingling from his burning touch.

'You know, you shouldn't have made the journey to Kald on your own, Anne,' he said, his brow creasing again. 'It's dangerous. If you'd sent a messenger I would have ridden out to meet you.'

'I wasn't on my own. I was with Lord Stanton and—'

'Damn it, Anne, I don't want to hear about him,' he grated, stepping closer to her, ambushing her senses with the familiar spicy scent of him. And then she wondered— was he jealous? Just as she had been about the serving girl? Was that why he was being so cold? Was he hurting too?

He gripped her wrists with his hands and heat raced up her arms, as if he was binding her with red-hot bonds. She welcomed it. She longed to go back to being his.

'Now tell me what you're really doing here.'

He was staring down at her in such a heated, penetrating way, making her feel as if he knew what she was thinking. And she didn't mind. She didn't want to hide from him or her feelings any more. She wanted to risk her heart and tell him how she felt.

'Why did you refuse my hand in marriage, Brand?'

'What?'

She wondered if her question had come out like a silent wail—that was how it felt in her heart.

'My father told me all about your conversation. Your agreement. But why did you reject me when my father offered me as your wife?'

This wasn't the carefully crafted speech she'd learned on the way here. It was all coming out wrong. But she felt so wretched and miserable, she didn't care.

She just needed to know the truth. She needed to know if he felt a fraction of what she felt for him.

'You know why.'

She shook her head. 'I don't, Brand. I need you to explain it to me.'

A muscle flickered in his jaw. He was not a man of words—she knew that. He was a Northman and a man of action—a warrior, a beautiful boat builder and a farmer. A protector of his people. And her saviour.

But she needed to hear this, so he would have to try.

'Because you always said you didn't want to be treated like an object. Because you said you were sick of men making decisions for you. I knew you didn't want to be just another Saxon woman, offered in marriage to form an alliance or in exchange for peace. I wanted you to be free to make your own choices, Anne, not to have your father make another one for you just to suit him or me. And because...'

He stepped back a little.

'What?' She closed the gap between them again.

'Because I wasn't worthy of you, Anne. I was so single-minded in my vendetta against Crowe that I hurt you in the process, and I couldn't forgive myself for it.'

Her father had been right. Brand was punishing himself. He didn't think he deserved her. But that didn't mean he didn't want her.

Hope soared inside her. If she could just be brave enough to let him know how she felt... If she could make him see himself the way she saw him, they might just stand a chance.

'But I forgive you, Brand.'

She moved closer towards him and, emboldened by the way his thumbs were gently stroking over her wrists, tried to put into words just what he meant to her.

'My father didn't send me. I came here of my own accord because I wanted to see you. It doesn't have anything to do with the boats. But I think you knew that anyway.' She swallowed. 'I came to tell you that I can't live without you. That I never expected to fall in love with a Northman, but I did—from the moment I saw you on the ramparts that night. You stole me away, heart, body, and soul.'

'Anne—'

'Let me finish. I have no regrets about any of it— apart from not throwing myself down in front of your horse and stopping you from leaving Termarth. I didn't know then that you had fought for my freedom to choose my own future, but I do now, and I choose you, Brand. I don't care that you are a Dane and I'm a Saxon. All I care about is that I will be yours and you will be mine.'

He pulled her towards him so suddenly, so urgently, she gasped. And he held her so tight, as if his life depended on it. At one point in time she might have struggled, might have gasped for air at being so confined, but not now. This was where she wanted to be. In this man's arms forever.

'It broke my heart to leave you, Anne. The day I met you when I was a boy was the best and worst day of my life. You were a glimmer of light in a dark time. My hope. And I've dreamed about making you mine ever since. But after I'd taken you from Termarth I realised that wasn't enough. I wanted you to want me too. I came to Termarth that night with vengeance in my heart, but when I left it was filled with love. I didn't believe I deserved you, Anne. I'm still not sure I do... But I promise I'll spend the rest of my life making you happy, making sure that I am worthy of you. *Ek elska þik*. I love you, Anne.'

Anne stared up at him and brought her hand up to cup his cheek. 'Growing up, I heard all kinds of stories about you, Brand the Barbarian, but the man you have become surpasses all those tales. You're so much more than you think of yourself. You're everything to me. You're a Northman with a huge capacity to love. And you have my heart forever. I love you too.'

Epilogue

The happy noise from the wedding celebrations going on in the longhouse could be heard from where Brand was leading his beautiful bride up the stairs to his room, his hands covering her eyes. She looked more stunning than he'd ever seen her, with intricate braids and little wildflowers in her hair. But it was her glittering green eyes and her breathtaking smile that had made him feel so happy as she'd walked towards him up the aisle earlier today.

'What's going on?' Anne laughed.

'I have something for you,' he said. 'An extra wedding gift.'

It had been the best day of their lives. They'd held the wedding down on the beach, and under the bronze autumn sun they'd spoken their vows. It had been the first time in his life Brand had felt tears in his eyes. They'd given each other family swords—a symbol that both families and kingdoms would protect each other from now on—and they'd stuck to tradition and carried out the bride—running up the hill, where the Danes and Saxons had raced each other on foot to the longhouse.

The Danes had won, of course, so King Eallesborough, and Lord Stanton, and all their Saxon guests had had to serve them ale throughout the evening. It had all been done in good spirits.

Brand was glad they hadn't fought the Saxons in some great battle at Kald. He wanted his home to be a place of peace, not a place of bloodshed. And over the past few months Kald had thrived. There had been no more attacks on his people, and they had used the gold he'd been given for the boats to buy more crops.

His people were happy. They said he'd done them proud. They told him his father would have been proud too, and he finally believed it himself. He was glad his legacy wouldn't be the slaughter of hundreds of men. No, the greatest battle in his life had been over his wife's beautiful face and body—a battle he'd had with himself. But, looking at her now, he knew he'd been victorious.

They'd enjoyed a hog roast feast and then, while the festivities still continued, they'd slipped away to be alone.

Anne tripped on a step, laughing in her long white silk gown, unable to see where she was going, so Brand picked her up and carried her the rest of the way in his arms.

At the top, he took her over the threshold, then placed her down gently, putting his hands over her eyes again. 'Ready?'

She nodded.

As he lifted his hands away, and her eyes adjusted to the steam-filled room, they fell upon the beautifully carved wooden barrel under the smoke hole. It was filled with hot water and scattered with rose petals. It was big enough for two and their initials had been carved into the side.

She looked up at him in delight. 'Did you make this for me?'

'I did. I couldn't have my Princess going down to the sea to bathe in the freezing cold water, now, could I?'

'Oh, Brand, I love it,' she said, clasping her hands together over her heart. 'It's incredible. It must have taken you ages.'

'You're worth it.'

She flung her arms around him and kissed him. 'You'd better not show it to my father,' she said, with a glint in her eye. 'He'll wonder why you were making this for me rather than building his beloved boats— after all, you are his oath man now...'

He growled, pulling her towards him. He knew she was teasing him. Over the past few days, in the run-up to the wedding, they'd hosted the Saxons, and Brand and King Eallesborough had got on well. Anne had joked that she'd hardly seen him—that her father was monopolising him and she was jealous.

'The only person I will ever make an oath to is my wife. And that was only ever going to be you, Anne.' He kissed her deeply, savouring the feel of her tongue moving against his. 'I love you, Anne Ivarsson. Now, shall we try it out?'

She nodded. 'Actually, I have a surprise for you too. Sit down,' she said, ushering him to the bed.

She reached up to unfasten the straps around her neck, untying her wedding dress, and his throat constricted. So it was going to be that kind of present... He was already hard with anticipation.

She let the material fall down her chest, skimming it over the flare of her hips and her thighs and he watched it sink to the floor. She stood before him naked, chewing her bottom lip. 'I got this for you,' she said.

And through a lust-filled haze his eyes flickered to the small inked flower on the indentation of her left hip.

'It's a primrose,' she said. 'To remind us of our first kiss. But I know that the primrose also means "I can't live without you", and I thought how true that was of me and you.'

He took her arm and tugged her closer, so he could inspect it better.

'Do you like it?' she asked, and he realised she was holding her breath. 'If you don't—'

'Anne, stop babbling.' He pressed his lips gently against the ink on her skin, making her shiver. 'I love it. It's beautiful. Just like you...'

And then his lips began to stray downwards.

Soon they were both naked in the water, and he was holding her wet body in his arms, as he'd dreamed of doing when he'd first seen her bathing on the beach. He was sitting on the bench in the barrel, and he pulled her onto his lap, weightless in the water. He gently lifted her up and then lowered her down again, impaling her on his huge, hard length. He gave her a moment to accommodate him, their faces just a sigh apart, and then she began to move her hips. His hands were on her bottom, coaxing her to move harder, faster, and when she cried out her orgasm, burying her face into his neck, he soon came spiralling after her, knowing that all his dreams had come true.

Later, as they lay curled up together in the bed, with Anne stroking the ink on his chest, they talked of their first adventure together as man and wife. They hoped to make a least one journey before any much-wanted children came along.

Brand was planning to take her to one of the little islands south of here in the *Freyja*, to celebrate their marriage, and neither of them could wait to be out on the sea again alone. He was looking forward to showing her how to swim, and in return she'd promised to teach him how to read.

Rolling on top of her, pinning her beneath him, Brand lowered his mouth down on hers. 'Thank you for making me the happiest man in the world,' he whispered.

'I'm sorry you didn't get your gold as part of the marriage bargain...' She grinned, teasing him again.

'If I have you in my life I'm the richest man I know. All I ever wanted was to steal your heart, Anne.'

She wriggled beneath him, stirring his desire all over again. 'You can steal me away whenever you like.'

And he did—over and over again...

* * * * *

ESCAPING WITH HER SAXON ENEMY

For Mom and Dad, Kristy and Simon,
and Auntie Maureen.

Chapter One

Kald Fortress, autumn 821

The bride and her entourage were late.

Ashford Stanton tried to curb his impatience by taking a deep, steadying breath and telling himself it didn't matter. It had been a long summer since he'd first seen her on the battlefield, and even though that day had affected him more than it should, her late arrival on this unusually warm afternoon had no right to bother him. He hated that it did.

Scanning his surroundings on the sheltered, windless beach, he made sure once again that nothing was amiss, that King Eallesborough was safe and everything was as it should be. Although nothing about this day could be described as ordinary. The excitement in the air was so thick he could almost reach out and grasp it, and Ash realised he was about to bear witness to a significant moment in history. If only his father was here to document it in his chronicles.

The sun was burning down onto the golden sand and a lick of perspiration gathered at the base of his neck. Running his hand over his hair, to try to tame the ends, Ash wanted nothing more than to wade out into the gently lapping surf and cool himself down. If he'd been in Braewood that's exactly what he'd be doing. But he wasn't at his father's fortress, or at his Saxon King's castle in Termarth. He was in enemy territory, and he'd rather be anywhere else.

Ash had been to Kald twice before and had tasked himself with learning the lay of the land. There was no denying the scenery here was a glorious sight, where vast blue skies met the sea, and salt marshes greeted the sand dunes and beautiful bays, but at this moment the setting wasn't doing anything to ease the tension strumming through his body. He took in the familiar view of the cliffs rising up from the beach, where the Northmen's hillfort loomed over the ocean, and studied the animated faces of the wedding guests, who were mostly Danes.

He drew a hand across his face. Excuses had chased through his mind about why he couldn't escort King Eallesborough on this trip to Kald for his daughter the Princess's wedding, but Ash had known not one of them would be good enough for his monarch. So he had reluctantly accompanied his King on his journey, offering his sword and protection, and keeping a careful watch over the fort's defences. He would continue to be on guard, to do his duty, yet he was disturbingly distracted.

Damn. This dark craving was a complication he

did not need. Which was why he was so eager for the wedding party to make an appearance—he needed to prove to himself that he would see the Danish shield maiden again and not feel a thing. He had positioned himself at the end of a row, where he could keep an eye on the people arriving, but he was only waiting for one.

Just at that moment a loud swell of rousing music announced the bride's entrance, and he rolled his shoulders, composing himself, before slowly turning around to look.

The bride glided past him to the altar and his lips twisted. He was actually glad his father couldn't be here to see such an occasion—he was already in ill health, and it might just have been the death of him. He had never thought he'd see the day when a Saxon princess would be married off to a Northman to form an alliance to keep the peace.

The possibility that this union had the potential to change perceptions and reshape Ash's own world hadn't passed him by, but he instantly banished the thought from his mind. There were a few secrets that were better left buried, so no one could get hurt.

Throughout his upbringing Ash's parents had told him stories about the Northmen's abhorrent invasions of Saxon castles and monasteries, destroying everything in their sights, raping and pillaging as they went. Those raiders came from faraway lands, navigating perilous oceans to land on Saxon beaches, take what they wanted from defenceless settlements and leave a trail of destruction in their wake. He had witnessed the tragic consequences of some of those attacks. Hell, he had suffered them his entire life.

Bitterness burned the back of his throat. He had grown up mistrusting and resenting the Danes, and yet his King had now agreed to an alliance with this clan who had settled in Kald, and Ash had gradually come to respect their leader, Brand Ivarsson. From what he knew of their people so far, they appeared to want peace, too. But the fact that he had felt the stirrings of attraction to one of them was incomprehensible. *Unacceptable.* Especially when the words his father had said to him when he'd last been in Braewood kept resounding in his head.

'Choose a wife of Saxon blood, produce an heir and protect my lands and power. Do this and make me proud to call you my son.'

He sighed. He had always sought the older man's approval, had longed for a kind word from him growing up, like a stray dog hungrily waiting for scraps. Yet Ash hadn't even wanted to take a lover, let alone a wife, these past few months, and there was only one person who was to blame for that.

His attention swung back to the maidens escorting the bride up the aisle, slowly moving towards him— one in particular.

Svea Ivarsson. The groom's sister.

The pull was too strong. His eyes were drawn to her like the enticing current of the sea, causing his blood to pound a little harder. Her dark blonde hair was lighter than he remembered, shining almost silver in the sunlight, and it tumbled down to the base of her spine in a mixture of intricate braids, curls and flowers that swayed as she moved. She had eyes like the ocean—deep-set, blue and wild—and skin as silky-smooth and pale as the sand beneath her bare feet.

She was a natural beauty, with her slender curves strapped into that close-fitting dress, and yet he knew she was strong. He'd seen her handle a sword and shield and it was a vision he'd struggled to erase from his memory these past few months.

He'd never seen a woman wield a blade before, and he'd been enthralled. He still was. Yet he knew he should not be. He didn't *want* to be.

As Svea moved towards him her piercing gaze lifted to his and a shot of awareness bolted through him, igniting a fresh pulse of desire. But just as quickly as their eyes met hers iced over, her back stiffened and she turned away.

He made a fist with his hand. Svea didn't even like him, and had never tried to hide it—not since the day he'd met her and told her to 'show mercy' on the battlefield. He would just have to stamp out this attraction, regain the control he was renowned for.

He would never forget the barbaric fight between her brother and Lord Crowe, the leader of a mercenary Saxon force... It had been one of the most brutal fights he'd ever witnessed, heightened by Svea charging forward at the final moment, ready to help her brother and run her sword through their enemy.

Stunned, Ash had stepped in and demanded she stop. He hadn't known what he knew now—that Crowe had killed their father. And although he understood her pain, and Crowe had since been thrown into a cell in Termarth, he knew she wasn't pleased to see him here. He'd made himself her adversary by being an acquaintance of Crowe's, by getting involved, and she'd been hostile ever since.

Standing beside the bride and groom throughout the ceremony, her back turned against him, she was like an icicle glimmering in the sunlight.

Ash had scouted the grounds more than once during the wedding feast, and later went to sit in a corner of the crowded longhouse next to a small open fire, away from the raucous Danes and the rowdy Saxon soldiers. He scowled. Normally, he wouldn't stand for his men partaking in such revelry, but the King was in fine spirits, rejoicing in his daughter's happiness, and had allowed them all one night of merriment.

Ash wasn't sure he would ever be able to relax in such surroundings. He had never been one to let his guard down—not for a moment. He hated festivities at the best of times, preferring his own company. He thought it stemmed from the few family gatherings he'd experienced growing up, when he had been made to feel like an outcast.

He scanned the longhouse again and saw Svea working her way around the guests, brandishing a jug of ale. She smiled easily among her people, exchanged a little banter, and he felt his interest spike again. The irony wasn't lost on him. His father had given him an ultimatum, had demanded he find himself a Saxon bride to secure the Stanton legacy— and now he couldn't take his eyes off this woman.

A *Danish* woman, who had hated him at first sight and would probably try to kill him if he ever made a move. Not that he was going to. He just had to get through tonight, and then he and his men would be leaving this place for good. He would never have to see her again.

He sat up straight in his seat, all too aware that she was drawing closer, pouring ale for his men, and any moment now would reach his table. He schooled his face in anticipation.

She stopped short when she saw him, as if deciding to take a different route around the hall, even looked as if she might stalk past him. It was nothing new. Due to his fierce reputation and formidable looks, people always kept their distance. He'd learned to live with it, even welcomed it, yet now it irritated him. Perhaps that was what had him opening his mouth, calling out to her...

'Svea.'

She seemed to waver, to consider ignoring him, and then obviously thought better of being so rude, and finally forced herself to turn towards him. He felt another punch to his gut when her beautiful blue eyes reached his.

'Ah, Lord Stanton. Would you care for a drink?' She held up the jug. 'I don't think I've seen you touch a drop all evening.'

Her narrow nose drew his gaze down and he studied her full, soft lips, which were a pretty petal-pink, although her smile looked stiff and her voice was clipped.

He gave her a brisk smile in return. 'Thank you, but no. I am here out of duty, not pleasure.'

Her gaze turned glacial, her face taut, and he knew instantly that she liked his kind as much as he liked hers. Was she just putting on a show for her brother's guests, as he was for his King?

'And ale only serves to cloud the judgement, don't you think?'

'Well, we can't have that,' she mocked. 'We all know your *sound judgement* is what's keeping us all in check.'

His brow furrowed at her blatant disrespect. He was used to being revered and well-regarded by the people of Termarth. 'You must be referring to my judgement on the Crowe situation—my wisdom in demanding that you show mercy to a man already broken and on his knees…' Clearly she was just looking for someone to blame—and he was it.

'Wisdom…was that what it was? Or interference? Crowe killed my father, Lord Stanton. You took the side of my enemy and denied me my revenge.'

He could detect the anger simmering beneath her words, the fire in her personality, and it was igniting an unwanted spark inside him.

Ash inclined his head slightly, as if to acknowledge the weight of her claim. 'I didn't know that at the time.'

'Would your actions have been different had you known?'

'Probably not. I don't believe in taking the law into your own hands. What you did was reckless.'

Her eyes flashed in the flickering firelight. Svea was headstrong, she was impetuous—she was everything he'd been brought up to see as dangerous in a person. And judging by the way his lower body was responding to hers, she was most certainly a danger to him…

'I'd waited years… I think that was long enough to consider my feelings on the matter.'

He sighed, but was careful to maintain his steady tone. 'I have had the man locked away—a satisfactory outcome for us both. Yet, if I'm not mistaken, you've avoided me each time we've met since.'

She shrugged one slim defined shoulder, unwittingly drawing his attention to the material of her dress stretching across the generous swells of her breasts. 'You flatter yourself, Lord Stanton. To ignore you would imply I am even aware of your presence.'

He clicked his jaw. He found her scorn irritating, but her indifference was maddening. Her hand on her hip, she gave him a challenging stare. His eyes dropped to her shoulder, where a dark, intricate design swirled its way over her collarbone and behind her hair. It looked like the twisted branches of a tree, winding up her neck. She had another dark symbol he didn't recognise etched into her wrist. He wanted to tug her closer and inspect it, but he didn't dare touch her. Her whole demeanour screamed for him to stay back.

'Some people may find your status as the King's right-hand man something to be lauded, but others know it's easy to make it in this world with a father in high places,' she added.

He forced a dismissive laugh, but her open assault on his position in life took him aback. And he understood. She was still angry. She wanted to lash out and hurt him, as he had hurt her in denying her the chance to avenge her father's death. But if only she knew the truth... How he'd had to fight to make it in this world, cast out of his parents' home when he was just a boy, unwanted. And he still had a battle on his hands even now, to keep his title and his inheritance. His pride.

'Anyway, we are at my brother's wedding, and unfortunately I have a duty to be gracious to *all* his guests—you included. If you don't care for a drink, I shall have one for you. I suddenly feel in need.'

She lifted a tankard from a nearby table and proceeded to pour herself a cup of ale. Raising it up in the air, she made a toast. 'To the happy couple. And I hope you enjoy the rest of your evening...'

'Doubtful. I have no interest in weddings.'

'We are in agreement about that, at least. *Skol!*' she said, before downing the tankard of ale in one go. Afterwards, as if to disrespect him further, she drew her sleeve across her mouth, wiping the tiny beads of moisture away.

He stared at her, incredulous. He had never known a beautiful woman try so hard to disguise her allure. It intrigued him. 'Still, you played and certainly looked the part today,' he said. He wanted to rake his eyes over the soft, feminine curves of her body, but he was careful to keep them trained on her face. He knew how important it was to treat a woman with respect. 'Up until a moment ago, I thought you looked lovely.'

Her face darkened and she gave an unladylike disdainful snort. He wished the words back the moment he'd uttered them, knowing he'd made a mistake.

She placed the empty tankard down on his table. 'You seem to have a knack of imparting your opinion upon people who don't want to hear it, Lord Stanton. And, as I've been sweating like a pig on its way to the smokehouse all day, I think you should save your compliments for the bride.'

Svea abruptly turned and walked away from him, her dress swishing around her bare ankles, leaving him stunned once again. She wasn't like other women. He had certainly never met one who would scoff at a compliment, drink like a man, or wield a sword like a warrior. He'd never seen a woman with such patterns on her skin before. And no woman had ever spoken to him with such outright contempt. Well, except for his mother.

Svea didn't seem to care what people thought of her. She was just totally herself, and he envied her for that. He'd been ruled by honour, family reputation and others' opinions his whole life.

Was it his chastisement of her behaviour or the compliment that had had Svea stalking away from him? he wondered. Her anger at him seemed unwarranted, misdirected. After all, the man who had killed her father had been locked away, stripped of his wealth and titles. Ash himself had made sure of it. So why was she being so churlish? He wished she wouldn't be. It only served to light a fire in him.

He shifted uncomfortably in his seat and watched as she went about her chores, trying to make herself look as undesirable as possible, seeming not to care, and yet, curiously, it was having the opposite effect on him. He flattened his palms, spreading his fingers out on the table, pressing his boots harder into the floor. Desire could be crushed, like all emotions. And he should know—he had become an expert in doing just that.

Not many men intimidated her. Not any more. But *he* did.

Of all the overbearing, condescending, arrogant men she had ever met, Lord Stanton had to be the worst!

Svea wondered if it was the way he towered above everyone else, or the way he kept himself apart from the other men, sitting alone, brooding, his dark watchful gaze raking over everything and everyone. She had the feeling he never missed a thing. He reminded her of the ravens of her god Odin, his eyes and ears. He was all-seeing. All-knowing. And yet it was as if he himself wanted to go unnoticed. Only he failed miserably.

With his incredibly broad shoulders and a robust, powerful body that emanated sheer strength, he could never blend in. The way he wore his black hair, slicked-back and pulled into a tight knot, his beard neatly trimmed, defining the harsh angles of his face—it all drew attention. He just didn't seem to belong. Everything about him made her wary and she wasn't alone—even his men were mindful of him, in a respectful way, sensing it was safer to give him space. They were right.

Svea didn't want to go anywhere near him, and had even attempted to ignore him when he'd called out to her. She hadn't wanted to face him, lock eyes with him, or hear his patronising words. She felt on edge around him, as if he was judging her—probably because he was! He had expressed his stern disapproval of her behaviour the moment they'd met, and she had felt the censure in his deep brown eyes ever since.

Since her parents had died, no one apart from her brother had ever chastised her. How dare Lord Stanton think it was his place to do just that? Ridiculously, it made her want to rebel, to fight against it, to provoke him to react. It would certainly be interesting to crack that cool resolve of his.

The drinking of the bridal ale had gone on long into the night, and Svea had been careful to keep her distance from him, but she'd still imagined his dark, reprimanding gaze on her, following her as she went about her duties.

She had been shocked when he'd complimented her on her appearance, and it had caused a strange heat to flare in her stomach. She didn't seek, or want, any man's approval—least of all his! The men in Kald knew better than to comment on her looks. They saw her as one of them—a farmer, a fighter. It had taken years, and hard work on her part, to get to this posi-

tion, but now she commanded their respect and camaraderie, and finally things were the way she liked it.

Eventually dawn arrived, and with it her chance to
escape outside, away from all the people in the hot,
overcrowded hall. She rushed to take off the restric-
tive wedding attire and hoped she'd never have to wear
that dress again. Brand owed her a debt for that. She
changed into riding gear, much more to her taste—
an embroidered blue tunic and a leather tabard over
woollen breeches.

She wrapped her trusty belt around her waist and,
thinking back to Lord Stanton's comments about her
actions against Crowe, fastened her bracers and boots
tightly in anger. She couldn't believe he'd called her
reckless. She added a touch of black warrior paint
around her eyes, hoping her fierce appearance would
be enough to ward off any more scrutiny from the
reclusive Saxon lord.

The sun was beginning to rise, with golden streaks
lighting up the sky, as Svea galloped along the cliffs
to the rocky summit, following the longship as it set
sail down the river and out into the wide, open sea.
Seated astride her beloved horse on the headland,
with the wind blowing in her long hair, she waved
her brother and his new wife off on their honeymoon.
She had ridden alongside them as far as she could, and
now she watched as the ship grew smaller and smaller
on the horizon, until it finally disappeared from view.

She swallowed down the lump in her throat. She
was pleased Brand had found happiness, but she
would miss him desperately while he was away. The

wedding had been a mostly joyous occasion, but it had sought to remind her that she could never have what he had—fate had made sure she would never marry. As she'd watched his hands being bound to the Princess's during the ceremony, to signify that their lives were now tied to one another, she had known she would never belong to a man as his wife, that she could never be someone's property. Instead, she would continue to be a warrior and protector of Kald.

In marrying a Saxon princess Brand had helped to protect their lands and their people, through forging an alliance between Kald and Termarth, yet she had often wondered how he could love one of their kind, especially after what had happened to their father. *What had happened to her.* She could never be at ease in a Saxon's proximity.

Svea had been all too aware of the King's men at the wedding, yet she would never let them know they unnerved her. She wouldn't give anyone that satisfaction. She had learned to cover up her fear with a veneer of nonchalance and scorn, and so far it had served her well.

As she steered her horse to ride back down the hill towards the fortress, she was relieved to see the royal guard were readying their horses to leave, about to depart these shores for their own kingdom. Soon she would be able to breathe easily again.

Cantering back into the central square, she saw it was crowded with men in military dress, forcing her to slow her steed, Max. She took in the soldiers' glazed eyes and weary frames. It was clear the men had drunk far too much of the sweet, fruity ale because their movements were slow and laboured.

The formidable Lord Stanton was the only one who had abstained. He had always been controlled on the few occasions she'd met him before—and this time had been no different. He still had that superior, detached air about him this morning, but her brother respected him, so she had promised to keep her animosity towards him in check. She had promised to behave.

Approaching the convoy, she pinned the Saxon Lord with a look, ready for a fight. She knew he wouldn't like what she was about to say.

'King Eallesborough, Lord Stanton… Good morning. My brother asked me to ride out with you to the forest path, to see you safely on your way. We've had a particularly wet season and the marshland has become lethal, even washing away a few of our livestock. I'll be able to show you a way around it.'

Lord Stanton pressed his knees into his horse's sides, nudging his animal forward, his dark brow forming a line. 'There is no need for that, Svea. I am more than capable of finding the way back.'

'I'm sure…' She shrugged. 'Nevertheless, I made a promise to my brother. And I'll enjoy the morning ride.'

He matched the Danish warriors of her clan in both height and width. Despite the words she had spoken to him last night, about how he'd gained his position as the King's most trusted adviser and general, she could certainly see why his men would follow him.

She'd wanted to lash out and attack his position, but he had a reputation for winning many battles, and a collection of face markings to rival those of any of Kald's warriors. Combat scars from fighting her own kind, perhaps? But, unlike her brother and the other Northmen she was accustomed to, Lord Stanton was impeccably dressed in full regalia and shiny chain-mail, professing his loyalty to the crown.

'And what of your safety when we part ways? I cannot leave you unattended.'

'Your concern is unnecessary, Lord Stanton. Two of my men will be joining us, and they'll be only too happy to accompany me on the return journey.'

A muscle flickered in his proud face—the only sign that he might be irritated. She imagined he was used to getting his own way. Well, not today.

'All right. If you insist.' He glowered at her.

'I do.'

She turned in the saddle and sought out her men, Kar and Sten. She was secretly glad her Danish shield brothers were coming with her. It bolstered her confidence. Despite the fact that she'd tried to harden herself to situations like these over the years, she wouldn't normally choose to surround herself with so many Saxon men. It made her insides quiver.

'Bring up the rear,' she commanded them.

Spurring her horse into action, she took the lead as the convoy of Saxon soldiers began to depart the fortress. The sun was rising quickly in the grey sky, burning off the clouds ahead, and a sliver of excitement danced down her spine. Soon they would be saying goodbye to their newfound allies and then she would be free to enjoy her ride along the magnificent shoreline back home.

Except for a few hunts and fishing expeditions, and one life-altering trip to Termarth a long time ago, she had never been far from Kald. The circular wooden walls had been her sanctuary these past years—somewhere to heal, somewhere she could feel safe. And now she knew her enemy was behind iron bars she finally felt ready for a little adventure. A little freedom. She would certainly need it after spending the morning with Lord Sensible!

He was keeping pace with her at the front of the group, riding beside her, and it was unnerving—like having a constant shadow looming over her. She could feel his dark gaze on her and it was making her agitated. She wanted to enjoy the scenery, but his presence was distracting. *Stifling.*

Giving him a sidelong glance out of the corner of her eye, she could see his large, tanned hands holding the reins of his steed, his strong thighs in total control of the animal. She had never seen a man look so tidy, so immaculate. The sun was glinting off his burnished armour, making him look like some kind of god, and she found it strangely fascinating. It made her want to make him look a bit dishevelled, ruffle his hair, see how he would react. *That* was disturbing.

She sat up straighter on her horse, trying to block him out. She refused to be intimidated by his perfect demeanour.

'You ride well, Svea,' he said, his deep, authoritative voice finally breaking the silence. 'I've never seen a woman ride astride before, rather than side-saddle.'

'Then you obviously haven't met a proper woman before, Lord Stanton.'

'I'm beginning to realise you are one of many talents...you ride, you drink, you fight—you even have control over your men. I'm impressed.'

'To impress you was far from my intent,' she said, rolling her eyes. She couldn't be sure if he was complimenting her or mocking her, and neither was acceptable to her.

'What's next for you, I wonder?' he added, ignoring her sarcasm.

She tipped her chin up. 'My brother has entrusted the fortress of Kald to my care while he's away, and I don't mean to let him down.'

His look of shocked surprise pleased her. Good. She wanted to confound him.

'And the men don't mind a woman being in charge?'

'I will see to it that the people of Kald are looked after and safe. I don't need any extra appendage for that, do I?'

His eyes narrowed on her. No doubt he didn't approve of her base words.

'You have your own fortress to rule over, do you not?' she continued.

He nodded tightly. 'It's my father's stronghold, actually.'

She had heard of the impressive garrison of Braewood, and of his father's deteriorating health, and she wondered why Lord Stanton spent his time in the service of the King rather than ruling his own people. There had been rumours that he had been ostracised, but she couldn't be sure if that was true—it might be hearsay. If he was viewed unfavourably by his family, perhaps he wasn't all that he seemed...

'I'm not afraid to get my hands dirty, Lord Stanton. Are you?'

There was a pause, as if he was choosing his next words carefully. Then, 'Not at all. But I'm also not one for playing lord of the manor,' he replied. 'King Eallesborough has need of my sword, and I would prefer to keep busy on the battlefield.'

She could understand that. She knew what it was like to have to expend energy just so you could sleep at night. And yet she couldn't help thinking that his serious, considered approach to everything was at odds with his reputation as prodigal son and ruthless warrior. He was certainly a conundrum.

Increasing the pressure on her horse's reins, Svea returned her focus to navigating the tricky marshland. She was glad when the forest finally came into view in the distance—the point where they would part ways—and it gave her a burst of courage. After passing a particularly deep section of water, she applied her spurs to the horse's sides and picked up the pace, galloping out across the thick mud. But all of a sudden, her horse reared up, throwing her backwards in the saddle.

'Whoa...' she soothed, stroking his mane. 'What is it, Max?' The animal raised his head, and his ears tilted forward. 'What can you hear, boy? A deer or a fox, perhaps?'

'At this time of day? Doubtful,' Lord Stanton said, slowing his horse to pull up alongside her. 'You should be more careful, Svea.'

He scowled at her, before holding up his hand for his men to halt behind them. She swallowed down her irritation at his patronising tone. Who did he think he was?

He cocked his head, listening.

Max's ears twitched again and his nostrils flared. Her animal could detect danger. Svea knew it. She felt a trickle of unease flow through her as she used her hand to shield her eyes from the sun and scanned the horizon to see if she could see anything.

'Something's out there. Max is not easily frightened... He has good instincts.'

'As do I... I'll investigate.' Lord Stanton dismounted his horse and walked forward a few paces. 'Wait here.' His stern voice deepened, as if he meant to emphasise the instruction.

Svea shivered. She felt unsettled—as if she was being watched, as if she was waiting for something. But what? She searched their surroundings again. Apart from the braying of the horses and the murmurings of the men behind them, it was quiet. Too quiet.

She couldn't just sit here and do nothing. She jumped down after Lord Stanton, following him as he waded through the marsh.

He turned around and fixed her with a hard look. 'I told you to wait.'

'And I don't take orders from you.'

He pressed his lips together, as if to stop himself from shooting back a retort, and his long, powerful legs continued to stride purposefully through the knee-deep water. She wondered what words he'd bitten back, almost wanting him to lose all restraint, to see him retaliate.

He moved with confidence and she waded after him. When they reached dry land on the other side, nearing the line of trees, a flock of birds ascended from the dark ferns, screaming overhead. Apprehension swirled in her stomach and she reached for the hilt of her sword. Something was wrong.

Crouching down on his haunches, Lord Stanton inspected the ground. 'Look—there's footprints. Lots of them. Someone's passed through here before us.'

All at once the trees erupted into action and an explosion of men thundered out of the forest, roaring loudly, taking them by surprise. Max reared up behind them, screeching, before swiftly taking off across the plains alongside Lord Stanton's startled horse.

'It's an ambush!' he shouted.

A swarm of arrows came cascading over the trees, hurtling down upon them, and it took a moment for Svea to register what was happening. They were under attack. And then everything descended into chaos.

Svea raised her sword and shield, and before she had time to think she was fighting an unknown enemy. Iron clashed against wood, sending shields splintering, as wave after wave of burly men lunged in their direction through the marsh.

She had put herself in the heart of battle many times, and she'd learnt how to hold her own. But that didn't prevent the intrusion of violent, upsetting memories of her past each time she came up against a male enemy. Driven by her need for self-protection, she sought strength from her darker emotions, her rage, in order to overcome the unwanted fear. She'd make these raiders sorry they'd ever attacked them.

Beside her, she was aware of Lord Stanton fighting, all too conscious of his powerful strength. His actions were fierce and deadly. No warrior was a match for his strength. She had never seen a man fight like that, with such lethal precision. She suddenly felt glad he was on her side.

It was all a blur of swords clashing and water splashing around their ankles. She fought off one man, then another. Her slight figure meant she was quicker and more nimble on her feet than most. Men were often shocked to see a woman fighting, and she used their surprise and hesitation for her gain.

What did these men want? Were they opportunists, or had they planned it, knowing the royal convoy would be travelling this way?

Back to back, she and Lord Stanton seemed to be making progress, warding off some of their attackers. Then, without warning, a giant of a man suddenly bore down on her, striking her in the face with his shield, and her sword clattered to the ground. She fell, landing on her back in the cold murky marsh, and he loomed over her, his weight pressing her down into the waterlogged earth.

'Aye, this one's a woman,' he leered, summoning his mate. 'We could have some fun with her.'

No. Not again.

Her heart began to pound in a stampede of terror. Memories crashed over her and she froze at his words. She knew what it was like to be a toy for men to play with. And she would never, ever allow that to happen again.

Her wide eyes met Lord Stanton's, her consternation meeting his concern, and she saw him charge towards her, all lithe legs and dynamism. Unable to move under the brute's big body, she watched in awe as her ally dispatched the man who stood between them, and it spurred her into action. Using the anger that was surging through her to power her body, channelling her aggression, she kicked and thrashed and managed to shove the beast off her—before he was pulled backwards with force by Lord Stanton and quickly dealt with.

He gripped her elbow to help her up, firm but gentle. 'Are you all right?'

She wasn't sure. She wasn't so shocked by what was happening—she was used to fighting—it was more the onset of memories that had rattled her. On any normal day she usually had her fears under control. But now her legs were trembling, her breath shaky. And those feelings were only intensified by the disturbing warmth of Lord Stanton's large, supportive hand curled around her arm.

'I'm fine,' she lied, fiercely pulling herself out of his grasp and reaching for her sword, which lay on the ground. 'I'm ready to fight again.'

'No!' he barked, taking her arm again with more force this time and dragging her backwards. 'Svea, look.'

She glanced round to see a shallow expanse of water now lay before them and their convoy—who were quickly being surrounded by the rest of the raiders who had charged out of the forest. And, to her horror, she saw that they were rounding up prisoners—the King included. She looked on in dismay as her men—her loyal friends who were usually so strong—reluctantly dropped their weapons in defeat.

'Quick. Come with me. This way,' Lord Stanton said, tugging her into the treeline, hiding them from view.

She struggled against his hold, trying to resist retreat. It went against every bone in her body to fall back, to surrender when people needed her help, when she'd been wronged. But Lord Stanton was too strong.

'What are you doing? We have to help the King… our men…'

She attempted to wrestle with him as he pulled her further into the dense forest. Rage ripped through her blood now, that ambushers had dared attack her, threaten her, and she wanted to fight back. She was so angry. And what was Lord Stanton doing? Why wasn't he fighting? Why was he sheathing his sword?

And why was his touch sending flames flickering across her skin?

'Stop it!' he growled.

'We can't just leave them!' she said, her hands trying desperately to push him away, to release herself from his hold.

This wasn't the man she'd just seen, who had fought so effortlessly, so fearlessly... This wasn't the man her brother had spoken of, who wasn't scared of anyone or anything.

'We can't just give up. We need to fight!'

'And we will,' he said, releasing her arm in favour of gripping both her shoulders. 'Believe me, there's nothing I want more than to make those men sorry they attacked us. But we need to think. Be strategic. Our men are surrounded. If we keep fighting it will be just us against a small army.'

She wasn't sure if it was his words that helped to appease her, or his large warm hands grounding her, but she stopped trying to hurl herself back into the fray. She shucked him off and wrapped her arms around her waist.

'And you nearly got yourself killed, dammit!' he growled. He ran his fingers through his hair, tucking the strands that had begun to come free back into the knot.

That was the least of their issues—she'd survived, hadn't she? In fact, she'd seen off five or so men before she'd been thrown to the ground. It was the King they should be worrying about. Although now the adrenalin was wearing off she had to admit she did feel a little edgy. She'd lost her horse. Her friends had been taken captive. She'd been attacked! And *he'd* saved her—a Saxon!

She swayed on her feet and he caught her by the elbow again.

'Are you sure you're all right?' he asked as he eased her down onto a fallen tree trunk.

'Don't touch me!' she spat.

'A woman like you shouldn't be fighting, Svea. You'll just be seen as bait—a temptation to these men. I told you not to come!'

Anger erupted inside her and she leapt back off the tree trunk, her face riotous. 'I'm as good a fighter as any of your men!'

A woman like you. She didn't like the vitriolic way he'd said it. What did he mean? Was her reputation at stake here?

The rage that had erupted inside her was quickly replaced by cold dread, and she ran her hand over the metal *kransen* around her arm. A symbol of her virginity. She felt a fraud for wearing it. But she was sure neither her brother nor his new wife would have said anything about her past...not to this man. Yes, he had been Princess Anne's guard before she'd married Brand, but he was still practically a stranger.

Feeling unsteady on her feet, she slumped back down again. She did not want to be seen as a *temptation*. Never. And the fact that he had described her as such—as bait—sent a warning signal through her. She had to get away from this man.

Lord Stanton seemed to have the opposite idea. He drew a hand over his face, as if to gather his thoughts, then slowly crouched down in front of her. He looked into her eyes.

'I'm sorry. You're right,' he said calmly. 'You fought well, Svea. I didn't know women could fight like that. You were as good as any of my men.'

She nodded, mute. She didn't know what she'd been expecting him to say, but it hadn't been that. A prickle of awareness edged along her skin. She thought she preferred the cold, reproachful Lord Stanton—not this man who was looking at her with concern, whose voice had turned gravelly and warm while he was apologising. It unnerved her more than his usual disapproval.

'Where did you learn to fight like that?' he asked.

She frowned. He wanted to make conversation? Now? When they should be fighting or forming a plan? 'My brother taught me.'

Their people had been greeted with conflict from the Saxons since the day they'd arrived on this island. Their clan had come here in search of a better life and had put down roots, but they'd had to fight for their lives and their land on many occasions.

Since she was just a young girl she had made it her mission to learn how to use her mother's sword and shield. She had determined never to be defenceless or vulnerable again. She had made Brand train with her for hours, every single day. At first he'd overpowered her each time, but slowly she'd learnt to be more nimble, more decisive. He'd taught her how to use her environment to her advantage and how to build up her body strength through swimming and lifting heavy things.

Soon, she'd started to beat some of the men in Kald, who were twice her size and strength, in practice fights. And the day she'd bested Brand he'd scooped her up and whirled her round in the air as they'd grinned at each other in delight, knowing she was finally ready.

'He's taught you well. But you're putting yourself at risk, being out here among all these men. You must see that.'

He reached up and stroked a strand of hair from her face, attempting to tuck it behind her ear, but she stiffened, recoiling from his touch and casting him off with her arm.

'And now you're hurt.' He stood, nodding to her forehead.

She frowned, putting her fingers to her temple. She hadn't realised she was bleeding. She could not understand him. One moment he was chastising her, the next he was troubled by her plight.

'I'm fine…it's the others I'm worried about. Lord Stanton—'

'Ashford,' he said. 'That is my name. You can call me Ash.'

Ash. It suited him. She swallowed. 'We can't just leave them…'

'Of course not. I don't intend to,' he said, prowling over towards a clearing to peer through the trees.

Svea let out a breath she hadn't realised she'd been holding. She shook her head. 'Who are these men? What do they want?'

'I don't know. I don't recognise them.' He crouched quietly, observing like Fenrir, the giant black wolf of her gods, stalking his prey from the shadows of the bushes. Fearing his strength, the other gods had bound Fenrir, and she wondered if she ought to do the same to Ash...

'They're Saxons, aren't they? *Your* people.'

He ignored her barbed comment. 'Perhaps they thought we were carrying treasure. Or maybe they want to harm the King for some reason.'

'I thought you were meant to be the King's best soldier. Why are we even in this position?'

His gaze swung to her, narrowing. 'I am. Which is why I'm still alive to rescue him, like I rescued you.'

She glanced away. She couldn't argue with that. And she thought how absurd it was that she had fought alongside this Saxon soldier, as an ally, when all she saw when she looked at him was danger. But he had an extraordinarily strong body and, despite her skill with a sword, she knew he would probably be able to overpower her if he wanted to. Like Fenrir devoured the sun...

She would die trying to stop him, though.

'So what do we do now?' she said, looking away and picking at a piece of bark on the fallen tree, as if to give her hands something to do, her eyes something to focus on other than him.

'I will follow them. See who they are...what they want. I'll make sure nothing happens to the King.' He was firm, decisive. He walked back towards her and knelt down in front of her again. 'Svea, I want you to return home. We're near enough to Kald for you to go back. You can raise the alarm, be on the alert, and wait there for me to sort this out.'

Her face shot up to his. 'Wait? Never! They're my men, too. I'm coming with you.'

She couldn't believe what she was saying. She didn't want to be alone with this man. She had sworn to hate him. She didn't know him, or what he was capable of. For all she knew he might have dragged her into the forest as a ruse to attack her.

With that thought in her mind she glanced around, checking her surroundings, looking for a place she could run and hide if she needed to. But she had never been afraid to take risks, and she couldn't just sit idly by while her men were in trouble. Lord Stanton was about to find out she could be just as assertive as him.

He shook his head. 'It's too dangerous. I'll be faster, and better, on my own. I can't vouch for your safety—'

Did he really care about that? 'I'm not asking you to protect me!' she bit out, interrupting him.

'Your brother would want me to make sure you are safe.'

She launched herself off the log and shook herself down, defying him, preparing to leave. 'I can fend for myself, and Brand knows it. He taught me how to do just that. Besides, we don't know what's waiting for us at Kald, either—if the fortress has been attacked.'

His dark eyes studied her, glowering. But her final comment seemed to sway him. He must have realised she was right. They didn't know if this was a two-pronged attack—if there were other men who had watched them leave Kald this morning, seen an opportunity and advanced upon the settlement…

She shuddered. She hoped not. Not while it was in her care.

'All right,' he agreed slowly. 'But on one condition. From this moment on you will do exactly as I say…'

'And if I don't?' She tilted her chin up in defiance, forcing herself to look into his deep brown eyes.

He took a step towards her until his large, intimidating body was just a whisper apart from hers. She stopped breathing. Panic and that new, peculiar heat flared in her stomach. She really hoped he wasn't going to touch her again…

'Don't push me, Svea.'

She'd seen the way he fought earlier, his skill with a sword. It had been fierce, deadly. It was a far cry from his usual civilised veneer.

'You don't scare me, Ashford Stanton…'

He grinned then, a slow, seductive smile, and her heart began to clamour, ricocheting in her chest. She had never seen him smile properly before…and he was striking. She felt her legs begin to tremble again.

And now she knew she was lying to him, and to herself, because he was the most overwhelmingly attractive man she had ever seen, and the reality of their situation began to dawn on her. No one knew where they were. They were all alone out here in the forest, just the two of them, and the truth was it scared her to death.

Chapter Two

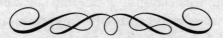

Ash cursed himself. He should have seen this coming.

Keeping low within the undergrowth so as not to draw any attention to themselves, they followed the convoy of captives along the forest edge for a while, throughout the midday sun, listening to the band of ambushers throwing insults at the King, the soldiers, but mainly the Danes.

Ash knew this wasn't good. He'd thought maybe they were opportunists, simple thieves, but the longer they trekked on, the more it seemed they had a destination—and a purpose—in mind.

He was angry with himself for letting his men drink too much ale last night. They would have been able to fight better with their wits about them. And he was even more furious with himself for agreeing to let Svea escort them to the forest. If he'd stood firm she would be safe at home right now. That was if Kald hadn't been attacked, too. But seeing her stand up to him this morning, dressed in body-tight armour, her eyes shimmering with an inner determination, he had relented. She had weakened his resolve and look what had happened.

They'd been trudging through shoulder-height bracken and muddy ground for hours, Svea in her soaking wet clothes. It had been hard going and he was beginning to feel concerned about her. He could see that she was flagging—not that she'd ever admit to it. She was far too stubborn and proud. Each time he slowed down to wait for her she just pushed herself harder, catching up with him and then stalking past, careful not to brush against him, pressing on without even taking a break.

It was infuriating. Despite her feminine, curvy frame, which she tried and failed to hide under heavy chainmail, she was stronger than most women, and yet her vulnerability still reached out to him, piercing his heart more sharply than any sword could.

She was tense in his company—he would have had to be blind to miss that. There had been a few times he'd tried to help her climb over fallen tree trunks, gripping her elbow to assist her, but each time she'd tensed, practically shrinking beneath his touch, like a snail withdrawing into its shell, and instantly shrugged him off. She avoided his gaze, holding her body away from him, often crossing her arms over her chest as if she were putting up a barrier between them. And he noticed how she kept a firm grip on the hilt of her sword at all times.

Was she just wanting to be ready in case they had to fight again, or was it him she was afraid of? It was possible. He knew his imposing looks struck fear into many.

He had been momentarily in awe of her skills with a sword, impressed by her fearlessness—until she'd almost got herself killed. When he'd seen that man knock her to the ground, pressing her under the water with his weight and making lewd comments, Ash's blood had run cold. It had only confirmed his suspicions that having a woman on the battlefield was a terrible idea—especially one of such beauty. He was painfully aware of the reaction she could induce in men, and what beasts they could be. He'd suffered the ramifications of that kind of behaviour his whole life.

His fierce need to protect her had made him see red. His control had slipped and he'd dispatched those men in cold fury—no regrets. He didn't want to look too closely at that part of him—at what kind of blood ran through his veins to make him behave like that. He had been so determined not to let anything bad happen to her, he even wondered if he'd sacrificed the King's safety for her own. And yet, even though he knew he had failed in his duties, he couldn't bring himself to regret it. He would make the same choice again.

He couldn't understand why he felt so protective of her. He didn't want to feel this way. For a man of his standing to like a Danish woman—he was certain it would all but ruin his reputation. But still, he admired the way she'd handled herself, the way she'd been so brave, crushing her emotions, caring more about the safety of her men and her people back at Kald than the fact she'd been attacked herself.

It was honourable, but foolish! She needed to take better care of herself from now on, especially now they were on the same side—allies fighting a common enemy.

After what felt like an age, the Saxon men and their weary captives finally slowed as they approached a clearing in the forest. On closer inspection, Ash realised it was a temporary camp, where another thirty or so men were waiting for them. His heart sank. He'd been trying to put a brave face on for Svea, keeping positive, thinking that perhaps they could stake out the group, wait for them to rest, then strike. But their enemy's numbers were increasing, and as he watched the men roughly tie up their hostages, he realised an extraction of the King was starting to look impossible.

Ash found himself and Svea a sheltered spot under a canopy of russet trees, where they could rest at a safe distance out of sight while still keeping a close eye on their quarry. And he himself was glad for the respite. Cold and shivering, but trying hard not to show it, Svea sat down quietly and leaned back against a tree, careful not to rustle or crunch the leaves underfoot. He would offer to sit next to her, to warm her up, but he didn't think she'd entertain that idea. Instead, he unclipped his cloak and cast it down over her.

'Here,' he said. 'You need this more than me.'

She accepted it almost grudgingly, her fingers brushing against his, making his heart skitter ridiculously. What was it about her that bewitched him so?

Svea reached for the little leather water satchel from her armour, and when she took a huge swig, quenching her thirst, Ash ran his tongue over his lips. Hesitantly, she passed it to him, careful to evade his touch.

'Thanks.'

She looked like a different person from the feminine beauty who'd strolled through the hall towards him yesterday, her hair now plaited into tight braids and piled on top of her head, tight coils cascading down her back. Her face was streaked with dirt, her tunic was torn in places from the brambles and she had a nasty gash to her right temple. But she was no less attractive.

He liked the fact that she didn't conform—he found it intriguing. She was certainly unique in both her looks and her behaviour. And he knew he would have to start trying harder at fighting these disturbing feelings.

He reluctantly removed his tabard, which bore the banners of the crown, deciding it best to lose the royal colours in case they came across anyone and needed to go unnoticed. He tore a square from the material and soaked it in a nearby bubbling brook, squeezing it out before coming down beside Svea and pressing it against her forehead.

'You're still bleeding.'

She jerked away from him. 'I told you not to touch me! I can do it,' she said, wrinkling her nose, snatching the material from him.

He sighed. He wondered if they were really so

different. He always tried to keep people at bay, too, but he did it for their own good. He had the feeling she was trying to protect herself. Over the years he had come to prefer keeping people at a distance, but with Svea he was finding that distance infuriating. Against his better judgement he wanted to reach out and reassure her, comfort her, but he knew she didn't want him to. Was it just his touch that repulsed her, or were there other reasons?

Shunned, he stalked to the stream and filled the water satchel. What had he expected? His unusual face and large body had always unsettled people—caused them to stare, then glance away. Even as a boy the people of Braewood had sensed he wasn't the same as them. He had been reviled for being stronger, faster, taller... He had never fitted in. And even though they hadn't known why, they'd known he was different so they'd treated him as such.

There had been so many times when he'd longed to join in with the other children in the fortress square, happily playing together, comfortable in their own skin, but he'd always felt he had something to hide, so he'd chosen to keep himself apart. Nothing had changed since—he still carried a great deal of guilt for who he was, and he'd grown to accept this life of solitary freedom.

He sat down opposite her, stretching out his long legs next to hers, careful not to touch her.

'So they're clearly not thieves. But why would fellow Saxons want to seize your King?' she whispered.

'I don't know. But I wonder if he was anticipating

something like this would happen. He was insistent that I come to the wedding with him. A lot of people across the kingdom didn't agree with your brother marrying the Princess, and they certainly don't support the alliance between Termarth and Kald. It's caused a divide between the Saxon people.'

'Do you?'

'Do I what? Approve of a union between Danes and Saxons?' He shrugged. 'It doesn't really matter what I think.'

'You always seem to have an opinion on everything...'

His lips twisted. He prided himself on speaking his mind about all things bar his own family history.

'I like the idea that Termarth could become a place where all people would be welcomed.'

He wondered, in a place like that, if one day even he could be accepted for who he was. But first he'd have to learn to accept himself... He admired Brand and Anne for speaking out about their feelings, not caring what people thought of them. He wasn't sure he could ever do it, or subject himself to such scrutiny. Not when he knew just how hurtful it could be.

'When you have seen the things I have seen, it's hard to trust, to believe our people could live together.'

The accounts of Northmen raiding Saxon lands and then not leaving, but staying to create settlements, had become much more frequent lately. He knew the King hoped this marriage union would bring his people more security from these clans through forming an alliance with one. Many people didn't agree. There was too much anger, too much hate.

'It is hard for us to trust you also,' Svea said, her voice heated. 'Our past is marred with atrocities carried out upon us by your kind.'

'You chose to come here,' he countered, holding her gaze. 'To *our* land.'

'We didn't have a choice!' she spat, suddenly incensed. 'What would you have had us do? There isn't enough land to farm where we come from. It was leave or starve. We were just young children when my father put us in a boat and we sailed across the sea to find a new home. He was *that* desperate. And we lost my mother to the ocean on the way here. It wasn't a decision that was taken lightly…'

He was shocked at the revelation and felt a sudden pang of sympathy for her. He took a moment to digest what she was telling him.

'I didn't know that,' he said. He wondered how the loss of her mother at such an early age had affected her. Hell, he knew the feeling of abandonment all too well. Only his parents had chosen to leave him, Svea's mother hadn't. She had drowned. Her story was tragic.

'You don't know a lot of things—about me or my people.'

Ash didn't like the thought of her being a starving hungry child. He'd experienced that himself at times, despite the fact that she thought of him as having a privileged upbringing, and it wasn't something he wanted to relive, nor that he would wish on anyone else.

'You're right,' he conceded, inclining his head in acknowledgement. He realised he didn't know any-thing about her, and against his better judgement he wanted to. 'But I'm willing to learn. That must have been a terrible choice for your parents to make—and awful for you. You must miss your mother very much.'

He stretched out an arm to tug a few blackberries from the burgeoning hedgerow beside him and held them out to her. 'Are you hungry now?'

She leaned forward and he tipped them into her palm, his fingers brushing against hers, and the tiny touch triggered another ripple of awareness through his body.

'You have to admit, you are in the minority. Many of your kind come here looking for spoils or trea-sure,' he said.

'Well, we came looking for survival. We risked our lives in search of a new home. We're not what you think—we're not like some of the others. Kald was un-inhabited when we arrived on these shores. We didn't steal anything—we just created a settlement and have found ourselves having to defend it ever since.'

Deep down, he already knew what she was saying to be true—her clan *wasn't* the same as the North-men who had attacked Braewood all those years ago, who had done so much lasting damage to his home, his family…

Despite his innate hatred of her kind since child-hood, he hadn't been able to eradicate his dark obses-sion with the Norse people. When he was just a boy, there had been many a time when he'd crept down to his father's chronicle room and pored over his writings and drawings by candlelight, trying to understand these warriors and garner more information about his heritage. Once, his father had caught him, but instead of putting a loving arm around his shoulder and explaining it to him, he had whipped him and sent him back to his room, frightened and alone.

He had so many questions—about Svea, about her people, about where they'd come from, their beliefs... It fascinated him. Maybe if she told him, he could learn a thing or two about himself. Maybe it would help him to accept who he was...

He pulled a few more juice-filled berries from the bush and popped them into his mouth. Their sweetness tasted good as they burst on his tongue, and helped to placate his rumbling stomach.

'Then I agree with the King and your brother. We should attempt a truce between Danes and Saxons—try to be friends. Perhaps we could start with us?' He offered her a hopeful smile.

Svea scowled in contempt. 'I'm not sure I want to be added to the list of your friends—you don't have a great history of likeable allies.'

His face fell. He realised she was on the offensive again. Her penetrating blue eyes were accusing, her demeanour hostile. She reminded him of the beautiful long-necked swans he'd seen gliding along the river in Termarth. They were graceful and agile, yet if you went anywhere near them they hissed and began to flap their wings. Svea was like that. So hostile. And she seemed unwilling to set aside their original differing views.

Ash inclined his head. 'You're talking about Lord Crowe again.' It seemed she just couldn't let the subject die.

'Tell me, when you rode alongside him, did you know what kind of man he was? What he was capable of?'

He sighed. 'I didn't know he'd killed your father, if that's what you mean. And I still don't understand why. Your brother said it was some kind of attack because you were Danes?'

She nodded and bit her lip.

Was there more to this than she was letting on? he wondered again. He couldn't claim to be a fan of her kind, but he would never attack someone just because they were a Dane. If Crowe had done that, it really was despicable.

'I'm sorry. About your father.' He realised now that the death of her father must have been even more painful after losing her mother at such a young age.

'He was a good man.'

He nodded, and then, because he felt the need to share something of himself, and to keep her talking, he added, 'My mother died when I was young, too, but of natural causes.'

It had been a strange day when he'd learnt of her passing. He didn't remember feeling upset—he just remembered his father's anger towards him, as if it had somehow been Ash's fault. So he'd stayed away. Ash had wished her back—of course he had. But he'd never truly known her. Not really. She hadn't ever wanted to be close to him. Hell, she hadn't been able to stand the sight of him. Not ever.

He'd stayed out until dinner time. And then the guilt had crept along, like the clouds darkening the sky, and he had chastised himself for feeling so numb, for not caring as much as he should have, making him wonder what kind of person he was. The kind of person who couldn't even shed a tear for his own mother.

He cleared his throat. 'My father is currently in ill health,' he added.

'Yet you're not at his side? You're not close?'

He shook his head. 'We never have been.'

His relationship with his father had been just as strained. When he'd returned home that night he'd been sent to bed without any food, for not showing respect for his late mother. For not being with his father.

The simple fact was that his parents had never been able to love him, and he understood why. He'd known from a young age—from the day his father had told him the story of how he'd come to be. And yet he didn't blame them...only himself. Even at Svea's words now he felt guilty for not being with his father, as she clearly thought he should be.

He shrugged. 'He wouldn't want me at his bedside, that's for sure.'

'Any siblings?'

'No, although I have always wished I had.'

He had often longed for a relationship as close as the one that Svea clearly shared with her brother. The closest thing to it that he'd experienced was the rapport that had been built up between himself and the King and his men, meaning he would do all that he could to get them back. But having a sibling would have meant there would have been someone to soften his parents' scrutiny. Someone better placed than him to continue the Stanton line. But, no, his father had tasked him with the responsibility, and he'd threatened to deny Ash his inheritance, strip him of his lands and title, if he didn't comply.

'Married?'

He glanced up in surprise when she spoke, as if she was following his line of thought. 'No,' he said. 'I told you I wasn't keen on weddings.'

Of course there had been women over the years, but none of any significance. He was always careful to keep his emotions and his true self tightly locked away—for their sake more than his.

He saw the colour rise in her cheeks as she glanced away.

'I wasn't sure if that was because of a bad experience or just your lack of enjoyment of the festivities. You don't strike me as the kind of man who would enjoy a good celebration.'

'No?' He raised his eyebrows. 'I decided a long time ago never to marry or have children.'

It was for the best. All he wanted was to forge his own path in life—but because he'd been born into the Stanton family, that seemed impossible.

He hadn't heard from his father for years—until he had received word that Aethelbard had become ill and Ash was needed at home. He'd been called back to Braewood and told he was required to take a Saxon bride to secure the family's future and his father's fortress. So far he had refused. How could he marry a woman who didn't know him and could never know the truth about him? It wouldn't be fair. Besides, he'd never met a woman he'd wanted to share his secrets with.

'It's the least you could do!' his father had insisted.

Ash knew just how fortunate he was that his parents had kept him—a bastard boy with the blood of a monster running through his veins. He owed them his gratitude, and he'd spent his life trying to win his father's affection. But he couldn't bring himself to perform this final act and make the man proud. His father had gone so far as to say that if Ash hadn't married a Saxon lady by the time he passed away, he would renounce his lands and titles—and destroy his honour by revealing Ash's true identity.

If he carried out his father's orders the responsibility of ruling Braewood would fall to him, and he had mixed feelings about that. It was his ancestral home, his birthright, and yet he'd barely spent any time there as a child. He'd been sent away to a monastery when he was a young boy, kept out of sight of his parents so he couldn't cause them any pain. He'd felt unwanted, rejected. He had been taught to read and write and pray with birch whips, not with love and nurture. And there had been long hours of work and barely any food.

It had been a lonely existence, a childhood of captivity, and he'd learnt to live without affection and a proper home. He'd longed for the day when he could escape. And as soon as he'd been old enough he'd left. He'd returned to Braewood briefly, but he still hadn't been made to feel welcome, so he'd learned how to fight, taking his anger out on the battlefield, and worked his way up the ranks.

He'd thrived on the glory of winning, finally receiving the praise and accolades he'd always longed for as a child, and he had made his own success, becoming the King's loyal warrior through talent, not his family name, despite what Svea thought.

He glanced around, studying their surroundings. He admired the mature trees and listened to the soothing sounds of tumbling water. He felt at home in the wild like this, or out on the battlefield—not cooped up in some fortress, hosting feasts and ruling others. He knew he couldn't put off what his father was demanding of him forever, and yet even knowing this he was drawn back to his companion's face. Svea looked exhausted, her eyes heavy and her lips taut, and yet she was still achingly beautiful.

She avoided his gaze as she wrapped the cloak tighter around her. At least she hadn't refused that. He might not have to worry about her catching her death just yet.

'It's probably just as well you don't want to marry. I doubt anyone would have you anyway,' she mocked.

He grinned. 'You're so frosty, Svea. Is that why *you're* not married?'

Her eyes narrowed on him. 'I'm not married because I don't wish to be. I don't need a man to complete me, and I certainly don't want one ruling over me.'

'Does your brother agree? Is he not in charge of arranging a marriage for you?'

'No!' she spat. 'My brother would never make me do anything I didn't want to do!'

He believed that to be true, and he was beginning to wonder which of their families was more barbarian after all. Svea had a family who cared about her and had her best interests at heart, which was more than he could say for his father.

A loud clamouring of horses' hooves approaching the Saxon camp stole his attention, sending his senses soaring. Rising quickly to peer through the trees, he saw a large balding man jump down off his steed and speak to some of the ringleaders.

Ash cursed under his breath, lowering his head.

'What is it?' Svea asked, coming to stand beside him, lifting herself up on tiptoes, trying to get a better look herself.

'I know who that is.'

'Who?'

He pointed towards the man with ruddy porcine features. 'That's Lord Crowe's brother—Cecil. From Calhourn.'

'What? No!' she gasped.

He turned towards her and watched as she took a step back, her face turning ashen.

Ash began to pace, thinking out loud. 'This isn't some random attack by bandits,' he said. 'This was planned. Thought out. Now it all makes sense. Calhourn soldiers must have taken the King as a hostage—to help Cecil rescue his brother.'

'See!' Svea fumed, rounding on him, a scowl carved into her beautiful features. 'You should have let me kill him when I had the chance. Then none of this would be happening.' She stabbed a finger into his chest. 'This is all your fault.'

He frowned, looking at the place where she'd jabbed him as if it burnt. Maybe she was right. Perhaps he should have let her avenge her father—at least then she wouldn't hate him so much, and the King might not have been captured.

He turned his attention back to the men, assessing the situation, wondering what they were planning.

'Do you think they'll demand an exchange? Crowe for the King?' Svea whispered, appalled.

He nodded. 'Possibly...'

Concern chilled him now. This was worse than he'd first thought. He felt certain they'd be heading to Termarth next—and at present the kingdom was at its weakest, with the King and some of Ash's best men having been taken hostage.'

'We need to do something,' Svea said. 'I know what Crowe is capable of. What if his brother is the same?'

And as if his worst fears were coming true, Ash watched as some men grabbed Kar and Sten and bundled them forward to stand before their leader. When he saw Cedric roll up his sleeves, a sneer carved into his face, the hairs on the back of his neck stood on end. This couldn't be good.

'This is for my brother,' Cedric spat. He curled his fingers into a fist and struck the first blow, which landed against Kar's jaw. Ash heard Svea gasp beside him. She reached for the hilt of her sword, her face pale, her knuckles turning white, and he knew she was about to rush forward, about to try to stop this display of brutality, to help her men.

Instinctively, he gripped her arm and wrapped his other hand around her mouth, tugging her back against his chest. 'Svea, don't!' he whispered.

No sooner had his muscles tightened around her soft curves than her whole body stiffened.

'Look away,' he ordered as Cedric began to rain down punches on her friend, seemingly for sport, while laughter erupted from his men.

The Dane, unable to fight back as his hands were bound, sank down to his knees. Ash's blood ran cold. *Coward*, he thought of Cecil. To attack an unarmed man.

Memories of being bound and beaten on the cold monastery floor when he was just a boy ripped through him. At first he'd been shocked. When he'd arrived at the monastery, although he'd been devastated that he'd been abandoned by his parents, he'd thought he was in safe hands among men of faith. He'd been wrong. He remembered that feeling of being alone, being hurt. The pain, and also the un-justness. Everyone deserved a chance to fight back.

Svea began to lash out, struggling in his arms, but he held her fast, his muscles strained. He twisted her in his embrace and pressed her tightly into his chest, his arms wrapped around her back. She made every effort to free herself, her words muffled as he pressed her harder into his body.

'It'll be over in a moment,' he said. 'Keep quiet. Don't do anything foolish.'

Cedric continued to kick the Danish warrior and Svea stilled, her initial rage seeming to subside, but with each and every sickening blow she flinched in his arms. Ash ran his hands up and down her back, attempting to soothe her. She reminded him of a feral, frightened mare which had once bolted from Braewood's stables. He'd been tasked with talking her down, trying to get her to a safe enclosure.

After what seemed like aeons, the brutal beating finally stopped when Kar lay battered and bruised and still on the ground. 'It's all right. It's over,' Ash whispered, stroking Svea's hair. He fancied she almost leaned into him, or was that just wishful thinking? 'He's hurt, but he'll live.'

Svea suddenly pushed at his chest with her hands, staggering away from him, her face mutinous. 'You should have let me help him!' she fumed.

'You against all those men? You're crazy,' he said, disturbed by her behaviour.

Ash was barely holding his own annoyance at bay, furious with the Saxon men for their actions and his inability to help Kar, but just as angry with Svea for her extreme risk-taking yet again, and it took every shred of his resolve to carefully control his voice and tone.

'Are you trying to get us both killed? This reckless independence of yours is going to get us into trouble.'

He was incensed with himself, too. For the way his body was responding to hers.

She stepped further away from him. 'I can't bear the thought of someone being hurt and no one coming to their aid. And you seem to lack the courage to do what needs to be done.'

'Oh, I know what needs to be done. And the first thing is to teach you a lesson in obedience, Svea. You're irrational, rash, and therefore you make poor judgements—you rush in, regardless of the consequences. Your brother may have taught you how to fight, but he should have taught you how to control that temper of yours.'

If there was one thing he'd learnt from the monks at the monastery, it had been how to endure pain, to stay calm—how to use his anger to make him stronger, to show restraint, tolerance and self-control. All traits he prided himself in now.

'You're not my leader, Ash. And I'm sorry we're not all as controlled and perfect as you!' she bit out, before crumpling onto the ground, as if sinking in despair. 'It's hopeless,' she said, burying her head in her hands. 'They'll kill them, won't they?'

Ash came down beside her, his unusual flare of anger quickly giving way to concern. 'If they want Lord Crowe to be released they'll need as much advantage as they can get,' he said gently. 'If they were going to kill your men I think they would have done it already.'

'Evil runs through their blood,' she said bitterly. She ran her hands over her metal armband absentmindedly.

He stared down at her. Did she really believe that such a thing was possible? That malice could run in a bloodline? If that was the case, what did it mean for him? He hoped it wasn't true. It was his worst fear.

He reached out to take her chin between his thumb and forefinger, lifting her beautiful blue gaze to his. 'We have to hope they're safe for now—at least until they get to Termarth, if that's where they're heading. It might just buy us some time to raise troops.'

'What are you suggesting?'

'That we go to Braewood and raise the *fyrd*— an army of free men willing to fight for the King. We can't fight Calhourn soldiers without help—their numbers are too great.'

'Aren't we closer to Kald? Why shouldn't we go back there and get my people?'

He sighed. He should have known she'd try to fight him on this. 'I mean no offence, but this is a task for Saxon soldiers, not Danes.'

Over the years he had built up an army to protect Braewood and Termarth from possible invasion by the Northmen, and now he was going to use those men to rescue Northmen and the King from Saxons. Everything was all wrong—including his feelings. How could this be happening?

'We're all meant to be on the same side now, aren't we?' she said, sarcasm lacing her voice. But nevertheless she seemed to accept his answer. She stood, shaking down her clothes. 'How far away is it? Your fortress?'

'My father's home, not mine,' he corrected her. 'It's half a day's ride at most. But first we'll need to steal a horse...'

They'd waited until nightfall, when the men in the camp had eaten and drunk themselves into a stupor, and now all was quiet. Keeping low, Svea followed Ash as he crept within the shadows of the trees, skirting around the tents, her heart in her mouth.

They reached the place where the horses were tied up. If they were seen, they would surely be captured, and then all hope would be lost. They wouldn't be able to get help, and the King and her men were depending on them.

As they approached the horses, tethered to various trees, some of them let out a whinny, shuffling about, and she held her breath, glancing at Ash. He nodded to a black stallion and they moved either side of it, Ash gripping its bridle and stroking its nose, Svea quickly untying the rope.

Her legs felt like water, and yet Ash seemed so assured, so calm. 'Ladies first...' he whispered, motioning for her to climb up as he held the animal in position.

Svea went to mount the horse, and Ash gripped her elbow to help her ascent. Why did he insist on touching her? Every time he did, it sent a shot of heat through her and she didn't understand it. It wasn't unpleasant, and yet she didn't want to feel like this—

not with him, a man who was more male, more virile than any she'd met before.

Her body was still burning in all the places where he had held her in his uncompromising hold earlier. When she'd been encased in his muscled arms, he had been too strong for her. She had been angry and scared at what was being done to her friend, but the tingles he'd sent dancing up and down her spine when he'd smoothed his hands over her back had been equally terrifying. And when he'd tenderly stroked her hair, she had been horrified when she'd almost sunk into him, seeking more of his comfort.

She knew how attraction worked between a man and woman—she'd seen it unfold many times between her people back at home in Kald—but she'd never experienced any of those feelings for herself. She'd meant what she'd told Ash earlier, about not needing a man to complete her. She was happy as she was. Or as happy as she thought she could ever be, given what she had been through. She had decided for herself that she would never marry. She would never feel the same way other men and women did towards each other. She had accepted she would never know that attraction. Until now.

It was no surprise that she felt shaken and confused— first they'd been ambushed, then her friend had been attacked, and now they were tiptoeing around their enemy's camp, trying not to be discovered. But she knew her feelings also had a lot to do with the man at her side, his hands now curling around her calf as he steadied her position.

Ash gently took the rope from her and she was conscious of his fingers grazing hers, sending ripples of heat through her. When he began to lead her and the animal away from the rest of the horses she hoped it wouldn't make a sound. Just one whinny and they'd be surrounded in an instant. They'd probably kill Ash and do unthinkable things to her.

A cold hand of fear clutched her throat. No matter the strength she portrayed, hoping that if she behaved that way long enough it would become reality, that she would truly be as strong as she seemed, deep down she wondered if she would ever escape the fear and the memories. She rarely spoke about it, just buried it, never wanting to burden her brother with her dark thoughts. In a way, she was trying to protect him from the past, too, by putting on a brave face for them both.

'What about you?' she whispered down to Ash. 'Don't we need a horse for you?'

'Shh,' he said, pressing one long finger over his lips.

It seemed to take them a lifetime to reach the undergrowth a safe distance away from the camp. When they hit the dense forest again, she allowed herself to breathe more easily. Her shoulders finally released their tension. They'd made it undetected. They could be on their way. But her relief was short-lived.

'Shuffle forward. I'm coming up.'

'What?'

'Move up,' Ash said.

Panic floored her. Did he actually intend to ride behind her? To share the horse? She looked down at him in horror. The horse looked strong enough to carry both of them, even Ash's large frame, but that wasn't her concern.

'Why did we just take one horse? Why didn't we take two?' she asked, her throat tight.

He must have seen her startled look, heard the alarm in her voice, and she didn't want to show him she was afraid. But she couldn't help it.

'Because that would have drawn too much attention. They may not notice one go missing, but two... The last thing we need is men on our tail. Come on, Svea. Move up.'

And without warning he suddenly mounted the horse behind her. She let out a strangled protest as his legs straddled hers and his arms came around her. Again.

His large hands gripped hers, firm but gentle, taking the reins from her, and she instantly let go, breaking the connection, letting him take control. So much for standing up to him, she thought. And where was her false bravado when she needed it?

She closed her eyes briefly and blew out a series of breaths, trying to stay calm. She was all too aware of his chest pressing against her back, his thighs tightening around hers as he spurred the horse on, and she tried to make herself as small and as rigid as possible.

'Just relax,' he said.

Relax? How could she possibly relax? She was aware of his every movement, of the taut muscles in his thighs rubbing against her legs, his mighty arms surrounding her, embracing her, and she was conscious of her bottom moving against his groin. She cringed, shrinking further into herself.

Earlier, when they'd been rushing through the brambles, his company hadn't been so bad. They'd moved in silence, tracking the convoy, both wrestling with their own thoughts. But now, sitting pressed up against him in the moonlight, cloaked in darkness, it was unnerving. There was an almost intimate quality to it, and she wished she could escape his potent touch, push him off the animal and gallop far, far away.

She always made sure she was never alone in male company. And she never got physically too close to men, even when they were just talking. She protected herself at all times. So this...this was her worst nightmare.

'What's the matter?' he asked, his deep voice tickling her ear.

She shook her head fiercely. 'Nothing.'

'Are you sure? You're like a little spider, playing dead.'

She squirmed at his comment. Rather a fly caught in a spider's web, she thought. Trapped between two large arms. 'If you must know, I don't like being touched. By anyone. Let alone a Saxon and a brute like you.'

She was annoyed with him—and with herself, for the conflicting feelings rushing through her. The touch of most men made her wither, as if reducing her to ashes, yet his touch set her ablaze, set her alight from the inside. It was disturbing, and she didn't know how to deal with these new and terrifying feelings apart from trying to banish them, block them out as if they didn't exist.

She felt him sigh. 'You're safe with me, Svea. Believe it or not, your boyish looks and fierce mannerisms aren't that tempting!'

'Good!' she raged.

But she felt him grin into her ear, and couldn't decide if he was teasing her or not. She always wanted to be seen as one of the men in Kald—it was what she strived for—and yet, ludicrously, she felt wounded by Ash's comment. Did he not find her attractive? And why did that bother her? It was a good thing, wasn't it?

She forced herself to focus on the dimly lit path ahead, telling herself she could do this. She could do anything to protect her people, even be in close proximity to a Saxon. A dangerously attractive Saxon. She tried to reassure herself that he would have attacked her already if he'd wanted to. He had not once been heavy-handed with her. Instead, he'd saved her life, had shown concern for her safety—had even attempted to patch up her injury. There was no reason to think he would harm her now. He had been careful with her so far. Besides, he didn't even think she was womanly.

She suddenly felt a pang of loss for her mother, and all she could have learnt from her if she'd still been alive. Talking about her earlier must have brought old emotions to the surface. She'd only had her father and brother for guidance, and although she knew she had been lucky to have such a strong bond with them, there were things her mother could have told her—about dressing like a lady, about men both good and bad and how they behaved. That might have been useful.

After everything that had happened that fateful day in Termarth she'd felt her mother's absence more than ever. She would have done anything to see her one more time, to have her cradle her close in a protective way, as Ash was doing now. And more than anything she wanted to know if her mother would have been proud of the woman she had become.

They moved through the stillness of the forest in a shroud of silence for a while, but it was too much— she felt the need to fill the quiet, rather than focus on Ash's warm breath on her cheeks, his arms around her waist.

'I don't like spiders anyway,' she said.

It was the first thing that came to her mind, and she winced at her ridiculous words. Why was she still talking about spiders?

'No?' That light edge to his voice was back. 'Don't tell me you're scared of them?'

'Not exactly. But anything that pretends to be something they're not… It's creepy.'

She felt Ash's hands tighten on the reins. It had been a minor reflex, but she'd noticed it all the same. She had the notion that her words had somehow offended him, which was absurd. He had thick skin— she doubted anything she said would bother him. But his body had definitely tensed.

All of a sudden he began to slow the horse. To her

surprise, once the animal had halted, Ash lowered himself down, picking up the reins and leading them through the bracken.

'What are you doing?'

Had she said something wrong? And why was she now missing his warmth? It was absurd.

'Giving you some space. That's what you want, is it not? Now we're a safe distance from the camp we can afford to slow our pace a little. I had the feeling our riding together was making you uncomfortable.'

She felt sure she heard him mutter the words *'and me, too'* under his breath.

'You're right,' he said. 'We should have taken two horses.'

She couldn't understand his conciliatory efforts. Ash wasn't acting like a typical Saxon male, who just took what he wanted where women were concerned. Despite the fact she'd just been getting used to sitting so close to him, to being in his arms, he seemed to be putting her thoughts and feelings before his own and it caught her off guard.

Had she got him all wrong? It made her feel guilty.

'Aren't you tired from walking all day?' she asked.

'I'm used to being on my feet. Don't worry about me… Unless you *want* me to get back up?' he said, looking up at her and flashing her a grin in the moonlight.

She shook her head vehemently. Of course she didn't!

'You don't need to hold the reins, you know. I'm perfectly capable of riding on my own,' she snapped.

'I know that. When are you going to stop think-ing I'm doing things to control you, Svea, rather than to protect you.'

She swallowed. She wasn't handling any of this very well.

'I'm sorry,' she said, feeling a swell of emotion ris-ing in her throat. 'I think everything is overwhelm-ing me. My brother has been gone one day and look what's happened. I've allowed his men to be taken hostage, and who knows what's happening back at Kald. On *my* watch. I've let him down.'

She knew she shouldn't be saying these things—not to Ash...it made her look weak. But she'd uttered the words before she could stop herself, exposing her vulnerability by revealing her worries and fears. It was something she very rarely did.

Maybe Ash was right. Maybe she *was* rash and foolish...perhaps she *did* have a temper and made poor judgments. It wasn't the first time her fiery na-ture had got her into hot water... She had always thought if she lashed out first, with words and actions, it was the best way of protecting herself, of prevent-ing herself from getting hurt.

She thought back to all the times men had made a passing remark about her, perhaps just trying to give her a compliment. She'd overreacted, often draw-ing her sword, and Brand had had to calm her down. There had been evenings when men had brought her a drink and she'd thought they were trying to get her drunk. She'd responded with fire and aggression. Her thoughts flew back to when she'd been out walking in the woods and had come across a man. She'd attacked him as a form of self-defence, only to discover he had been unaware she was even there.

Perhaps she was all the things Ash had said. She made a silent vow to herself now that if they were to survive this, she would try to change.

He halted the horse again and looked up at her, his dark eyes softening. 'You couldn't have done anything to prevent this, Svea. You fought well, and you're doing everything you can to get your men back.' He started walking again. 'If it's any consolation, I feel the same. I keep going over everything in my head. I shouldn't have let my men drink last night, for a start—not when we had a journey ahead—and I shouldn't have allowed you to come with us as our guide.'

She couldn't believe he was admitting that he felt he was to blame. Most men never did that, and she knew from being in his company for just one day that Ash wasn't one to show his emotions. But she liked it that he had. It took a strong man to admit when he was at fault, even if she didn't see that he actually was. He'd done everything he could to fight and protect his men.

'Some guide... I actually don't know where I am now.' She laughed bitterly. 'Do you?'

'Yes, fortunately I know this forest. There's a little grove up ahead. It's sheltered and hard to find, even more so in the dark. We can stop there and rest for the night. I doubt anyone would find us there. We should be safe.'

Svea tightened her grip on the reins and the horse faltered. 'You want us to spend the night out here?'

He glanced up at her again. 'What's the matter? Never slept rough before?'

'Many times—but never with a Saxon male. And I certainly won't be doing so tonight.'

Especially as her body was responding to him in ways it had never behaved before, sending her thoughts and feelings spiralling. She felt panicked. Confused.

'We should push on,' she said, realising her voice was slightly high-pitched. 'If we carry on now, surely we will make it to Braewood by morning?'

'To carry on in the dark when we're both exhausted and can barely see would be madness. Look, I have promised I won't touch you again, if that's what you're worried about, and I mean it. I'm not going to hurt you, Svea. Just…trust me.'

He was asking the impossible. He didn't know what had happened to her in the past, and she wasn't about to explain. But she didn't think she could ever trust a man—let alone a Saxon man. Not after what Lord Crowe had done. Never…

An owl's cry ripped through the otherwise silent night and Ash saw Svea give an involuntary shiver.

'You should try to get some rest now, Svea.'

They'd travelled the rest of the way to the grove in silence, her body stiff, the atmosphere tense, and when he'd tied the horse up to a tree, he had allowed her to lower herself down without offering his help.

Normally he would have provided his assistance, but she'd made it very clear he wasn't to touch her, so he'd stayed away. He wondered what had happened to make her shy away from touch. He had the strong desire to rectify it, to show her just how pleasurable it could be, but he knew she wouldn't let him. And he had told her she could trust him.

He'd been pleased when she'd opened up to him, even enjoyed her nervous babbling—until her unintentional words had hit their mark. For hadn't he been pretending to be something he wasn't his whole life? He'd tried to be a child his parents would want. He'd tried to behave the way the monks had wanted him to at the monastery, but it had never been good enough. Now in the service of the King, he had found satisfaction basking in the glow of his monarch's approval, but he knew he was still suppressing a part of him, lying to himself and others. Why did he want to hide that dark side of him so badly? Why did he care so much what people thought? He wished he could be more like Svea in that respect.

'I still don't see why this is necessary,' she pouted as she settled down beneath a large oak, her arms tightly crossed over her chest. It was hard to see anything in the darkness, but by the sound of her voice, she was most displeased with his idea to bed down here for the night.

'You'll feel better for a rest,' he said. 'And try not to worry about our friends. We'll get them back, Svea. I won't let you down.'

He was determined. He would save them, for his

own self-respect. For his King and his men. For the people. They were relying on him. But mainly, he knew he would see this through for her. She cared about her men and he knew she wouldn't be content until they'd rescued them, so neither would he.

'Tomorrow will be a better day.'

'How can you be so sure?'

'Well, it can't be any worse, can it?'

He passed her his cloak again to keep her warm.

'Don't you need it?' she asked, uncertain, reluctant to accept his gesture of kindness.

'I'm not cold. I'll be fine.'

'Are you going to get some rest?'

'Perhaps. I just want to make sure we weren't followed, so I'll keep guard for a little while.'

She fussed around a bit, trying to get comfortable, but for someone who had protested they shouldn't stop, and was worried about being alone with him, she fell asleep pretty quick. Ash smiled. He knew the moment she'd given up fighting her exhaustion, as her breathing changed. It became deeper and steadier. He knew he mustn't touch her—he'd promised, and he wasn't going to go back on his word, but after scouting the grove a final time, he came down as close as he felt appropriate to her, hoping his proximity would keep them both warm. The ground was cold but with the first layer of fallen leaves of the season covering the earth, it wasn't too hard.

Tomorrow, they'd be back at his father's fortress and Svea would have a nice warm bed to sleep in. It would be harvest time in Braewood now. The men would be in the fields, threshing and ploughing, and the women would be grinding the grains. Yet despite it being his home, the image of Braewood didn't exactly conjure up many memories of comfort or happiness. He'd wanted to stay as a boy, but he'd been sent away. Now as a man, it was hard to feel a connection to the place. He wondered how the people would feel if he did become ruler there, after his father passed. Would they still whisper and cower away from him, as they had when he was a child? Or would he now be able to command their respect? Did he even want to, or would he feel like an imposter, walking the hallways?

He wondered how his father would react to him bringing a Dane through his door. Not well at all, he thought. In fact, he couldn't imagine either he or Svea receiving a warm welcome. His people had hated her kind for years, and they had good reason, but he was starting to see that not all Danes were the same. It gave him hope. He was starting to see her for who she really was—someone who was willing to help others before herself, someone strong yet kind. Could it be possible that one day his people could see her like that, too?

And she was breathtakingly beautiful. He knew his feelings towards her, as a Saxon lord, went against everything his people deemed acceptable. He was expected to marry a respectable Saxon lady. If anyone were to find out he was attracted to a Danish woman, it would not go down well. To many, she was seen as a heathen. And he had to conform, do what was expected of him, as he always had done. But he couldn't deny that he was starting to like her. A lot.

Svea rolled over in her sleep towards him, as if trying to get more comfortable, and he could just make out her face in the darkness. With her high cheekbones and full, lush lips, he had never seen a more stunning woman, despite what he'd told her earlier about her boyish ways. He wasn't sure if he'd said that to reassure her or to protect himself. But who was he kidding? He wanted nothing more than to draw her into his arms and feel her soft curves pressing against him. But he couldn't. He mustn't. She was still being aloof, refusing to warm to him even though he had saved her life.

He turned on his side to face her. He was weary from their day, but still he felt the stirrings of desire in his groin. It had been torture holding her perfect body so close in the forest, having her lash out and thrash against him, and then having her sat between his thighs on the horse, wrapped up together in the darkness, her intoxicating rose petal scent tickling his nose, and it had only made things worse—his body had reacted with force. He had never had such a strong reaction to someone before, which was another reason why he'd got down.

But it wasn't just her body he was enjoying getting to know. He was finding he liked talking to her. He wanted to hear about her past, her opinions, her gentle, lilting voice washing over him. And he wanted to share his views and opinions with her, too. That was new to him—usually he didn't reveal anything of himself to anyone.

No one had ever cared to listen about how he felt about things when he'd been growing up. No one had even wanted to talk to him, or share his company. He had often sought solace in the stables in Braewood, making friends with the animals, and then at the monastery, he made it his role to look after the horses they used for transport. It was only when his actions on the battlefield had begun to get him noticed that men had started to ask for his advice and had wanted to be around him and seen at his side. Now the men were keen to serve him and the King requested his frank assessment of situations often, and it was easy to give a point of view on something impartial. He wondered if they would still respect him if they knew the truth about him. He doubted it. But when it came to expressing his own feelings, his hopes and desires… No. It was just something he didn't do. Yet with Svea…there was something about her that made him let down his guard, just a little. Ash wondered if there was a part of him, the unknown part, the part he usually crushed and tried to deny, that was making him attracted to this woman, as if like was being drawn to like?

Svea suddenly threw an arm out in her sleep, her hand coming to land on the side of his chest—and he stilled. If ever he had wanted to test his true character, this was it. His greatest temptation had been put in front of him, just a whisper away, so close he could smell the floral scent of her hair…but he wasn't allowed to go near her. Talk about torture. Yet he was determined he wouldn't be the person his mother and father had always dreaded and feared he would grow up to be. They imagined him as a monster, and yet, he only cared about Svea's safety. That was the reason she was here with him now, as he believed she would be safer under his protection than back home at Kald.

Damn. Why did he think stopping to rest was a good idea? He should have listened to her. Instead, he was being punished. Her fingers curled ever so slightly into his body, and he groaned, throwing an arm over his forehead. Here he was, sleeping out in the woods, knowing a battle almost certainly lay ahead to rescue his King and his men, and yet all he could think about was this woman at his side. He stretched out his weary body and closed his eyes. He had the feeling this was going to be a very long night indeed.

Chapter Three

When Svea woke, and she realised she was staring into the extraordinary face of Ashford Stanton, her fingers resting against his solid chest—she gasped. Instinct had her snatching back her arm in horror. She had warned him not to come near her, had made it very clear she was not to be touched, and here she was, draped all over him! She was appalled. Thank goodness he was still asleep and would never know.

Sitting up, being careful not to wake him, she raked her hand over her tousled hair and her sleepy face, glad to see the grove now bathed in early-morning sunlight. It was a pretty, tranquil place, and Ash had been right—if anyone had been following them it would have been hard to find them here. He had done well to discover it in the dark.

She stared down at her companion, watching the steady rise and fall of his broad chest, and took the opportunity to openly study his handsome, now familiar face. The harsh angles of his brow and jaw were softened by slumber, and his usually neat tied-back hair had come undone and was loose around his shoulders. She smiled. One day in her company and she had managed to mess him up a bit.

He'd made the right call to stop—she felt much better for the rest. Although she couldn't believe she'd managed to fall asleep, considering the company she was in. It boosted her belief in her ability to heal from the past. It was as if she'd known deep down she could trust him. And he'd been true to his word. He hadn't touched her. She was so incredibly grateful, her heart went out to him.

She took in his scars, some faint, some deeper, and wondered how he'd got each one. What pain had he suffered and what battles had he endured? He didn't share much about himself, only thoughts and opinions on others and the world around them, and she wondered what emotional scars he carried. She knew from experience that they always ran deeper than the physical ones.

Debating whether or not to wake him, so they could be on their way, she realised there was a disturbing part of her that wanted to lie down again next to him, to seek out his warmth and see if he would pull her close…run his fingers through her hair as he had done yesterday.

And what would happen if he did? Heat bloomed low beneath her belly again and she bit her lip. Her thoughts scared her—she had never wanted a man to touch her before. Ever. Not after what had happened in Termarth.

'Enjoying the view?' Ash said lazily, suddenly opening his eyes.

Svea started at his low, deep voice, mortified that she'd been caught staring. 'No!' she spat, turning away and feigning disgust, her cheeks heating. 'You had an insect crawling on your face and I was thinking about swatting it. Hard. That's all.'

He grinned. 'I'm glad you didn't. Did you sleep well?' he asked, sitting up and immediately pulling his hair back into its band. She'd noticed he seemed to be a bit of a perfectionist when it came to his appearance, keen to look neat and tidy. Part of her wished he'd left his hair down...she rather liked the relaxed Ash.

'Not really.'

She didn't know why his smile grew wider. 'Well, tonight you can look forward to a more comfortable bed at Braewood.'

For some reason that thought didn't put her at ease at all. She was so far out of her familiar territory already. Usually it was she and Brand who would host guests, in their humble surroundings at Kald. She prided herself on preparing good food and creating a welcoming environment for the villagers and any travellers in the longhouse. She liked looking after people. She had learnt that from her mother when she was little. She would always help her prepare food for the evening meal. And cooking a feast and looking after guests was a way of keeping her memory alive.

But Svea had never been a guest at someone else's home, let alone a Saxon's fortress. She wasn't sure what to expect, or how she should behave, and she felt a knot tighten in her stomach.

They exited the forest and traversed over rolling

multicoloured landscapes, Svea riding the horse and Ash keeping pace alongside her on foot. She was glad he was more talkative this morning. When he was un-forthcoming, as if he was holding something back, it made her feel on edge. But today he was asking her questions about Kald and her family, as if trying to better understand her, to work her out, and when she answered he seemed to lean in and listen intently.

It helped the journey to pass more quickly. And it was a distraction from her rumbling stomach. They'd had berries for supper, and more berries and nuts for breakfast—she was craving some decent food.

She told him of her days spent training the men and women of Kald to fight, and how she enjoyed catching fish and going hunting. And she revealed that, although she enjoyed being creative, she was terrible at needlework—once again letting him know that she didn't conform—but that she wasn't bad at cooking and holding the fort.

It helped to distract her from thinking about him and his athletic body, managing to keep pace with the speed of the horse, and the image of his wicked grin that morning when he'd caught her staring at him. She was desperately trying to cling on to her anger against him. It was easier than admitting she might actually be starting to like him.

The thought scared her. She had never *liked* a man before and it was unnerving. Frightening. Why did it have to be a Saxon? Why did it have to be this man?

Ash had pointed out the borders of Braewood, and they stopped at a couple of streams to let the horse quench his thirst, and then at a few high points which offered teasing glimpses of the sea in the distance. She knew she should be pleased they were nearing their destination, but upon seeing the various landmarks, and hearing Ash talk about his home, her nerves only increased. She was, however, delighted to learn that the fortress was located on the coast. The ocean had always helped to calm her.

The first thing she'd done when she'd been well enough, after she'd been attacked in Termarth as a girl, was go into the sea to wash away the dirt and the shame. She had stayed in there so long, trying to get clean, trying to wash off the stain those men had left on her body, that she hadn't cared about the cold.

Brand had come looking for her, and had finally had to drag her out. He'd wrapped her in furs and sat her by the fire, fussing around her. But she'd done the same again the next day, and a swim in the sea had become her daily source of comfort since. It helped her to feel clean, almost pure again, during the time she was in there, and she also felt closer to her mother, knowing that somewhere she lay deep beneath the surface.

She would need to seek the ocean's strength in Braewood as she wasn't sure how she would be received there. Ash himself had admitted that his people didn't get along with Danes.

'I promise you will be safe and under my protection, Svea,' he said, as if he could sense her apprehension.

Suddenly a thundering noise sent vibrations across

the field and had them both snapping their heads round. Svea gasped at the chilling sight of a group of heavily armed men on horses rising over the crest of the next hill and hastening down the valley like a swarm of giant ants. They were heading straight for them, and she and Ash were out in the open. There was nowhere to hide.

Before she knew what was happening Ash was pulling her down from the horse, his large body backing her against the animal's side.

'We don't have much time.' He gripped the gilt circlet around her upper arm and dragged it down to her hand.

'What the—?'

With some force, he crushed it, moulding it into a shackle-like band around both her wrists. 'They're Saxon soldiers. I can tell by their armour. And, given the direction they're travelling in, carrying spears and at such a speed, they can only have one possible reason to be out here. One destination in mind. They must be joining Crowe's men against the King.'

No. The realisation that the Saxons would be surrounding them within moments, and knowing what most Saxon men were capable of, made her heart lurch. This couldn't be happening. Not after how far they'd come. Not now they were so close to Ash's home and to getting help.

She shook her head, her mind wanting to deny it. But looking at Ash's grave face made her realise how dire a situation they were in. Just how many more times could she find herself in situations like this? It was why she had worked so hard to be one of the best on the battlefield. But, despite her show of strength, it was as if the gods were taunting her, forcing her to relive her attack through memories over and over again. She knew the past few days had heightened her emotions, but she wasn't sure how many more times she could pretend to be all right about it.

'Can't you tell them who you are? That you're a Saxon, too?'

'It's not me I'm worried about! By the colour of your hair, your eyes—hell, even the markings on your skin—they'll know you're a Dane,' he said, sounding almost annoyed with her, his hand coming up to curl over her braids and pull them down over her neck to cover up the dark swirls. 'It will be better for you to be seen as my property, not my ally,' he said, nodding to the makeshift bonds to explain why he'd created them. 'Give me your sword.'

Her hand gripped the hilt firmly. 'No!' It was her mother's sword and her only protection. She prided herself on being able to defend herself or die trying...

'I'm your protection now,' he ground out. 'Please believe I'm doing this for your own good. I don't want to frighten you, Svea, but now is not the time to argue.'

She scowled, gripping the sword even tighter. By the deafening sound of the horses' hooves, and the feel of the ground rumbling beneath her feet, she knew their enemy was almost upon them.

'Svea,' he pressed, leaning in close. 'You're an incredibly beautiful woman and those men... Most of them would probably love to get their hands on you. I don't want that to happen, do you?'

It was as if he was iterating her deepest, darkest fears. A shiver ran down her spine as his words hit their mark. She tried hard to make sure she wasn't attractive to men, had thought it was working, even on him... Yet he was saying he thought she was beautiful? No man had ever dared tell her that before—for fear she might pummel them. But Ash...

His warm hand covered hers, coaxing her fingers to release the weapon. 'Now give me your blade.'

The sword slipped deftly from her fingers into his.

'Put this on,' he said, handing her his cloak. 'Keep it wrapped around you. Keep yourself covered up. Don't draw any attention to yourself.'

Suddenly voiceless, and defenceless, she let him drape the woollen garment around her shoulders. If he was worried, she knew she should be. And she felt as if this time she had even more to lose.

Ash tugged her to the back of him and they stepped away from the shelter of the horse just as the large group of riders bore down on them. 'Stay behind me. Keep your head down. And don't say a word,' he whispered.

The armed men reined in their horses and came to a stop in front of them, surrounding them. Ice-cold dread flowed through her. She had been surrounded like this before...

'Good day to you.'

A man with a menacing appearance cantered forward, he and his horse heaving from the exertion of their ride. He removed his crested helmet and smoothed down his greasy hair. He reminded her of a peacock. He had a mean, conceited face and his eyes raked over their attire, assessing Ash's Saxon armour and no doubt realising he must be a man of status if he could afford a slave.

'And to you.'

She noticed Ash was careful not to place his hand on the hilt of his sword, not wanting to incite any conflict. He just stood proud, assured. But with the point of view of someone who was beginning to know his behaviour, from spending so much time in his company, she saw the tension visible in his neck and in the rigidity of his stance.

The leader turned his eye to his spear, which he was twirling in his hand, as if the long, sharp weapon somehow proved his manhood. Svea resisted rolling her eyes. She wished she could snatch her sword back from Ash.

'We're looking for a Saxon camp in Alderbury Forest. Have you passed through that way?'

Ash nodded. 'Aye, we saw it. You're heading in the right direction. If you keep going, you'll be sure to come across it.'

The man's eyes narrowed on them. 'Then you must have heard. Calhourn soldiers are rallying men to march on Termarth. The people have had enough of our King making friends with the Danes. Won't you be joining us?'

Svea was suddenly very relieved Ash had had the foresight to discard the tabard that marked his allegiance to the King. She realised he wasn't like most men who rushed in, using brute force. He preferred to use his mind. He had been right when he'd suggested she could learn a thing or two from him.

Ash inclined his head casually. 'I may well be. But I have a situation of my own to sort out first.' His voice was unwavering, as if he was in total control. And his response had been non-committal. She knew he was trying to calm the situation before it escalated. But how did he do it? How did he hide his anger so well? She had struggled with that for years, taking her resentment out on all men—especially those she encountered on the battlefield. His acting made her wonder what else he kept hidden behind that austere appearance. How had he become so adept at hiding his emotions? And why?

'Saxon lords have been promised more land, gold and spoils from the fight, if that helps to sway you. But it seems you have already found spoils of your own.' The man smirked, trying to peer around Ash.

Svea felt sick as the man's blatant beady-eyed stare scraped over her. She felt the slow creep of dread sweeping across her skin and saw Ash's fingers bunch into fists at his sides, while a muscle flickered in his jaw.

'We have orders to kill those who oppose our cause. If you're not with us, you're against us... Of course I'd be happy to keep quiet, but my silence is going to come at a cost.'

She felt Ash take a deep, steadying breath. 'I'm not

a bargaining man. But even if I were, I have no silver to pay you. And, as you can see, I'm travelling light.'

'From where I'm standing, it looks like you have all the riches in the world. Especially to me and my men, who have been riding for two days. We could do with some entertainment. Tell you what—just hand over that pretty slave girl of yours, soldier, and we'll allow you to be on your way.'

Svea swallowed. Normally she would have reached for her sword, lashed out by now. But she was beginning to realise she didn't just have herself to think about. If she started a fight she would need Ash's help to finish it. They really were in this together. And Ash had taken her weapon, so she had no choice but to do as she'd been told.

Ash reached for her, his hand clenching roughly around the metal bond he'd created. She gasped.

'What? This thing?' He lifted her wrist as if to show she was his property. 'She belongs to me. She's a good worker—and unfortunately, my lords, she's not for sale.'

The man's lips curled into a sneer. 'Everything has a price. And she's just a heathen, only good for one thing. She's certainly not worth losing your head over.'

Svea staggered forward, livid. 'Give me a sword and I'll dismember you both…' she said scathingly, unable to help herself. So much for trying to change.

'Quiet!' both Ash and the brute barked in unison.

'The girl is mine,' Ash said. 'If you want her, you'll

have to fight me for her. You and me…a weapon each. Is she worth losing *your* head over?'

Svea's stomach rolled. Why did it always come to this? Was it something she did, or just the way she looked, that drew these men to her?

'The victor gets the girl and may carry on his journey.'

No! Svea thought. This was her worst nightmare come true. The stakes were too high. If Ash should lose, then she would lose everything. Herself. Her sanity. *Him*…

The man grinned. 'You're on.'

His warriors cheered, suddenly coming to life, as if they'd been starved of amusement on their travels. She didn't understand how anyone could enjoy watching two men battle to the death. But they obviously thought their leader had a fighting chance.

Even as her mind whirred, trying to think of a way out of this, it was already happening. All around her the horsemen began widening a square, setting the course on which her fate was to be played out as she stood there dazed, despairing, immobilised by her fear of what was to come. How had she somehow, once again, become the property of men? A possession they thought they could own, negotiate over, and do what they liked with…?

The peacock got down from his horse and shook off his cloak. Ash removed his sword from its scabbard, rotating his shoulders, moving his muscles in readiness to fight.

'Ash…' she whispered. 'Please don't do this. Perhaps…perhaps you should hand me over,' she said, her mouth dry.

It was her absolute worst fear, but she would sacrifice herself to save her men if she had to. And she knew she needed Ash alive to do that.

He looked at her as if she had gone mad. He took a step towards her and stroked a finger down her cheek. 'Never.'

She swallowed. 'You need to get home, raise the *fyrd*. Think of the King. You said so yourself—we're his only hope. If something should happen to you…'

His dark face rarely gave anything away. And yet by the crease in his heavy brow she could tell that he was angry—with her, for suggesting he give her up, and with these men.

'Then I will have died fighting for a worthy cause,' he said, his eyes levelling with hers. 'And I will meet my death with honour, should it come to that. But, Svea, if something happens to me I want you to run. Run fast into those trees over there. Find somewhere to hide. Just don't look back,' he whispered. 'Promise me you will do that?'

She nodded, numb, tears threatening. She hardly ever cried—and especially not in front of men. She didn't know what the matter was with her. She just knew she needed him to win. To stay alive.

When Ash turned around the man was ready for him, and immediately—unfairly—struck the first blow. His blade sliced through Ash's chin, and Svea gasped in shock at seeing his blood. Another scar to add to his many others…

'Brace yourself,' the peacock sneered at her. 'It won't be long till you have a new master.'

Svea pulled back in disgust, wrapping her arms around herself. She felt sick to her stomach. How had it come to this? Just yesterday morning she'd been waving her brother off on his honeymoon, ready to run things in Kald for a while, looking forward to a time of peace. And she'd been delighted to be sending the Saxons home, pleased that she'd never have to see Lord Stanton again.

But now her world had been turned upside down. The Saxons were at war between themselves, as well as with the Danes, the King had been captured, and the very man she had thought she despised was now fighting for her life.

She placed her hand against the horse, offering the animal reassurance while seeking its warmth and comfort for herself.

The man's jibe spurred Ash into action, and he circled his opponent. When he finally used his sword his movements were fluid, fast, and he instinctively warded off the jabs coming at him from every direction. The peacock fought in a nasty way, raining down frantic, dirty blows on Ash, and Svea winced with every clash of metal.

But it was as if Ash had been training for this his entire life. It soon became clear that the stranger was no match for her champion. Brutal and brave, Ash fought without fear of death, reminding her of her fellow Northmen. And when his hair came free of its bond he began to look like one, too. She had never seen such a skilled warrior. In any other fight he would have been spectacular to watch, but as her destiny was entwined with every slice of that sword, this one was unbearable. She almost turned her face into the horse's flank, but knew she must see every moment of this fight.

The slashings and stabbings became quicker and more ferocious, and when the peacock's blade sliced through Ash's waist Svea gasped. But incredibly Ash carried on, as if he hadn't felt a thing, bearing down on the stranger. Svea and the men on horseback watched in awe. She could tell both men were tiring now, under their heavy chainmail and weapons, but Ash seemed to be drawing on a last reserve of strength, and with one final, brutal blow he knocked the weapon out of his opponent's hand and the man fell, scurrying backwards, his face forlorn.

Reining in their agitated horses, the Saxon riders looked on in mute horror as their leader surely faced imminent death. Svea's heart lifted just a little. After the words he'd threatened her with, she wouldn't be sorry.

In a desperate last-ditch attempt to regain his blade, the peacock crawled along the ground—but Ash was swift, conclusive. He pinned the man to the floor, his boot on his chest and the tip of his sword to the brute's chin.

'Who *are* you?' the peacock asked.

'I am Lord Stanton of Braewood.'

A hushed gasp rippled around the group. The man gulped against the sharp blade. 'Lord Stanton... I did not know it was you.'

Svea studied Ash. She knew of his reputation, but she hadn't realised he instilled such fear and reverence in total strangers.

'Perhaps you should ask who you're speaking to before threatening a man in future. And you are?'

'We are riders from Rainhill, my lord. I am Ealderman Elrick… We are *allies* of Braewood, my lord. Of your father.'

Ash's scowl deepened. 'Any allies of Braewood should know better than to behave this way against a fellow Saxon. Against a fellow man and a woman, no matter what their kind.'

Svea's heart began to pound a little faster. It was in that moment she realised her brother had been right, Ash was a good man.

'But she's just a pagan, my lord.'

Ash edged his sword a little further into the man's skin, and he winced.

'All people deserve to be treated with respect. Do you understand me?'

'Yes, my lord.'

'Now, all of you leave us—before I do something I regret.'

Ash sheathed his sword and released the man from underneath his boot. The peacock rolled away, scuttling to stand and race for his horse.

As soon as the men began to move off the hillside Ash tried to compose himself. He took a few deep breaths, which helped his anger at those men to subside. How was it that so many men thought they could do what they liked, take what they wanted, without suffering the consequences?

He knew many Saxon men who thought they could do what they desired to Danish women. They saw it as their right, and it disgusted him. Especially now he was beginning to respect and admire Svea for all that she was.

He had fought bloody and hard, and his muscles were weary—but he'd do it all again if he had to.

'Are you all right?' he asked, turning to Svea while wiping his brow with the back of his hand.

When he'd seen those men approach, all he'd thought about was keeping her safe. And when Elrick had leered at her he'd seen a look of pure dread pass across her features. He'd hated to see her so vulnerable, and again he had scolded himself for his foolishness for letting her leave Kald in the first place. When the man had said he would be her new master, he'd wanted to run him through. The thought of any man laying his hands on her was too much to bear.

'Me? Yes.' She nodded, her lip trembling. 'You?'

He pressed a hand to his chin. 'I'll mend.'

But as he crossed the distance between them his lower abdomen burned with pain and he winced. He hadn't noticed it before...

'You're hurt. Is it bad? Let me see.'

'It's nothing. I've had worse.'

'Let me look. Sit down. Over there,' she said, motioning to a low part in the field wall.

He shook off his heavy chainmail to reveal a dark stain spreading across his tunic, and cursed. Svea knelt down before him as he cautiously peeled off the material, lifting it away to reveal a gash to his stomach, above his right hip. He sucked in a breath at the pain.

She gave his wound a quick glance, but he noticed she avoided staring at his bare torso for long. She was either squeamish or had never seen a man's body before. Her cheeks reddening, she averted her gaze, and he thought it must be the latter.

She began to root around looking for something. But he knew all he could do now was wait till they reached Braewood before trying to patch it up.

'What are you doing? Looking for more berries?' he asked, trying to make out that his wound wasn't important.

'Oh, please, no more berries,' she groaned. 'No, I'm looking for some meadow wort.'

'What's that?'

'A plant. I will try to clean the wound, but it will help with the pain.'

'I can cope with the pain,' he said, bemused.

Still, she rummaged about in the undergrowth for a second, and then her face brightened. 'Aha—here!' She crushed some green leaves between her fingers and added them to her water satchel before handing it to him. 'Drink.'

'How do I know you're not trying to poison me?' He grinned, taking a sip. 'I think you might like to.'

She tutted. 'Why do you say that?'

'You did say something about dismembering me...'

She smiled guiltily.

'And I think you still resent me for stopping you from taking revenge on Lord Crowe.'

'That doesn't mean I want you dead.'

'Thank goodness. I don't think I'd stand a chance against that sword of yours. Which reminds me— here,' he said. And he pulled her blade from his scabbard, handing it back to her.

Her face relaxed and she smiled in pure relief. He smiled back as they locked eyes with each other for a moment.

'This is my mother's sword.'

'It's very beautiful.' He didn't break eye contact.

'I could have taken him myself, you know.'

'I know.' He shrugged.

She poured some of the water onto a corner of his cloak. Then she lifted his tunic again and tentatively began to wipe the blood away from his wound with the damp material. There was a slight tremble in her fingers. He blanched.

'This might sting for a moment,' she said, biting her lip. 'Sorry.'

She dabbed gently at the wound, doing the best she could. He leaned back a little, to give her better access. She was so close he could smell rose petals again.

'You know, you could have just handed me over to save your own skin…to protect the King. Why didn't you?'

'Perhaps for the same reason I saved you on the battlefield instead of the King. Instinct.'

She sat back on her knees, halting in what she was doing. 'I thought that was merely circumstance.'

He shrugged, holding her gaze. And then, his eyes falling to the crushed *kransen*, he reached out and caught her wrists. He prised the crumpled metal from her skin, and feeling brave, perhaps because he'd just saved her life for the second time, continued to hold her for a moment, tracing his fingers over the marks where it had been. He hoped she wouldn't stop him.

'I thought it might be hindering you or hurting you,' he said. 'I'm sorry. For damaging it.'

He knew Dane women wore these metal bands as a symbol of their virginity, among other things, and that if she were ever to marry it would be replaced with a crown on her wedding day. He felt bad for ruining it.

'It doesn't matter. It wasn't precious to me,' she said, her voice almost a whisper. 'Thank you, Ash. For saving me from those men.'

'Anyone would have done the same.'

'I don't think so… And I thought you didn't believe in taking the law into your own hands?' She smiled, repeating the words he'd said to her a few days before, at the wedding feast.

He released her and she leaned forward again, having another try at cleaning his wound. He drew in a breath at the sharp discomfort.

'What was that reaction about, anyway? The way those men all backed away when you gave them your name?'

'You sensed that, too? I'm not sure. But I have a feeling that when we get to Braewood we will find out.'

What had his father been up to? he wondered.

And just how much trouble could he cause from his sickbed?

'The way you fight… You remind me of a Dane. How is it that you are not afraid of anything?'

He studied her. Was that what she thought? If only she knew the truth. That deep down he was afraid of who he was, and of what other people would think of him if they discovered the truth. It was something that had haunted him his entire life—the thought of the damage his secret could do to his honour if word got out. He feared that he was monstrous—although every moment he spent with Svea helped to confirm to him that not all Danes were like that. It was good for him. *She* was good for him.

'Actually, I am,' he said. 'I'm afraid of the rain.'

'The rain?' she asked.

'Yes,' he said, shaking his still-loose hair. 'Because it makes my hair curl.' He gave a mock shudder.

She stared at him, incredulous. And then she let out a laugh—and it was the most delightful sound he'd ever heard.

'I can't believe that you, of all people, are making a joke at a time like this.'

'Me "of all people"?' he asked, his eyebrow raised quizzically.

She shrugged. 'I confess I thought you were boring. Haughty. I did not know you had a sense of humour.'

'I hide it well.' *As with other things*, he thought. 'Now *your* hair… It's blonder than when I saw you last. Almost silver,' he said, reaching out to take a strand and curl it around his fingers.

Amazingly, she let him. 'It's the lye soap,' she said, her voice husky.

'Does it work on men's hair, too? I was thinking of trying out a new look.'

She giggled again. 'I'd love to see that.'

He smoothed her hair over her shoulder, feeling braver now, brushing his fingers over the sensitive skin of her neck to reveal the dark, twisting design on her collarbone. Her skin was warm to the touch and incredibly soft.

'What is this?' he asked, taking in the design of what looked to be a huge ash tree, complete with swirling roots and a mass of branches rising up her neck. He envied their ascent into her hair. He'd been wanting to take a closer look at the design for days, weeks…

'It's *yggdrasil*, the Norse tree of life—it has many meanings, but I chose it to represent a sign of growth. It's also one of the only trees that can take blows without splintering.'

'I like it.'

'I did it myself. It started out as a…a healing exercise… And then I began to enjoy the creative process. Afterwards, others started to ask me to do designs for them—things that said something about their beliefs or their personalities.'

He nodded. His fingers dropped to her arm and he took her slim wrist in his hand once more, turning it upwards. He knew he was pushing his luck—

that she might tense and cast him off at any moment. Skating his fingers gently up and under her sleeve, he pushed it backwards, making her shiver under his touch, and he revealed more dark swirling patterns on her skin there.

'And this one? What does it say?'

'This is the Helm of Awe. It offers protection against the abuse of power. It also helps to curb my fear.'

His smile slipped. 'Did someone hurt you, Svea?' He continued to hold her.

'A long time ago, yes. I had a bad experience.'

His thumb smoothed over her delicate skin. 'What kind of bad experience?'

She looked up into his eyes. 'The worst kind.'

His heart crumbled for her. His stomach churned.

With his other hand he reached out to touch her cheek lightly, reverently. 'Was it Crowe?'

'Yes.'

He cursed under his breath, felt a sudden spurt of rage shafting through his body. 'You're right. I should have let you kill him when you had the chance.'

For an instant she looked shocked that he was conceding she'd been right, and then suddenly she came up on her knees and kissed him. It was a soft, gentle kiss on the cheek, and so spontaneous it took them both by surprise. It was as if she was thanking him for finally agreeing with her. For being on her side. For understanding.

And then, just as quickly as she'd done it, she bowed her head, flustered, as if she was as disturbed and confused about their newfound friendship as he was, and rose to her feet.

He took a moment to collect himself before tugging down his tunic. Perhaps she had kissed him to banish dark thoughts about her past. He realised he would love to kiss her back, to show her not all men behaved like that, and how his touch could be pleasurable.

A huge drop of rain spattered against her hair, his arm, and he grinned. 'Great,' he said, trying to lighten the mood. 'Curls it is.'

She smiled in response. 'Is it any better?' she asked, nodding to his wound.

'Totally cured.'

Chapter Four

They'd been passing teasing glimpses of the sea through the trees for a while when finally, underneath a large grey storm cloud, the three blackened turrets of Braewood Keep came into view. Ash grimaced. He had always thought the building said a lot about who he was. It served as a stark reminder of an attack that had left its mark on the fortified tower, never to be forgotten. He saw the flawed keep as a reflection of himself...commanding, one of the country's greatest strongholds, yet scarred, damaged by the past. And no one had ever cared enough to restore it to its original condition.

Svea had insisted on him riding, due to his injuries, but he had refused, until finally she had agreed to share the horse with him to speed up their journey. And this time she hadn't held herself so stiffly away from him, but had allowed him to pull her back into his chest, letting him hold her. And strangely, despite the pouring rain and their sodden clothes, now they were so close to reaching their destination, he didn't want to be there. The moment they went through the gates they'd no longer be alone. This might be the last time he'd ever take her in his arms, and he was reluctant to let her go.

He didn't know the brutal details, but now he knew that Crowe had hurt her he felt sickened. It explained a lot about the way she behaved, the way she put up such a tough front, but it only made him want to protect her, look after her, even more. The tender kiss she'd given him earlier had taken him aback—but it had also given him hope. Perhaps she didn't think of him as such a brute any more... He didn't know how that could be the case—he surely looked more dishevelled, bruised and intimidating than ever.

He wasn't sure the people of Braewood would even recognise him. He usually tried to look immaculate, to fit in, to suppress any notion that people might have that he was anything other than a Saxon lord. But his previously pristine chainmail was dirty and ragged from the journey, from fighting, and his shoulder-length hair was hanging loose. Even his beard was longer than usual, but it felt strangely liberating.

Yet he knew his father wouldn't approve. He looked more like a Dane than he ever had.

Aethelbard Stanton had built the settlement of Braewood inside the walls of a Roman town and it had grown over the years. But Ash's father had focused his attention on the high fortifications that wrapped around the fort. It had been a lifelong project, almost an obsession for him, to construct an impenetrable imposing wall, in case the Northmen should ever return.

As they drew closer Ash noticed a commotion going on outside the main gate. There seemed to be people strewn about, sitting in little self-made shelters erected against the stone walls, shivering in the rain, trying to keep feeble fires going.

'What is this now?' he muttered.

Suddenly he felt weary. They'd had a long trip across the countryside and the rain hadn't ceased all morning. They were soaked through and cold, and he wanted to get Svea in front of a fire with a hot meal as soon as possible.

He slowed the horse as they approached the throng of people, and resisted putting his hand to the hilt of his sword.

'Lord Stanton,' the gatekeeper said, recognising him and rushing forward. 'Welcome home.'

'What's going on here?'

'They're Danes, my lord. All of them. Every day more of them arrive, seeking shelter after their settlements have been attacked.'

He felt Svea tense at the man's words.

'They say they only wish to help tend our lands in return for shelter and food, but your father refuses to let them in, my lord. Yet still they will not leave, saying they have nowhere to go. Some are sick or wounded—and many have young children. But Braewood soldiers have been forbidden from helping them.'

Ash nodded, and took a moment to assess the situation, scanning the faces of the men and women huddled together. Some were elderly, some were mothers tending to their babies. One thing was abundantly clear—they couldn't stay out here. His father was so bloody stubborn. How could he turn them away?

These people were just like Svea and her clan. It was plain to see they were not a threat—they had just come here in search of a better life and hadn't yet found it. But he had the means to change that, despite having to go against his father's orders.

He turned the horse so he could address the crowd. 'Friends, I am Lord Stanton of Braewood, and you are most welcome here.'

The Danes, cold and fatigued, looked up at him with desperate hope shimmering in their eyes. But it was Svea's release of breath against his arm that was his true reward. He wanted to please her.

'You will all be given food and shelter. I only ask that you leave your weapons at the door.' He turned back to the gatekeeper. 'Now, open the gate and get these people inside.'

They all stepped back as the large wooden fortress gates opened. Ash and Svea passed through first, coming to a halt in the square, and he jumped down, holding his hand out to Svea to help her descend. For once, she accepted, and when she reached solid ground he lingered, holding her gaze and her hand a moment longer than necessary.

Forcing his attention to the scene going on behind him, he turned to some of Braewood's men. 'Open those grain stores. And this one.'

And as the settlers began to tentatively stumble through the gates, hesitantly handing over their blades or arrows, he spoke to them once more.

'You have my word that you will be safe here, under my protection. And we shall find work for you on the land if you wish to earn your keep. I shall send food and water imminently.'

Ash was furious with his father. He had always been willing to give up his lands, his position here, thinking it the best for his people, but he was starting to wonder if that was the case. Looking around him, he wondered if his father and his outdated thinking was doing more damage than good. And the thought of having another sparring match with the man made Ash feel jaded.

He wondered what Svea was making of all this. It wasn't exactly a good first impression.

The thought surprised him. Did he want her to like it here?

Murmurs of appreciation and thanks rumbled through the people as he and Svea helped them move their few belongings. Ash picked up a small child who was crying and carried the boy inside the safety of the fortress walls, while Svea tended to the wounds of those who had been injured. Once a fire had been lit the people seemed in better spirits, and Ash saw an opportunity to pull Svea to one side, tugging her arm to follow him.

'You did well out here. Thank you,' he said. He tipped his head in the direction of the hall. 'Come on. I'll show you around…get you settled in.'

She stiffened, shaking her head. He saw the trepidation in her eyes and he understood it—especially after hearing what a welcome the other Danes had received from his father. He wanted to reassure her, tell her he knew all too well what it felt like to be an outsider here. He'd suffered prejudice for being different his entire life. And he vowed to never make her feel like that.

'That's not necessary,' she said. 'I can stay out here, with the other Danes. It looks perfectly comfortable...'

Once again the thought struck him that she wasn't like other women—the ones in his King's court, or the ladies his father wanted him to marry. Svea didn't care for riches. She didn't even care for her own safety or comfort compared to that of others.

But there was no way he was letting her stay out here. He wanted her with him, or as close to him as she'd allow. To hell with his reputation.

'Svea, you're my guest here.' He slipped his hand downwards from where he held her upper arm to take her hand in his. He didn't care if anyone saw. Or what they thought.

He entwined his fingers with hers and gave them a little squeeze. 'You're coming with me. No arguments.'

Svea should have protested. She should have stayed outside with the other Danes and drawn a line under everything that had happened. But the instant his fingers had curled around hers she'd relented. She'd let him take her hand and she had followed him inside.

She had to admit she was curious to see the inside of Ash's home, to try to understand him better. Outside, it was even grander than she could have imagined. The stone fortifications were so high and forbidding she doubted any enemy would ever get through or over them. And yet the tall tower of the keep, which rose up into the rain clouds, was rather ominous—especially with just three remaining crumbling turrets, which seemed to have been ravaged by an old fire.

Stepping inside, she saw there was a fire burning in a large hall which wasn't too dissimilar from the longhouse in Kald, with benches and animal skins and furs scattered about. It was cosy and inviting— or was it the heat radiating from Ash's hand holding hers that was making her feel warm? It was as if she could feel every contradictory rough and smooth part of the long, large fingers steadily holding hers, offering her reassurance. But as a portly lady jostled towards them, giving Ash a warm smile, he discreetly released her from his grip. She immediately missed the contact.

'My lord, you're home! What a pleasant surprise. Good heavens—just look at the state of you! Are you hurt? What has happened?'

'We've had a long and somewhat eventful journey, Ellette. This is Svea, a friend from Kald.'

Svea and Ellette acknowledged each other with a little nod, and the woman's eyes swept over her wet warrior's attire. Svea had the feeling this woman didn't miss a thing.

'We could both do with a wash and a decent meal. And the people outside are starving hungry—could you send out a cauldron of hot pottage?'

'Certainly, my lord.'

'I assume my father has heard I'm home? We've probably caused quite a commotion.'

'Yes, he knows. And, just to warn you, he's not best pleased, my lord.'

He nodded. 'I thought as much.' He turned back towards Svea. 'What do you want to do first? Wash or eat?'

Ellette looked surprised that he was giving her the choice, letting her decide her actions. So was she…

'Wash, please.' She was desperate to get out of her heavy chainmail and wet breeches.

He nodded. 'Would you be able to find Svea a room and some clean clothes?'

'Of course,' Ellette said. 'This way then, love. Svea, is it…?'

Svea followed the woman hesitantly, and they headed towards some winding stairs. She was strangely reluctant to let Ash out of her sight and break the camaraderie between them. He had been a strong leader outside in the courtyard, giving clear directions with authority, and the Danes had looked at him with respect and admiration. As had she.

He gave her a reassuring smile. 'I'll see you shortly.' They climbed a few more steps. 'Ellette?' Both women turned back to look at him. 'Where is he?'

The woman nodded to a small room on the right. 'In there.'

Ellette led her up the stairs to a narrow corridor and opened a little door at the end. Svea took in the large room before her. It was very grand compared to her simple farmstead back in Kald. There was a large bed in the middle, covered in various furs, and there was a small table and a barrel to bathe in. She stood awkwardly by the door as Ellette helped a servant to fill it, bringing bucket after bucket of steaming hot water. She tried to offer her assistance, but Ellette batted her away.

When the door was finally shut on her, and she was alone for the first time in days, she just stood there, taking it all in. The bed looked comfortable and inviting, and she longed to sink down onto it, to rest her weary body, but she didn't want to get it damp from her wet clothes, so she quickly untied her braids and removed her dirty, sodden garments, dropping them to the floor.

Tentatively, she stepped into the barrel. At home in Kald she was quite happy bathing in the sea, with the icy surf invigorating her body, but this was a whole new experience. Sinking under the surface, she let the warm water lap against her skin. It felt wonderful, and helped to soothe her tired and aching muscles.

She tipped her head back, allowing the water to soak into her hair, to ripple across her face and clean away the mud and the rain. She wondered if somewhere in this fortress Ash, too, was washing off the blood and grime from their journey. She hoped his wound was all right. It hadn't looked too deep…she thought it just needed to be kept clean.

Once again, the memory of his bravery astounded her. He was an incredible man. Her thoughts strayed to his body...or to the glimpses of it she had seen when he'd lifted his tunic. The smooth, tanned skin on his stomach was rippled with muscles, as if he had been carved from stone. And she knew what it felt like to be pressed tightly against them, after riding encased in his powerful arms today.

She had insisted he ride, as she'd been worried about his injury, but he'd been stubborn, saying she should take the horse, and of course she'd refused. Once they'd settled on sharing, her body tucked into his, she'd realised she actually liked it. She'd enjoyed the feeling of being wrapped up in his arms, and even managed to relax back against him.

She was surprised at herself. What had he done to her to break down her well built-up defences in just a matter of days?

His proud, handsome face came into her mind, and that wicked grin he'd given her this morning, when she'd thought he'd been asleep, his hair tousled around his neck.

She felt that heat shift low in her belly again. This was all so new to her. How did he have such an impact on her mind and body?

She drew her fingers down over her breasts, slowly lathering her soft, sensitive skin with the soap that had been left for her, feeling her rosy nipples peaking beneath her touch. And then she started to clean her stomach, and lower, suddenly feeling brave and wanting to explore those tingling feelings further. She moved her fingers slowly downwards to reach between her legs, where she was experiencing flickers of excitement when she thought of him. She tentatively ran her fingers through her neat curls and below, parting the intimate folds of her skin.

She thought of Ash's large hands stroking over her shoulder, running through her hair, and she began to probe, pressing her finger against the tiny nub that was screaming out to be touched. Her head tipped back as she circled it, opening herself up with wider, firmer movements, delighting in the incredible sensations she was creating, in this wonderful newfound pleasure rocking through her body. She spread her legs wider, moved her fingers faster, thinking of his thighs pressing against hers, her bottom shifting against his groin, his dark brown gaze watching her...

A knock on the door brought her to her senses.

She sat bolt upright in the barrel, shocked. *What on earth was she doing?*

Her cheeks hot, her heart pounding, she wiped the water out of her face. 'Yes?' she choked.

'It's just me, love.' It was Ellette. 'I have some clean clothes for you. Can I come in?'

Svea tucked her knees to her chest, trying to cover herself. She wasn't used to anyone seeing her without clothes on. She had always been a private person. She only ever bathed in the sea in Kald when she was sure no one else was around.

'All right.'

The kindly woman stepped through the door and

politely averted her gaze, simply laying out a gown on the bed for her. 'There you go, love. Just shout if you need anything, and come down when you're ready.'

The moment the woman shut the door again Svea launched herself out of the water. She didn't know what had come over her, getting hot and bothered daydreaming over a man. A Saxon man!

She found a comb and roughly drew its teeth sharply from her scalp through her locks, appalled by her behaviour. She had always seen her body as something to be fuelled, to be used for strength... It had been used by others and had pain inflicted upon it, but it had never been used as a vessel for her own pleasure. She had never thought to touch herself before—or wanted to until now.

The polished metal circle on the table was useful as she tied her hair into fresh braids. At home, she had to use water if she wanted to look at her reflection— she needed one of these metal things. She took in her rosy cheeks and bright eyes and barely recognised herself. Who *was* this woman she was becoming?

Gingerly lifting the purple silk gown, she admired the soft material and fingered the intricate stitching. The under-dress was easy to slip on, and the peplos she pulled on over the top fitted perfectly. She had never worn such a fancy garment. It was beautiful— not like her usual clothing at all. She toyed with the idea of putting her trusty tunic and breeches back on, but they were nowhere to be found. Ellette must have picked them up and taken them to wash. So, sighing, she drew the silky material together at her waist with the gold-laced braid and studied herself again in the shiny metal circle.

She would never usually wear anything that would draw attention to her cleavage, or her waist. She'd had to for the wedding, because Anne had requested it, and Brand had begged her to wear a pretty dress to please his bride, but that had been once only. She usually hid her figure under masculine clothes. She usually made her own garments—badly.

She smoothed down the silk skirt, feeling nervous. What would Ash think of her wearing this? Why did she care?

She was curiously apprehensive as she slowly made her way back down the spiral staircase, wondering what she would find in the hall. Her nerves were as tightly wound as the steps. Was it to be just her and Ash having dinner together? Or would the people from the settlement be there? That was what happened at home in Kald. Everyone piled into the longhouse for the evening meal, catching up on the news of the day, sharing stories. In comparison, it was very quiet here.

But as her foot hit the bottom stair she heard raised voices. She halted, straining to listen. It was Ash, and another deep voice she didn't recognise. She pulled back a few steps, hiding herself from view.

'Well, she's no longer here, is she? She doesn't decide!' Ash barked, before slamming the door on whoever he was arguing with and striding out into the corridor. She watched as he smoothed a hand over his damp hair, cursing under his breath, before storming into the adjacent hall.

Svea had never heard him raise his voice before—he'd always been so calm, so measured. She wondered who or what could have made him so angry. His father, perhaps? She wondered why they didn't get on. She would do anything to have one more day with *her* father. She missed him all the time. The pain had eased over the years—Brand had helped with that—but she would always remember what a wonderful man he had been. Did Ash not look up to his father in the same way? And if not, why not?

She waited a moment or two longer before descending the last of the stairs and entering the hall. Ash was seated at the central firepit, warming his hands in front of the flames, deep in thought. There was a large wooden table which would probably seat thirty men, but it was only set for two, so she assumed whoever he'd been talking to wouldn't be joining them.

Good. Greedily, she wanted him all to herself.

Her stomach growled in response to the thought of food and Ash glanced up, his tense face brightening when he saw her. His brown eyes met hers, burning almost amber in the candlelight, and her heart stuttered. And then they swept over her in approval, his gaze darkening, and she felt a responsive heat flare low in her belly.

She suddenly wondered what it would be like to have his fingers touch her where hers had been moments before, when she'd been bathing, and her cheeks flushed at the erotic thought. She had never wished for such a thing to happen before. What was he doing to her? He was making her long for things that surely could never be.

Usually she'd do something to make herself look less attractive, or to detract attention from herself, but she didn't think she could even move. He looked rakishly good-looking. His dark hair had been tamed into a neat knot again, and he'd trimmed his beard back to a shorter style. It was the first time she'd seen him without his armour, in normal clean clothes, and the way his tunic clung to his sculpted body was mesmerising. Magnetic. Her mouth dried.

He rose to meet her, stepped towards her. 'Svea, you look…'

'Like a girl?' she said, preventing him from giving her a compliment.

'You took the words right out of my mouth!' He grinned wolfishly.

'Yes, well, I usually wear a tunic. I'm not used to such fine clothes.'

'You wear them well.'

He looked her up and down again, and she was surprised to find she didn't mind. Normally she'd do anything to avoid a man's scrutiny.

'Very well.'

His eyes were proprietorial, and she realised she liked it. His words from before floated through her mind. *The girl is mine.*

'Whose are they?' she croaked.

'They were my mother's.'

'Then I'm honoured.' She patted the skirt a little. 'She had very good taste.'

His brow furrowed a little. 'Shall we...?' he said, motioning to the table. 'I believe you are hungry, as your stomach was protesting.'

He pulled the wooden bench out for her and she sank onto it. Most men weren't so considerate.

No sooner had she sat down than Ellette brought them both some bread, and a bowl of wheat stew with vegetables. It smelt delicious.

'Please eat,' he said.

Svea had thought she was starving, but now, sitting across from him in this huge hall, adorned with hunting trophies and shields, barrels of ale and more candles than she'd ever seen, dressed in this glamorous gown, she suddenly felt jittery. It didn't feel real. And her emotions were playing havoc with her appetite.

'Where is everybody?' she asked. 'You saw what the longhouse in Kald was like at the wedding. It's that chaotic every day.'

'Most people will eat later—now they are all out in the fields. It's harvest time. Others will be on the ramparts, or in their farmsteads. We don't spend much time feasting together here. My father has never been one to host gatherings.'

'He lets this hall go to waste? Still, are you pleased to see everyone? You must be glad to be home,' she said.

'In a way,' he said, making light work of his meal. 'What do you think of my father's stronghold?'

'It's impressive.'

'If a little unwelcoming? Go on—you can say it.' He grimaced.

'No, Ellette has been lovely. Too kind, really. But the place seems rather empty.' She suddenly felt a pang for her home, her friends. Ash's stronghold was huge, and yet most of the people were outside rather than inside. It seemed hollow, somehow, as if it was a body missing its beating heart.

'It's always been that way,' he said.

'Do you not wish to change it?'

When he frowned, she wished she'd been more careful with her words.

'That's up to my father. Despite his illness, he's still in charge.'

'You were the one making decisions today...'

'Which I may come to regret.'

'You couldn't leave those people to die out there in the cold. Winter is on its way. They were starving, hurt... You did the right thing, Ash.'

'My father is most displeased that I went against his orders.'

So it *was* his father he'd been arguing with.

When Ellette came to remove their plates Svea tried to help her, standing to gather their dishes. She wasn't used to having someone wait on her.

Ash gave her a bemused smile.

'It's all right, love, I can do it,' Ellette said. 'You sit down.'

'I'm intrigued...' Ash smirked. 'Are you going to wipe your mouth on your sleeve now? Or were you acting out just for me?'

She blushed. Thinking back to the way she had behaved at her brother's wedding, she cringed. Although she wondered... If she made such a display of disrespect now, would he stop looking at her with that heat in his eyes? A small part of her welcomed it, perhaps even wanted to explore it, but she also wanted to run far, far away.

She was glad when Ellette came back, breaking the tension, and placed a steaming pie in front of them. 'Braewood's best blackberry pie, my lord. I hope you enjoy it.'

More blackberries! Svea couldn't believe it.

Ash stared at the pie as Ellette began to carve into it and scoop a large serving into a bowl. He avoided Svea's eyes. 'Thank you, Ellette. It looks delicious.' His lips twitched.

'Blackberries freshly picked this morning.' She passed him and Svea a bowl each. 'Enjoy them,' she said, before bustling away.

As soon as Ellette was out of sight he raised his eyes to Svea and a little giggle escaped her lips. It was infectious. He let out a mischievous chuckle, too, and suddenly they were both laughing together...

'Whatever is the matter?' Ellette asked, returning moments later with a jug of water.

It just proved to make things worse.

Tears streamed from Svea's eyes, and she realised she must have needed the release. It had been an intense few days. Perhaps Ellette's pie would be the perfect remedy, but even so she didn't think she could stomach another blackberry for the rest of her life. Or at least this season!

Ash relaxed back in his chair, smiling at her. And she smiled back warmly. He was such a handsome man, and he had treated her kindly. She was ashamed of the way she'd spoken to him that night at the wedding…especially now he'd saved her life— twice. Just a few days ago he had been her sworn enemy, and now they were sharing jokes…

The thought had her straightening, and she reached over for her cup to take a sobering sip of water. She felt guilty for laughing while her friends were suffering, and for enjoying Ash's company so much.

'I've asked Ellette to look after you while I'm gone,' he said, coming forward to lean on his elbows, suddenly serious, too.

'Gone?' All humour left her.

'I need to ride out to the neighbouring burhs. Each has promised to provide men when the King or Braewood is in need. We won't be helped by the fact that those men we met on the road passed through here on their way from Rainhill—my father fed them and agreed to send men to assist Crowe.'

Svea gasped. 'The men who tried to kill you?'

His lips narrowed. 'Yes. My father and I have had words. I will not let Braewood be associated with those who are an opposing force to the Crown—or the Danes.'

Hope soared inside her. And she realised, despite what he'd said about it being his father's home, not his, that he did care about Braewood and its reputation.

'No wonder they balked when you gave them your name. They must have known you'd oppose your father's wishes. They must have known you're the King's right-hand man and they could be hanged for treason.'

He nodded. 'Indeed.' He pushed his chair back and stood slowly. 'I will go now and rally the troops…see if I can patch up some of the damage my father has created between us and our allies.'

'Now?' She liked it that he was so determined to rescue their men.

'I'm conscious that we have little time,' he said.

'Then I shall come with you,' she said, rising, too. 'I will go and change.'

'No. Not this time,' he said brusquely.

'But—'

'Svea,' he warned her. 'It won't help our cause.'

'You don't want me with you?' An unexpected pain lanced her in the chest, pretty close to her heart. 'I thought we were in this together.'

'We are. But just for this part… If I'm seen with you it will sway opinions, affect decisions. I know it shouldn't matter, but unfortunately it does. The men need to know this battle is about Saxons versus Saxons. I'm sorry to be so blunt.'

She nodded, accepting what he was telling her. She could understand how having a Dane with him might put others off joining them. Hadn't she felt the same about Kald aligning itself with Termarth? She was glad he was sharing his plans with her, including her, but she didn't want him to leave her, and she didn't want to be here in this Saxon fortress without him.

He softened his voice. 'Besides, I'll feel better knowing you're safe here.' He came around the table towards her and took her hand. 'And as for wanting you with me...I think by now you know that I do...'

Her throat felt thick with emotion. She couldn't talk.

He reached out to take her chin between his fingers. 'I'll be back tomorrow. By nightfall, hopefully.'

'You haven't even had a chance to rest your wound...' she whispered.

He leaned in and planted a gentle kiss on her forehead, trailing a hand down her spine, sending tingles dancing after it.

'Don't worry about me, Svea.'

But the trouble was, she did.

After seeing Ash and his men off on their journey, Svea decided she couldn't spend the rest of the day dispirited, wishing he'd allowed her to go with him, wishing she'd ignored his orders and followed him anyway.

She was intrigued to see the ocean in Braewood, so she pulled on his cloak, which had finally dried out by the fire, and made her way down the steep escarpment to the sand beneath. The cloak smelled of him...musky, woody...and she felt a pang in her chest. She had spent so much time in his company it felt odd not to be with him.

Braewood was a beautiful place, the fort having been built into the top of a cliff. The beach was more vast, more wild than the sheltered bay in Kald, and she longed to head into the waves and swim off her fears, her anger—everything that had happened over the past few days. But she wasn't sure if it was customary for a woman to do such a thing here. And she knew better than to solicit any unwanted attention.

Instead, she unlaced her boots and dug her toes into the cool sand as she looked out to sea, watching the birds soaring above, hovering over the water and then diving beneath to capture their meal.

She wondered what her brother was doing now—whether he was enjoying his first days of married life out on the sea. And then she thought how much she had changed in such a short amount of time—changed from the girl who had scorned his wedding. She was starting to think that maybe it wouldn't be *all* bad, being bound to a man… Of course, that depended on who the man was…

Ash's face filled her mind. How could one man have had such an impact on her—and in just a few days?

She realised now that she hadn't ever really faced what had happened to her in Termarth. She'd spent years fantasising about getting revenge on Lord Crowe, wallowing in her anger. And even when the man had been locked away she still hadn't been able to put it behind her. She hadn't truly confronted her feelings, not wanting to share them with Brand or anyone in Kald because she felt ashamed, and because she didn't want to cause them any pain.

But she was starting to think she needed to talk about it to someone…because she was missing out on things. Although she enjoyed her life in Kald, she was beginning to believe she could be happier. And perhaps she had a right to be.

She walked the length and breadth of the beach, paddling in the icy water tumbling onto the shore, admiring the different rock formations, the grasses and seaweed. She was hunting for pretty shells, thinking she might take them home as a reminder of this magnificent place, when in the clay-like wet sand she came across a small pointed item. She crouched down, washing it off in the salty surf, uncaring that the bottom of her skirts was getting wet, and studied it.

It looked like a tooth. The tooth of a sea dog—those great beasts with dark black fins that rose out of the water. These teeth were a symbol of protection amongst her people, and she knew it was quite a find. She tucked it into the trim of her dress, deciding she would perhaps make it into a necklace and give it to Ash when he returned. If anyone deserved protection it was him. He had earned it.

Svea wondered what it was that kept him from this beautiful place. He had said he didn't get on with his father, but was that the whole truth of it? When they'd arrived, he'd turned heads in the fortress square. The people—both Saxons and Danes—had clearly respected him. What was holding him back from taking up his position here? It was an impressive place, almost as grand as the King's castle in Termarth, and it offered a glimpse of Ash's power to come.

She thought of her daily life back in Kald—how she swept the floors, looked after the livestock and trained the farmers to fight, while Brand and his men made boats or built up their defences. It was a hard but rewarding life. She wondered what the lady of a Saxon fortress like this would spend her days doing. If *she* were to ever be in that position, she decided, she would want to be busy, to help. She couldn't be waited on, or spend her days sewing. She would want to explore, swim, hunt, work the land—basically do all the things she did in Kald, but on a larger scale.

Why was she even thinking like this? Her thoughts disturbed her. And anyway, Ash had told her he would never marry...

She wondered why. He hadn't said...

Heading back inside, she set about exploring the warren-like corridors and the dark, secret rooms that branched off from the main hall. Despite her initial reservations, she was pleased to find that she felt safe. Nevertheless, it was strange to be in Ash's home without him being there. She wanted to share this with him, for him to show her around. She wanted to hear his witty observations and see the place through his eyes.

She found the pantry and the larder, and took in all the jars and goods, wide-eyed. Food in Kald was always scarce. She also found a little chapel, where the Saxons must go to pray. Her church was in the woods in Kald, or out in the open on the beach. There, she felt close to her gods.

She was in awe when she found the armoury, and wanted to try out each and every blade and bow, but quickly closed the door to stop herself. Still, her curiosity had been piqued, and the more she roamed, the more she realised she was hoping to learn more about the man she was beginning to have feelings for.

When she entered a small library, she came upon scroll after scroll of diary entries. It was at times like this she wished she could read. Instead, she studied the bejewelled covers, and the pictures inside, tracing her fingers over the drawings on the delicate parchment. She recognised Braewood fort, although in the images there were four turrets, not three, and there were drawings of a beautiful woman—Lady Stanton, perhaps?

But as she turned the pages the images became darker. Fires. Warriors attacking people. Warriors with markings on their skin and boats that looked like longships. Bodies stacked up everywhere, images of death...

She slammed the pages shut, her blood running cold. Had Danes attacked Braewood fortress? It would explain why the building was damaged, and why her kind weren't welcome here. She cast her mind back to what Ash had told her in the forest, about Danes ransacking settlements. Had he witnessed such atrocities first-hand? Had he been hurt? If so, did he blame her? And why hadn't he said anything? He must despise her people. And yet he had stood up for her against those men earlier...

Needing answers, Svea picked up her wet skirts and went to look for Ellette in the back room of the hall.

'I was hoping to be of some use to you,' Svea said

to the woman. 'How can I help? I can scrub, or peel, or even wash pots.'

Ellette was clearly taken aback by her offer of help, tutting. 'Lord Stanton would never forgive me if I let you do such a thing,' she said, placing a large pile of vegetables on the table.

'I am perfectly capable. And he doesn't need to know,' Svea said, winking. She picked up a knife and a swede and began to peel it, delighting in the mundane task, needing to feel useful. 'Besides, if I help I'm hoping you might consider making a little extra for the settlers outside.'

The woman smiled conspiratorially. 'Yes. Let's do that. But we must keep it between us. Lord Aethelbard is in a black mood again. He doesn't need to know.'

Svea had warmed to this woman instantly, and liked her a lot. She wondered how long she had been in Ash's life. How well she knew him.

'I have been exploring Braewood this afternoon. Why is it, do you think, that Ash—Lord Stanton— doesn't live here? It's a wonderful place.'

Ellette sighed heavily. 'It is Lord Ash's choice, my dear. Truth be told, we don't see him much at all. It would seem he prefers not to come.'

'But why?' Svea asked, shaking her head. 'I don't understand.'

The woman shrugged one plump shoulder. 'No one knows for sure, but if you ask me it was his mother and father's fault. He was never close to them, and they were both very cold to the boy when he was growing up.'

'How so?' Svea dunked the chopped pieces of swede in a large pot and set about peeling another.

'Well, I don't know all the facts, but his parents sent him off to a monastery when he was just a boy. They said he was too feral. They had a strained relationship from the start. He was always different—bigger, stronger than the rest of the boys—and he wanted far too much freedom. He used to roam about the shoreline all day long, and they wanted to tame the wildness out of him. But he was only eight when he left this place…just a child.'

Svea felt a dart of sympathy shoot through her for that little boy. She tried to picture him, with dark hair that curled up at the ends which he just couldn't tame, sad and serious brown eyes… She had lost her mother around that age and it had devastated her. But she'd been able to lean on her father and brother for love and support. Whereas Ash—had he had no one? Her heart went out to him. She wondered what harm such early isolation might have done to him.

'He came back years later, so handsome and very refined. But he was sullen…rather stifled, if you ask me,' Ellette continued.

That would explain a lot, Svea thought. Why he was so reserved at times.

'But between you and me, his father still couldn't love him. It was all such a shame. So he left again—went off out into the world to make his own way. He worked without their support and look at him now—prominent and influential. A favourite of the King.'

Svea thought back to her judgement of him that

day on the marsh. How she'd accused him of being privileged because of his family name. She chastised herself. How wrong she'd been. She wondered why he hadn't set her straight. Why had he allowed her to believe things that weren't true?

'You'd think his parents would finally have been proud of him, wouldn't you?' said Ellette.

'Weren't they?'

'No. It's said his mother couldn't stand the sight of him even then. She died of the sickness soon after that time. And his father… Well, he can't even say a kind word to his son now, on his deathbed. But you didn't hear any of this from me, of course.'

Svea nodded, but her thoughts were on Ash. She wondered what impact his bleak upbringing had had on the man he had become. He must be carrying around some deep-rooted scars. Despite his grand home and her meagre one, and if you could see past their Dane and Saxon blood, perhaps they weren't really so different.

Ellette tumbled her chopped vegetables into the large black pot of boiling water. 'Apparently Lord Aethelbard has made some demands about what his son needs to do to inherit this place when he's gone, to keep his lands and title. I believe one of them is an arranged marriage to Lady Edith of Earlington…'

An unexpected stab of jealousy shot through Svea, winding her. She took a deep breath, fighting to get herself back under control. She instantly berated herself, thinking how ridiculous that was. She couldn't possibly care—she was against the institution of marriage herself. But the thought of Ash entwining his fingers with another woman's, placing a soft kiss to her forehead, was not a pleasant one.

'But the young Lord has refused. They say his father will not die until he agrees! They're both very stubborn.'

Svea felt a slight trickle of relief at the woman's words. She knew Ash was determined, and he had told her himself he didn't want to marry, but now she wondered why. Was it just to spite his father? Was that the reason?

'Lord Stanton hasn't even tried to bend to his will,' Ellette continued, lowering her voice to hushed tones. 'We all hope he does, of course. It would be wonderful to have a lady to look after the place again. And the young Lord would be a good leader—just look at how he dealt with those people outside.'

Ash had made sure the Danish settlers had all they needed before he'd left, and Svea was glad he'd stuck to his word. She'd come to realise he was not the man she had first thought—he was so much more.

'Was there a fire here once, Ellette? I was wondering what had happened to the keep...to the turrets.'

'Oh, yes, but that was before my time, dear. There was an attack by—'

'Danes?'

'Yes, dear. They arrived on the beach unexpectedly and attacked the settlement here. They were savage—they destroyed everything in their path, or so I've been told. But that was before the young Lord Stanton's time, when his father had just taken over here. It wasn't long after Lord Aethelbard and Lady Stanton were married.'

Svea nodded, deep in thought. 'That must have been terrifying for them.'

It also explained why Lord Aethelbard had built the walls up so high. She wondered if he lived in fear of the Danes attacking again, and she sighed. Why did some of her people give Danes such a bad name? But she realised whether Saxon or Dane it didn't matter— some people were good and some people were bad.

Once the stew was ready, she took another large cauldron of pottage outside for the settlers. They were extremely grateful. She checked on a few of those who were sick, or wounded, and relit their fires, fetching more wood. She sat and spoke to them for a while, listening to their stories of crossing the ocean and building up settlements here, only to have them destroyed. It made her realise how lucky she was that they'd kept Kald safe all these years.

They all thanked her for her kindness, and it helped her to feel a little less guilty as she retired to her comfortable room and slipped beneath the wool and animal skins.

Even though she was bone-achingly tired, she couldn't sleep. Her thoughts kept returning to the man she had spent the past few days with, his intense deep brown eyes focused on her. She wondered where he was now. She wished he hadn't had to travel so soon—especially as his wound hadn't had time to heal. She hoped he was all right. She imagined him meeting with other Saxon lords, trying to convince

them to help. And then she wondered if any Saxon
maidens would be at those settlements.

A vision of a hall full of pretty women, all delicate and lovely, smiling at the handsome lord, filled
her mind and she tossed and turned in the bed. She
tried to tell herself that Ash knew if they were to have
any chance of rescuing the King, and her friends, that
he had to act swiftly, so he probably wouldn't have
time for any pleasantries… Besides, he'd told her he
didn't want to marry or have children. But did that
mean he didn't enjoy the casual company of women?
She knew how promiscuous the men and women in
Kald could be…

No, she could not bear to think about it!

Trying to think of something less disturbing, she
wondered what the real reason was that Ash didn't
want to rule here. She made up her mind to ask him
when he returned, and to learn more about him—if
he'd share more with her. And, in turn, she would
have to share more with him. Was she ready to talk
about her past? She thought perhaps she finally was.

Although Svea tried to keep herself busy, the next
day dragged excruciatingly slowly as she waited
for any sign of Ash and his men. She helped in the
fields for a while, much to Ellette's disapproval,
and checked on the people in the barns, whom Lord
Aethelbard had thankfully left alone. She went for
another long walk on the beach. She fetched eggs
and milked some of the cows, and she played with
the Danish and Saxon children in the square.

As the day began to fall away she even tried to

sew, but it was no use. At dinner time she picked at her food, not really hungry, and when dusk started to close in she found herself watching the fortress gate, waiting for his return. Her eyes were trained on the wooden entrance like a predator, checking and re-checking for any sign of men on horses. And then she paced.

At every sound she started—only to be disappointed when it wasn't him. What the hell was wrong with her? When it grew darker, she began to imagine the worst. She hoped he hadn't been hurt.

Finally, she succumbed to fitful sleep on a bench in the hall.

Chapter Five

When Ash returned he found Svea curled up, asleep by the fire. Her beautiful blonde locks fell gently across her cheek and he drew them back tenderly, so he could see her face. His heart ached. He'd only been gone a night and a day, but he'd missed her. And he'd raced home as fast as he could just to get back to her, encouraging his men with promises of extra mead and food for their families.

It had made him begin to wonder what it would be like to have her waiting at home for him always… it would certainly make Braewood a more attractive place to settle down. And yet he knew that was a fantasy, and it could never be.

He crouched down and gently touched her shoulder to wake her. 'Svea.'

She stirred but didn't wake, and he took the chance to trace his finger over the dark lines on her neck, learning their pathways. The intricate knotwork fascinated him. *She* fascinated him.

Her blue eyes opened slowly, and when they focused on him her lips curved up into a smile. His heart swelled.

'You're back,' she said languidly, trying to push herself up into a sitting position. 'I was beginning to worry.'

'About me? I told you not to.' He smiled.

She shrugged a shoulder as if in a sleepy haze. 'What did the people of the burhs say?'

'They've promised to join us. Tomorrow morning. Then we'll ride out together to Termarth.'

'That's wonderful,' she said, throwing her arms around him. 'Thank you, Ash.'

His whole body tensed in surprise. She had never shown such a warm display of affection or gratitude towards him before. Well, apart from that sweet kiss that kept playing on his mind. He was glad he had made her happy, and he hoped his success in rallying the troops would convince her of his good intentions. His arms came up to hold her and he tugged her into his body, just for a brief moment.

'Do you think Cecil Crowe and his men will have made it there by now?' she asked, pulling back.

'Hopefully not yet. It would take a while to move that amount of men—especially with hostages on foot. We've done all we can for now, Svea. I promise we'll get them back. Please try not to worry.'

'So who will be coming? Who is joining us?'

'Ealdorman Buckley of Earlington, Lord Crompton of Bartham and Lord Fiske of Bellton. All well-respected lords of their lands and fierce fighters. They've promised at least thirty men each.'

Svea nodded. 'Ellette mentioned Earlington earlier. She said you had a...connection there.'

Ash's eyes narrowed at her tone, at the uncertainty in her eyes. He knew Ellette's mouth had a tendency to run away with her. Had she been talking to Svea about Lady Edith and his father's hopes for Ash to wed her? Was Svea jealous?

His lips curled upwards. 'Just because my father wants something to happen, it doesn't mean it will. I missed you while I was gone.' He trailed a finger down her cheek. 'I have brought you something...'

She sat up straighter.

From behind his back, where he'd placed it on the floor, he pulled out a long-stemmed flower. Huge, bright and yellow, it looked like the sun.

Svea's face beamed as she gingerly took the stem from him. 'It's beautiful! I have never seen anything so joyous before.'

'I know. I saw it and thought of you. You can eat the seeds, too, as I know you're always hungry.'

'Thank you,' she said, laughing.

'Are you hungry now?' he asked. 'I'm starving.'

She nodded.

'Come on, then.'

He gripped her hand in his, entwining his fingers with hers, pleased when she let him, and led her through the hall and down the corridor to the larder. It was late, so most of the settlement's people had retired to bed, and he was glad. He wanted some time alone with her.

He tugged her into the food store and stared up at the shelves, taking in all the various pots and jars. 'What do you want? It looks like we have cheese, soup, stew... Or how about some honey on bread?' he asked.

'That sounds good. Anything but blackberries.'

And they both grinned.

He reached for the honey pot and carried it over to a table in the kitchen. Reluctantly, he released her hand as he unwrapped a fresh loaf and carved off a few slices before smearing them with the amber liquid. Svea hoisted herself up to sit on the table, her legs dangling, and he passed the honeyed bread to her.

'So, what did I miss while I was gone?' he asked, before taking a bite of his own bread. 'What did you get up to?'

'I spent a while with the Danes, getting to know them. They are really lovely people, Ash. And they are so grateful you let them in.'

He nodded. 'I did wonder if I'd return to find them turfed outside the walls again. I'm very glad that's not the case. But it makes me wonder if my father is more unwell than he's admitting. He wouldn't normally give in without a fight.'

'I haven't heard a peep from him. It's been very quiet. I went for a lot of walks on the beach, and explored the fortress a little. Actually, I did come across your father's library,' she said guiltily.

His brow furrowed and he put down the remainder of his slice of bread. 'And?'

'Well, I can't read, so the words didn't mean anything to me, but the pictures...'

She stared at him, with questions in her brilliant blue eyes. But he didn't want to talk about it—not now. Just for one night, he didn't want to be reminded of who he was. He didn't want to talk about the past. He didn't want anything to dampen his good mood at being with her again.

'He's very creative, my father,' he said dismissively. 'We should find you a blank book. You could draw some of your designs in there. I'd like to see them. Do you like the beach?'

'I love it. It's so beautiful. I don't know how you can bear to be away from this place.'

Usually it was easy to stay away. But not with Svea here.

'Did Ellette look after you like I asked her to?'

'Very well. And, don't be cross with her, I persuaded her to let me help with some of the household tasks. I did a bit of work in the fields, and with the animals. I also helped with the cooking. I needed something to take my mind off things.'

He wondered if those 'things' had included him. He knew he had barely thought of anything but her while he'd been gone. She never ceased to amaze him. This was meant to be her chance to relax and recuperate after their journey, but instead she'd helped his people, worked on the land and in the kitchen.

'What did you make?'

'Pottage, bread…all sorts. I enjoyed it.'

He stepped towards her and wondered at the pull she had. He'd felt it from the moment he'd seen her that day in Kald, wielding that huge sword above her head, and the attraction was growing stronger all the time—as if there was some invisible line between them, reeling him in. He just wanted to be near her, close to her. More than anything he wanted to make her smile, like she made him smile. And that was a rare thing.

He dipped his finger in the flour on the table and lightly touched the tip of her nose. 'I have told you I missed you. Did you miss me?'

She smiled, dusting it off. 'It was strange being here without you.'

He watched as she pinched a little of the white powder and flicked it at him, her eyes glinting with mischief.

'Is that your way of saying you missed me, too?' He grinned.

And then she leaned back, laughing at his flour-covered beard.

'I'll get you for that,' he warned.

He grabbed a handful and she jumped down off the table. 'Ash, no!' she said, laughing, and as he threw it at her she squealed and ducked behind the table.

He had never had fun like this. He'd seen the other children playing when he was younger, but he'd never joined in. And as an adult he'd always been serious. But there was something about Svea that made him want to shake off those restraints and feel alive.

He moved after her and she tried to make a run for it. But he was too quick, and he grabbed her round the waist and deposited the flour in her hair. She gasped, and then both of them fell about laughing.

'What on earth is going on here?'

The stern voice came from the doorway. They both glanced up to see Ellette in her nightgown, holding an oil lamp, looking vexed.

'I'm so sorry, Ellette. We'll clean it up, I promise,' Svea said, straightening.

'Yes. Make sure you do! And don't wake Lord Aethelbald...there'll be hell to pay,' the woman said, turning on her heel.

Svea bit her lip, trying not to let out another giggle.

'We'd better clean ourselves up first,' Ash said, still laughing, unconcerned about Ellette and her wary gaze. He probably should care about what people thought of his bond with Svea, but surprisingly he didn't. 'Come with me.'

Taking her arm, he tugged Svea through a door and out to the back of the settlement. His fingers strayed down her skin to take her hand in his again, and they walked down the steep path towards the moonlit beach.

'So, what do you think?' he asked, giving her a playful nudge.

'Of what?'

He pointed to the sea. 'A late-night swim.'

'What?' She laughed nervously.

'You *can* swim, can't you?' he asked, goading her.

'Of course I can,' she said. 'Actually, I've wanted

to swim since we got here, but I wasn't sure if it was the done thing here in Braewood. In Kald, we swim all the time.'

'Well, you'll be pleased to know we do, too.'

'Even at this time of night?'

He shrugged. 'We need to wash all this flour off. And at least no one else will be around to see. We'll have the place to ourselves.'

When they reached the sand Ash began to pull off his boots, and then his tunic. He stopped when he realised Svea was just standing there, her eyes wide, staring at his large muscled chest, chewing on her bottom lip. A look of confusion crossed her face, and he stilled. Was he making her uncomfortable? That was the last thing he wanted to do. He'd thought they were having fun. He'd thought they both needed this. But perhaps his large body was off-putting—especially covered in its tapestry of scars.

'I can't swim in this dress. I'll sink!' she said, turning her attention away from him and focusing on her skirts.

Well, she wasn't saying she didn't want to go in…

He looked her up and down and realised she was right. She could go in naked, but he had a feeling she wouldn't agree to that.

'Here,' he said, passing her his discarded tunic. 'Put this on.'

She gripped the material tight, holding it to her chest. She still wasn't sure, and he wanted to reassure her.

'It's just a swim, Svea.'

'Then turn around,' she said, and he grinned.

He had known she wasn't one to shirk a challenge.

So he did as he was told, even though they were cloaked in the late-night darkness, so he could barely see her anyway. He listened as she tussled with her gown, and then heard it drop to the sand. The response in his groin was instant. *Damn.* What he wouldn't give to turn around, stride over to her and take her bare body in his arms. But he knew he mustn't. He had said it was to be 'just a swim' and he would stick to his word.

He knew he had to take this slowly. He couldn't be sure what Crowe had done, or just how badly it had affected her. It made him feel sick, just thinking about that man laying his hands on her. He guessed he had caused her some serious damage, given the way she held herself, the way she behaved, and he needed to build her trust—especially where her body was concerned.

'Ready,' she said, stalking past him and running into the water.

The material of his tunic barely reached the top of her thighs, and the sight made him harder. He followed her, laughing. The thought dawned on him that he would follow her anywhere. When he was with her he felt lighter, warmer, as if all the burdens that lay heavy on his mind had abandoned him, or become less somehow. She filled a void in his life and fulfilled his need for fun and friendship. Of course he knew it was much more than that. But to someone who'd never had it, fun and friendship would do for now.

He heard her gasp at the coldness of the water and she slowed her approach into the waves. He waded in to the same depth and saw her eyes dancing in the darkness. His breeches were soaked and clinging to his muscles. Usually he would swim naked, but he kept them on for her.

When the water was deep enough to lap against his wound, he sucked in a deep breath.

'Are you all right?' she asked.

'I'd forgotten all about it till now.'

'Hopefully the salt water will do it good.'

He loved it that she seemed to care about his injury. He wasn't sure anyone had shown him such kindness before.

He dived beneath the surface and swam out deeper, releasing all the stresses and strains of his journey, before returning and coming up for air beside her. She took a breath and copied him, and they swam alongside each other. She was strong and kept pace with him, carving her arms through the waves. He should have known she'd be a good swimmer.

When they both surfaced, she grinned up at him, breathless. 'I love the ocean. It makes me feel so small and insignificant... Back in Kald, if I had a bad day, I'd go for a swim and it would clear my head. It always helped to put things into perspective. And it helps to make me a stronger fighter.'

He nodded. He didn't like the thought of her having bad days. 'You could never be described as "insignificant", Svea,' he said. 'But I understand what you're saying. I used to come to the sea after an argument with my father, to wash all my worries away.'

Suddenly serious, Svea reached out and touched his arm. Her fingers were cool against his skin. 'Why don't you get on with your father, Ash? Ellette said he was cruel to you, when you were growing up.'

His brows knitted together. 'He did his best.'

She stared at him, removing her fingers and placing her hands on her hips.

'What?' he said, and shrugged.

'Is that all you have to say? All you're going to tell me?' She shook her head at him, frustrated.

He wiped the water out of his eyes, drawing a hand over his face. He didn't want to talk about it. It would ruin the mood. He didn't want to burden her with sob stories from his past. He didn't want to tell her why he didn't get on with his father because he didn't want to share that with anyone. Especially her.

'There's not much to say.'

He wanted to change the subject to something safer. Something less personal. He didn't want to revisit the past. Not tonight.

'But that's not true, is it?' she bit out. 'You fire questions at me all the time, Ash—about my family, my beliefs, where I come from. You're always delving deeper, wanting to know more. But you don't offer me the same courtesy. I ask you questions and you tell me nothing of yourself. How am I supposed to know who you are?'

Hope bloomed inside him at the fact that she wanted to know him. And yet at the same time a pain burned in his heart and he subconsciously rubbed the spot on his chest. What she was saying about him was true—he did keep himself firmly locked away. But he couldn't reveal this part of himself because he didn't want it to change how she felt about him—he didn't want it to affect their new camaraderie. He was hoping she was beginning to like him, as he was her, and he was scared that the truth would ruin it.

Silence echoed all around them. There was only the sound of the tumbling waves onto the shore and their gentle breathing. Why couldn't she just hold all her questions for tonight? But, no…she seemed to be giving him time to explain, and he didn't know what to say. He didn't want her to know who he really was.

She gave him a last exasperated look before throwing her arms up in the air and beginning to wade back to the shore.

'Svea, I thought we were having fun. Where are you going?'

'I'm getting out. It's far too cold in here for my liking. *Icy*.'

Was she talking about him? He knew she was right—he was keeping her at arm's length with his words, while wanting to draw her closer with his actions. And that wasn't fair—and it clearly wasn't working. But he wasn't used to sharing the details of his life. People weren't usually interested in hearing about it and he liked it that way. No one—not even the King—knew much about him at all. He was independent, only beholden to himself. If he told her she would know his secret, have a hold over him…

He caught up with her on the beach, followed her as she stalked up the sand, the wet tunic clinging to her skin, water dripping down her pale thighs. He tugged her arm to pull her round to face him. 'Svea, wait.'

'I've told you so much about myself, Ash. Don't you think I deserve to know something about you?'

'All right,' he said, his hands on his hips, shaking his wet hair. 'What is it that you want to know?'

'Anything! Everything,' she said. 'I want to know what happened here. What happened to make the turrets of the keep blackened by fire? Why are the walls built so ridiculously high? Why don't you get on with your father? Why did he send you away when you were younger?' She sighed, pausing for breath. 'I want to know why you live in Termarth, and not here. And what are your plans—what are your hopes for the future?'

'Is that all?' he asked sarcastically. He raked his hand through his hair, expressing his annoyance.

'No! I have lots more questions… What are you planning to do when all this is over? Will you be going back to Termarth once you rescue the King?'

'I doubt he'll have me.' He laughed bitterly.

'What do you mean?'

'I swore an oath to protect him and I let him down…'

'You didn't. You haven't. Not yet.'

'I did, Svea,' he said, taking a step towards her. 'Because it wasn't the King I was driven by desire to protect. If it had been, *he* might be standing here with me now—not you.'

She swallowed.

He lifted a hand to peel a wet strand of hair away from her face. 'It's the same reason I fought those men yesterday. You want to know something about me? Something truthful? I couldn't bear the thought of any man touching you, Svea, unless that man was me. And now I really want to kiss you, if you'll let me…'

Her blue eyes were huge, and she looked so beautiful. She was trembling, but he wasn't sure if it was because of the cold, or because of what he'd said. She hadn't moved or said a word, so he moved closer to her, his chest almost touching hers…

'Svea, say something.'

'I—I've never done this before.'

Ash's hands came up to cup her cheeks, his large thumbs caressing the corners of her lips, and he pressed his body gently against hers. Every part of him. She felt the instant flicker of excitement.

'It's all right. I'll coax you through it.'

His dark, heated gaze was fixed on her and his movements were slow, as if he was giving her time to say no, to change her mind, and she felt her legs tremble hard. But, for the first time in her life, she knew she wanted this to happen.

Smoothly, reverently, he pulled her face towards him, lowering his head at the same time. Her eyes fluttered shut as he covered her lips with his. His cool, salty skin was at odds with the warmth of his mouth, and as his tongue swept inside hers she gasped at the thrilling and tender feelings rushing through her body.

Her knees buckled, she began to sway, and he caught her with his arm, hauling her closer. As his silky hot tongue delved deeper, rolling over her like the ocean waves, drawing her in, pulling her under, sending searing heat charging through her, she curled her toes into the sand. His other hand trailed down to brush over the sensitive skin on her neck. His thumb was at her throat, circling her pulse, and an insane need lanced her.

She had never imagined a kiss could feel so good, sending signals to every part of her body, telling her she wanted more. And it was as if Ash could read her mind, because his hand drifted down to cup one full, heavy breast in his palm and she moaned. She'd thought she'd never allow a man to touch her again, but as he gently kneaded, softly squeezing her flesh with his fingers, pressing his thumb lightly against her pebble-hard nipple through the wet material, she welcomed the sensations he was creating. And as he twisted and teased the hard peak, his lips still ravaging her mouth, a low moan escaped from her throat and her head tipped backwards.

He took a moment to stray from her mouth, his lips roaming down her neck, kissing and licking, tormenting her with his clever tongue, moving to the base of her ear, all the time whispering how beautiful she was. Excitement pooled between her legs. Then he came back to her lips again, claiming her mouth once more.

Her thoughts flashed back to the kiss she had given him in the field—and how he'd said it had cured him. This was the same for her. His kiss was giving her confidence, telling her that she could do this. That she was healed. Needing to prove it—to herself and to him— she bravely pressed her hips closer, letting him know that she wanted this. That she'd meet him halfway.

Her fingers were trapped between their bodies, and she splayed them out against his solid chest, wanting to explore. She glided them upwards over his smooth, firm skin, to curl around his neck, her fingers delving into the wet hair at the base of his neck. She was drawing him closer, pushing her tongue into his mouth to deepen the kiss.

He growled, his careful control seemingly about to break. And his response delighted her. She'd finally done it. She'd broken his steely resolve. Feeling triumphant, she recklessly writhed against him, wanting to cause more of a reaction.

He gathered her closer, his hands drifting down her back and cupping her bottom, tugging her against him so she could feel his huge, hard length, and then his fingertips dipped lower, to the bottom of the tunic, swirling over the backs of her thighs. They travelled upwards, beneath the material, seeking out her most intimate places…

And she panicked.

'Ash, stop!'

With a violent shove she pushed him away, fiercely removing herself from his hold. Her actions were so sudden they shocked them both.

Her face flushed, her hair dishevelled, she couldn't bring herself to look at him. She felt so ashamed. Instead, she grabbed up her dress from the sand and ran.

Chapter Six

'Svea, let me in.'

'Go away.'

'I'm not leaving till we talk about this,' Ash said through the heavy door.

He rested his forehead against the wood. She'd left him standing out there on the beach, his ragged breaths coming in bursts, wondering what the hell had happened.

Well, he had a pretty good idea—she'd panicked and changed her mind. And now he was standing outside her door, trying to persuade her to let him in. He wanted to check that she was all right. He knew they couldn't go to sleep before they'd talked.

Damn, he felt like such a fool for rushing things. Why had he behaved like such a brute? He'd promised her he wouldn't touch her, but he'd broken his word time and time again, ruining her trust.

But the taste of her kiss had been intoxicating… the feel of her body against his too much of a temptation. And she'd seemed to come alive under his touch. She'd pressed herself against him as if she wanted him, squirmed against him as if she needed satisfaction... And he'd wanted to give it to her. He'd never wanted anything so much.

'Svea, you're going to have to face me eventually. Can you please open the door?'

He pressed his ear against the wood and heard gentle footsteps behind the door, as if she were pacing up and down. He softened his voice. 'You can't just bury your head in the Braewood sand and pretend it never happened. You can't hide from me forever. Come on...you know I'm right...'

Finally he heard her pad over to the door, and slowly she opened it a little. He took in her wide blue eyes, her flushed cheeks, her lip caught between her teeth. Thank goodness she'd had the sense to change into dry clothes—a long white nightgown Ellette must have given her. She looked stunning, with her damp long blonde hair tumbling down over her shoulders. This virginal vision of her didn't help to ease his desire, but at least she was wearing more material than before. He swallowed. More material was good. He didn't know if he'd have had the strength to stay away from her if she'd still been standing there in that clinging wet tunic.

He, too, had had the sense to pull on a dry tunic and breeches before coming up here, although his feet were bare and he hadn't warmed up yet. But that probably had more to do with her cool treatment of him rather than their late-night swim.

'Can I come in?' he asked.

She sighed, as if resigned, and pulled the door open a fraction wider, leaving it ajar before walking over to the bed and sinking down on it, wrapping her arms around her waist.

He walked in and closed the door behind him. But he was careful to stay beside it. He wasn't sure how she was feeling about him—she was certainly giving off mixed signals. It seemed she couldn't even bring herself to look at him. Instead, she was studying a little mark on the wooden floor, swirling her pretty toes around it.

'Are you all right?' he asked.

'I'm fine.' Her toes stilled, but she didn't move her eyes from the mark.

'Do you want to tell me what's going on?' he asked, careful to remove any censure from his words.

She shrugged a slim shoulder, chewing her bottom lip some more. 'I'm sorry,' she said quietly. 'For what happened out there...'

'Which part, exactly?'

She glanced up at him quickly, looking conflicted, her face heating, and then she looked down again. 'The last part. I thought...I thought I was ready. I thought it was what I wanted.'

'And it isn't?'

'Yes. No.' She shook her head, frowning. 'I don't know.'

She seemed to be annoyed with herself, not with him so much. It made him brave enough to push himself away from the door and slowly make his way towards her.

He crouched down before her, so their eyes were level. He was starting to think this was more to do with the 'bad experience' she'd mentioned on their journey from Kald rather than with him. But unless she told him the full story he couldn't help her.

'Svea, do you want to tell me about it? About what happened with Lord Crowe.'

She shook her head, cringing at hearing the man's name.

He reached out to take her cheek in his palm, bringing her eyes back to his. 'It might help.'

Tears welled in her eyes and she wrung her hands. She opened her mouth to speak but no words came out. She swallowed and tried again. 'I've never told anyone about it before...' she managed, her voice wavering. 'My brother told our people in Kald, after it happened. But I find it hard to speak about it. It's too painful.'

'I know all about pain. And I know it's hard to talk about bad things that have happened in the past. Why do you think I say so little?'

She gave him a sad smile. 'You have bad memories that consume you, too?'

'Yes. And I know it hurts to remember... But perhaps, if you share them, I can help?'

She nodded. 'I want to try. And I know that you deserve to hear the truth, Ash. Perhaps, if I tell you, it will help to explain why I behaved as I did out there on the beach. Maybe you'll forgive me.'

She took a deep breath and he realised she was about to begin—to tell him her story. He thought how brave she was. Far braver than him. He rocked back on his haunches, giving her some space.

'Lord Crowe and his Saxon soldiers took everything from me—my father, my dignity and my innocence.'

Ash felt her words pierce his chest. This was even worse than he'd imagined, and now he wasn't sure he wanted to know the details—they'd surely make him sick to his stomach. But he knew he couldn't stop her now. She had to tell him everything, no matter where that might lead them.

'When I was young, my father took me and Brand to Termarth. He was a boat builder. He wanted to trade. On the way home we went to a mead house for a drink. We were minding our own business, just chatting, when out of nowhere Saxon soldiers approached us, surrounded us.'

She brought her legs up to tuck her knees under her chin.

'A few of them made some crude comments—about how I looked, about us being heathens—and my father, being a typical Northman, wouldn't have it. He saw it as a mark on his honour. He stood and drew his sword to fight the leader of the group, but they weren't interested in fighting fair. They beat him—and then they killed him.'

She pressed a hand to her throat and swallowed, as if to dislodge the lump of emotion there.

Ash raised himself off the floor and came to sit next to her on the bed, suddenly feeling inadequate to soothe her pain. 'I'm so sorry, Svea.'

'Brand and I were reeling from what had happened, just standing there, trying to comprehend what they'd done. Through the shock and the pain, I think we realised we might be next, so we tried to make a run for it. Brand managed to get away, and I was glad, but I wasn't so lucky. The men grabbed me. The leader—Crowe—ripped at my clothes, and while his men held me down he raped me. When he'd finished, he let them take turns with me. I had just turned twelve.'

Ash squeezed his eyes shut, trying to fight the horrific images flooding his mind. He dragged a hand over his face. His heart went out to her for what she'd gone through, what she'd suffered. It was horrific. It seemed Saxon men really were no better than the Danes.

She wiped her hands over her face, trying to hide her tears. 'They left me for dead,' she said, and anger laced her words now. The anger which had likely been her constant companion these past years, making her the hard, fierce woman she had become. 'And I vowed never to let a man take advantage of me again.'

He wanted to reach for her, to comfort her, but she was so deep into her harrowing tale he wasn't sure she'd want him to. Especially now he knew why she'd shied away from him and his touch. She no doubt saw it as something to be feared.

'It took a long time for me to recover. They'd hurt me. Badly. I decided that when I was strong enough I'd make those men pay for what they did. I spent most of my days learning to fight, so that the next time anything like that happened I could protect myself. And others.'

Ash didn't trust himself to speak. Rage was surging through his blood. How could Lord Crowe and his men have done that? He should have let Svea kill him when she'd had the chance. He'd like to kill him now.

'Svea, I had no idea...' he tried, his voice hoarse.

He wondered how she'd got through the grief of losing not one but both parents and then dealing with this as well. He knew she was strong, but this... She was extraordinary.

'How could you have?' She shrugged.

'I can't imagine how you must have felt when you came up against him on the battlefield that day. I shouldn't have interfered.'

'You didn't know. And, in case you hadn't noticed, I'm quite good at hiding my pain... I think perhaps we're rather similar in that respect. After that day in Termarth, after I was attacked, I became a different person. I'd do anything to avoid men looking at me. I never wore pretty clothes again. I decided to dress in a way that didn't attract attention.'

That explained a lot, he thought, thinking back to her actions in the longhouse in Kald and the way she warded off male scrutiny with her fierce mannerisms and warrior clothing. Although she'd still drawn *him* in... And despite all that had happened to her she was still compassionate and kind, putting others before herself. He admired her courage and strength of mind. After the ordeal she'd been through, he couldn't believe she'd ridden out with a convoy of Saxon men to the forest, or insisted on coming with him to Braewood when she must have been downright scared. *Damn.* If he'd known all this he would have been more careful of her feelings.

'And I can honestly say I have never wanted any man's attention. Ever...' A crease appeared in her brow. 'Until now.' She found that mark on the floor again and scuffed her toe against it. 'These feelings I have when I'm with you... They frighten me.'

He studied her beautiful face, now fully understanding her behaviour. She wanted him, as he wanted her, but she was confused. And afraid. And he could see why. If only he'd realised the extent of the trauma she'd suffered before he'd kissed her on the beach... Yet she'd wriggled and writhed against him, encouraging him, enticing him into taking things further, thinking it was what she wanted—and then she'd panicked.

His large arms came around her, pulling her into his chest. He didn't want her to be scared of him. He would have to prove to her that he was trustworthy, that he could be gentle, that he would never hurt her.

'What are you—?'

'Just holding you. Nothing more. You're safe with me, Svea.'

He hoped she knew him well enough by now to realise that this was only to show her he cared—nothing more. He just wanted to give her the comfort she needed.

And to his relief, after a long moment, her body

began to soften, sagging against him, and he stroked her hair, hoping it would help her tension and worries ebb away.

Svea wasn't sure how long she'd been sitting like that, on the edge of the bed, wrapped in Ash's warm, secure embrace. Being held in his robust arms helped to make her feel stronger and more at ease. He had listened to her without interrupting or passing judgement, and then he had soothed her, saying kind words, making her glad she had told him about her past.

It was as if a little of the weight she carried had been lifted—as if she had removed a barrier between them by revealing her deepest, darkest fears. And now she thought she would be happy to stay like this forever, in his comforting hold, under his protection...

Her thoughts reminded her of the gift she'd made him and, wanting to give him something in return for the beautiful sun-like flower, and for the kindness and comfort he had shown her, she pulled away from him slightly.

'I had forgotten. I've made you something,' she said shyly.

'You have?'

She nodded and stood, pacing over to the table where she'd left the necklace. She held it up and carried it over to him, suddenly feeling slightly embarrassed. What if he didn't like it? Did men like him even wear such things?

'It's a sea dog's tooth. I found it on the beach. It's quite a rare find. I added a cord to make a necklace.

Our people…we believe such teeth offer protection. I was worried about you when you were gone. I thought you could wear it to keep you safe.'

He smiled, and she could tell she had stirred his emotions. As he reached out to take it from her gratefully, his fingers brushed against hers. Tingles rippled through her again, and she was surprised to still be feeling desire for him, despite what had happened on the beach. Even after running away from him.

'Thank you. I love it.' And, as if to prove it, he instantly pulled it over his head. She smiled back. 'But are you sure you don't want to keep it?' he asked.

'No, it's for you.'

'No one's ever given me a gift before.'

She raised her eyebrows. 'Never?'

He shook his head.

'Not even as a child?'

'No.'

She knew he wasn't close to his father, but she was determined to find out about his late mother, too. How could she not have loved him or treated him with kindness? It made her angry, and she hadn't even known the woman.

'Actually, there is something else I was going to ask you for, but now you've given me this I feel greedy,' he said, fingering the necklace as if it was something to be cherished.

Her breath hitched. 'What is it?'

What could this man want from her? She felt as if she would give him anything. Anything he wanted. If she could.

He gently reached for her still-damp hair and cast it over her shoulder. She shivered. His large fingers caressed the pattern-covered skin there. Next, he turned his attention to her wrist and turned it upwards, running his hands over a circular symbol with lots of little spears coming off it. She could tell he was fascinated.

'You said you drew these yourself?'

She nodded, stunned at the little sparks of excitement travelling along her arm.

'I want you to give me a marking like yours,' he said, smoothing the material to reveal the dark, swirling lines. 'Here,' he said, moving her hand to place it on his chest.

She gazed up at him.

'Will you?' he asked.

'You want me to ink your skin?' she asked, slightly amazed. She would never have thought him the type of man to want that. Not when she'd first met him, anyway. She had thought him so immaculate, so sensible and self-contained.

'Yes.'

She laughed, delighted. How was it that he continued to surprise her? 'But are you sure? They're permanent. Once they're there, they're with you for life. And aren't they seen as a Northmen thing?'

He shrugged. 'Not necessarily. Besides, I feel like being reckless. Rebelling. It must be the company I'm keeping.'

She grinned wider.

'So…' He raised his eyebrows. 'Will you do it?'

'I'd be honoured.'

'What do you need?'

'You want me to do it now?' she asked, incredulous. He certainly wasn't wasting any time.

'If you're not too tired,' he said. 'I don't know about you, but I'm not ready to sleep just yet.'

'All right.' She smiled. 'Let's do it.'

And she reeled off a list of the things she would need, including a rose thorn, some wood ash and a few herbs.

Ash reluctantly left the room, telling her he'd be back shortly, and thankfully it didn't take him long to return with the things she needed. She felt a flutter of excitement about creating a design on his chest. It would be incredible to do it for this man whom she was starting to care for. It would help to seal the tentative bond they'd created between them.

She quickly made the mixture and gathered everything together on the table before nervously announcing that she was ready.

'Where do you want me?' he asked.

It was an interesting question... She almost responded with a flirtatious remark, but instantly thought better of being so brazen. She was still shaken by what had happened outside. She could still recall the feel of his tongue in her mouth. Did she want that to happen again?

She realised she did—but would he want to kiss her again, after she'd so callously pushed him away before? And, if he did, how far would they get before she panicked again?

'There—on the bed. Prop your feet up and lie back a little. You'll be here a while.'

He pulled his tunic over his head and cast it down onto the floor, before leaning back, getting comfortable. He was a glorious sight. Her face heated a little as she studied her blank canvas. The tooth necklace looked at home, resting on his muscled chest, and, sweeping her eyes down, she realised she had never had a more perfect body to work on.

'Is this going to hurt?' he asked.

'Scared of a little pain?' she teased.

'Never.'

She knew it to be true. He was the bravest man she'd ever met.

She cleared her throat. 'So, what design do you want?'

'You decide. Choose something that has meaning to you—to both of us. I trust you.'

Svea looked at him in wonder. How could he place so much trust in her? And if he could do that, could she do the same? Could she reciprocate, and trust this man with her own body?

She knew what she was going to do.

She dipped the rose thorn into the wood ash and leaned in, hovering above him. His body was so beautiful it seemed a shame to mark it at all. Apart from the slight smattering of hair in the middle, the rest of his chest was smooth, with only a few scars here and there. She tried to focus, because this was important, but as she rested her hand on his skin, and felt his solid muscles bunching beneath her touch, she was distracted.

She had never worked in such intimate conditions before—on a bed and in candlelight—and she had certainly never been attracted to the person she was marking… She was all too aware of his warm breath fluttering across her cheek, his dark, steady gaze on her face, and her heart began to pound.

'Do you get this close to all your subjects?' he asked lightly, reaching out to curl one of her braids between his fingers.

'No! And do you mind?' she said, pulling her head away. 'I'm trying to concentrate.'

He grinned, as if he knew the impact he was having on her.

She forced herself to apply herself to the task at hand, drew in a deep breath, and began drawing the outline of her design.

It took a while to get the knotwork just right, and the shading to her liking, but after a while the pattern began to take shape. It started to take on a life of its own. Ash seemed to drift away with his thoughts, allowing her to focus, and she felt as if it was going to be her best work as she poured her heart and soul into it.

She was so glad she'd told Ash about her past. She knew she couldn't be with him without him knowing the truth, and she realised she did want to be with him. No man had ever made her feel this way before. No man had attracted her as he had. And no man had been so strong, yet so gentle. And although he was a Saxon, and she was Dane, and she wasn't sure what future they could have together, she still *wanted*…

His skin was warm and sticky beneath her touch,

where she'd been resting against him, and it was doing funny things to her…making her feel hot and bothered, with heat melting between her legs. It was as if a swirl of intimacy enveloped them.

Finally—reluctantly—she pulled away to study her work, leaning back and tipping her head to the left and then the right. She instantly missed having an excuse to lean over him, to touch him at will. She almost said she hadn't finished…

But he was looking at her expectantly. 'Well?' he asked.

'All done,' she said, biting her lip.

This was the worst part—when her subjects studied her work. She hoped he'd like what she'd done. It was too late if he didn't.

He grinned. Then he sat up and swung his long legs off the bed, heading towards the shiny silver circle she'd studied herself in the day before. His dark, serious eyes raked over the design in his reflection. Two small birds in flight, black and beautiful but fierce, were spread across the top right-hand side of his chest…

'They're ravens. A powerful symbol for both our people, representing thoughtfulness and wisdom… When I first saw you, you reminded me of them,' she said.

He ran his fingers over them.

'Our god Odin has two ravens sitting on his shoulders: Huginn and Muninn. Huginn is the sensible one,' she said, pointing to the one on the left. 'He is a little like you. And Muninn is more passionate.' She blushed. 'Also like you. Each day Odin sends them off around the world to ask questions and garner wisdom and knowledge. That's like you, too. You're always asking questions,' Svea added, talking quickly now, almost babbling. She still couldn't be sure if he liked the design or not. 'They represent power, offer protection, and strike fear into your enemies.'

She swallowed.

He came back to sit next to her on the bed. 'Svea, they're perfect,' he said, looking down at them, unable to take his eyes off the creatures, stroking his fingers over them in awe. 'They say everything I want them to say and more. Thank you. I think you're very talented.'

'Do you really like them?'

'I couldn't have chosen better myself.' He reached out to stroke a long, tanned finger down her face. 'And I think I like myself more with a part of you on me.'

'I liked myself more after I'd covered my skin in patterns. After Crowe. It was as if I was somehow claiming my body back for myself.'

His lips thinned into a hard line at the mention of that man and he took her hand in his. 'Svea, thank you for telling me about what happened. For helping me to understand. I'm truly sorry I stopped you on the battlefield that day, meaning you didn't deal with him as you wanted to.'

'I did, though. Just seeing him, facing him again, made me feel stronger. Watching him fall to his knees, seeing him so weak...and then knowing you'd locked him away—it helped a lot. Although I can't bear the thought of him being set free…'

'We'll stop them, Svea. I promise,' he said, leaning forward and lightly kissing her forehead. And then he pulled back. 'Crowe… Is he the reason you don't want to marry or have children?'

She nodded. 'After it happened—after the attack—a woman who had the art of healing told me I was so badly hurt, that those men had caused so much damage, I was unlikely to ever have children.'

His brow formed a dark line. 'I'm so sorry, Svea…'

At first she had been completely and utterly devastated. She'd always thought she would grow up to be the mother of many children. She'd imagined herself as a wonderful mother, just like her own. And she'd had to grieve for those children who would never be, for an imagined life that would never happen. She'd felt ashamed that she wasn't like other women…that she was barren. For a long time she'd felt unable to see the light—until one day she'd decided to find another reason for living.

She'd decided to invent a new Svea. And she'd poured her time and effort into becoming a warrior and a protector of her people. And over time she'd come to realise not being able to conceive was a blessing…

'Don't be sorry. At the time, I was just so glad I wasn't with child. That would have been awful… the final blow. I could never have had a child by one of them. Can you imagine? I would have hated it. I would have seen their faces in it every moment of every day, thinking it would grow up to be a monster, just like them...'

Ash nodded, but his features tightened and his body tensed, just as it had on the horse the other day, before he'd got down. He looked almost crestfallen. Had she said something wrong again?

He stood, dropping her hand and slowly pushing himself away from her, and she instantly felt the distance. He picked up his tunic and pulled it on, covering up his ink and his beautiful body, and headed towards the door. She realised he was about to leave, and she didn't want him to. She wanted him to stay. But he obviously had other ideas.

Had she said something to put him off? Her mind raced for an explanation. Why was he suddenly trying to get away from her as fast as he possibly could? She shook her head, as if she'd missed something. Something important. Was it because she'd confessed that she was unable to conceive? Did that matter to him? Did that change things? Perhaps he no longer saw her as womanly...

'I'm sorry for all the injustice you've suffered at the hands of men, Svea.' He bowed his head. 'No one should have had to endure what you've been through.' He pulled open the door. 'It's late. I will leave you now to get some rest. It's going to be a long day tomorrow.'

And then he was gone. He walked out into the dark corridor and closed the door behind him and she felt robbed, deprived... She didn't know what she'd been hoping for, but after the intimacy they'd shared it hadn't been this. It was as if a cool breeze had burst through the door, taking him with it. He'd left so suddenly, without giving her what she needed. He'd left her wanting…

There was no way she was going to be able to get any rest—not without knowing why he'd left her. Not without some kind of explanation.

Chapter Seven

Ash stared at himself in the polished metal slab on his table. Hauling off his tunic and throwing it on the floor, he took in the new design on his skin and ran his fingers over the lines. For a long while, lying on Svea's bed, letting her brand him with her creative gift, he'd thought he had never been so at peace. So content. It had been a beautiful, private time between them, when they'd let their guards down and accepted a mutual trust between them.

He had never wanted her to finish. And yet when he'd seen the exquisite design that captured his whole self so perfectly he had been overwhelmed. As Svea had explained the design he'd heard the words she'd used to describe him… *Thoughtful. Wise. Sensible…* His heart had bloomed. He knew he tried his best. *Passionate. Powerful. Protector…* She knew he would do anything to keep her safe.

He had so desperately wanted to believe that he was all those things she believed him to be. And then… *Monster…*

His blood chilled. It was always there, lurking beneath the surface, his dark, sordid secret. Unbeknown to her she had wounded him to the core, describing his darkest fears.

He stared into his own brown eyes and his hardened face as he had done many times before, wondering if they were the features of a monster, desperately searching for any sign of resemblance between him and his mother, hoping that this time he would see a glimpse of her face in his. But he couldn't see her at all. Which meant only one thing—he must take after his father.

Monster...

He slammed the metal slab down onto the wooden table in disgust. He was striding across the room and then back again, when suddenly there was a soft knock on the door.

Ash stopped pacing the floor and cursed. What could Ellette or his father want at this time of night? Reluctantly, he went to open it.

It was Svea.

Svea was at his door.

His heart thumped wildly in his chest.

She was nibbling on her bottom lip, still wearing that wholesome virginal nightgown, and she was glancing up and down the corridor as if she was worried that someone would see her.

'Can I come in?' she whispered.

'How did you know where to find me?'

'I explored. While you were away.' She shrugged. 'Sorry.'

His lips twisted—at least she was honest. And she was more interested in discovering things about him than anyone had been before, although he knew she shouldn't be. He should have kept his distance... made sure she stayed away. He wasn't good. Not for her. Not for anyone.

Even so, he held the door open wider for her and she ducked under his arm and came inside. He closed the door and leaned against it, feeling at a loss as she stood in the middle of his room, wringing her hands. The place was a mess, his tunic discarded on the floor alongside his boots and sword. What was she doing here? And why had he let her in? He was playing a dangerous game.

'I like your chair,' she said, pointing to the corner. 'And you have a wonderful view of the beach,' she babbled, motioning to the other wall.

'I know,' he said darkly. Surely she wasn't here to talk about his furniture or the pretty scenery outside? 'It's late, Svea. What is it that you want?'

She screwed up her face and he winced at his harsh tone, his direct words.

'Ash,' she said, turning round to face him. 'Did I say—or do—something wrong?'

'No.'

'Is it the ink—do you not like it?'

'It's not the ink, Svea. I told you. It's perfect.'
You're perfect.

'Was it what I said about me being unable to conceive? Does that matter to you? Does it make me somehow less attractive?'

'What? No! I don't care about that. I told you I don't want children, Svea…'

'Then what is it? You bolted from my room like a startled stallion, as if I'd put the fear of Odin into you. I—I was hoping you'd stay…' Her words seemed to dry up. Then, 'Ash,' she said, stepping towards him, 'I don't know how to do this…where to begin. But… Don't you want to spend the night with me?'

He sucked in a breath. It was all he wanted—to hold her against him, in his arms all night—and yet something was holding him back…something dark and scary on the borders of his mind. It was like a huge black cloud, brimming with awful secrets, and he was so afraid it would burst. He wanted to keep it hidden and not to have to deal with it.

He stood rigid, rooting his feet to the floor, but it was as if fate was working against him, sending her his way, breaking down all his defences, forcing him into cracking under the pressure. He didn't deserve her, so he couldn't make a move towards her. No matter how much he wanted to.

Could he?

'I can't,' he said, his voice strained.

But she didn't seem to be listening. She closed the distance between them, coming to stand just a whisper away from him. She placed a delicate hand on his bare chest. 'Ash, don't you want me? Is it because of everything I've told you? Because I'm…tarnished?'

'That's not it,' he said furiously, shaking his head, frowning, shocked that that was what she thought.

Was that how he'd made her feel? He was such a fool.

He raked a hand through his hair before reaching out to gently grasp her upper arm, wanting to reassure her. 'Svea, you know that I want you. More than anything...' His voice didn't sound real.

'Then kiss me. Please, Ash.'

He squeezed his eyes shut for a second. He wanted to. He really did. But she had been so honest with him—she had laid herself bare, all her scars and insecurities. He was in awe of her bravery. Because he was still lying to her. He was lying about who he really was. And if he'd disliked himself before, he despised himself now. He knew there was no way he could lay a hand on her without her knowing the truth about him. It just wouldn't be fair.

He searched her face for answers, but even as he was trying to muster up the strength to push her away, to let her down gently, he watched her as she fumbled with the fastenings at the neck of her nightgown, untying the collar, her fingers trembling.

His heart was in his mouth. There was nothing he wanted more than to peel away her clothes and explore her beautiful body, to show her how she deserved to be treated, how pleasurable touch could be. And yet if she knew his story—knew what blood he had flowing through his veins, what his father had done—would she still want him?

He covered her hand with his. 'Svea, no.'

She shrank back. Her eyes were filled with confusion, darkened with hurt. He knew he had to tell her his secret, that it was a risk he had to take… He knew that she was worth it. And he knew that if he didn't he'd lose her anyway.

'There's something you don't know about me. Something that I need to tell you before you decide to do this.'

Her blue gaze focused on him, and she seemed to steel herself for whatever was to come. 'What is it?' she asked.

He knew there was no going back now. If he wanted her he had to fight for her, and the first thing he had to do was be courageous and honest—just as she'd shown him how to be.

He took her hand in his and walked her over to the bed. She sat on the edge and stared up at him, concerned. He kneeled on the floor in front of her. He wanted to look her straight in the eyes when he told her. With a kind of morbid fascination, he wanted to see how strong a reaction she'd have to his hideous revelation. He needed to see if she was repulsed…if there was a moment when her eyes changed from looking upon him as a man to seeing him as a monster…

Where to begin? He had never told anyone this before, and his hands were actually trembling. He didn't think he'd ever been so nervous—not even in the throes of battle—but he was determined. He had to do this—for her—and he took a deep breath to steady himself.

'Have you ever seen a cuckoo lay its eggs in the nest of another type of bird, so the other bird has to raise the cuckoo's young?'

Svea frowned, confused.

He knew it was a strange way to start a story, but if he could just make her see... 'Those little cuckoo chicks are monsters. They kill all the others to survive.' He stroked a hand over his beard, hoping the picture he was painting would help with getting his message across.

But Svea shook her head. 'Ash, what are you talking about?'

He swallowed. 'That baby you said you could never have...by one of those men... You said it would have been a monster child.' He took a deep breath. 'Svea, what I'm trying to tell you is *I* was such a child.'

Her breath caught. 'What?'

'Those drawings you saw in my father's chronicles... You're a clever woman—I'm sure you worked it out. Danes attacked our shores years ago, when my father and mother had just married. It was swift and brutal. The people of the settlement didn't stand a chance. One night, when they were asleep in their beds, savage warriors landed on Braewood beach and raced up to the fort, destroying everything in their path, setting the keep on fire. They took some of the women and children with them—presumably as slaves—and killed many of the men. And what Crowe did to you—the way he attacked you—that's what a Dane did to my mother.'

Svea's wide-eyed horrified gaze studied his face as if he'd removed a mask and she was seeing the real him for the first time. She was searching his eyes as he had been doing moments before she'd knocked on the door. Perhaps she was looking for clues to his ancestry…signs she hadn't seen before in the wide set of his jaw, his pronounced brow.

'She was raped—and I was the result of that brutality. And what you described…how you'd have felt if you'd been with child by Crowe or one of his men… was exactly how my mother felt about me. She and my father had to look upon me every day. I was a constant reminder of what had happened to them. Until they couldn't bear it any longer. Until they sent me away to a monastery where the monks tried to beat the Dane out of me. For years.'

'Ash…'

She looked sickened, and he was glad he'd told her. For if the knowledge of what kind of man had made him, how he had come to be and what kind of blood he had flowing through his veins repelled her, it was right she knew before she decided to let him fold her in his arms and take her to bed.

'Born an illegitimate child, I have Norse blood flowing through my veins, Svea. And I have no idea of what kind of person I really am, who my real father is, or what I'm capable of. Which is why I act the way I do…why I keep people at bay for their own protection. It's why I don't drink ale, why I dress the way I do and why I have to stay in control. I need to keep guard over my behaviour at all times. I am worried that somewhere beneath the surface lies a part of that man who attacked my mother.'

He stood and paced the floor, the usual feelings of guilt for what his parents had suffered and the shame of who he was, of how he'd been created, burning through him. But then he came back to the bed, unable to keep his distance from her, his hands on his hips. And now he could add a sense of misgiving and foreboding apprehension to the mix of his feelings, because he was wondering what Svea was thinking. He was desperate to know.

'I was happy living a solitary, reclusive life until recently, when I met you. You wanted to know why I don't live here... It's because I don't feel worthy. I was never made to feel I belonged in Braewood. This place has never felt like my home because I was banished from here when I was a small boy, when my own family couldn't bear the sight of me. Neither could the monks at the monastery I was sent to. They believed I was a devil child. So they made me pay for the crime of being born every single day. Of course my father commanded that my lineage be kept secret in Braewood, for the sake of his pride and the family's reputation, so no one knows the truth—but I do. I feel it. I've felt like an outsider for my whole life. People stare at me as if they know I'm different. And when I see the crumbling keep, the blackened turrets—they're a constant reminder of what happened, of what I am. A monster.'

'No!' Svea shook her head fiercely, her face pale, a tear streaking down her face. 'You're not a monster, Ash. You can't honestly believe that. I know I don't.'

'You said it yourself! You said you wouldn't have wanted a child knowing it was born out of violence. Well, that's what I am... Take a good look. Even my own mother couldn't love me.'

'What I said was wrong,' she said passionately, standing and moving to meet him in the middle of the room. 'Because I've never met a man like you. You're no monster, Ash, you're the best man I know.'

He stared at her, his hands loose at his sides. He didn't trust himself to move, because he couldn't quite believe what he was hearing. He'd told her the truth, his deepest, darkest secret. He'd been trying to warn her off, tell her she ought to stay away, that he didn't know what he was capable of. And yet she was still leaning towards him, reaching for him, putting her hand on his shoulder.

'If these last few days have taught me anything, it's that people can be good or bad whether they're Saxon or Dane. And you, Ash, you're the best of both. You're one of the good men.'

Tentatively he took her hands in his, wanting to draw strength from her touch. 'How can you be sure, Svea? Because I'm not...'

'What happened to your mother and father was awful—tragic, even. But it wasn't your fault.' She squeezed his fingers and looked up at him, her blue eyes shining with affection. 'Your parents were victims of an appalling attack and they had no say in what happened. But they did get a choice in how they brought you up. Those poor birds don't kick the cuckoo chicks out of their nests, Ash, they take care of them, raise them as their own. You're an innocent person here.'

He looked at her, uncertain, still not sure he agreed with her. But he didn't want her to stop talking. He wanted to hear more of the affirming words she was saying. He needed to hear them from her. She was such a positive force in his life. He'd never liked himself very much, but he knew he needed her approval as he needed the very air that he breathed. And if he was to touch her, to make love to her, he needed her consent.

'If you want to know what I see when I look at you, I'll tell you,' she said. 'I see a brave, strong man who is loyal to his King, to his family and his people. A man who cares about others, whether they're Saxon or Dane. A man who is more beautiful, inside and out, than anyone I've ever met before. A man I can trust, wholeheartedly. Please don't push me away, Ash, because of something that happened years ago—before our time. Not when I've never wanted any man to touch me like I do you.'

She bravely pressed her body against him and he rested his forehead against hers.

'Just for one night, Ash, can't we try to forget about who and what we are?'

A hectic beat started clamouring in his chest. He couldn't believe it. He couldn't believe she was saying she still wanted him after all he'd told her. She wasn't repelled or disgusted as he'd thought she might be, which meant she was either insane or he was, to still be standing there, while she was in his room, asking him to lay his hands on her.

And then, in case he needed it spelled out for him, she pulled him down next to her and sat on the edge of the bed again.

'I want you to kiss me again, Ash. I'm going out of my mind. Don't you know it's rude to keep a lady waiting?'

He laughed, and the tension of the past few days—hell, *years*—seemed to melt away beneath her delicate touch. He brought his hands up to hold her face. He pressed a soft, tender kiss against her lips.

'More,' she whispered, leaning into him.

He grinned against her mouth and kissed her again. But this time it was a deep, open-mouthed kiss that stole their breath away. And as he kissed her he lifted her backwards, laying her down on the soft furs.

He stretched out beside her, his arms wrapping around her back, pulling her into his body, while continuing to take his time kissing her. He couldn't believe this was happening...that all his desires were coming true. But he knew that this time he had to take it slowly. Whatever she was saying about what she wanted, he knew he had to make sure she was truly ready. He'd made a mistake in rushing her before, sending her running from his arms, and he wasn't going to let that happen again.

Svea's fingers chased over his bare chest and moved around his sides to explore his broad back. Her touch burned, her fingers like tiny flames flickering against his skin, trailing over his muscles and scars. They came back to linger over his hard nipples, swirling through the hairs on his chest and the fresh marks on his skin. And he watched the emotions cross her face as she explored him. Wonder, excitement, hesitation… He wanted her to learn all the soft and hard ridges of his body, and then she wouldn't be afraid of him.

'I like it that there's a part of me etched into your body…' She smiled. 'Forever.'

'Me, too,' he said, kissing her forehead before pulling her beautiful mouth back down to his and letting his tongue become more demanding, more inquisitive, until she was responding, pressing her body closer to his. 'I want to give you something you'll remember forever, too.'

He broke away to leave a trail of delicate kisses down the column of her neck, wanting to probe and examine every part of her with his tongue. He glided it over her swirling patterns, following the lines there, and then down over her collarbone, and the pulse flickering at the base of her throat. Drawing the collar of her gown aside, exposing more skin, he let his hands curve down over the thin material. Carefully, he took one of her breasts in his hand, cupping its weight, and she gasped when his tongue followed in hot pursuit over her swollen skin.

He stared up into her eyes. 'Shall I take this off?' he asked, his hands smoothing over the material that was suddenly annoyingly in the way. He didn't want there to be any barrier between them.

She nodded, her cheeks flushing, and he pulled her up to a sitting position. She wriggled the material free of her bottom and then he took over and lifted her arms up in the air, bringing the gown over her head before discarding it on the floor.

When he knelt over her she was quick to bring her knees up, to cloak her breasts with her hands. 'You've probably been with lots of women...' she muttered, suddenly shy.

He reached out to place his hands over hers. 'None that have made me feel the way you do.'

As his fingers curled around her fingers where they gripped her skin, he slowly peeled her hands away, and she finally gave in, exposing herself, lying back on the bed and offering herself up to his heated perusal.

'None as beautiful as you.'

Pressing her arms above her head, he hovered over her, wanting to kiss her again—and saw her freeze. He lifted himself away immediately, remembering what she'd told him, realising it would make her uncomfortable to be pinned down beneath his weight. The last thing he wanted was to bring back those memories. No, tonight they would be creating new ones.

He stretched out beside her again. 'I'm not going to hurt you, Svea,' he soothed, bringing her mouth towards him and kissing her again until she relaxed against him. 'In fact...' he grinned wickedly '...if my body makes you nervous, what if I promise to only touch you with my lips—for now?'

'Just your lips?' She frowned and looked unsure, as if she didn't understand.

'Yes. I can't hurt you with my lips.'

He started with her mouth, loving the feeling of having his tongue inside it, and he made it last. Having her naked beside him, it was torture not to touch her with his hands, but he knew the delayed gratification would be worth it. It was the most passionate kiss he'd ever experienced, and it soon had her pressing her naked thighs together, squirming against him. He was desperate to touch her there, to push his hand between those delicate blonde curls, nudge between her legs and seek out her intimate places. But he knew he had to show restraint. He had to wait until she was ready.

He moved to her temple, to place soft, sweet kisses there, and then down to nuzzle her ear, his slow torment causing her to thrust her breasts towards him, wanting more. The temptation of her dark, hard nipples was too much. He was drawn to them, wanting them in his mouth, between his teeth, and he groaned. His tongue glided over her naked shoulder, over her collarbone and then down, his open-mouthed kisses laving her perfect breasts, and she writhed beneath him. He sucked a dark, tantalising bud into his mouth, gently dragging his teeth over the slick skin, and she gasped.

Her fingers roamed through his hair, holding him in place, as if she never wanted him to stop. But he had another destination in mind, and as his head lowered, his tongue swirling over the smooth, sensitive skin of her stomach, her hands gripped onto his shoulders.

He moved even lower, and she gasped, trying to sit up, to stop his descent.

'Ash, what are you doing?'

'It will feel nice. I promise.'

* * *

Propped up on her elbows, Svea licked her lips, nervous, as she watched Ash's mouth move over her body, caressing her with his tongue, his beard grazing her, sending a blaze across her skin. He placed delicate little kisses to her hips, and then down over her smooth, naked thighs. She tipped her head back, giving in to all the incredible, exciting sensations he was causing.

And then his face was right *there*, hovering at the apex of her thighs, over the tight curls that hid the most secret parts of her, and she gasped.

'Svea…?' he whispered.

She knew what he was asking. He'd promised only to touch her with his mouth, and he wanted her to part her thighs, to expose herself to him, to give him better access. But could she be so brazen? Were such things done?

He nuzzled her with his nose and she slowly, wantonly, spread her legs, blaming pure unbridled lust, unbelievably *wanting* him to take possession of her with his mouth. She threw her arms over her heated face in flustered, feverish submission. His lips touched her sensitive nub—the one she'd found while bathing and had rubbed and stroked, thinking of him—and now he was doing exactly that…with his tongue.

She cried out, unable to help herself. It felt so explicit, so intimate, so incredible, and she raised her bottom off the bed to meet him, desperate for more. She hadn't known such acts were allowed. But now she knew, she never wanted him to stop.

The exquisite sensations building inside her were intense, like a restless tide rolling, swelling…and she was riding the crest of his wave. As his masterful tongue glided all the way along her crease with breathless precision, seeking out her core, the wave crashed and shattered into a million pieces against his mouth, the release so extreme she thrashed about in wild abandon, holding his head in place and crying out his name.

It took a while for her body to stop shuddering, and she didn't know how long they lay like that, neither of them moving, his head resting on her thigh. He must be giving her time to get her breath back, but she wanted him to come up, to hold her in his arms again, so she tugged at his shoulder.

He dragged his body up towards her and grinned. 'Was that so bad?'

She blushed, draping an arm across her forehead as he kissed her again. 'You know it wasn't. I didn't realise such a thing was even possible.'

He grinned. 'There's a whole world of possibilities I want to show you, Svea, if you'll let me.' He splayed a possessive hand over her breast.

She giggled. 'Did they teach you to do that in the monastery?'

He grinned. 'Not exactly. I don't think Abbot Æbbe would have approved.'

She sobered. 'Was it all bad…while you were there?' She couldn't bear to think of him being mistreated. She ran her fingers over the scars on his chest. 'Is that where you got these?'

'Some. Not all. Some are battle wounds.'

'What did they do to you?'

He shrugged. 'Tried to beat the Dane out of me. I'm not sure they succeeded. I think they knew I would never grow up to be a monk! Sometimes I went without food. And there was always work to do, no time for play. But it was no worse than what the others suffered, I'm sure.'

She had the feeling he was making light of it, but she didn't press him for more information. She hoped he would feel able to tell her in time. She suddenly felt lucky that she had had such a loving family, despite losing her parents when she was so young. At least they'd taken care of her. Ash had never had that, but she wanted to take care of him now.

'I did make good use of the library there,' he went on. 'And I had an excellent education. In that respect I was fortunate. I was taught logic and philosophy, geography, how to read and write—all skills that have helped me serve the King well.'

'I would love to be able to read and write,' Svea said.

'I could teach you,' he said. He rolled onto his back and pulled her so that she was lying beside him, her head on his chest. 'Actually, a lot of the runes describe you. Let me show you.'

Using his fingers, he drew what felt like a cross on her back. 'What's that?'

'The g-rune—Gyfu. It means gift. *You're* a gift, Svea...'

Next he drew a vertical line, with a loop to its right.

His fingers were so gentle it made her shiver. 'What's that one?' she murmured.

'That's Wynn—meaning hope...joy...perfection. And one more,' he said, drawing a line with two small diagonal lines coming off it. 'This one is Ansuz, known as the Rune of the Ash.'

She smiled up at him. 'I like that one. I like them all.'

'So no, the monastery wasn't all bad. I think the worst thing was feeling so alone. And, of course, not being by the sea. I missed the ocean.'

'I would miss that, too. But Termarth isn't by the sea...' she said thoughtfully. 'Do you like it there?'

'I like the people.' He continued to stroke her back with his fingertips. 'They have come to mean something to me.'

'You know, there were rumours at one time that you were going to marry the Princess.'

He raised his head off the bed. 'Anne?' he asked, surprised.

'Yes. Brand was not happy. I think he felt threatened.'

Ash grinned. Slowly his fingers roamed down to squeeze her soft, smooth bottom, kneading the sensitive flesh.

'He didn't have anything to worry about. There was never anything between us. It seems I prefer my women on the wilder side.' He kissed her lips again. 'And I want to see how wild I can make you, Svea.'

As if wanting better access to her secret places, he pulled her on top of him, so his fingers could dip further below. 'This time I'm going to touch you with my hands. Everywhere...'

His words ignited a fire within her, and she writhed against him. And then he stroked down the crevice of her buttocks, gently, lightly teasing.

'Ash...' she spluttered, the anticipation of his intimate touch no longer making her nervous, but wet—and wild. Just as he'd requested.

'I have told you, Svea. I intend to leave no part of you untouched.'

His fingers delved deeper, down to her soft, silky entrance, and he gently, carefully, pushed a finger inside her.

She gasped, tensing around him, gripping his shoulders.

'Is this all right?'

'Yes...' she choked.

And as he began to slide his finger in and out, accelerating his speed, she spread her legs to straddle his hips, giving him better access. But she didn't know how much more of this sweet torture she could take. What was he trying to do to her?

'I want to touch you here,' he said, pressing deeper, 'with my body. And I promise it will feel like this, but better.'

He gently withdrew, moving upwards to caress her tiny nub, circling it with his clever, skilled finger before easing it inside her again. Her intimate muscles clenched around him, the sensations driving her wild.

She was excruciatingly aware that so far she hadn't touched him in return, nor given him any pleasure. She had just taken. Not that he'd given her much choice. But she knew now that she must. She wanted to please him, more than anything, but she didn't know what to do. She suddenly wished she'd listened to the women talking about their men and what pleased them back at home, in the longhouse. But she'd always shied away from such conversations.

How ridiculous, she thought, that she was suddenly more nervous, more fearful of this—of wanting to please a man—than of fighting in a battle or running a fortress. Tentatively, she moved to the side of his body, let her hand cover the ridge in his breeches, her fingers trembling. His breath caught.

'Ash,' she said. 'Will you show me what to do… what you like? I want to please you.'

As if all her wishes were coming true, he tugged down his breeches so they were both naked, and she enjoyed the feel of her bare legs entwined with his. He rearranged their position, drawing her back into his chest, her bare bottom pressed against his body. And then he took her hand in his and wrapped her fingers around his shaft.

Kissing her neck, he showed her how to move her hand up and down, and he groaned. She continued to move her hand as he'd demonstrated, and he brushed her hair aside so that he could kiss her neck, her shoulder.

When she ran her thumb over the top of him, experimenting, he gripped her body tighter, his muscles bunching. She thought he must like it, so she did it again.

'Svea, that feels so good…'

She moved a little faster and his hands came up to cup her breasts, gently crushing them, and she turned her mouth to find his. As his kisses became open-mouthed and explicit she felt her body quiver, those flames flickering between her legs again, making her squirm, and she wriggled her bottom backwards against his groin.

As if he could read her mind—or her body—he let his hands roam down to stroke between her legs again, needing no pause before easing his fingers inside her again. And when he withdrew, his hands caressing her body, she felt the slick wetness of her excitement on her thighs.

'Svea, I want you,' he said.

It came almost as a question, and she knew he was asking her if she was ready.

Her heart began to pound, and nerves fluttered low in her stomach, but she knew she wanted this. He was still curled around her body and, gripping him tight, she guided him to her entrance.

She brought her hand up to hold his jaw. 'I want you, too.'

'Trust me?'

She nodded.

It was an invasion of great gentleness. He moved carefully, slowly, and she loved him for that, but as his hard, silky skin pierced her body she gasped at the sudden breach and he stilled.

'Are you all right?' he asked, his voice raw.

'Yes.'

'Do you want me to stop?'

'No,' she said, and she took a deep breath, willing her tight, tense body to relax around him, to welcome him in. 'Please don't stop, Ash.'

And as he stroked and soothed her, whispering how beautiful she was into her ear, she slowly began to relax around him and he edged further inside. Her breath caught, but this time it was a gasp of pleasure, not pain, and she felt a ripple of heat flood through her. Suddenly she wanted more, gripping his thighs, tugging him towards her, and with a single sudden thrust he slid deep inside her. All the way.

'Svea...?'

'It feels good. *You* feel good.' She had never imagined it could feel like this, and she felt a swell of emotion bloom within her.

He rolled her onto her stomach, so that he lay on top of her, and surged inside her again, making her cry out in wonder at the unexpected, insane pleasure rocking through her. She spread her legs wider and he thrust harder, pinning her to the bed. But she welcomed it now. This was her choice. She wanted Ash to take ownership of her body. She wanted it to be branded with his touch. She wanted to be completely and utterly impaled by her beautiful half-Dane.

He continued to kiss her neck, her shoulder, stroking his hands down her body as she grabbed a fistful of the furs above her head. And then his fingers roamed down, digging into her hips and pulling her up slightly, so he could move his hand beneath her, between her legs. Ruthlessly he pressed his finger to her nub and thrust hard inside her, over and over again, setting a torturous, yet unhurried pace, as if he wanted to savour every moment of his taking of her.

The pressure was building again, and she knew she was on the brink. She didn't know how much more she could take. She began to grapple wildly with the furs, needing something to take hold of, to anchor herself, and then she finally felt his muscles tense as he slammed into her once more, harder than ever, and she screamed with pleasure, feeling herself splinter and shatter as she revelled in every last moment of her total surrender to this man.

Chapter Eight

When Svea next woke, the sun was streaming through the smoke hole, lighting up the room as Ash had lit up her world last night. She gave a satisfied stretch of her aching muscles. Despite the heaviness of her limbs she felt as if she was floating...lighter than she'd felt in a long, long time. She luxuriated in the memory of their lovemaking, and turned, expecting to find Ash lying in the bed beside her, wanting to ask to do it all again, but he wasn't there. The large bed was empty.

She sat bolt upright and scoured the room with her eyes, but he wasn't there. If it hadn't been for the raw ache between her legs, reminding her of the intimate things they'd done together, she might have thought she'd been dreaming. Instead she smiled. She felt wonderful, elated. But where was he? Had she overslept? When had he left her? And why hadn't he woken her?

She dashed out of bed and snatched up her gown from the floor. She threw it over her, then reached for a blanket to wrap around herself, in case she should meet anyone in the corridor. She tiptoed out through the door and stealthily raced into her room, rushing to put on the clean breeches and tunic Ellette had left for her.

She could hear people milling about—at work in the square, making a commotion downstairs in the hall. At home, she was usually one of the first up, and she felt guilty she had stayed so long in bed. She skipped down the staircase in a hurry, hoping to find Ash by the fire, or perhaps readying the horses for their departure.

She charged into Ellette in the doorway.

'Ah, there you are, dear! Are you hungry?'

Svea shook her head. 'Actually, I'm looking for Ash—Lord Stanton. Have you seen him?'

'He left a while ago, love. He said that I should leave you sleeping.'

'What?' Panic thundered through her. *No!* He wouldn't have left without her—would he? Not after last night.

'Left to go where?'

'Ealdorman Buckley and the Lords Crompton and Fiske arrived at dawn this morning. It took me by surprise. I wish the young Lord had told me they were coming—I would have had a meal prepared. Anyway, Lord Stanton said they were all heading for Termarth, to help the King and his men. He said I wasn't to wake you. He said to give you a message, though. Now, let me try to remember what it was…'

Svea bit her lip anxiously, her heart pounding.

'Oh, yes, he said to tell you he knows you'd want to come, but he doesn't want you getting hurt. He said it's best you stay here, where you'll be safe, until he returns.'

Betrayal clawed through her chest like a giant wolf, fighting its way out, and a rage strong enough to set another fire burning through Braewood Keep took hold of her. Thus far they had been a team. She'd thought they had formed a plan to help the King, his men and her friends, and they would see it through together. But he'd left without her, as if he didn't need her. How could he?

She dropped down on to a bench to steady her shaking legs. Yes, she was a woman. But first and foremost she was a warrior and protector of Kald. She wanted to fight for her people. She wanted to be useful—not some feeble Lady who stayed at home, waiting for her man to return. She couldn't believe he was denying her this opportunity, denying her honour. Did he not know what was important to her— did he not know her at all?

And surely he would want her with him at his side? Especially after everything they'd been through? After everything they'd done together last night? If it had been up to her, she wouldn't have been able to let him out of her sight.

She knew what Ellette had told her was true—that Ash probably was worried about her and wanted to protect her and keep her safe—but even so she felt hurt and let down.

Cold, hard determination settled in her stomach.

She wouldn't stand for it. She would not be restrained or suppressed at the hands of a man. Ash did not control her. He had asked her to trust him before he'd entered her body last night, and he had been careful and considerate with her, but look where it had got her. He'd lulled her into a false sense of security and now she felt foolish. She felt as if she'd been duped. He hadn't even had the courtesy to wake her up and say goodbye, face to face.

She stood, making her decision. They couldn't be too far ahead. If she left now, she might just be able to catch up with them. She didn't know the way, but an army like that would have left clear tracks on the ground. She knew she would be putting herself in danger, riding out alone and across open countryside, but she didn't think she could bear it, sitting here, waiting for news. Surely this was a risk worth taking?

Her mind kept running over the past few days for any signs she'd missed that he'd never intended her to go with him. *'We'll ride out together to Termarth.'* That was what he'd said. But when he'd said 'we'll', she'd thought he had meant he and she. Had she got it wrong? Or had that once been his intent and he had changed his mind since their lovemaking last night?

Either way, she sensed that he'd been dishonest, and now she felt totally and utterly used, stranded and alone, and she resolved never to let him make her feel like this again.

As she wolfed down the bread and milk Ellette handed to her, and strapped herself into her chainmail and boots, she fired questions at the woman about which direction Termarth was from here, and how many men had joined Ash today. She readied a horse in the stables and mounted the animal, a fierce conviction solidifying inside her.

Ellette fretted about her, trying her best to persuade her not to go, but she'd made up her mind. She was unshakeable on the matter. And if anything were to happen to her at least she would know she'd tried to make a difference, that she'd been a part of something.

She said goodbye to Ellette and some of the Danish settlers, then spurred the horse on and exited the gates. She instantly found the trail and followed the footprints through the mud, galloping at speed across undulating landscapes, leaving the glittering blue-green ocean behind in the distance. The countryside was vibrant and beautiful, a rainbow of rich colours underneath the crisp sunlight, but she didn't have time to stop and admire the view.

She realised she was finally getting the ride she wanted, and a taste of freedom—only it wasn't along her beloved shoreline at home. She was heading towards enemy territory. But she wasn't afraid. No, what frightened her was the fact that, despite her anger towards him, she was still desperate to see Ash. She wanted to look into his eyes and see if he felt the same as she did after last night. That it had been incredible. Life-altering. She wanted to know that he didn't have any regrets.

She could still feel the taste of his lips on hers, the touch of his burning skin, his long fingers gently kneading her body. And she still wanted him… Badly. To think she had settled on a lifetime of celibacy… Oh, what she would have missed out on. The things he'd done to her…she had never dreamed they could feel so good. The way he'd taken possession of her mouth, and all her intimate places, first with his tongue and then with his body… It had been exquisite. And she wanted more.

But she knew she should not. Not without an explanation. Not without an apology. She deserved better. He had wounded her in leaving her, and she knew from past experience that she didn't heal easily. It was as if he'd been trying to be kind, attempting to take care of her and keep her safe, but in doing so he'd acted as if he were superior, patronising her. As if she wasn't good enough to fight alongside them… as if he was embarrassed about her.

She wouldn't stand for it.

Early afternoon came and went, and she realised she had never ridden so fast, or for so long, without a break. She was starving, and she was worried about the horse, who must be starting to tire, too. She passed hedgerows laden with berries and felt a pang in her chest. She wanted to stop and pick some from the brambles, to taste their sweet, tangy juice on her tongue, so they'd remind her of him. But she knew she had to keep going if she were to have any chance of catching up with him.

She felt tears fill her eyes, and she tried to make sense of the mixed-up mass of emotions she was feeling. How had one night rocked her to the core, altering her perceptions and her opinions? And as she passed fields of cows, with cute little calves at their hooves, for the first time in her life she wondered what it would be like to be a mother, to have a child to cherish and a husband at her side.

The direction of her thinking scared her. She had spent one night in bed with a man and now she was daydreaming about marriage and children—things that could never be. She was appalled with herself. Hadn't Ash told her himself that he never wanted to marry or have children, and she had repeated the same. She couldn't even conceive. No, their lovemaking had only been for one night. She'd said so herself... Just one night of pure, unequivocal pleasure.

She tried to ground her thoughts, thinking back to the things Ash had told her about his upbringing, and she realised he had never had someone to look after him—not properly. Ellette was probably the closest person he'd ever had to a mother, on those occasions when he'd been allowed to stay in Braewood and see her. Underneath his strict, serious demeanour, she wondered if somewhere there was still a lost little boy, ill at ease with himself? She wondered if her affection could change all that.

She had cared for him when she'd thought he was a Saxon. And she'd wanted him when she'd discovered he was a Dane, too. How could his mother and father not have found something to love in him, as she had? And then she felt cross with herself all over again. What was she thinking? She needed to stir up her anger towards him.

When she came across the embers of a still-warm fire, her heart lifted. She knew she must be getting close now.

'Just a bit longer and then we'll stop,' she coaxed her speedy companion, urging him on.

So on they went. Her legs were roaring with pain now—from gripping onto the horse so tightly, from pressing her knees into its sides, and perhaps from the new experiences she'd discovered last night.

Well, she had hoped for an adventure while Brand was away. She'd certainly got one.

She felt a pang of homesickness and realised she missed her brother. She wanted to see him again and tell him all about Ash, about everything they'd been through. She wanted to share her joy and her frustration. She wished he could be at her side to solve all this.

Finally she caught a glimpse of the tall silver ramparts of Termarth Castle, looming on the horizon. The sight filled her with unease and a deep sense of foreboding. The last time she had been here awful things had happened. Things that had changed the course of her life. She hoped that this time things would be better, but her dark memories were combined with fresh thoughts of her men being hurt by Crowe and his brother. They haunted her.

She knew she must be close to Ash and his soldiers now. And then, like a vision in a dream, they appeared in the distance, their flags and banners flying in the wind. It looked as if they'd chosen a barbican on a bridge as their base. They seemed to be erecting tents, lighting fires, making camp for the night.

She pulled her shoulders back and held her chin high. She'd done it. She'd made it. She'd show him...

The horse seemed to sense the end of their journey was near and upped his pace for the final few fields that stood between them and their destination. But Svea was suddenly wishing he wouldn't be so speedy. She even found herself reining him back, slowing him down, as she wondered what Ash would say when he saw her.

Suddenly nervous, she had the feeling he wouldn't like the fact she'd gone against his orders. Or that she'd ridden a day across open countryside on her own. No doubt he would call her foolish, and reckless. But why did she care? She was angry with him.

The last thing she wanted him to think was that she had traversed hills and ravines at breakneck speed just to see him, though. Because that would be madness. No, she thought, thinking back to how she'd felt when Ellette had said he'd left without her that morning, stirring the rage that was still simmering in her stomach. She needed to make it clear she was only here to save her men. They were her priority. She was here for the fight.

The camp was a flurry of activity. Ash's men were putting up tents, and the leading Lords were huddled inside the central pitch, discussing the ways in and out of Termarth Castle.

Ash knew the kingdom and all its strengths and weaknesses better than anyone—he had prided himself on learning every entrance, every crack and crevice, anything that could be used against them—and it felt wrong to be sharing the information with others. But he knew that he must if they were to have any success in securing the King's fortress.

The trouble was, he was struggling to focus. His mind kept swaying back to Svea and all the incredible things they'd done together last night. The way his body had fitted inside hers so perfectly. It had never felt so good.

And yet he'd surely ruined it when he'd left Braewood without her this morning. It was awful to know that after the intimacy they'd shared, the connection they'd made, she would have spent the day furious with him for leaving her behind. For not even saying goodbye. Because he knew Svea. And he knew she would have wanted to come, to be a part of this, and she'd be livid that he'd kept her out of it.

It hadn't been a quick decision. He'd hardly got any rest last night after they'd made love, watching her sleeping in his bed, her long blonde hair framing her beautiful face, cascading over her bare shoulders. She'd looked perfect, like a goddess, and he'd realised there was no way he could take her into battle. He just couldn't bring himself to wake her, watch her put on her armour and ready herself to fight.

Call him selfish, but he couldn't stand the thought of her getting hurt. It was better this way. The emotional pain she would have felt at hearing he'd left without her, and the pain he was feeling now, were a small price to pay to keep her safe. And he'd thought he would be able to focus better without her being here, because he wouldn't have to worry about her.

Only he couldn't seem to concentrate at all. His thoughts kept returning to the weight of her breasts in his hands, the taste of her under his tongue and the feel of him moving inside her. He hoped she was all right. He hoped that when this was all over and he returned she would be able to understand his reasons and forgive him. If only he could rescue her men, she might even be proud of him.

A commotion near the gate of the barbican drew his attention and he stood quickly, making his way through the throng of men to see what was going on. The soldiers parted for him as he strode forward and he finally broke through the lines, his hand on the hilt of his sword, ready to face whoever had arrived.

Shock, quickly followed by a rush of joy, jolted through him.

It was Svea.

Svea was dismounting from a large black stallion and the men were leering and laughing, surrounding her, delighted to have a beautiful woman in their midst. They were all trying to help her descend, welcoming her to the camp.

His breath caught. He blinked, as if he didn't believe what he was seeing. But when he opened his eyes again she was still standing there, like a vision of strength and beauty, holding her sword and shield. Pleasure ripped through him. She was here, as if he'd dreamt her into life, so he wouldn't have to wallow in his misery at being apart from her any longer.

'I'm here to see Lord Stanton,' she boldly announced to the men.

And he wanted to charge towards her, saying, *I'm here*, to take her in his arms and never let her go.

But as he stepped forward her eyes locked with his and sanity returned. Ice met fire as she glared at him across the courtyard, seemingly undeterred, even though she was surrounded by an army of men. Was she insane? Why had she come? Her ignorant determination sent lashings of anger—and desire—to his groin.

'Svea, what the hell are you doing here?' he barked, suddenly furious. She'd blatantly ignored his order that she wasn't to leave Braewood. She was so wilful! She was beyond control! Had she not learnt a thing while being in his company? Did she not know that her actions could get her into trouble?

'I have come to fight. To save my men.'

A stab of disappointment that she hadn't said she was there for *him* unsettled him, but he instantly discarded it, incensed now. His lips narrowed. 'I told you not to come.'

'And I told you I don't take orders from you.'

A rumble of surprise from his men that she should speak to him so, in front of them, made his fury burn harder.

He beckoned to his squire, Wolf, and asked him to take Svea's horse and give it hay and water. And then he gripped Svea's arm—hard—and walked her over to the bridge, away from the eyes and ears of the soldiers.

When they realised their leader was dealing with the woman they began to disperse, seeming to lose interest. Good. He needed to talk to her, to scold her, and he didn't want an audience.

When they had reached a fair distance away, she flung herself out of his grasp and rounded on him, anger blazing in her blue eyes.

'How could you?' she spat, more enraged than he had thought possible. 'You lied to me, Ash. You made me believe we would do this together.'

'I changed my mind.'

'You can't do that. This isn't about you. It's about your men. My men. Your King. You told me yourself I fight as well as any of your men, and you need every warrior you can get. So why did you leave me behind?'

'You know why,' he barked. 'I don't want you fighting.' He thought he would do anything to ensure her safety. He'd even put her before his King. 'I don't want you out here, among all these men, in the camp or on the battlefield.'

'It's not your choice to make.'

'It's no place for a woman.'

She reeled back at his words. *'No place for a woman?'*

'No. I made a mistake last time in letting you come. I should have stood my ground all those days ago when we rode out from Kald. I've regretted it ever since.'

She gasped.

'You should never have left home that morning. Catastrophe has followed us ever since,' he bit out.

'And that's *my* fault?'

'Keep your voice down,' he said, conscious that the soldiers would be able to hear their raised voices, that they were causing a scene. 'Of course it's not your fault, but as I keep telling you—you're a liability, Svea. Why can't you see that? Just take a look around you. You're a weakness in our armour.'

She stepped back, looking shocked at his cold words.

'A weakness?'

He knew that he'd hurt her, and he hadn't intended to, but he was angry. Angry with her for leaving Braewood by herself, because by doing so she had put herself at risk. He still couldn't quite believe she'd travelled all that distance alone. It was thoughtless. What if something had happened to her? He wouldn't have been able to bear it. And now turning up at a camp full of men...

How did he know she'd be safe unless he kept a constant eye on her? It was selfish of her. Now he'd have to guard her, and that wouldn't do his sanity any good. How would he keep his desire for her in check? And as for the imminent fight... He needed to focus on that, and having her here was not going to help him. But, worst of all, he was worried he wouldn't be able to protect her on the battlefield, and that scared him more than anything. He would never forgive himself if something happened to her.

She closed in on him, tipping her chin towards him. 'A weakness in the fight for your King and my men? Or a weakness to you, Ash...? Maybe I'm not the one who is at fault here. Do you do this with all your women? Make love to them, then leave without even so much as a goodbye?'

'Svea?'

They both turned in the direction of the familiar voice. Shock and surprise crossed Svea's face until pure joy won over them. All her anger dispersed and her face lit up.

'Brand!'

Ash watched as she suddenly turned from him and ran into the Northman's arms. Brand clasped her close. A bolt of jealousy churned in his stomach. It was the scene he'd dreamed of moments before—only she was launching herself into her brother's arms, not his.

'Hi, Sis.'

He hoped beyond hope that the formidable Danish warrior hadn't heard their argument. He didn't think Brand would be too happy to learn that Ash had seduced his sister. And he felt like a brute, because what she'd said was true. He *had* made love to her, then left her without so much as an explanation or a goodbye. Perhaps it was cowardly. But he had done it for her own good.

He felt so damn frustrated—with her and himself. The last thing he wanted was to argue with her, and he hadn't meant what he'd said about regretting that she'd ever left Kald. To regret that would mean he wished last night had never happened, and he wouldn't change that for the world. It had been the best night of his life.

'I might have known it was you when I heard a scene at the gate,' Brand was saying to her, laughing.

'What are you doing here?' she gasped in delight.

'When we came ashore in Rainhill we heard of the King's plight and we knew we had to cut our honeymoon short. I came as quickly as I could. Anne is worried about her father. We all are. And I have heard about Kar and Sten.'

Svea nodded, her eyes welling with tears, but she quickly blinked them away.

'What are *you* doing here?' asked Brand.

'I was just wondering the same thing,' Ash added, scowling.

The warrior's blue gaze lanced him. 'I heard,' Brand said, and he raised his eyebrow, looking between Svea and Ash as if he was seeking an answer to a question he hadn't asked.

'I was telling Svea the battlefield is no place for a woman,' Ash said, suddenly glad he was such an expert at masking his emotions. 'Will you tell her I'm right?'

Brand's brow furrowed. 'Have you not seen my sister fight, Lord Stanton?'

'I have.'

'She's one of Kald's best warriors,' Brand added.

'I don't doubt it. Still, I'd prefer it if she was safe at home.'

'Is that so?' Brand said, his lips widening into a smile and his wise, penetrating gaze suddenly all-knowing, as if he had recognised something in Ash. 'Well, she's here now, and there's not much we can do about it, is there? Come on, Sis,' he said, turning to Svea and draping an arm around her shoulder, leading her away. 'Let us get you some ale. And perhaps you can fill me in on what you and Lord Stanton have been up to these past few days.'

Ash and the ealdorman and the other Lords, along with some of Brand's men from Kald, were gathered around the campfire. Brand had shown Svea to the food area and she'd devoured a bowl of stew. Then they'd found her a tent of her own to sleep in by moving some of the men. Now her brother had begun introducing her to the Lords.

Svea was overjoyed to see Brand. She was sorry he'd had to call an early halt to his honeymoon, but she knew they'd have a better chance of rescuing their men, and the King, with him at their side. And when he told her he'd taken Anne back to Kald, and everyone there was safe, she had almost wept with relief. She hadn't realised how worried she'd been. She would have blamed herself if anything had happened there while she'd been away.

She'd filled him in on most of the details—how they'd left Kald and been ambushed, and how Ash had saved her life not once, but twice. She'd even described how they'd decided to head to Braewood to raise the *fyrd*, only leaving out a few minor things—like how she thought she was falling for Ash, the way he made her feel, and the fact that he'd kissed her and made love to her all last night...

She looked across the fire at Ash now, and he was

more sullen, more brooding than she'd ever seen him. The cool censure in his eyes earlier had chilled her. She knew he was angry with her for defying his iron will, and she understood why. But she was angry, too—firstly because he'd left her when she had a right to be here, and now because of all the hurtful things he'd said to her when she'd arrived...

Had he meant them? Did he really regret everything that had happened between them?

Their eyes met over the flames and heat soared through her body. He was absently toying with the tooth necklace she had given him. He was the only man not drinking ale, and she realised she had come to respect his control, despite how annoying it could be. She thought perhaps it was his discipline and restraint that had helped her to trust him, to allow him near her—the reason why she had felt safe to let him touch and explore her body. And yet at the same time she wanted to smash down his wall of authority, his rules and regulations. She wanted to see him lose control where she was concerned...

Some of the warriors began to tell stories around the fire and she enjoyed the camaraderie, being one of the men again. She was increasingly aware that Lord Fiske, to her left, kept telling jokes, trying to impress her, and while she laughed in response, humouring the man, she noticed Ash wiping his palm on his breeches, leaning forward to stoke the fire roughly with his other hand.

Was that jealousy burning in his eyes?

Being this close to him and not being able to talk

to him, or touch him, was torture. She wanted to know what he was thinking. She hated to admit it, but she would give anything to be in his arms again. She didn't know what was going to happen out on the battlefield tomorrow, and she had an urge to make every second count. She was starting to feel as if she'd wasted too much time in her life already.

She was glad he'd rallied the troops to fight—he'd done well—and yet she couldn't help wishing they were alone. What she wouldn't give to be back in that grove with him now, just the two of them, or back in his bed, in his strong embrace. She couldn't make sense of her feelings. How could she still want him when she was so angry with him?

She wiped her hands over her face and, suddenly feeling weary, knowing they had a big day ahead of them tomorrow, stood and bade them all goodnight.

'Do you need some help finding your tent in the dark?' Lord Fiske asked, rising alongside her. 'I'd be happy to escort you.'

Ash was up like a shot, his movement sudden, sharp. But Brand spoke words to appease him, to steady his breathing.

'There's no need for that, Lord Fiske,' Brand said, getting out of his seat slowly. 'I'm heading that way myself.'

Looking between Ash and Brand, knowing better than to make a scene, or reveal to the Lords that there was anything between her and Lord Stanton, Svea looped her hand through her brother's arm and let him lead her away from the men, through the little tents to find hers.

'Will you be all right in here on your own?' Brand asked, concern clouding his features.

She was glad he was here. It made her feel as if she'd done the right thing in coming. It was right that they should fight together to take their revenge on the men who had killed their father.

Brand had taken care of her for as long as she could remember. She understood why he blamed himself for what had happened to her in Termarth, for not being able to help her, but she wished he didn't. She knew he suffered from his own memories of that day, and from terrible guilt. And he must miss their father and mother, too. But while he'd grieved their loss he'd also cared for her, looked after her well. He'd taught her all she needed to know to be independent, he had shown her love, and she would always be grateful to him for that.

'I'll be fine.' She gave him a fierce hug goodnight.

For a long time now—since her father had died—he had been the only man she'd needed in her life. Just lately, she'd wondered if that was changing. Perhaps she didn't need him so much any more. Perhaps she could set him free to look after his new wife and any children he and Anne might have. She would love to be an aunt one day—especially if she couldn't have her own children.

Brand started to walk away, before stopping and turning back. 'Svea? I know it's nothing to do with me, but don't be too harsh on Lord Stanton. I know you're angry with him for what he did, for leaving you behind, but I believe he has your best interests at heart.'

'I know that.'

Brand had told her Lord Stanton was a good man back in Kald, when he'd asked her to escort him and their guests to the forest. He'd warned her to be nice. She had known Brand was a good judge of character, but still she'd felt irritated, not wanting to give the Saxon Lord the time of day. She'd wanted to rebel. But now... Now she felt differently. She knew Lord Stanton's deepest, darkest fears, and she knew how he felt when he moved inside her.

'I know you want to fight, Svea. And I'm not going to deny you that chance. We need your skills. But I also know how much I care about Anne, and I wouldn't want her anywhere near this place... I can understand how Lord Stanton feels.'

'What are you saying?'

Had he seen something between them?

'Just that maybe he had good reason to act the way he did. When you care about someone, you'll do anything to protect them. Don't stay cross with him forever. Life's too short.'

She nodded, swallowing the lump in her throat. She knew he was right.

'Goodnight, Svea.'

She watched him go, before giving a heavy sigh and passing through the cloth door of her tent. A hand on her arm startled her, spinning her round, and she gasped.

Ash.

Relief and elation swept through her, but she instantly masked her delight. She didn't want him knowing she was pleased to see him here, inside her tent. That it was what she had been hoping for.

'What—?'

He reached for her and pulled her up against his body hard, claiming her mouth with his. She knew she should push him away, but she liked the way he was holding her tight, drawing her in, deepening the kiss, as if he needed her just as much as she needed him. And she couldn't help it. Her legs weakened, along with her resolve, and she sank against him. It felt so good to be back in his arms.

When they came up for air, she knew she should step away from him. 'I'm still angry with you.'

But he reached for her again. He wasn't letting her go.

'As I am with you,' he said, as his mouth ravished her lips and nipped and nibbled along her neck. 'But I still want to be inside you, like I was last night. I can't think of anything else. It's all I've thought about. All. Day. Long. Tell me you want that, too.'

His words sounded rough, raw. She whimpered with lust as his lips hunted down her breast.

'I couldn't bear those men fawning all over you out there. It made me insane with jealousy…'

His words pleased her, as did his searing touch. She was glad he cared and that she was having such an effect on him, as he was on her.

'Svea, I'm sorry. For what I said earlier. Believe

me when I say it comes from my fear of you getting hurt. Of my not being able to protect you.'

His fingers stole down between her legs and she knew he must have found her damp. She knew that she was. She writhed against his hand.

'I never asked for your protection, Ash.'

He stroked her fiercely through the material and her legs buckled, so he pushed a muscled thigh between hers.

'I know that, but you have it anyway. Watching you sleeping naked in my bed, you looked so perfect, too precious to take into battle. I need to know you'll be safe.'

'You have to take risks in life, Ash. Like I did with you last night.'

'Were you sore this morning?' he asked, softening his touch.

'No… I just…wanted more. And I turned to find you gone…'

He groaned. 'Please, Svea… Give me permission to pleasure your body. Put me out of my misery. Tell me that you want me inside you again.'

She liked to hear him beg. It gave her confidence a lift.

She tossed her hair back over her shoulders and his arms came up and around her again, pulling her close, trying to trace the soft swells of her breasts. But the cold chainmail of her armour was in his way. She pushed him down onto the bed and stood before him. She unclasped the metal and it fell away. He moved his hands towards her belt, unfastening it, using the ends to pull her towards him. And then his mouth was on her stomach, placing hot, hard kisses over her skin.

She lifted up her tunic and pulled it over her head. She burned wherever he placed his lips. It felt so good to be acting on the pent-up feelings of the day at last. To finally have this release. To be close to him again. And to know that he still wanted her.

He started to rise towards her, to kiss her beautiful breasts, but she pushed him back.

'No. Don't touch me, Ash. I want you to watch.'

She wanted to show him that he might have conquered her body last night, but she'd let him—it had been her choice. She wanted to show him that he could make demands, try to control her, but she'd make her own decisions.

'This is your punishment. For leaving me in Braewood.'

He swallowed.

She unlaced her boots slowly, felt his eyes on her breasts as they moved enticingly as she bent over and pulled off the leather. Then she untied the cord on her breeches and pushed them down to the floor, stepping out of them.

Naked before him, she watched him draw in a ragged breath, saw his eyes darken. He seemed to be finding it hard to breathe. She felt a sudden intimacy wrapping around them, as if she was about to let him in on a secret, and she enjoyed the feeling of being in total control, of having power over him for once. And as she moved her hands over her own body, over the swollen swells of her breasts, and rolled her nipples between her fingers, she watched the pulse throb in his neck.

'Svea…'

She thought back to how she'd wanted to ruffle his feathers on the marshland, when she'd barely known him. Well, she was certainly doing that now.

'I have a right to be here, Ash. I'm not like one of your Saxon women. I follow my own desires. You can't tame me.'

She parted her thighs and her hands stole down between her legs. His eyes dilated, his hard cock straining against his breeches as he followed her every movement, clearly not wanting to miss a second of what she was doing.

'Do you know…I touched myself here when I bathed in Braewood? I thought of you.'

'Svea…' he choked.

'I'm thinking of you touching me here now. Do you want to touch me here, Ash?'

She didn't need to ask him twice. As if he could bear it no longer, he launched himself towards her, sinking to his knees, and laid claim to her with his mouth.

His hands came round her to hold her buttocks, to fasten her to him, and she was glad. She didn't think she could stand without his support. His tongue glided along her opening, nipping at her little bud of pleasure, and she held on to his shoulders for dear life. She had him exactly where she wanted him.

The pleasure was mounting, already too much, but she wasn't ready for it to be over—not before he thrust inside her. She pushed at his shoulders and he reluctantly pulled away, breaking the connection. His eyes were two huge pools of fire, and she sank down onto his lap, straddling his thighs. She gripped his face between her hands and kissed him hard, her tongue entwined with his. She was in a hurry now, wanting him naked, like she was, and she frantically pulled at his tunic, tugging it out of his breeches and dragging it over his head.

He laughed. 'What have I created?'

She could feel his erection beneath her and she wanted to release him, free him. She roamed her hands down to the top of his breeches, loosening them. He lifted her up in his arms, as if she didn't weigh a thing, so she could pull them off and out from under him.

She ruthlessly took hold of him, as he'd shown her how to do the night before, and he groaned, resting his forehead against hers. He reciprocated the pleasure, his hand prowling between her legs, finding her soaked. It was a battle of dominance, over who could give the most torment, but his fingers soon won, slipping inside her and claiming her body once more, wreaking havoc on her senses.

She began to move her hips up and down, riding his fingers and the fierce waves of pleasure until she could take it no longer. And then a thought occurred to her. If he could torment her with his tongue, maybe she could do the same to him. And so she dipped her head to where she was holding him in her palm, and put her tongue to the tip.

He groaned loudly. His hands twisted into her hair, bringing her mouth down further onto him. She had no idea what she was doing—she just knew she wanted to torture him as he was her. She wanted to send him to the brink. She wanted to set him free, make him wild. She took him to the back of her throat and he swore. She smiled and did it again, and he bucked beneath her. Oh, yes, he'd definitely lost that cool control now. All restraint was gone.

All at once, in a swift movement, he growled and pushed her down onto her back, lowering her so she was stretched out beneath him on the floor. And he parted her thighs wide with his legs.

'Is this all right?' he asked, as his large body hovered over her.

She appreciated that he was checking on her, but she wasn't afraid any more. She just needed him. 'Yes. I want you. Now, Ash.'

She lifted her arms to place her hands around his neck, pulling him down on top of her, and then he was right there, at her entrance. He used his hard, silky tip to stroke up and down her crease, opening her up to him, and as his tongue probed inside her mouth he guided his cock inside her. Every muscle in her body tensed at the invasion, the blinding pleasure, and she bit down on his lip to stop herself from screaming out. He felt huge inside her body, filling her up, and incredible. He thrust again, beginning to up the pace, moving faster, longer, harder, deeper. But she still wanted more. She wanted everything he could give.

Her arms roamed down his back to grip his bottom, her fingers digging into his flesh to frantically pull him further inside, and she wrapped her legs around him, taking him all the way in. He was so deep she didn't know where she or he began or ended. They were just one, moving together, their tangled, thrashing bodies slick with sweat. And as they both came in unison, in an explosive, powerful climax, they pressed their mouths together hard, so no one could hear their euphoric roars.

Afterwards, Ash lifted her sated body and carried her to the bed, tugging her against him and holding her in his arms. He stroked her back and arms with his fingertips, soothing her trembling limbs.

'Ash, I want you to tell me you're glad I'm here,' she said, her breathing still nowhere near resembling normal.

'I can't do that, Svea. As much as I was pleased to see you earlier, and as much as I wanted to make love to you again, and even after having the best sex of my life, I could never be *glad* you're here, about to fight a vicious enemy. But, having said all that, I will be your shield on the battlefield tomorrow.'

'And I'll be yours,' she whispered.

Chapter Nine

More than a hundred warriors raised their huge wooden shields as they lined up to create a wall on the plains outside Termarth. It would be a formidable sight to their enemy, and yet Ash couldn't help wishing they were on the other side of the imposing stone ramparts.

He knew this place inside out, and defending it from the outside was a bizarre prospect. One he had never imagined possible. He felt as if he had let down all the people within the walls.

Sworn to protect them, he had left the kingdom undefended when he'd travelled with King Eallesborough to Kald for his daughter's wedding. From Ash's own upbringing he knew that you couldn't look after something from afar—it would slip beyond your grip. The distance between him and his parents had become irreparable. And now, just looking at the damage his absence had caused to Braewood and Termarth, it only helped to prove his point.

Saxon rebels had taken the kingdom, and the King

and his subjects as hostages. He hoped the corrupt Crowe brothers hadn't done any serious damage to either. He wasn't sure Termarth would recover. The dark castle walls loomed ahead of them, reaching up into the threatening sky, and he tried to push down the sense of impending doom. The way he saw it, they had two options. They could lay siege to Termarth in an attempt to rescue the King—although he knew that would cause many casualties—or they could try to negotiate. Negotiate with a man who was starting a conflict between his own people and whose brother—who Cecil must have set free by now—had raped Ash's new lover. Neither option was appealing.

The leaders of the *fyrd*, as well as Brand and Svea, had discussed it earlier that morning, and they'd decided to try to talk first, to see what the Crowes wanted, hoping to avoid as much bloodshed as possible. But, frankly, if Ash had the chance to run his blade through those men he wouldn't hesitate.

He looked across at Svea, on the horse at his side, and wondered how she was feeling. Covered in warrior paint, her hair tied up into a mass of intricate braids, she looked dangerous. And he knew it to be true. Hadn't she brought him to his knees last night? But the last time she'd been to Termarth she'd suffered brutality and lost her father. He hoped she wasn't suffering an onslaught of painful memories. He hoped he'd given her some incredible new ones to strike out the old.

The croaking call of ravens screeching overhead caught his attention, the birds flapping their wings against an ominous ashen sky, and Svea turned to face him. They exchanged a look. He hoped seeing those beasts of battle now etched into his skin was a good omen. He felt the heavy throb of his heartbeat, his muscles tightening in readiness. He hoped he could lead them all to victory.

'Just promise me you'll be careful,' he said, trying not to focus on all the things that could go wrong, already doubting his decision to allow her to make her own choices and fight.

She rolled her eyes. 'I will, Ash. Promise me you will stay safe, too.'

He nodded.

He had slipped from her arms and her bed before dawn this morning. Before anyone had been awake to notice. But it had taken all his strength to leave her. Sprawled out naked between the furs, she had been everything he'd ever dreamt of, all he wanted, and his chest had hurt. He had never had trouble leaving a woman's bed before. He had never wanted to repeat any night he'd spent with one. He had never been interested in sharing confidences or creating intimacy. But this woman...

He couldn't bear her being out of his sight, out of his arms. They belonged together.

Even now, as he urged his horse forward to the gate to request a word with Lord Crowe, he didn't like the distance he was putting between them. If he was apart from her he couldn't protect her. But he tried to focus on the large looming entrance, and on what he was going to say. His words might make all the difference. First he would insist on seeing the King and the other hostages. Only after he'd seen them would he ask about their terms for peace.

But then his gaze fell upon the large cart which Crowe's men were rolling out towards him. His eyes narrowed, and he put his hand to his sword. He wouldn't put it past the brothers to attack without warning…

Nothing could have prepared him for the sight he was about to see. He wanted to look away but he was unable to. He was transfixed, trying to make sense of the horror before him. It could only be described as a massacre.

He reeled back on his horse, wanting to put some distance between him and the cart. Because there, stacked up, were the dead bodies of his men, his best soldiers, his friends, and also those of the Danes, Kar and Sten. He forced himself to look, needing to sear the image into his memory. Some had suffered knife wounds, others had had their necks stretched, making their faces contorted, and it turned his stomach.

He knew he was to blame.

He'd vowed to Svea that he'd get them back. He'd asked her to put her trust in him. But he'd taken too long. He hadn't been able to protect them on the marshland and now, because of his delay in rallying the troops…

He heard Svea's blood-curdling scream behind him and turned to see her dismount from her horse and run towards the bodies, her sword above her head.

But Brand was at her side in an instant, folding her in his arms, smothering her cries, holding her tight.

Ash felt the slow trickle of failure pass through him. This was all his fault. He'd let her down. And he would now have to accept the consequences...the repercussions of his actions.

He stared at the harrowing sight before him. There was one thing Ash now knew with absolute clarity. He knew that Svea had been right—it didn't matter if you were Saxon or Dane, all men could be evil, no matter what blood flowed through their veins. He felt his nostrils flare, his fists clench and unclench. He had to push the pain down, deal with it later and let the rage take over.

It was as if an unspoken understanding had passed between the ealdormen and the warriors. There would be no talking. No negotiation. This was the rallying cry that made these accidental allies come together against one enemy, and they would fight for their lost men, for their King, for vengeance, to the death.

As a loud rumble of thunder ripped across the sky, Svea opened the battle by throwing a spear towards the Saxon on the gate, honouring her god Odin, and then there was no hesitation. All stealth and strategy was cast aside, and with a combined guttural roar they launched into attack, the shield wall of men advancing on the towering fortifications.

Soldiers began to scale the castle walls while storms of sling stones started flying over the ramparts, raining down on them, trying to halt their ascent. Ash and Brand led the cavalry charge to the gate, cutting down swathes of men there, before taking up a battering ram to hammer down the gate.

Everything seemed surreal. Ash felt numb. He had seen many battles and confrontations, but never on the King's own soil. He felt sickened that it had come to this. He couldn't believe he was laying siege to his own home. He hoped the King would one day forgive him—that was if he was still alive. His body hadn't been among the others, which gave Ash hope that he might not have totally failed Termarth, as he'd failed Svea and his men.

It didn't take long for them to break through the iron. Ash knew all the weak spots, and the men infiltrated the castle walls, converging on the inside to join the fray. It was confused carnage, with casualties suffering horrific injuries already scattered about, men in brutal combat wherever you looked. The panic from the people was tangible as they ran around, screaming in the chaos, and he shouted for them to take shelter, to get to safety. The sight of him back on home soil seemed to calm some, and inspired others to join him and fight.

The battle was bloody and brutal. Ash dispatched men as they came at him. But his attention was divided. He had one eye on his enemy and one eye trained on Svea as she fought fiercely, holding her own. If anything happened to her it would be more than he could endure, even though he knew he no longer deserved her. Not that he ever had.

It was a relentless battle, ruthless. Rampant fires were breaking out all over the place, thick black smoke choking the fighters, and arrows and bodies ricocheted off the walls as the fight raged on. He just hoped they could salvage the soul of the kingdom after this.

Suddenly a flaming arrow struck a cart behind him, engulfing the men there in flames. Ash's armour burned and he unclipped it, shucking off the hot, heavy metal and his scorched tunic. His skin prickled with pain. He welcomed it. He saw it as punishment.

Seeing their chance to attack him while he was down, a group of Crowe's men approached, surrounding him, but their skills were no match for his fury. He sensed the conflict was turning. They were overpowering their enemy...the fighting was coming to its climax. The men on both sides were tiring, but still they fought on, with a grim determination.

Suddenly realising that Svea was gone, that she wasn't at his side, Ash swung his gaze around the courtyard, over the devastated market stalls and burning food stores, the roofs on fire, wildly searching for her face among the mayhem, his heart pounding in his chest. How had he lost her?

His eyes finally fell upon her on the bridge, but his blood chilled. She was challenging the Crowes, a ferocious look on her face, and he watched the sickening showdown begin to unfold. He couldn't be sure how coming face to face with her attacker would be making her feel—he just knew he needed to get to her. *Now.* He was in awe of her bravery, but aghast at her notion that she could take on two of Calhourn's fiercest warriors by herself. She really was untameable, like the wind now whipping across the barricades, the driving rain lashing down upon them.

He turned to see Brand fighting off two men, and the Dane nodded in a silent plea for Ash to go after her.

Running up the stone steps and along the ramparts towards her, his breath coming in short bursts, Ash saw she was being overtaken. He knew he wouldn't make it to her in time. He grabbed up a spear. Quick, decisive, he threw it, narrowly missing her, but hitting his target. Cecil Crowe tried to duck, but he didn't stand a chance against the deadly accuracy of Ash's throw. The man slumped to his knees. Svea spun round to look at him in astonished admiration.

But the sudden demise of his brother had spurred Lord Crowe into action and he lashed out, knocking Svea's sword out of her hand and seizing her from behind. A savage struggle ensued, but Ash was right there by her side. Where he should have been all along.

'Let her go,' he said, pointing his sword at the man, moving slowly and deliberately towards him.

He saw the rage in Svea's eyes at once again being caught in the grip of this monster. But she no longer seemed afraid—just angry as hell.

'I'll kill you!' she was screaming, thrashing under his grip.

Seeing the balding beast's hands on her was nauseating, bringing up images of what he'd done to her when she was just a young girl. Ash wanted him dead just as much as she did.

'Lord Stanton, I thought we were allies...' Crowe sneered as he continued to tackle Svea. 'Surely you're not going to take the side of a heathen over a friend? Drop your weapon and I'll consider not killing the girl...just hurting her a little. We could even share...'

'Never.'

His hair around his shoulders, his tunic gone, revealing the dark warrior patterns on his chest, Ash realised he looked more like a Northman than ever. And finally, in that moment, he was ready to embrace it.

'You're a traitor to your kind, Stanton,' said Crowe.

'On the contrary. I'm a Northman, and you make me proud to call myself a Dane.'

He glanced down to the courtyard and saw Brand had put down his opponents and was lighting a spindle of arrows. He hoped the King would forgive them for this.

He gave Brand the signal and then yelled, 'Svea— move!'

Instantly, she jabbed her elbow into Crowe's ribs and leapt away. Ash grabbed her and pulled her into his arms, to safety, just as the torrent of firelit arrows hit the bridge, covering the entire entrance to Termarth in flames.

And as the city wall collapsed, taking the Crowes' bodies down with it in an almighty avalanche of wood and stone, the deafening rumbling sound reverberated around the castle, drawing the battle to a close.

* * *

'Are you all right?' asked Ash, his large hands on her shoulders, his eyes raking over her face, her body.

It reminded her of when he'd dragged her into the forest that day after they'd been ambushed. He'd had the ability to ground her even then.

'Yes,' she said, shocked by what had just happened. Was her nemesis really dead? Had her lover saved her life for a third time?

He patted her body, as if checking that she hadn't been hurt.

'I'm fine, Ash, really.'

'Hell, Svea, what were you thinking, taking them on by yourself?' he scolded her. 'When are you going to learn?'

She shrugged, feeling numb. 'I don't know. I couldn't let them get away with it. What they'd done. I didn't think—I just knew I had to stop them.'

Her jaw hardened. Did he think it wasn't her place? Because if it wasn't hers, whose was it? She had more right to be angry with those monsters than anyone.

He turned away from her. 'I have to go to the King. Find out if he's still alive.'

She didn't want him to leave her. She wanted him to stay and comfort her, to talk about what had happened and how she felt about it. But even as he was speaking he was moving away, determined. He was set on his purpose, his priority being the King, and he seemed distant, detached. Had he been hurt? she wondered.

He headed down the stone steps, increasing the

distance between them before halting and turning back. 'Just…try not to get into any more trouble while I'm gone.'

Svea nodded, watching him go. Was he all right? She hoped so.

She looked around her in despair, taking in the devastation and destruction. She didn't know what to do first—where to start. Everything was in disarray. Little fires were still burning…bodies were strewn about everywhere. She sank down to her knees amid the chaos. People were wailing, clambering over wood and stones to get to safety, and the farmsteads and grain stores had been burned to the ground.

She had never seen such a bleak sight, and she felt overwhelmingly tired. But she didn't care. *They'd won.* They'd taken down Crowe and his brother and reclaimed the castle. They'd achieved what they'd set out to do all those days before, despite the heartbreaking losses they'd suffered along the way.

Ash had been nothing less than heroic, leading the men into the fray with grit and determination. And he'd rallied the people, encouraging them to take up arms against the enemy. He was right. She'd rushed in again, having seen the Crowes and not wanting to let them out of her sight, not wanting to allow them to get away. But once again she'd been foolish. She should have waited for help, because of course they'd overpowered her. Two against one.

And all those feelings had come rushing to the surface. Fear, yes—but mainly anger. Anger that they still had their hold over her. But then, thank goodness, Ash had appeared at her side, saving her again.

She'd nearly got herself killed, and she was furious with herself. She promised herself she would never be so reckless again. She hoped there would never be a need. She had to listen to Ash and stop taking risks. When he'd pulled her away from Crowe as the bridge had given way beneath her feet she had felt more shaken than ever before. Being back in the arms of that man had been more than she could bear. But then he'd fallen, and she'd watched as the brute had taken his last breath.

She hadn't been able to believe it. Crowe and his brother were finally dead. She was finally free of them. They could never harm her again. She'd wanted to throw her arms around Ash, bury herself in his shoulder, draw on his strength and comfort. But he'd gently placed her feet down on the solid stone steps and, after checking she was all right, he'd left her, without even holding her close or kissing her.

Something was wrong, but she wasn't sure what. Was it just that he was angry with her for putting herself in danger?

She looked around for him now, wondering if she might spot him in the distance, a shining light amid all this mess and darkness, but he was nowhere to be seen. She prayed he would find his King safe and well.

Instead, Svea saw Brand coming towards her, striding through the clouds of grey smoke. His face was unreadable and she held her breath, hoping he was bringing good news.

'The King's alive,' he said, coming down beside her, with drizzling rain and a look of sheer relief washing over his features. 'We scoured the castle and found him locked in the dungeons. He's shaken, but unharmed. And he's very grateful to us all for saving his life and his crown.'

Elation ripped through Svea. She was glad the King was safe. It meant all the loss of life hadn't been for nothing. And it would mean a great deal to Ash. She knew how guilty he felt for not saving the King on the marsh, but now he had redeemed himself. Her heart swelled. All would be well.

She stretched out her arms and allowed Brand to lift her to her feet. They began to pick their way through the rubble, trying to find survivors, attempting to clear up some of the mess. The storm dragged on, and despite the cold and wet seeping through their clothes they were glad of the rain, as it helped to put out the fires, halting the damage to the castle walls.

It was a long, painstaking afternoon, which took its toll on their bodies and their thoughts. By nightfall, the King had organised a celebratory feast in the grand hall but despite their victory the mood was sombre. The ordeal of recent weeks had worn them down. The people were weary—they had lost too much.

Looking around the grand hall, adorned with paintings and gold and garnet decorations, rich, soft furnishings and roaring fires, Svea sat in wonder. But none of the trinkets and trophies drew her eye as much as the man at the end of the table, who sat at the side of the King.

Ash. She hadn't seen him all day—not since he'd saved her on the ramparts—and she longed to talk to him, to hold him, to thank him, to love him. She wondered how he was faring after losing so many of his men. By the looks of it he had suffered some bad cuts and burns himself. She wanted to take care of his injuries, check that he was all right, but she hadn't been able to get near him. He was back in the service of the King, and his monarch must have need of him.

The King stood at the head of the long table, a goblet in his hand. He was a tall, proud man, with grey hair and a beard, yet he looked frail, more weary than Svea had ever seen him before. After rapping on the table for silence, he extended his thanks to his warriors and his subjects, his eyes shining with pride and tears, and said he wouldn't have his crown if it wasn't for them, the Crowe brothers having intended to take it for themselves. He congratulated them on their victory and made a toast, raising his mead.

The masses in the grand hall clapped and cheered. And as everyone rose to clink their jars of mead Svea stole another look at Ash. But instead of joining in with the salute, he remained still, his usually impassive face looking more downcast than she'd ever seen it.

Over the past few days, he'd remained focused on the goal of rescuing his King and their men. But now... Now he was back to being serious Lord Stanton, right-hand man to the King. Efficient, but removed. He'd withdrawn again, reverted back to being that lone soldier she'd shied away from at the wedding in Kald. He seemed almost impregnable, sitting there brooding, and it sent a shiver of unease through her body.

She knew he must have a million tasks to do and, knowing him, he would be engaging in them so he didn't have to deal with feelings of grief for his men. She knew now that he was an expert at crushing his emotions, and probably had been since he was that young boy who'd been unloved and abandoned by his parents. But surely he had time to speak to her? To check on her? Surely he wanted to?

Because she wanted to speak to him—she wanted to talk about the day, the battle, to go over the details with him. She wanted to tell him how she'd felt when she'd come face to face with Crowe. She wanted to share her feelings about it with him and hear his in return. But he hadn't even once looked her way. It was as if he was withdrawing from her, from everyone— as if he wanted to be alone. But why?

She found it infuriating. She was hurt, too. She had lost two of her beloved shield brothers, and she needed him. She wanted to seek comfort in his arms and in his bed. Could he not see that? Did he not care?

His eyes were devoid of any emotion, and wary apprehension ebbed through her. This man, sitting so far along the table from her, silent and resolute, wasn't the man who had taken her swimming in the sea and shared laughter with her in the kitchen in Braewood. Nor was he the man who had made passionate love to her last night. No, this man had the weight of the world on his shoulders. Did he not realise he'd suc-

ceeded in his task? That he was the people's hero—
and hers?

She willed him to lift his eyes and look at her.
To walk over and say something. Anything. But he
didn't. It was as if he was a longship, adrift at sea,
and she was a beacon on the cliffs, trying to catch the
helmsman's attention. But he never looked her way.

It had been the longest night of her life. Svea had
tossed and turned and just hadn't been able to get
comfortable, despite stretching out in the biggest,
grandest bed she'd ever seen. But every time she'd
closed her eyes she had seen Ash's molten brown gaze
and his back turned against her as he'd walked down
those steep rampart steps. She'd drifted in and out of
sleep, and when she'd finally woken in the morning
she'd had a terrible sense of foreboding she hadn't
been able to shake off.

She had risen early, and now she was taking a
stroll around the castle, flanked by Brand and King
Eallesborough, assessing the damage. The King's
men had been working since dawn, lifting the rubble
away from the main gate, and they were making good
progress. The entrance was almost clear.

But Svea couldn't focus. She hadn't seen Ash this
morning, it seemed he was nowhere to be found, and
she was starting to feel edgy—as if something had
happened…as if something was terribly wrong. What
if his injuries were worse than they'd seemed? What
if they were infected and he had a fever and he was
lying in a bed somewhere in the castle needing her?

But what if it wasn't that at all? What if it was simply that now they'd seen their mission through he didn't need or want her any more? That, whatever they'd experienced together, he now wanted it to be over? She shuddered at the thought.

Last night, even the delicious meats, the sweet honey-based mead and the music hadn't been able to lift her spirits, and she had been glad when they'd all retreated to their rooms for the night. They were the most luxurious, magnificent spaces she'd ever seen, and yet she knew she would trade it all to be back in Ash's room in Braewood in a heartbeat. She would do anything to be in his arms. And all night, on hearing every footstep or noise outside her door, her heart had jumped, hoping it was him, that he'd finally come to her.

But he hadn't.

She wondered why he'd shut himself down, not speaking to her, keeping her at bay. She had barely slept, and she felt bone-achingly tired. And now, as she and Brand followed the King as he began to climb the stone staircase that led to the battlements, overlooking views of the golden rolling fields, the glowing copper leaves on the trees marking the passing of time, she could no longer bear it. She had to say something.

'King Eallesborough, I hope you don't mind me asking, but have you seen Lord Stanton today?'

Brand glowered at her, as if what she was asking the King wasn't appropriate, but she ignored him, instead focusing on the Saxon monarch. He had a calming presence, and she hoped he would see that she was worried and take pity on her.

He turned to look at her with concern in his wise green eyes. 'No, Svea, I'm afraid not,' he said.

And then he surprised them both by sitting down on a pile of rubble, shaking his head before burying it in his hands.

'Is everything all right, Your Majesty?' Brand said, stepping forward. 'Shall I send for a healer?'

'I am quite well, thank you. It's just... You know how you think you know someone like the back of your hand, and then...I don't know...someone chops off that hand? That's how I'm feeling this morning.'

'What's happened?' Svea asked, stepping towards him, her heart beginning to race. This didn't sound good, and she had the unsettling feeling it had something to do with Ash. *Her Ash.*

The King sighed. 'Lord Stanton came to see me last night, in my private quarters. He asked to be released from his oath of fealty. It came as quite a blow. He's served me loyally for years...'

Svea's heart was in her mouth. The King clearly thought as highly of him as she did. What was Ash thinking?

'He said he feels he's let me down. He blames himself for everything. Of course I told him he hasn't, but he won't hear it. He said that none of this should ever have happened. That he feels the men's blood is on his hands.'

Pain lanced her. How could he feel that way when he'd saved Termarth?

The King looked up at Brand and Svea before continuing. 'He went on to tell me how his father was a Dane. I'm not sure how I didn't see it before... I mean, now that I know I can see it as clear as day. You can just tell, can't you? Look at the two of you,' he said, and smiled, gesturing to their strong bodies and dark markings.

Svea thought back to the day before, when she'd seen Ash charge towards her on the ramparts. His chest bare, his ink on display for all to see, his extraordinary muscles rippling, he had looked almost superhuman—like a demi-god. But he was a Saxon and a Dane. Her demi-Dane.

'He should have known it wouldn't be a problem to me. My own daughter married a Dane, after all,' he said, standing, placing a hand on Brand's shoulder. 'A good man. But it is to him. He said people knowing will compromise his position here. He thinks it will confuse the soldiers and the people—that they won't know which side he is on. He seemed almost... ashamed.'

Svea winced in pain, as if the King's words were puncturing her body. She knew Ash was worried about the blood he had flowing through his veins, and she had tried to convince him he was no monster. She had thought he was concerned about the actions of his father, the fact that he'd been conceived in rape, and what kind of person that made him. She hadn't thought he was actually *ashamed* of being a Dane. And if that was the case, he was ashamed of the part of him that was like her.

She bristled with hurt and disbelief. Was he embarrassed to be with her? Had he been avoiding her, pushing her away, because so many others were around? And when he had told her he would never marry and have children, had that been the truth? Or was it just that he would never marry a Dane? That he would never marry *her*...?

'He told me he had decided to return to Braewood,' the King continued. 'He explained that his father is unwell and needs him.'

Pain exploded in her chest. *She* needed him.

'He told me there are many men who could replace him and be my oath man, but only he can rule Braewood after his father. So it is time for him to leave.'

The tightness in Svea's ribcage was making it hard to breathe. He was abandoning the King after all they'd been through. Would he really walk away from her? Abandon her, too? But could she really expect any more, given that those were the actions he had learnt from his own parents? Ash didn't owe her anything. He had made her no promises. Only that he would give her pleasure... And he had—and it had been glorious. But short-lived. Now she was suffering great agony.

'He kept on saying he needed to make amends... to put things right. I know his father is keen for him to marry, and for him to take up his position at Braewood. But he will be greatly missed here.'

Svea felt distraught, tormented. Ash had taken her to bed, made love to her, and now he was leaving without giving her a reason, without helping her to understand. How could he? Would he now agree to his father's demands? Was he contemplating marrying Lady Edith after all? Someone who could give him a child? She felt sick. Would he even say goodbye to her?

Bitterness burned through her body. She knew the differences between them were insurmountable, and she knew she had been insane to think they could ever be together—his father certainly wouldn't allow it, not while he was still alive. And yet there had been a part of her that had foolishly hoped and dreamed... But now those dreams were unravelling. Spiralling away. He was leaving her. Again. But this time she couldn't go after him. Because this was different. She wasn't sure it was her place. She would have to let him go, and she wasn't sure she could endure it.

Excruciating grief rumbled through her and she nearly sank to her knees. It was only her pride that kept her standing.

They'd survived the battle of his lifetime, and they'd been victorious, and yet Ash didn't think he'd ever despised himself more than in this moment as he made his way through the devastated castle square towards Svea.

People congratulated him as he passed them by, applauding his bravery, his win, and he nodded his head in thanks. But inside he'd never felt so defeated.

He had confessed his guilt to the King, over not being able to save him on the marshland in Kald, but King Eallesborough wouldn't hear it, instead spoiling him with words of praise he didn't deserve. It only sought to make him feel worse, as Ash didn't believe any of it. It made him more determined to leave.

It was his fault they were in this position. If he hadn't followed his desire, instead of his fealty to the crown, those ambushers might never have taken the convoy. If he'd been quicker in raising the *fyrd*, his men might not have been butchered. He might have been able to save the Danes. But, no…he'd spent his time seducing a beautiful shield maiden, convincing her to trust him, and then he'd let her down.

And now everyone knew he'd lied about his identity.

He'd always been worried that the King would find out about his lineage and he'd be stripped of his lands here in Termarth, his title and his pride. He'd believed he'd destroy his family's honour if the truth were ever to come out. As a child, he'd desperately tried to hide the darkness within him, seeking his parents' approval. They had planted the seed of shame in him and it had grown like a vast tree, mushrooming, sprouting, the branches expanding in height and breadth, right down to the tips of his fingers.

And finally, standing there on the ramparts yesterday, his chest bare and his ink on show, his hair around his shoulders, it had been as if that tree had shed its leaves, naked for all to see. It had become obvious he had Danish blood in his veins, and he couldn't deny it any longer. He'd had to carry the weight of his secret on his shoulders and in his heart all his life and he couldn't do it any more. He was exhausted from trying to hide it. So now the truth was out.

Sitting in the throne room where the King's witans often took place, his monarch had listened to his story—the one he'd revealed to Svea that night in Braewood—and Ash had been ready to take whatever punishment came his way. But, stroking his hand over his well-groomed beard, the King had just listened, nodding, accepting. He'd merely asked what side Ash would choose if he had to decide between Saxons and Danes, and Ash had replied, 'The right side. The peaceful side.'

Ash had told his King he was stepping down from his position. If *he* wasn't proud of who he was, how could others look up to him? How could he ask others to follow him? How could anyone place their trust in him again? He knew he'd never forgive himself for any of it. Through his actions he'd lost everything. His self-respect. His men. And the woman he loved.

And he would soon lose his father. So he'd come to a decision. He had to go home—back to the place where his life had begun. Now his secret was out his father didn't have that hold over him, and he would try to resolve the differences between them before it was too late. Doing that would at least create the foundation for building a future he was proud of.

Digging into his last reserves, he crossed the final steps to where Svea was standing. It would take the last of his strength to tell her he was leaving, to say goodbye to her. It might just destroy him. But he knew that this time he had to do things right.

When she glanced up and saw him striding in her direction she didn't smile. And when he saw the stubborn set of her jaw, the cold flare of condemnation in her eyes, he knew that she despised him. That she couldn't forgive him. He knew that it was over.

'You're leaving.'

It was a statement, not a question. Her voice was toneless, and her face emptied of all emotion.

The King's maids must have found her a gown to wear, because she was dressed in a fresh tunic and peplos, although she had rolled her sleeves up ready to tackle hard work.

She was the most incredible woman—so strong, and always helping others. She looked stunning, and he still wanted her. He'd wanted her from the moment he'd laid eyes on her, her face turned up towards the sun, her blade glimmering in the light. He had fought those feelings, not wanting to care for her. But they'd been much too strong, breaking through his resolve. And now he realised he loved her. He always would. She would be his biggest sacrifice.

'I am. I have decided to take up my familial obligations—to take responsibility for my people in Braewood. It's time.'

She nodded, continuing to pick up shards of rubble and toss them into a barrel, as if his words meant little to her, as if she was once again indifferent to him. Her heart was like that stone, hardened against him, he thought. And he was but a bridge, broken perhaps beyond repair. What he wouldn't do to have her reach out and touch him, say some of the kind words she'd said to him the other night, to build him up. He desperately wanted her to tell him not to go...not to leave her. He knew she had the power to sway him.

But of course she didn't.

He hadn't saved her men, as he'd promised. And out there on the ramparts it had been too close. She had almost got herself killed. He'd almost lost her, not been able to protect her. And the fact she'd tried to fight the Crowes by herself, not trusting him to do it, just proved what she really thought.

The silence stretched between them, and he scuffed the floor with his boot. 'How long do you intend to stay in Termarth?' he asked, and he cringed at his own pleasantries, feeling the words drying up on his tongue.

'A few days at most. Brand wants to get back to Anne in Kald as soon as possible.'

At the mention of his name Brand came over to greet them, breaking through some of the tension. 'You're returning to Braewood, Lord Stanton?'

'I am.'

Ash and Brand gripped and shook each other's forearms.

'I wish you a safe and speedy journey. It was an honour to fight with you,' Brand said. 'And I have been meaning to thank you for taking care of my sister while I was gone. For protecting her.'

Ash swallowed. *Not very well.* It was an effort to look into his fellow Northman's eyes. They had fought alongside each other as allies. But Brand knew who he was, what he stood for, whereas Ash had lost himself somewhere along the way. Or perhaps he'd never really known who he was. He'd only truly begun to understand himself, even to like himself, since he'd met Svea. And then he'd ruined it all.

'You'll have to come and visit us in Kald,' Brand said, looking between Ash and Svea.

Ash nodded politely, but he thought they all knew that would never happen. 'I've asked my men to stay here for a while and assist the King in rebuilding Termarth,' he said, feeling the guilt that he wasn't remaining with his monarch, adding to his self-loathing.

Afterwards, when the men returned to his father's fortress, he thought perhaps they could help him rebuild Braewood. Restore it to its former glory. He owed his father that.

Resigning himself to the fact that he wasn't going to be able to speak to Svea alone, and that she didn't want to talk to him anyway, he knew he had to draw the conversation to a close.

'Thank you for your help in reclaiming the castle and rescuing the King. It seems so long ago since your wedding,' he said, directing his words to Brand, although his gaze kept returning to Svea, 'but I hope you have a chance to enjoy the rest of your honeymoon. I wish I could go back and change everything. I'm especially sorry about your men. It's a great loss. I hope that you will accept my apology for my part in it.'

'Please, think no more of it. We all did what we could,' Brand said.

But Svea had turned her back against him, throwing herself into lifting more stones, and Ash had never suffered pain like it. Not on the battlefield, nor at the hands of his father and mother. She wasn't going to say goodbye.

With a final nod to the Northman, he turned on his heel. It took every drop of his willpower to walk away from her, to walk out of her life.

Chapter Ten

Svea heaved a basket of fish onto the table in the longhouse in Kald. She picked up an axe and one by one began hacking off their heads, before slicing them open and gutting the bodies.

She was aware of Brand, sitting at the end of the table. His hands were steepled in front of him and he was watching her in amusement.

'What?' she asked. She was not in the mood for laughter.

'Successful fishing trip?'

'What do you think?'

'Looks like it. Only you seem to be taking out your black anger on those poor, defenceless fish.'

'They're dead. They can't feel it,' she said, hacking harder.

'I suppose I should be grateful to be having a reprieve. I've taken the brunt of your aggression for a while now. Why the sour face and the bad mood, Sis? Do you want to tell me about it?'

'No.'

Brand sighed. 'Svea, winter is on its way, and this place is cold enough without you giving us all a chill as well. You're being unusually vile to everyone. We're all used to your feistiness, and we know you can be surly—we've always accepted why—but come on... It's been going on long enough, don't you think? Crowe is dead. You should be moving on with your life. But you seem to be more morose than ever.'

She tried to ignore him, wiping her hands on her pinafore and wrapping her shawl a little tighter around her. She gave an involuntary shudder. Brand was right—it was getting colder. It was going to be a brutal winter.

'A messenger came to the gates today,' he carried on.

'Oh?'

She wished he'd stop talking. She just wanted to get on with readying the dinner. She really didn't feel like making mundane chit-chat.

'The messenger was from Braewood.'

Her hand stilled on the axe for a second as a sharp twinge tore through her chest. Then she reached for another slippery silver fish and started hacking again. Only she felt a slight tremble in her hand. She didn't want to think about Braewood. She didn't want to think about Ash. It hurt too much. And she was angry with herself that just the mention of his name evoked this reaction in her. It had been a few months—she should have forgotten him by now.

'Don't you want to know what the message said?' Brand offered her a questioning gaze.

Images of Ash's proud, handsome face flooded her mind. She missed his dark gaze studying her face and the protective feeling of being in his arms. She swallowed, shaking her head, trying to rid her mind of the images. What had he done to her? Before him she hadn't needed any comforting embrace or protection. She had learnt to look after herself. And after he'd left she'd had to remind herself how to do so again. *Damn him.*

She suddenly felt the need to move, to pace, or to destroy something. 'Not really, but I sense you want to tell me.'

'Lord Stanton's father died last week.'

An icy draught passed over her and she shuddered. It really was cold in here, despite the fires burning constantly and the rushes from the sea shore covering the pounded earth of the floor. The winter frosts were starting with a vengeance and it had been icy, much more bitter than usual. Höðr, the god of winter and darkness, was close—she could feel him. Perhaps even more so as she tried to shut down her heart and her feelings. Everything felt so bleak lately. But curiously at her brother's words, at the mention of Ash's name, a flicker of something stirred in her body. He didn't deserve her pity, but still she hoped Ash was all right.

'His burial is the day after tomorrow. Only the family will attend. But afterwards Lord Stanton is hosting a feast in celebration of his father's life. We have been invited and I think we should go and show him our support.'

The axe slipped out of her hand and clattered to the table. 'No.'

Brand couldn't be serious. There was no chance of her going back there—not after the way Ash had left her, without so much as an explanation. Not after she'd discovered he was ashamed of himself as well as of her. And it would be far too humiliating to see him and his no doubt beautiful Saxon bride-to-be together...

'Svea, we're going,' Brand said, rising from his seat and coming towards her.

'You can go. I'm not.'

'He won't think much of that.'

'I don't care what he thinks,' she said, exasperated.

He hadn't cared what she thought when he'd walked out of her life after taking her to bed...after making her long for things she'd never wanted before. She'd hoped he would heal her, but she'd ended up more broken than before. Well, that wasn't strictly true...but it helped to tell herself that to stir up her anger against him, so she wouldn't wish for things she shouldn't.

'Besides, he won't want me there. I'm sure I'm a long-distant memory.'

'You don't believe that and neither do I. I think you owe him this, Svea—it's the least you can do.'

'Me?' Indignant rage shot through her.

'Yes, you! For pity's sake, Svea, he was like a broken man when he walked away from you in Termarth, after you treated him so callously that morning he came to say goodbye.'

'When did this become *my* fault?'

'You knew he was feeling that he was to blame for everything, and yet you didn't say a word. You just stood there, making him feel even worse.'

She gasped at Brand's words. Why was he trying to make her feel bad?

But he hadn't finished… 'And how could he possibly forget about you? You made sure you're there every time he looks at his own body, seared into his chest with that pattern. A pattern which, by the way, is the most incredible design I've ever seen you do. But that's beside the point. The man can't escape you.'

She was shocked at the way Brand was talking to her—although she had to admit the thought that Ash couldn't be rid of her, that he was carrying around a part of her forever whether he liked it or not, secretly pleased her. Well, *good*. Why should she be the only one to suffer?

'Since when are you on his side?' she spat.

'I'm not on either side. But he's in mourning, Svea.'

Well, so was she! She was mourning a relationship that could never have been.

'We know ourselves what it feels like to lose a parent,' Brand added. 'And Lord Stanton needs our support. Especially as on the same day of the feast the ealdormen will be holding a witan to vote for the next leader of Braewood.'

'What? Why?'

She turned to face her brother. Why would that be necessary? She was having difficulty continuing with her gutting of the fish now. The smell was turning her stomach and she felt nauseous. She couldn't concentrate.

'As I understand it, his father threatened to disinherit him if he hadn't married and produced an heir by the time he passed away. Lord Stanton hasn't complied with his father's demands—you *do* know that he has refused to marry, don't you?'

She bit her lip, shaking her head. She hadn't wanted to hear anything about Ashford Stanton since the moment he'd walked out of her life and she and Brand had returned to Kald. She'd feared the worst, thinking he must have gone back to Braewood and followed his father's orders. She perhaps should have known better. She knew how stubborn Ash could be...almost as stubborn as her... He had told her he didn't want to marry, and she should have believed him. He had never given her reason to think he would lie.

Brand nodded. 'He refused, and so his father renounced his claim to his lands and titles.'

She swayed on her feet, suddenly feeling lightheaded, so she pulled out a seat and sat down.

'Are you all right?'

She had been feeling so tired lately. She'd even found her usual enjoyment of her favourite pastimes waning. She'd been struggling to muster up the energy to go riding or swimming, and she was finding cooking for the masses exhausting. It was as if the passing of time had slowed these past few weeks, and everything seemed lacklustre.

'I'm fine. Really.'

'So, because he's been disinherited by his father,

Lord Stanton is set to lose everything. He must have really not wanted to get married. Not to a Saxon anyway.' Brand gave her a perceptive stare. 'I wonder why that could be...'

'But—but that's so unfair of his father!' Svea gasped, ignoring her brother's piercing gaze and his comment. 'Ash is the rightful heir. Braewood is his home. His legacy.' And he would make a wonderful leader. Those men had followed him into battle, hadn't they? She had thought she would follow him anywhere, too...

'I know. But if he himself doesn't think he's worthy the ealdormen may not vote in his favour. I was wondering if perhaps he needs someone to convince him otherwise?'

'What are you saying? I hope you're not suggesting *I'm* the person for that task.' Her heart picked up its pace. 'Especially when he's ashamed to be a Dane. Ashamed of me...'

'Is that what you truly believe?' Brand asked, stepping closer. 'I don't. Not for one moment. Don't let your own fear cloud your wisdom, Svea. That day after the battle I saw a man before me who had finally come to terms with who he was and how he'd come to be. He'd only ever felt ashamed because he'd lied about it, tried to hide it, and thought he'd lost his men's trust. *Your* trust. He wasn't sure how to put it right.'

She looked up at him, tears shining in her eyes. Could what Brand was saying be true? *Had* she let her own insecurities prevent her from seeing what had really been going on in Ash's mind? Had her own stubbornness stopped her from reaching out to him, preventing him from leaving?

She suddenly felt bereft. And so utterly foolish. But she had no experience in these things. She had never had feelings like this before.

'Oh, Brand. I didn't give him a chance, did I?' She gasped, bringing her hand up to cover her lips. 'I think...I think I was too blinded by my own hurt to see his pain.'

Her brother nodded, and then pulled her into a comforting hug. It was good to be held again. She took a deep breath and let some of her anger go.

'It's never too late, Svea. I still assert that Lord Stanton is a good man, and I believe that my sister, the one I know of old, deserves to be happy. She deserves to be with someone like that. My sister the shield maiden has always fought for what she wants, what she believes in. She's never let anything stand in her way. Even a man's mind.'

Svea felt a coil of cautious hope unfurl in her stomach at hearing Brand's words. Perhaps it was time to take one more risk... Ash had told her he didn't want to marry, and she might not be able to change his mind on that, but she could let him know she didn't hold a grudge against him and make him see that he was a good man. She could be brave and tell him that she would be at his side, no matter what. Unlike his parents, she would be there unconditionally.

Brand stepped away from her, holding her hands in his. 'So...are we going?'

Chapter Eleven

Standing at the site of the huge burial mound, gazing out over the crystal-clear ocean in Braewood, Ash had dressed for the occasion. He knew Lord Aethelbard would have insisted on him looking impeccable on such a day, so Ash had donned his finest cloak and breeches. But he'd chosen to keep his long dark hair loose and his beard full. He'd learnt he couldn't always keep his father happy. He had come to terms with that.

This was a glorious final resting spot, and Ash took comfort in knowing that his father was now re-united with his mother. He wondered if somewhere they were both looking down on him, and if they were proud of the man he had become. Possibly. Possibly not. But what mattered was that he was finally proud of himself.

After his father's threat about revealing his identity had been removed, when Ash had told the King about his real identity, it had been a great relief. After all those years of hiding his true self, feeling ashamed, worrying that the truth would come out, it had felt liberating to tell the world who he was. He'd felt like a free man—as if his chains had finally been cast off. He had expected to be shunned by some, and that would be nothing new. And yet here in Braewood the people had rallied round him, supported him. And all that had helped him to accept himself and start to like who he was.

He was glad he'd been with his father at the end. They'd never been close, but he was pleased he had come home for his final few months, during which he had tried to appease the man as best he could. He needed to be sure he'd done all he could to make amends, and he'd conceded to many of the man's wishes—all apart from one.

The burial had been a sombre affair—just the priest, Ash and a few household members. But afterwards they had invited guests into the mead hall for food, singing and dancing, to celebrate the life of the late ruler of Braewood.

Ash thought it strange that this might be the last night he'd spend in the fortress. He realised his emotions had come full circle within these walls. Born out of barbarity, he had suffered a cruel childhood here, and when he'd returned years later, moulded into the man they'd requested he become, he still hadn't been welcome.

But when the walls of Braewood had finally come into view after returning from the battle in Termarth Ash had realised he wasn't feeling his usual aversion to the place. He'd always felt the huge palisades and fortress walls had kept him either prisoner or exiled before, with the blackened turrets a sign of the darkness in his soul. But as he had glanced up at them that day a new determination had set in. He'd seen an opportunity to rebuild. A chance to change, to start again. He'd felt hopeful.

He'd realised that this was his ancestral home, despite his being born from violence, and he no longer saw it as a place of loneliness and solitude, for this was the place where he had found the most exquisite love and comfort in Svea's arms—if only for a short time. And those were the memories he chose to keep as his company.

He didn't know what the outcome of the witan would be today, but he would accept his fate graciously. He had no idea if the ealdormen would vote for him as their chosen leader, or if he would be removed from his seat here, but he had already made his peace with whatever happened next.

Taking in a lungful of sea air, he released it on a steadying breath. Whatever occurred today, he had determined he would go and find Svea and attempt to make amends. His heart had been restless since he'd left her in Termarth, and he knew he had to see her one more time. He knew he had to try.

Approaching the fortifications of Braewood fortress, Svea immediately noticed how different it looked since she'd seen it last. Although shrouded in winter mist, she saw the blackened turrets of the keep had been cleaned and rebuilt, so now there were four, and Ash's father's work on building up the walls to make them even higher seemed to have been paused. And there were no Danes camped outside.

She was surprised by how much seeing the place warmed her and lifted her spirits, despite the biting cold. She supposed it was because she had spent the best night of her life here, so it would always have a special place in her heart.

The journey from Kald had been hard going, as a light flurry of snow had begun to cover the ground. And it hadn't been helped by the butterflies in her stomach. Brand had decided they should take the long way, around the forest, and she hadn't argued—she'd actually been relieved.

She didn't want to see familiar landmarks and have her memories stirred. She didn't want to be reminded of all the moments she and Ash had shared together on their journey through the woodland to the coast. Although, looking around, she saw the landscape had changed since they'd escaped across the countryside all those months before, with the trees and hedgerows now barren. All the colours of the scenery seemed to have been leached, washed away, just like her happiness.

As they dismounted their horses and made their way into the fortress her skin was like gooseflesh. But, as much as she couldn't wait to get inside and warm herself by the fire, she was also aware she was hanging back behind Brand and Anne. They had received a warm welcome at the gate, but Svea wondered if Ash would be as receptive, and she was suddenly more nervous than she'd ever been. She was more nervous than the time she'd approached all those men at the barbican on the bridge.

Thinking back to her behaviour then, she wondered how she'd had the gall to do it—but she realised you could do anything when you were fighting for someone you loved.

She was pleased when they met Anne's father, King Eallesborough, just inside the doors. It was good to see him back in fine spirits and on a royal journey again, a new oath man at his side. She rather hoped the announcement of the King's arrival would be a distraction from theirs, as she didn't want to create a scene.

As they advanced upon the heavy doors of the hall, ready to make their entrance, she felt panic start to clamour in her chest. Maybe she shouldn't have come. What if Ash's invitation had been for Brand and Princess Anne only? What if he didn't want her here and treated her harshly—or, worse, ignored her?

She worried that Brand had got it all wrong—that Ash had moved on, or decided to marry after all. After everything she'd been through she didn't think she could cope with more heartache. But she knew she had to be brave and walk through these doors. Because not trying, not knowing, would be far worse. Because what if he did want her, but didn't think she felt the same? That would be a great tragedy. She tried to tell herself he would have asked the messenger to be specific if he hadn't wanted her to come...

She took a deep, calming breath. As the doors were pulled open the noise hit her first, followed by a surge of heat. She was astounded to see the hall was full, buzzing with a mixture of Saxon and Danish people, all mingling. It was a world apart from when she and Ash had sat at the table together alone, sharing an intimate candlelit dinner for two. She thought back to their laughter over the blackberries and smiled to herself.

Svea was delighted to see some of the Danish settlers again, who instantly came to talk to her and were excited to reveal that Ash had built them new farmsteads. They said they were working the land and had their own animals, and were all happier than they'd ever been. Svea was so pleased for them.

Then she saw Ellette, and the woman wrapped her in a fulsome embrace as if she was elated to see her. Svea felt her emotions rising to the surface and tried to swallow them down.

'You look tired, love,' the kind woman said, and ridiculously Svea felt her eyes sting with tears. She thought how amazing it was that you could feel so much warmth towards a person after only having met them once, but it had been during a time of heightened awareness—a time that mattered deeply, and the woman had taken care of her.

They exchanged a few words, and Ellette said that things had improved a great deal since Ash had moved home. Svea was glad. She wanted to ask how he was, and she wanted to ask about Lady Edith, but she couldn't bring herself to utter the words.

'Keep your fingers crossed for Lord Stanton today,' Ellette told her, before rushing off to tend to the cooking. 'We're all hoping the ealdormen vote wisely. It will change our lives.'

Svea wished she could go with her, to lend a hand, to hide away... But then her thoughts flew back to the way she had tried to cover up her body the night Ash had made love to her for the first time, and his insistence that she never hide from him again. Well, here she was. She had been brave enough to come, and now she was standing in the middle of his hall. She'd even decided to wear a dress, to show respect for the late Lord Stanton and because she'd thought Ash might like it.

But where the hell was he? Did he go over everything they'd spoken of and everything they'd done together when he lay in bed at night, as she did? Despite trying not to, she thought of him all the time.

She felt out of sorts among all these people, when she only wanted to see and talk to one. Finding Brand and Anne seated at a table, she made her way there and settled down next to them on the bench, but she couldn't focus on their conversation. She was distracted. Her pulse was racing.

And then, all of a sudden, Ash was there at her side, towering over the table like a bright star in the night sky. And her heart felt as if it would burst out of her chest. He welcomed the King, and Brand and Princess Anne, and then he was staring right at her, saying her name, and she didn't think she could speak.

'Hello, Svea.'

Her lips parted and she took a deep, savouring

breath. He was here. Taking in his rugged good looks, his molten, dark gaze and his long, loose hair, she thought he looked more handsome than ever before. Love blossomed in her chest and she wanted to stand up and throw her arms around him, tell him how she felt, that she'd never meant to let him go.

But instead she just sat there. She couldn't move. She knew she should say something about being sorry for his loss—anything—but she just couldn't get the words out. For the first time in her life she was rendered mute.

'We were very sorry to hear about your father, Lord Stanton,' said Brand, coming to her rescue.

Svea panicked. How could she even begin to broach the subject of her feelings towards him and close the chasm that had opened up between them when she couldn't even say hello?

Ash nodded, thanking them all for coming, and then, after focusing his gaze on her for another moment, he was gone. He was moving around the room, tending to his other guests, talking animatedly to the men, listening to the women. Her heart felt as if it would shatter. Was that it? Was that all he could say to her? Well, at least he'd said hello, which was more than she'd been able to manage…

Did he not care that she was here? She watched him move about, more at ease with himself than she'd ever seen him—as if he'd grown into himself these past few months…as if he was more comfortable with his body and who he was—and her heart ached. She wanted him to come back. She wanted him to look at her in that way again. And she never, ever wanted to let him out of her sight.

When a pretty woman, about her age, put her hand to his arm, leaned in to whisper something in his ear, and they both laughed, Svea blanched. Jealousy roared through her, and she realised she shouldn't have come. His father had died. It had been courteous of her to come, to see he was all right, but now she'd seen that he was, she should leave. Only she couldn't. Not without Brand and Anne.

'Who is that?' she asked discreetly, turning to her brother's new wife.

'That's Lady Edith Earlington,' said Anne.

Of course. Suddenly frustrated with herself—with him—wishing she hadn't made the journey only to feel ignored and humiliated, she excused herself from the table. She didn't want to sit there watching him smile at other women. It seemed he was happy, content, and he'd moved on without her. Whereas she... She felt tired, run-down, and she'd put on weight. She missed him with every beat of her heart. She missed him every moment of every day.

She was feeling so miserable, so bereft, she slipped out of the door and headed into the back room, looking for Ellette.

'Can I do anything?' she asked, when she found her, watching the woman fretting around in a hive of people cooking and pouring drinks.

But Ellette shook her head. 'No, dear, not today.'

And then she felt a large, firm hand close around her upper arm. 'What the hell do you think you're doing?'

Ash.

She had been gone just moments. How did he know she'd sneaked in here? Had he been watching her? Following her? The thought pleased her.

'I hope you're not even contemplating doing any work. You're a guest here.'

She shrugged, the feel of his touch burning her skin. 'I—I wanted to help. I couldn't just sit there, watching you talking to—'

His gaze narrowed on her. 'Come with me.'

He led her out through the back, as he had the night they'd eaten honey on bread and played with the flour. She wanted to return to that moment. It had felt so wonderfully carefree. Although she was suddenly struck with guilt that they'd never cleaned up the mess. Poor Ellette. She would have to make amends...

'Where are we going?'

Ash's hand was gripping her arm too tightly, but she didn't mind. He was here. They were alone. And she never wanted him to let go. Besides, she didn't think she could walk without him holding her up, her legs were trembling so much.

'The beach.'

'Won't you be missed?' she asked.

'I'm sure they can cope without me for a while.'

'Don't think for one minute I'm going for a swim—'

He stopped suddenly, pulling her round to face him so they were just a breath apart. And she was thrilled to be with him again, to have his hands on her skin, but incredibly nervous, too. Her stomach was in knots.

'What are you doing here, Svea?'

'I thought you'd invited me. I thought you wanted me to come…'

'I did. I just didn't think you would.'

'I wanted to be here. To support you. I'm so sorry about your father, Ash.'

Her words seemed to appease him and they began to walk again, a little slower now, and he softened his grip on her arm. But he didn't release her. Sneaking a sideways glance at him, she noticed he still wore a heavy frown. And he still wore the necklace she'd made for him. It was freezing outside, but she didn't mind one bit. He was here.

When they reached the sand, he turned to face her again. In the winter, the ocean had a raw, rugged, restless beauty to it, just like the man standing before her, and she wondered if Ash still swam during the colder months. She imagined his muscular arms carving up the waves. She wanted to know what he'd been up to these past few months. She wanted to know if he'd missed her.

'Did you manage to sort out your differences with your father before he passed?' she asked. Had it been worth it, his leaving her in Termarth? she wondered.

'I think my father and I had too many differences to rectify them all. But I'm glad I came back. I needed to know I had done everything I could.'

She nodded, understanding. Then she looked around. 'You've done so much here, Ash,' she said. 'Since you've been back. The keep looks so much better, and the settlers all seem happy…'

'What can I say? I'm trying to make up for my earlier failures,' he said, his lips curling upwards, although the smile didn't quite reach his eyes. 'You know me... I like to be busy.'

You know me. Her heart clenched. It pained her to hear him say it. It hinted at the past intimacy they'd shared. She'd thought she knew him. She wanted to know everything about him again. Always.

His grip on her arm dropped down to her wrist and he tentatively took her hand in his. How was his skin so warm when it was icy out here?

'Svea, I want to talk about what happened in Termarth. I owe you an apology... I'm sorry that I couldn't save your men. When I saw that cart being wheeled out through the gate, and Kar and Sten among the bodies, it was as if a huge wooden door closed on my life. I felt as if I had let you down. I felt as if I'd let them down.'

She shook her head. 'Their deaths... It was not your fault, Ash. No one could have saved them. Not you, nor I. I know you think their blood is on your hands, but it's not. Please don't hold yourself to impossible standards no one else would place on you.'

His dark gaze considered her. 'But when I left you were angry with me. You seemed to despise me. You didn't say goodbye.'

She never wanted to say goodbye to him. She thought it would break her. 'Yes, I *was* angry with you. But not about that.'

'What, then?' He looked confused.

She glanced down at the sand. She was reminded

of what Ash had said to her that night they'd first made love—that she was trying to bury her head in the Braewood sand. Well, not today…

'King Eallesborough told me you were leaving before you did. He said you had told him about what had happened to your mother, and that you were ashamed of the Dane in you. But that part of you, Ash, that part of you is in me… I was so hurt… I could tell that you had distanced yourself from me, and I thought you were ashamed of me, too, and embarrassed by whatever had been between us. When you came to say goodbye, my heart was splintering into a million little pieces. The truth is, I was too proud to ask you to stay.'

He stepped towards her. 'I had always worried I had something bad in me, Svea. And I'd felt the need to suppress it, to always feel in control…to keep at bay this *thing*, this barbaric act, that's defined my whole life. For as long as I can remember I've isolated myself as a means of protecting my family, my people…you. I'd spent so long thinking I must be a monster, believing that other people would see me as one…and I think the Dane and the darkness in me got muddled in my head.'

'I told you I don't see a monster when I look at you, Ash.'

'I know that. But don't you see? I was brought up to hate Danes. To hate myself. And then I met you. I didn't want to like you, Svea. I fought my feelings every step of the way.'

She understood what he was saying, and she

couldn't be angry with him for that. For hadn't she done the same? She had sworn to hate all Saxon men, including him. Especially him. And now she realised she had wanted to hate him because she had loved him from the start and her feelings had scared her.

His hand smoothed over the skin on her hand and he brought his other hand up to cup her cheek. 'It took falling in love with a Dane for me to realise the truth. That my parents had got it wrong and you'd got it right. That every person has the potential to be good or bad, no matter if they're Saxon or Dane. And I had started to have hope…to believe I was good. You made me think I really could be. Until I let everyone down…'

'You didn't, Ash.'

'I realised that day out on the ramparts in Termarth that I'd had enough of apologising for who I am. I was ashamed that I'd lied to everyone. I knew then that I had to embrace my heritage—especially if it meant I had a chance to be with you. And I thought the best place to do that was here. I had to lose everything, sacrifice everything, go back to the beginning and find myself. I needed to learn to like myself before I could ask anyone else to love me. Before I came for you. I realised the act of how I came to be no longer mattered, but how I choose to act did.'

He took a step closer towards her, their bodies touching now.

'My father insisted that I must marry a Saxon if I wanted to keep my title and inheritance…'

Svea swallowed. 'Lady Edith is very beautiful.'

'Perhaps to some. But she's not the woman for me. I told my father I wouldn't marry her. I told him I couldn't because I was in love with you.' He stroked her face with his thumb. 'My father forced me to choose between my inheritance and my feelings for you, and there was no contest. I chose you. Because you're the woman who taught me who I want to be, Svea.'

'And who is that?' she asked, breathless.

'The husband of Svea Ivarsson, shield maiden of Kald—if she'll have me,' he said, resting his forehead against hers, smiling. 'I have no idea what the witan will decide this afternoon—whether by tonight I will be the Lord of Braewood with a fortress to rule over, or be sent away with just the clothes on my back. But I do know that either way, if you say yes to marrying me, Svea, I will have everything I've ever wanted and needed. I shall be the happiest man in the world.'

She stared up at him, felt their warm breath mingling in the cold afternoon air. She had promised herself she would never belong to a man, that she would be a warrior and protector of Kald. But this man... It was his cool control and his gentle ways that had allowed her to let down her guard. It was his bravery and compassion that had made her trust him completely. And she wanted to be his. She wanted to follow him, wherever he went. To honour and obey him.

'If I say yes, does that mean you've tamed me?' she whispered.

'Never. I like your wildness far too much,' he said, and grinned.

But he had changed her—she saw that now. Whereas once she had been fierce and reckless, he had calmed her, taught her how to be gentle. He'd broken her in and she had adapted to his touch. And she wanted to be his, as he was saying he was hers. Forever.

'Then, yes, I'll marry you, Ash. Of course I will. I love you.'

A shout from the cliff above broke through their total absorption with one another. 'Lord Stanton, your presence has been requested in the hall. The witan have voted and made their decision. Please, come quickly.'

Nerves bunched in Svea's stomach. She hoped the ealdormen had made the right choice. That they had put their faith in Ash to lead them forward into a brighter future, as had she. But she knew, whatever the outcome, they would get through it together.

Svea began to move, to step away, to make her way up the path towards the fortress, but Ash gripped her, tugging her back towards him.

'Don't you want to go and find out—?'

'It can wait,' he said, pulling her up against him hard, bringing his lips down onto hers.

It started as a soft, slow kiss as he reacquainted himself with the feel of her mouth, his tongue caressing hers in a sensual bone-melting way, and then it deepened to become proprietorial, passionate, so unrestrained it left her breathless and achingly incomplete.

'Now we can go.'

He grinned, lifting his head away and pulling her

up the track, and her eyes narrowed on him. Well, two could play that game, she thought. *Just you wait till tonight, Ashford Stanton.*

It was the news everyone had been hoping for. Ash had been chosen to be the Lord of Braewood, ruler of the Saxons and the Danes.

Considered a man who had control, and the respect of the people, he was the only person the ealdormen had thought suitable for the role. They had seen his skill and bravery on the battlefield, and the way he'd shown compassion to the people of the burhs, including both Danes and Saxons, and there had been no one to rival him. And, due to the wisdom and foresight he'd displayed in bringing the *fyrd* together, the vote had been unanimous. It hadn't hurt that the King had made a point of saying that Lord Stanton was the best man he knew.

Svea couldn't have been more delighted that they'd rewarded his loyalty. Standing there in the hall, watching her lover being anointed successor to his father as Lord of Braewood, with everyone cheering and on his side, she clasped her hands together. She didn't think she'd ever felt so happy and proud—until, after they'd performed the ceremony, Ash thanked everyone and announced to the congregation that he was to be married.

He pulled Svea close for everyone to see his wife-to-be, pressing a soft kiss to her temple to show how much he loved her. It seemed he wanted the whole of Braewood to know how proud he was of his Danish bride. And she thought her heart might just burst with joy.

Everything was perfect. *Almost*. There was just one thing niggling her… But as people came to congratulate them and wish them well she tried to bury it, telling herself she'd deal with it later. She couldn't ruin this moment.

Brand was ecstatic for them, of course, spinning her around and telling her how happy he was for her, and he and Ash had taken themselves off to discuss the arrangements, their arms around each other's shoulders like brothers.

The drinking and merriment went on long into the evening, until finally people retired to their rooms or farmsteads, and others passed out on benches or curled up by the fire.

Staring down into her eyes, Ash took Svea's hand in his before leading her down the corridor to his room. The flutters of excitement low in her stomach, between her legs, were getting more fierce the closer they got to being alone. And the instant the door closed behind them they were in each other's arms, their mouths sealed together, tearing at each other's clothes.

Ash practically ripped her dress from her shoulder on one side, so desperate was his need to have her naked in his arms again, and she fell against him, laughing. One breast sprang free from the confines of the material and, holding her hands in his, behind her arching back, he let his mouth work its way down her neck to her heaving chest as he hardened against her stomach. She had missed him so much. She wanted him so badly.

But as his lips roamed lower that nagging thought popped back into her mind and her eyes flew open. She couldn't do this. Not yet.

'Ash, wait,' she said, struggling to pull herself free, to stand up straight.

'What is it?' he asked, looking at her through lust-filled hooded eyes.

'I need to ask you something.'

'Now?'

'Yes. It's important.'

He lifted his head slightly to stare down at her. 'What's the matter?' he asked again.

'Do you remember the day we were ambushed, and the conversation we had in the woods when we were first alone? We spoke about marriage and you told me you didn't want to father children,' she said.

'I remember,' he said, righting himself now, as if he'd realised she really did want to talk, and that it sounded serious.

'Why was that?' she asked. He had never explained to her why he had made that decision. 'Why don't you want to be a father?'

He frowned. 'I never thought I'd marry, let alone have a child. My father had been putting on the pressure, threatening me, wanting me to continue the Stanton line. I think he hoped that if I married a Saxon her blood would help to dilute my child's Danish heritage... At the time of our conversation in the woods I felt I didn't want to bring a child into this world if it was going to be anything like me. Why? Why are you asking now?'

'Do you remember what I told you?' she said, chewing her bottom lip. 'About what the healer said to me?'

He nodded, his brow furrowing deeper. 'She said she wasn't sure you'd ever be able to have children after what happened to you in Termarth...'

She swallowed.

'And that's all right, Svea,' he said, holding her face in his hands. 'If you're worried about my feelings on the matter, I'm fine with it. *You* are all I need.' He kissed her lightly on the lips and allowed his hands to roam down her back again. He pulled her close. 'Now, where were we...?'

'The thing is,' she said, resting her hands on his chest, pushing him back gently so he fell onto the bed. She unclasped the brooch on the other side of her dress, letting the whole thing drop to her waist, and then she continued to push the garment down to the floor. 'I can't be sure, but I think I may be...'

'With child...' he gasped, taking in her beautiful body, including her rounded stomach. He looked stunned—shocked, even.

'I was worried about telling you, knowing your feelings...'

And then his eyes met hers, and she saw they were glowing with love and admiration. Suddenly his arms wrapped around her stomach, pulling her towards him.

He planted a gentle, chaste kiss on her swollen belly. 'That was then...this is now.'

'So, you're not angry?'

'Angry?' He looked incredulous, and then he laughed. 'No, I'm not angry, Svea. I'm delighted. I'm—' His voice trembled and tears filled his eyes. 'I'm overwhelmed. Overjoyed. All my dreams are coming true. I have everything I've ever wished for and I don't know what I have done to deserve it.'

He pulled her down onto the bed and stretched out next to her, beginning to kiss her again with the lightest, softest kisses…everywhere. And she felt so cherished, so loved.

'This is the best news I could ever have had, Svea. The greatest gift you could give me apart from yourself.' He stroked her swollen breasts, and then moved down, over her stomach. 'Are you feeling all right? Have you been very sick?'

'I'm tired. And fat. But I feel fine!' She laughed.

'I can't believe you rode all the way here today in your condition,' he said. 'And in freezing weather.'

His hand splayed possessively over her small bump. Over their child. A child they had created through love.

She rolled her eyes. 'I'm not ill, Ash.'

'No, but you're precious to me, Svea, and I say no more risks. Do you understand me?'

'Yes, I understand.' She grinned, loving it that he cared about her so much. Loving it that he wanted to look after her, as she did him. Forever.

When he rolled on top of her and entered her at last he was remarkably gentle, slow and steady, and it was so torturous it felt wildly and romantically passionate.

When he was inside her, he stopped for just a moment, looking down into her eyes. 'Is this a risk?' he asked, concerned. 'To you or the baby?'

'No, thank goodness!' She laughed. 'Because there's no way I could stay away from your touch for so long...'

He grinned as he began to move inside her again, deeply, intimately. 'Thank you for helping me to love myself, Svea. I want you to know that this child will be loved, too—just like you will be—for the rest of our lives.'

Epilogue

Ash carried his beloved son, Bearn, into the chronicle room, where Svea was creating her latest image on a parchment inside one of the large books. It was similar to the most recent designs she had etched onto his body, and once again he admired her talent.

These days the chronicles weren't filled with disturbing dark images—they were filled with stories of a great escape, a battle, and an honourable hero who had won a fierce but beautiful shield maiden. And of a dark-eyed little boy with hair that curled at the ends, especially in the rain, who had a great big smile on his face.

Ash would always tell her that her latest was her best work, but she would shake her head and disagree. She always asserted that *he* was her greatest masterpiece.

When Bearn caught sight of his mother he smiled, stretching out his hands, and Svea wrapped her arms around her husband and her child.

'You both smell of the sea,' she said.

'We've been making great big fortresses out of the sand on the beach,' Ash said.

'He's going to be just like his father!' She laughed, thinking of the wonderful settlement Ash had built here in Braewood. 'He's going to create great things. Perhaps you'll do it together.'

Ash grinned. 'I hope so. Ellette is about to take Bearn for his bath. Do you feel like a walk? It's a beautiful evening.'

Svea nodded. 'All right. Just give me a moment to finish.'

The sun was beginning to set in the distant sky, and there was a glorious patchwork of pink and orange clouds floating above them. Svea was surprised when, instead of taking her down their usual favourite path to the beach, where they often enjoyed a moonlit swim together, Ash took her hand and led her through the settlers' farmsteads, past the barns and towards the crop fields.

'Where are we going?'

'I have something for you. Or rather, I have made something for you.'

She looked up at him, a wide, expectant smile on her face. 'What is it?'

'Come this way and I'll show you,' he said, tugging her through a low wall and into a field of...

She gasped.

Stretched out before her was a field full of hundreds and hundreds of beautiful sunflowers, their large, happy-looking faces all turning towards them in the late-evening sun. It must have taken him a long time to sow them, and even longer to grow them. And in the middle of them all was a stunning old tree, just like the one sprawling up her neck.

'Ash, it's—it's so beautiful,' she said, taking in the incredible sight before her.

'As are you. I wanted to create for you something so beautiful you might understand how it feels for me when I look at you.'

She stared up at him, her eyes shimmering with tears.

'I've been watching them grow and their faces... they literally turn and face the sun.'

'Like me, looking up at you?'

He grinned, and tugged at her hand, leading her along a little pathway, through the tall stems, to the base of the giant tree, where he had laid out a blanket and bowls of blackberries.

Svea laughed in delight. 'Berries! My favourite.' And they were, because they always reminded her of him.

'I thought we could celebrate the anniversary of when we met.'

They stretched out together under the branches of the great tree that must have been here for hundreds of years, with the sunlight dappling through the leaves, and he fed her the fruit, licking the juice from her lips.

'Ash, this tree...it's like the one on my neck. The tree of life.'

'I know,' he said.

'How did you find it?'

'When I came back to Braewood after the battle I came here to think. I came across this ancient tree and I realised why I'd always been drawn to you, and to your patterns,' he said, trailing his fingertips over the swirls on her body that matched those in the canopy above them. 'I realised that from the moment I first saw you on the battlefield we were connected somehow. That you were my home.'

And as Ash made love to her under the canopy of the tree, taking her to new realms of pleasure, sowing a new seed inside her, she knew there would be many more generations of their family to come. A mixture of Saxon and Dane.

In many, many years from now, in the distant future, Svea and Ash would no longer be here, but she hoped that they would have left a legacy. This tree with all its roots and memories…Svea's chronicles for people to read and decipher…a family. But mostly she knew that theirs would be a great legacy of love.

* * * * *

LET'S TALK

Romance

For exclusive extracts, competitions
and special offers, find us online:

- 🅕 MillsandBoon
- 🐦 @MillsandBoon
- 📷 @MillsandBoonUK
- ♪ @MillsandBoonUK

Get in touch on 01413 063 232